UNQUIET

BOOK ONE

KAY CAMDEN

UNQUIET

CHAPTER
1

IT WAS A quick stop at the store for milk and eggs, but that wasn't what Mick Svendsen brought home.

He heard the vicious metal-on-metal screech when he opened his car door. For once it wasn't coming from his work-in-progress car. The grocery store's lot was empty enough to amplify any noise, not that this one needed any help. A sound like that could only be bringing destruction, and his attention went straight to the target of his slow, appreciative drive-by in the parking lot a moment before. Now someone was standing beside that sweet Nissan 300ZX. A woman, tall and lean, in a brown puffy coat with a furry hood, her shiny black hair competing with the shine on that perfect paint job—no longer so perfect because of the crowbar shrieking across the hood.

Not my business, Mick thought. His mouth didn't listen.

"Hey!" he called. The wind bullied him across the parking lot, tearing his jacket open. No one should ever damage a car like that, not on purpose. It was bad for a person's karma. "There ain't many of those around anymore. You're—"

The pop of the windshield exploding cut him off. It paused his advance toward her. Anyone crazy enough to perform this kind of unabashed vandalism in broad daylight was crazy enough to use that crowbar on him.

She glanced at him then. Not caught, but expectant. Unashamed, undeterred. Not the slightest touch of guilt. A gust of wind hit again, lifting her hair all around her face as it shoved against Mick's back.

"Okay, maybe put the crowbar down." Mick unpocketed his phone, looking around for other witnesses only to find he was on his own. Stuff like this didn't happen in his small Missouri town. Or maybe it *only* happened in small Missouri towns. He figured people in larger places might have more street sense than to get mixed up in this.

She smashed out the driver's side window. Glass sprayed Mick and sprinkled the pavement around him. He turned away, feeling cold jagged pieces crawl down his shirt collar and settle in his hair, wondering how easy it would be to disarm a woman wielding a crowbar. The only woman he'd ever wrestled was his sister decades ago as a kid, and she was meaner and always victorious.

As she stepped to the rear of the car, Mick got the urge to throw himself across it. Which was ironic, because minutes ago he was fantasizing it would blow a crucial part while in town so it would find its way to his shop and become his project for the day. He didn't replace glass though. She needed to aim for the motor. The twin turbos. The thought was practically a sin.

"Tires!" he called out. He could fix tires. "All four of 'em. They want it. They're beggin'. You got a knife?"

Her insanity must be infectious because now he was sick in the head. But she'd stopped, and was facing him head-on now, reaching into her open coat. This is the moment he should've been dropping to the ground. She produced a shiny thing—*click*—a switchblade, now flipping through the air for Mick to catch—which he did, by the handle, with no idea how.

"Get to work," she said.

"Me? No way, lady, this is all you."

He couldn't believe no one had come out of the store or pulled into the parking lot. Time seemed suspended for the world, for everyone but him.

"Don't call me 'lady.'"

"Okay—ma'am?" Now armed, he approached. He eyed the crowbar. She eyed him eyeing it. Maybe it was a little weird to call a woman his age 'lady' and 'ma'am,' but there were no other good words, and 'beautiful' wasn't going to go over too well either, even though it was true. She wasn't from here, that was for sure. Everyone in Wyona came from similar looking genetic stock. Caucasian—and she had none in her. A face of planes and angles, a set of the darkest eyes perched over high broad cheekbones, matching silky hair parted in the middle.

Asian? Mick thought, knowing he was wrong, but it was the closest thing he had.

"Stop judging me."

"I ain't. I'm tryin' to figure you out."

Now he was close enough to see the web of red in the white of one eye. The bruise in the center of a split lip. Understanding struck bright and hard. This car was making a small payment for a much larger crime.

He folded the knife. There was complication here, a ton more than he could shoulder. He just wanted milk and eggs.

Then he wanted to go home and relax for the first time in weeks, on a surprise afternoon off from job number one due to splitting his forearm wide open. Business was slow enough at the shop for the boss to send him home, and for once he took it. Job number two started in a few hours. He was hoping to get some dishes done and change the lightbulb in the bathroom and collect his brain.

"Have you figured it out?" the woman asked.

The question was unbearably loaded, the answer too heavy for Mick's already piled plate. "I've gotta … Is there someone you can call?" He handed the folded knife to her. It dangled there while she watched him, like she was now trying to figure him out. Her fingers then brushed his as she took it back. The crowbar slid out of her hand, clanging on the cold pavement. The sound echoed through him, the last iteration settling at last in his heart.

He stepped back. Too much—too close. He couldn't even determine what. She was no longer a threat—to him or to the car. It was over; he was done here. But he couldn't seem to end it, couldn't get his feet to walk away. It felt more like he needed to come up with the next thing to say, to draw this meeting out, to fully unwrap it. That little brush of the fingers lingered, a promise of something about to begin or something that already had. Curiosity bit like a horsefly on the back of his neck, one he didn't even want to swat away.

"Where's your car at?" Because it was fair to assume the one she just trashed wasn't hers.

"I have no car."

There was no way to get around this town without a car. "What, did you blow in on the wind?"

She tilted her head, her severe eyes going soft like he was the butt of a joke. "I'm on foot."

"In Wyona?"

Something caught her attention behind him. Over his shoulder he spotted a top-heavy man in a flannel jacket moving at a good clip straight for them. Mick's brain gave him two quick announcements:

You're standing next to a very vandalized car.

You need to run.

He couldn't run. She would be left. She had the crowbar for defense but wasn't picking it up. She wasn't doing anything but staring at the guy heading toward them.

"Get in my car," Mick said. "Now."

She didn't need any more encouragement. They ran and got in, his tires chirping as he pulled through the space in front of him, using the short double row of cars as cover. Any guy who drove a 300ZX would know cars and would know the Brazen Orange GTO was the only one in town. Probably the only one in the state. Mick made a right out of the lot to avoid having to wait for a hole in both lanes of traffic because it felt like that guy was at his back bumper, ready to tear it off.

"Where can I drop you?" Mick asked, desperate to get himself out of the complication he just invited in.

"Here," she said.

They weren't even an eighth of a mile away from the crime scene. One main road through town, one route that guy would take to find a woman he probably knows is on foot. And there was nothing around but an abandoned firehouse, a used car lot, and a cattle pasture.

"I'd like to do better than drop you on the road." He didn't want to stop at all. That guy was probably gaining on them.

"There's nowhere else."

He glanced at her, but she wouldn't look at him. Two tiny earrings nestled in the curve of her upper ear, colorful beads dangled from her lobe. She hung her head, eyes closed. The shame he expected to see when he caught her with the crowbar was here now, evident in the slant of her shoulders and drop of her chin, palpable and picking at Mick's heart.

Damn it. Mick almost said it aloud. This wasn't a stray kitten, this was a woman, with a truckload of baggage that would not fit in his apartment alongside his own. Two jobs to support his father's homecare nurse and his single-parent sister and her three kids, the youngest with medical bills so insane it would make any hardworking person cry. Three jobs, he corrected. As soon as it got cold enough for snow. December in Missouri should be cold and snowy, not mild and windy like it had been. He'd be plowing at night as soon as that weather decided to hit. It left no time for sleep.

He couldn't bring this woman home. It was a wreck. He was out of milk and eggs. No spare room, no time to prepare one.

Watching his mirror for a 300zx, he drifted to the shoulder. She put her hand on the door handle, pulling it, but not enough to catch. Then she looked at him.

"I can't do this anymore." Spoken on an outward breath, it was a whisper so quiet it wasn't meant for him.

"Sorry, I…" *What?* Mick thought. *Can't help you? Don't want to help you?* He wasn't sure which it was. And the curve in the road behind him was too empty, too ready to spit that guy straight at him. His GTO wasn't fully rebuilt yet. He had to go easy on the horses or the spent shocks and struts would have them in a ditch. Using a project car as a daily driver wasn't ideal, but it was his only set of wheels. He should've kept the Honda.

But when a GTO is towed into your shop with more problems than the owner can afford to fix, the nice thing to do is take it off that guy's hands, right?

The woman was still in his car. Mick's brain, a disconnected mess. The road behind him still gaping. Continuing in the same direction would take him farther from home, where he needed to get some stuff done before his shift started. So he put the car in gear and took the road into Bryson's farm, knowing the driveway dumped into a gravel road that led to the back of the property with access to the route home. He'd talk himself out of it before he got there. Right now, it was a slick way to lose the 300ZX guy.

"Police station in Clarkson," he said five minutes later. The thought had gone straight to his mouth. The trip would eat up so much time.

"No police." Stiff, detached, she stared deadpan through the windshield. "I just need a couple hours to hide. Until he leaves." The last part seemed an afterthought. Insincere, for some reason.

Mick thought himself back to town, trying to think of somewhere she'd be safe for a couple hours. Everything was too close together. She'd catch too many eyes. People would wonder who the newcomer was, word would spread, and that guy would hear about it and find her.

"What if he don't leave?"

"He will."

"Then you get out—how?"

Her smile was small on her lips but big in her eyes. "The wind."

If only she could use the gusts shoving his car for something useful. He had two hands on the wheel to keep within the lines. If the wind would figure out which direction it wanted to blow, at least then he might be able to predict how to hold the wheel.

The monstrous sycamore in the front yard of Mick's place was fighting the wind, too. Behind it, the turn-of-the-century red-brick two-story with a stone porch sat unaffected, its many windows darkened by curtains. Mick parked behind the house, out of view from the road, on his landlord's grass. Old Mae would tear him up for it, but it was a better option than having to explain why he was housing a vandal. He wasn't the kind of guy to make a stray woman hide out in the ramshackle barn near the back fence, especially since it might finally surrender to gravity with the urging of the weather. So he took her to the steps leading under the house to his basement apartment.

"Don't move," he said inside, closing the door.

As he grabbed a pair of boots and a dirty sweatshirt that'd fallen off the armchair, he saw her cross her arms and lean against the closed door. Crap was everywhere, the whole apartment littered with stuff he never had time to put away. He took it all in like he was the guest, and whoever lived here was a slob. He moved armfuls into the bedroom and shut the door. Cleared the table of days' old dishes, dumping them in the sink. The whole time he watched her, how she stayed in that guarded position, her gaze following his every move.

Now cleared of books and half-folded clothes, the couch was free. He didn't know her name. Didn't want to call her 'ma'am.' "You're welcome to sit."

She didn't need to look at him; she already was. In one quick move she squatted, one arm toward the floor, fist opening like she was releasing a set of dice, only nothing was there. She stood to face him again. The leveled gaze, those dark eyes. He was glad they were small. Any bigger and that intense darkness would absorb him.

He shed his jacket, fixed the bandage that had partially unwrapped from his forearm. "I don't have much to drink. Water's pretty much it. You kind of interrupted my grocery run." He offered a small smile, hoping she'd see he wasn't being an ass about it. God, when was the last time he'd had a woman in his apartment who wasn't his sister?

"Forgive me," she said.

There was nothing for him to forgive. What she'd obviously been through wasn't her fault. And she hadn't asked for his help. He'd offered it. Not that he needed to say any of this, or that he could—because now she was chanting in some strange language and her eyes were being engulfed by a smoky cataract so otherworldly he backed into his tiny kitchen table, knocking it three feet across the tile.

A futile move. She was on him. A click of that switchblade as she spun him, his back to her front, blade against his throat. A sharp burst of adrenaline peeled through him.

Her voice, deep and gritty in his ear. "I don't like what you represent."

"Poverty?" he said. A sharp elbow to the ribs. "Ow!"

"What your kind have done."

"My—oh, shit, really? It's time to bash the white guy?" He swallowed to steady his pulse. Freaking out would get him nowhere.

"Your Viking blood reeks."

He laughed. "My what?" It wasn't funny. This dramatic a shift in the day was absurd, and his brain had already become unglued. Jagged metal tearing five inches of his forearm at the shop started the fun, now sharp metal splitting his jugular was going to end it. Was this how his father felt when the dementia started taking hold? Was it coming for him now?

No way. This wasn't happening, and he was going to stop it. This woman was as tall as him but not as strong. Armed, yes, but to hell with that. He wasn't about to be murdered in his own crappy apartment.

CHAPTER
2

WITH A KNIFE blade against his neck, Mick figured it out fast: this was a scam. He'd been set up. Rewinding the last thirty minutes to analyze it for clues distracted him enough to delay the auditory input of a knock on the door.

"Who's that?"

He took a moment to determine who it could be. He had nothing but a foggy fatigue even more present after the adrenaline dump. "No idea."

"Get rid of them."

The knife withdrew. So did her grasp on his arm. Well this was easy. Open the door and run. Those two things shone bright and clear in all the shock and rattled nerves.

He opened the door. He couldn't run. Because standing there was his sister, Kari, with the baby on her hip, her two other kids elbowing each other at her side. "Why are you parked out back? When I didn't see the car I thought you got in a crash or—" She caught sight of Mick's guest, her voice going instantly formal. "Oh, I'm sorry."

Mick didn't hear an apology. He heard confusion. Which was dead straight. A faraway part of him remembered her text from earlier, her frantic plea to replace a sick babysitter. And Mick had told her it was her lucky day—he'd gotten the afternoon off and could watch Doug and Janie so she could take baby Helen to one of her many appointments. Today's doctor was hard to get in to see. Canceling meant another long wait, time Helen should be using to get better.

He put a hand on the back of Doug's head to usher him in. "It's okay," he said to Kari. "We're good. You go on."

She shrugged off a kid's backpack and handed him the strap, mouthing, *You sure?*

"Yes. Go." He opened his hand to Janie, who'd gone shy because of the strange woman in her uncle's normally uneventful apartment. A guest wasn't just a rare event, it was a never event. "Come on, little birdie."

Janie took his hand. He'd hooked an arm around Doug, a casual hug to keep him from straying too close to the woman. Together, they watched Kari strap Helen into the back of her sun-bleached Buick and leave. Then Mick turned around to determine if his car vandal friend looked like the type to attack children, and if he should drag them to his car and get the heck out before she did. This woman had been the victim a few minutes ago. She wasn't anymore—far from it. But neither was Mick.

"So, looks like I'm babysittin' this afternoon. Rain check?" He injected as much friendliness as he could. Not that the kids would be fooled. They were too keen on these things now.

In his pocket his phone dinged. He took it out.

Kari: I'm SO sorry.

She knew how long it'd been since he'd had the time or desire for a date. He couldn't wait to tell her how much she'd saved him.

"You don't babysit your own kids."

"They ain't mine." Mick answered before realizing the inflection in her comment meant it was more than a judgment call. It was bait.

But why should this random woman care whose kids they were? What did she want from a guy who had nothing but a partially trashed used car and a messy basement apartment? The whole thing was so bizarre, maybe the parking lot scene had been a hallucination. The 300ZX hadn't followed him because it never existed in the first place.

Mick made a mental note to ask Kari when their dad first started showing signs of dementia. Surely thirty-seven was too young—even though this day might have a different opinion on that. He swiveled the kids aside so the woman could pass.

"Rain check," she said, her eyes hooked so deeply into him he could barely breathe.

Relief to see her leaving came on so hard he didn't notice the door open or close. One moment she was there, the next, gone.

Janie poked him in the leg. "Uncle Mick, who was that lady?"

"Just a friend."

She wrinkled her nose, not buying it. At six years old she could already see through every excuse and white lie, and she could spell, which made speaking to other adults over her head impossible.

"I got homework," Doug said, dropping his backpack to the floor. "I got to show you my new drawings first, though. Saber-toothed tiger dragon I did today. Yesterday, cobragator." He located the notebook and flipped pages, handing it to Mick once the right mythical animal combo was found.

Mick was too distracted trying to determine whether what had just transpired was real or the work of a sleep-deprived brain. An overworked brain. A brain setting one foot on the first step leading to inherited dementia. And he had no idea what he was going to feed them for dinner. "You kids want pizza?"

KARI KNOCKED ON the door several hours later—something she never did if picking up the kids. December's eager darkness had consumed the daylight. Mick's three small rectangular windows at the ceiling were black behind the thin curtains. Watching television with the kids left him nearly asleep in the dim light, so he flipped on the main overhead light and opened the door.

Her eyes were red from crying. He hated when she cried.

"You don't gotta cry alone in the car like that."

"Helen was with me. And she's asleep in the car, so I gotta—"

"You know what I mean. Hold it in so you can unload it at my kitchen table like old times." Not something he should bring up. But he wasn't just tired anymore, he was angry. He'd had too long to convince himself how badly he'd been scammed, and he was so tired of people, and the world, and that no matter how hard he worked he never got ahead. Everything was stacked so high against him there was no way to even see future financial security, much less aim for it.

"I don't want the kids to see. Were they good?"

Built into the question was also, *Is she still here?*

Mick started to push her back outside so he could explain in private, but his own eyes burned—not from despair, but fatigue—and the story was a long, unbelievable one that needed to be divulged in the happy light of day and not in the cold chill of a winter night. All that wind had brought winter in hard, judging from the intense drop in temperature in just a few hours. He waved her in so he could close the door before all his expensive heat got sucked out.

Instead, he said, "They're always good. Good enough to leave with Old Mae if this happens again and I can't—"

"Mick, I'm not expecting an elderly woman to watch my kids."

He was too tired to argue. He'd never won before, and he'd surely not win now. "So, more bad news?"

She gathered a brave breath. "Not exactly. Not good news either. But some possibilities. I'm tryin' not to get my hopes up."

Janie ran into her legs, clinging to her. She always got so needy when the TV made her sleepy. She had tried to cuddle Mick, complaining the whole time he was not soft like Mommy.

"Doug wants to spend the night here, but I got a U-Fill shift tonight."

Doug materialized behind them. "I can stay up, Mom. I'll draw behind the counter and stay quiet. And help Uncle Mick."

Kari gave Mick the look that said a million things. Among them: *You do too much for me. I can't ask you to do this but it would mean the world to him.*

"It's cool. It's only until midnight. I like the company."

"Yeah," Doug chimed in. "If I come, he won't be lonely." Nothing ever beat ten-year-old logic.

SEVERAL NIGHTS A week Mick worked the six to midnight shift at a 24-hour U-Fill gas station convenience store on the interstate. The owner could no longer afford to pay two clerks during the night. It was a lonely job, but a peaceful one. Business was slow but steady, one monotonous sale of gasoline and sundries to sleepy travelers and caffeinated truck drivers spaced by long stretches of quiet. Sometimes he got to run a junkie out of the unisex restroom. Sometimes he got to catch shoplifters and tell them to get lost. More often he had to chase raccoons out of the dumpster. They were sneakier than the junkies and shoplifters combined.

Mostly he spent the hours reading secondhand paperback Westerns behind the counter, drinking coffee and trying not to fall asleep. He hit the coffee as soon as he clocked in. Then he parked Doug by the door to the restroom with instructions to holler if someone came in the store, and he went to the sink to scrub his grease monkey fingernails with the scrub brush he hid on a ledge in the back of the cabinet. If his boss saw him working with dirty nails, he'd kill him then fire him. In that order. Usually he cleaned up at home, but sometimes he didn't have time if he got stuck late at the shop. And sometimes he was too busy stopping women from vandalizing cars then saving them from violent boyfriends then taking them to his apartment and getting nearly assaulted by them.

"*What?*" he said to his reflection in the restroom mirror after reliving the day's events for the hundredth time.

"What?" came from outside the door.

"Nothing, Dougie. Just talkin' to myself." He fixed the edge of the bandage on his arm and rolled his sleeve back over it. He should probably clean the wound again and apply a fresh bandage. He was too tired to care.

"Hey, it ain't Dougie anymore, remember?"

"Aw, shoot," Mick said, coming out. "You'll have to go easy on me, Douglas. Habits are hard for old folks to break."

"Not Douglas either. *Doug.*"

"Gotcha." Mick dragged the folding chair from the back room and set it up behind the counter in Doug's normal spot. Visible to Mick, invisible to customers. He rang up a bottle of chocolate milk and set it on the chair. Doug unzipped his backpack to retrieve his sketchbook and pencil and settled in, catching Mick's eye. Contentment, admiration, gratitude—it was the look a boy should give his father, not his uncle. Well, not *this* uncle, the man responsible for that child's fatherlessness. It always felt too much like Mick's fault. He'd befriended the guy; he'd introduced him to his sister. For years after that he'd watched the guy treat her like shit. Then one day Kari mentioned divorce, and Mick found her a lawyer and helped her stick to it—like Mick, she was also too nice, even to divorce a useless jerk—and waited through all the legal stuff, the threats, the ugly behavior, until one night he showed up at Kari's, high and violent and ready to punish the woman who'd divorced him.

Mick could never unsee her in that hospital bed. Swollen face, broken wrist, bruised neck. Then it was police and lawyers and reliving it all over on repeat. She survived it and got the asshole put behind bars, but not for long enough. Mick wanted to witness an execution.

He'd finally made his peace with the whole thing when the guy's meth addict brother cornered Kari at the elementary school, demanding she retract her story so his brother could make parole. Not that it would've even worked—the guy was out of his mind. More police, more lawyers, more bills she couldn't pay. But the creep was too sneaky to get busted on drugs, and the threats he'd made against Kari and the kids were her word against his. He was still out there somewhere, dead set on avenging his brother, a constant possibility of surprise visits, an everyday stomach-churning threat to Kari and the kids.

The most annoying part gave Mick the most guilt. If he hadn't hooked Kari up with that guy, there'd be no Doug, Janie, and Helen. And wishing them out of existence—if even to spare them—was the sickest part of all of it. He couldn't do it. So he had to accept the situation for what it was, and it was real horse shit.

Mick secretly wished Kari would find and marry a nice guy who'd protect her. It might be sexist, or a caveman ideal, but it was true. He wanted to check the pound for a Rottweiler or Doberman in need of a home, but the adoption fees were an unthinkable chunk of his paycheck, and Kari already had three kids. She didn't need another mouth to feed, another creature demanding her attention. The American in him whispered, *Buy her a gun and teach her to use it*, but the realist said, *Get real. Guns cause more trouble than they're worth*. It'd be more likely for her ex to take it away from her and use it on her. Or shoot her with his own the second she drew it.

"Cobrahawk. Fangs *and* talons. I kinda messed up the head, though."

Doug's drawing on the counter came into focus.

"That's the best one yet. Where d'ya come up with this stuff?"

His shrug was cool, cocky, and dismissive—the body language of a young man, not a little boy. "I just pick the most epic animals and put 'em together."

"How do you know a cobra and a hawk go together?"

"Dude, how do they *not?*"

Mick laughed. He picked up his coffee cup for a refill and noticed he hadn't even finished it. Doug was a lifeboat keeping him from drowning in fatigue. The couple ounces of coffee he had ingested did nothing but churn the anger that spiked earlier, giving it more life and more validation instead of making him alert.

He'd definitely been scammed. What she wanted from him was the mystery. If she thought he had any cash, she was crap at picking her targets. If she wanted to kill him, it wasn't going to go well on a second attempt—she'd lost her element of surprise. *Viking blood*, she'd said. It was so random. No one in his family made much out of where they'd come from. They were American and that's all that mattered. Fair and tall, he might've looked the part if he took off the jeans and hoodie, donned some furs and weapons, grown a beard and long hair, and hopped onto an old Viking ship. As he was, the blond hair had just enough shaggy wave to turn what could be intimidating good looks into boyish and relatable. People liked him before he opened his mouth. Not only for his genetic lottery win of physical looks but because of how he carried himself. Easy, inviting, friendly. He was simply just a nice guy.

Too nice, he thought. *An idiot.*

Because the moment that kept leaping back into his head was that crowbar sliding from her hand, its clang on the pavement that had traveled into him with a driving purpose. Gears engaging, a stalled engine finally firing up. That sudden brightness in her eye like she saw into him, saw who he was, and offered all her acceptance, her agreement. Her choice to give up whatever revenge she was carrying out and join him. It didn't matter what for. For something. Anything.

"No it didn't."

"What didn't?"

Mick ran a rough hand through his hair. "Nothin'. Just talkin' to myself again."

Doug stopped sketching to look up at him, lips tight, eyebrows drawn. The boy's thoughts were obvious because they matched Mick's own.

"It's not like your granddad talkin' to himself." Or was it? "I had a real busy day. Just tryin' to sort it all out."

MICK BUCKLED DOUG into the warming GTO ten minutes before midnight. It saved him from having to explain to Brenda, the woman who worked the next shift. He had no reason not to trust her, but he didn't want to test it. She had enough ex-husbands and tattoos to scare a guy like Mick. He stood at the door and watched his car until Brenda's Jeep brakes squeaked into her spot, then he was out of there.

His bed. That's all he could think about. Any bed, really. The floor even. He blinked himself awake all the way home while Doug sunk into the seat and nodded off, his little head jostling with the ride. *This is how exhausted people drive off the road and die,* he thought. *They just give in for one second and close their eyes.*

Not now, with Doug in there with him. He cracked the window and let the December night air in. The cold stung in his nose and throat, slapping him awake. At the house he jiggled Doug alert so he could walk inside and put him in bed in the tiny bedroom. He threw an old comforter on the couch, snagged a quilt off the chair, and fell into a dead sleep.

"Uncle Mick."

The whisper leaked right into his ear and pried him from sleep. Mick reached for the object poking his arm and caught a little hand. He couldn't see, his vision too blurry and narrow. "Yeah, what's up?"

"There's somethin' in my room."

Mick's eyelids were locked in a position offering only a mail-slot view. He strained his face, but they wouldn't unstick. The muscles themselves were still in a hard sleep. "It's fine, Dougie, go on back to bed."

"I heard scratches, then I saw somethin' movin' around on the floor."

Mice, probably. He'd tell Old Mae in the morning—no, on second thought he wouldn't. She'd say they were Nature's creatures and tell him to either keep a cleaner apartment or learn to cohabitate with the rodents he was feeding. And then he'd be nagged about keeping the apartment clean for months after that. And be reminded how the bad housekeeping was doing no favors to his love life, *and what about that sweet thing, you know, the Thompson girl, she always has such a nice smile...*

Yeah, a nice smile and zero chemistry with Mick.

He'd have to catch the little devils and take them to the old barn. And stop leaving dirty dishes out. Mick patted Doug on the arm. "Probably just a little mouse. Nothin' to be scared of. Go on back, bud."

"Uncle *Mick*. It wasn't no mouse."

"Wasn't *any* mouse." Mick sat up, rubbing his eyes, willing them to work again. The digital clock display was blurry but readable: 2:06 a.m. No way he could've been sleeping that long. It felt like nothing but an extended blink. "Okay, if I check it out, you goin' back to bed?"

Doug gave a grateful nod.

"All right."

Mick's head swam as he got up. At the bedroom door, he flipped on the light and had to step back out of the room the explosion in his head was so severe, nearly knocking Doug into the wall due to him being glued to Mick's hip. The table lamp on the nightstand was too far away, so he had to let his eyes water until they adjusted.

Together they did a sweep of the room. Closet, under the bed, behind the dresser. Doug looked for monsters, and

Mick looked for mouse droppings. Neither were found. So Mick tucked the boy back in and ruffled his hair. "Put that imagination to sleep, kid."

"Will you leave the door open?"

"Sure thing."

Mick shouldn't have turned on the light. He should've used a flashlight. He was wide awake now; he'd never fall back asleep. Flat on the couch, he had thirty seconds to worry he'd have to go in to work the next day on an hour and a half of sleep before he melted into the couch and was out again.

MICK WOKE IN a violent shiver, his teeth chattering, his fingers and toes numb. The couch had gone damp, bristly, densely hard. Through his eyelids the morning light fell at a strange slant with an intensity never allowed through his basement apartment windows. The air shifted, hissing in his ears, a restless tune of ghosts, of clean white bone and grinning skulls, brushing across him like an outside wind, cold, so cold—

He jolted upright, his eyes open. Dry leaves tangled in dead grass, trees, sky. He extended an arm, watched his fingers tremble in the cold. Beyond them, bare feet and legs. Bare everything. He went onto his knees, spinning around, looking for houses, people, cars—anyone to be witness to him outside, naked like this. It was a bad dream. A naked-in-an-inappropriate-place dream. Glossy red blood trickled from his wounded arm. Birds flew out of a nearby evergreen. He followed their ascent into the hazy blue sky. Which wasn't right at all. Mick didn't dream in color.

Sleepwalking. Dementia. Pop used to do this before we got him stable.

Up and running, one hand over his junk. This was real, and freezing to death wasn't on his to-do list. The ground had to be cutting up his feet, but they were too cold and numb to care. He knew it was morning, knew which direction was east. But he had no idea where he was, so knowing directions wasn't much help—although somehow, he had a vague recollection of the route he'd come, the path he needed to return on. The vantage point was off, though. Trees stood silent all around, a mix of harsh bare limbs and pine needles smacking him as he ran by. The canopy grew denser with more evergreens filtering subdued morning light. Ahead, a wash of brightness. He ran toward it and was ejected onto a barren winter field. At its farthest edge sat the old barn. Beyond it, a glint of Brazen Orange Metallic. His car was a salvation he ran to, his apartment door a slab of wood suitable for worship.

Then he remembered Doug.

He turned the knob—locked. And the door was too solid in the jamb to be locked with only the knob, which meant the dead bolt was locked too. Impossibility shuddered through him so strongly he took the steps back to the lawn and looked up at the house to make sure it was the right one. An identical house with an identical '06 GTO was a bigger impossibility than sleepwalking and locking the door behind him, so he slipped around the corner of the house to the big planter where Old Mae had buried a spare key. It was still there. He blew off the dirt and let himself into his apartment, grabbing a jacket off the hook by the door to wrap around his waist. Doug sat in his coat at the kitchen table, back stiff, watching the door.

"Dougie, I'm sorry, so sorry."

"Where'd you go?" His voice was small, held tight so it wouldn't tremble.

"I don't—how long was I gone?"

Doug shrugged. It was apparent the time didn't matter. What mattered was Mick wasn't there when he expected him there. Doug's father was gone, all ties cut, and the only man Doug knew had just left for no known reason. A scab reopened, a pain reignited.

"Okay, let me get some clothes and we'll figure this out."

Chapter

3

Doug pointed to the pile of Mick's clothes on the couch. Mick had no idea why he'd take them off to go outside in the middle of the night or how he'd explain all this to Doug. He didn't lie to kids, not if he could help it. Getting dressed didn't give him enough time to come up with a believable white lie anyway, especially since the long rip in the back of his shirt consumed his attention. Tearing up clothes in his sleep was a new strange tic he could've done without.

"Truth?" he said, sitting in the chair facing Doug. "I'd never step out on you like that and not come back. You have my word. We clear there?"

Doug took a tight breath. Nodded.

"As for where I went … I guess I went outside and fell asleep. Just wait till your mom hears about this. She'll slay me."

Doug smiled a little at that, not because he wanted to but because he couldn't help it. All the kids loved it when Kari laid into Mick. They giggled until the giggling itself became funny, and then there was no stopping them. Their mother was too sweet to do any of the things she threatened them with, but to Mick, all bets were off.

"And I guess I lost my key out there, so Old Mae's gonna slay me again when your mom's done."

"You broke the window too." Doug pointed.

Still thawing, Mick hadn't even noticed shards of the old glass dangling in the frame. He crossed the room and found more glass on the floor and nearby armchair. This house was simply too remote to attract break-ins.

Then he remembered the woman he'd brought there.

"Well, shoot," he said, letting himself back outside to investigate. What he found was more glass outside—more than what he'd found in the apartment. He was no detective, but he could make an educated guess: this window was broken from the inside.

Doug sidled up beside him, hands in the pockets of his coat. "You think it was an animal or somethin'? Like a coon?"

"Nah, they're too smart to want to break into my place. Nothin' for them in there." He didn't bother pointing out the window was broken from the other way. "I'll fix this later. Let's get some breakfast in you."

"Can I help you fix it?"

"Sure thing." He gave Doug a fist bump. He had no idea when that was going to happen. He needed the daylight and wouldn't be off work until after dark. Tonight was his night off. Maybe he could borrow the cordless work light from the shop. If he could fix the window fast, maybe Old Mae wouldn't have to know about it. He needed to get the frame out and drop it at the hardware store for new glass on his drive into work.

All he had was dry cereal since he was out of milk. He dug out some peanut butter granola bars and found some discount brand orange soda in the back of the fridge to substitute for orange juice. Kari was going to kill him. Doug was going to elect him president.

Leaving Doug to savor his liquid sugar breakfast, he took the window frame off the hinge and collected a trash bag and duct tape to patch the hole so it would at least be weatherproof while he was at work. He searched the utility room before remembering he'd left the stepstool in the bedroom after replacing a light bulb.

In the bedroom he found something else entirely. It took a long moment for his overworked system to process the sludgy black mess trailing across the laminate floor to a puddle of the stuff leaking from under the bed. The odor—rotten, spoiled, dead, like decomposing leaves or an unkempt barnyard. Too many surprises and not enough sleep in the last twenty-four hours left him unable to see it for the otherworldly thing it was. He hollered through the doorway. "Doug, you spill somethin' in here?"

Doug had slept in there. Even if he hadn't done it, he would've noticed it.

"No, sir," came the reply.

"You see this mess?"

He heard Doug's kitchen chair scoot. Then he appeared with his can of orange soda in hand. "What mess?"

"Did you see this when you got up?"

"No, sir." His eyes got big with the innocent recognition of how something might look like his fault, but he had no proof why it wasn't.

Mick didn't mean to frown at him, but he found himself doing it. He just didn't understand how anyone could miss such a strange mess. "Was it too dark to see?"

"Guess so. I didn't turn on the light. I thought you were on the couch, but you weren't, so I waited out there for you. Ew," he said, pinching his nose closed. "Smells gross."

Together they squatted to peek under the bed. Together they leaned forward; together they jolted back.

"Holy shit," Mick said as Doug said, "Holy moly."

Without the gooey puddle, the small object under the bed would've looked like a deflated ball. A broken toy, discarded, in no way threatening. Balls didn't often come in such an unusual textured black, though, and they didn't leak dirty motor oil. These ideas alone were also no threat. But a primitive part of Mick recognized it would've been a threat—or it had been a threat. And if this object were a thing he could name he'd say it, identify it for what it was so Doug didn't have to scoot behind him and look so terrified.

Mick noticed then how off its shape was, how incorrect and grotesque. Two extended pieces, one flipped over the object's main bulk, the other lying on the floor. Limbs? Maybe, but pointy on the ends with several curved barbs. Two shorter ones bunched at the end. Also pointed.

"What is that thing?"

A name would help. It would take the unfamiliarity out of the mix, allow the threat to be sized-up and processed. It's a copperhead. Cancer. A terrorist. Then at least Mick would know what he was dealing with and plan accordingly. He felt like a kid again, imagining a monster under his bed, unable to name it and deal with it.

"No clue." Was this what Doug had seen moving around on the floor last night? Mick didn't want to ask and remind him—it brought it all too close, and his pulse was already hitting hard. Mick was too young to have a heart attack. Standing, he got a hanger out of the closet. "You want to head on back to the kitchen and I'll pull it out?"

"I wanna stay with you."

"You probably don't wanna see this."

"S'okay. Do it."

Mick did it. It took a couple tries before he got the hanger hooked solidly enough to drag the thing out, and when it slid from the shadow under the bed into the light, both Mick and Doug scrambled backward, Mick knocking Doug's soda from his hand as he shoved him back.

Chalky gray hide. Beady brown-red eyes. A gaping mouth lined with double rows of sharklike teeth. The limbs Mick had identified were indeed arms, extending from a muscular upper body that would've packed some punch in upright form. The lower body was smaller. The whole thing was structured like a miniature gorilla, with two exposed bony ridges extending from the front of the head and running down its back. Shiny black claws extended from every digit. And the thing's gut was a slimy black hole of gore.

"What the hell is that?" Mick shouted, still pushing Doug backward out the doorway.

It looked like it belonged in some kind of fictional underworld, a creature of death, a dealer of pain. It was wrong for the known world, for Mick's world, for the bedroom where he'd put his nephew to bed and dismissed complaints of scratching noises and something moving around.

Mick didn't curse, but he was cursing now. He was fighting mad. This was one thing too many. Held at knifepoint in his own damn home. Sleepwalking naked in the cold, abandoning his nephew. No food in the house and a damn broken window he didn't have time to fix. Now a gory carcass under his bed?

"No," he said. He wasn't accepting it. He needed to go to work, hit the grocery store, and fix that window. He needed to clean up his apartment and pay his bills. He didn't need to dispose of any strange corpses. He didn't have the time or the know-how, and he didn't want anything to do with it.

He caught the sound of Doug's voice then, and he tuned in.

"...has to be, don't ya think? We need to take a picture, because people always say they see aliens, but no one ever has any good pictures and if we—"

"No pictures. I don't think—" Mick couldn't think.

"I kinda feel sorry for it. It looks super scary, but do you think it woulda hurt us?"

With those teeth and claws and its pit bull build, it was only built for dishing out hurt.

"Maybe it was friendly," Doug continued. "What do you think killed it? You think there was another one that ran away?"

Images scattered across Mick's memory. His shivering hand extended in front of him in the angle of bright morning sun, the hibernating forest all around. A crash of breaking glass throwing reflection into the night. A dark streak in a dark room, charging, motion halted, a flop onto the floor.

Mick's ringtone shrilled from the other room.

"I gotta clean this up," he said, suddenly aware of how important that was.

"Can we show Mom first?"

One problem: He didn't have time to clean it up. He had to take a shower and go to work. Time was ticking hard upon him, and the phone wouldn't shut up. Strangely enough the sight that bothered him the most was the spilled orange soda. He picked up the can. "Hey, grab me a towel from the kitchen, will ya?"

Doug brought one, wetted from the sink. "It gets sticky unless you use water."

"Stay back. I don't want you near that thing."

"Will you bury it proper?"

Mick wanted to incinerate it, but he wasn't going to tell Doug that. "Yeah, I'll say a prayer and everything."

"Do you think it has an alien family?"

"I hope not."

The phone started up again. Mick wiped the soda off the floor and pushed Doug out of the room, shutting the door behind them. The whole thing would be gone when he got home from work, he knew it. It was all a big hallucination. He was going to sit Kari down and ask her if she remembers the early years of Pop's dementia. Between the two of them, they might be able to determine what year it started. Not the year Pop was diagnosed, but the year he first started speaking of strange things and getting lost in the house and calling them the wrong names. Did their grandpop have it or anyone else up the line? Maybe if Mick got on some drugs right now, his wouldn't get as bad as Pop's. He couldn't afford to check out of life, not with a sister and a father who both depended on him. Speaking of, today was his day to check on Pop after work.

SATURDAYS WERE THE busiest days at the shop. Good for making the time slip by. Not good for busting up knuckles, sweating through his coveralls, and pretty much every other reason. Mick's arm was bleeding through its latest bandage. Only he knew what he'd done to it before waking up naked in the woods that morning, and he *didn't* know. After finishing up a brake job, he wiped his hands on a rag and went out back for a mid-morning break by the dumpster. He remembered the two phone calls he'd missed that morning and checked his voicemail. One was an unknown number, no message. The other was Pop's home nurse calling to say she had a family emergency and had to catch the earliest flight east. She had no idea when she'd be able to come back, so he probably needed to find a new nurse.

"Really?" he said to the dumpster.

It said nothing back, which was a relief. He put a hand in his pocket and jingled his keys, the ones he thought he'd lost in the woods when he was locked outside. Turns out they were on the counter where he'd left them the night before. Could he have sleepwalked outside, dug up the spare key, locked the door behind him, then buried the key again? It was possible, but the dirt in that planter hadn't been disturbed. He would have noticed that.

He sent a text to Kari: *You bring Doug or I pick up? I get off at 5.*

She texted right back: *I talked him out of it.*

So Mick wouldn't have his helper for the window. Worried she'd heard about the alien corpse because it actually was real, and Doug saw it too, and it was still lying on his bedroom floor, he texted, *Why?*

Because I missed him last night and I'm selfish. :)

She was always saying Doug was her anchor.

OK, well I need to talk to you. Tomorrow?

Mick's boss came outside with his reading glasses on, a box of rolled bandages tucked under his chin and freshly washed hands held up to dry in the air. "Let me see that arm, cowboy."

"Hey, Virgil, you mind if I borrow that cordless work light for the night?" Mick rolled his sleeve up. Virgil was both owner and grandpa of the shop and arguing with him wasn't a worthwhile use of anyone's time.

Virgil unraveled the old bandage and let it drop. "As long as it comes back with you Monday, it's all yours. You finally doing some work on that Pontiac?"

"Nah, just a window in my place. Hoped to get it fixed tonight." Mick cringed at the cold sting of antiseptic. With his other hand he jingled his keys again. "Hey, you ever heard of an animal breakin' a window out?"

"A wild animal?"

Mick regretted asking. It sounded crazy. *He* wanted to be the first one to determine he was crazy, not anyone else. "Yeah, I don't know. Never mind."

"Can't think of an animal that'd do that. Human animal, maybe. You have any smart ass neighbor kids who like to throw rocks?"

ON THE DRIVE to Pop's place, Mick had himself convinced the alien carcass in his bedroom was a dream. It couldn't really be an alien. A monster? Demon? It didn't matter. The morning had been normal. He and Doug had eaten dry cereal, granola bars, and orange soda at the kitchen table, then he'd driven to Kari's, watched Doug hop from the GTO and sprint up the lawn to the open door where both he and Janie waved from the porch, Janie's finger-in-light-socket hair cuter than anything he could dream up. Kari gathered them inside and Mick went to work. He was so tired and stressed, he'd combined real life memory with dream memory. Which wasn't a healthy thing, but it wasn't dementia.

He'd brought the work light because the hardware store had called to say his glass replacement was finished. The broken window *was* real. And still a mystery. But the glass was fixed now, in his trunk and ready to go back into the frame and make the whole thing go away.

"Hey, Pop," he called as he opened the door. "Got you some groceries."

He'd gotten himself some too—actual vegetables and bread and fresh catfish for dinner, plus the eggs and milk he'd missed out on the day he'd brought that woman home. She was still a mystery too, responsible for the new set of busted knuckles he'd earned when he was thinking about her instead of the wrench he was pulling at work.

"And I got you a cake. Pop?" It always gave him the sickest fright when the house was quiet like this.

From the old portable tube TV on the kitchen table, a pioneer family stared back at him in black and white, their covered wagon behind them. Normally Pop would be in the opposite chair, arms crossed, one fist against his chin as he absorbed a history program he'd probably viewed ten times. Mick dropped the bags on the counter. He packed the cold stuff in the fridge and freezer while trying not to think about this being the day he'd find Pop on the floor and he should've moved him into his place with him and it was all his fault—

Stop, Mick thought. The nurse said he was perfectly capable of living on his own as long as he had people checking on him often. Mick's apartment was too small for two people who needed their own privacy, and no way was Mick moving back in with his father. Either situation would mean Mick would never have a social life. But he already didn't have one, so he couldn't really see the difference.

Mick took the hall to the larger bedroom's half-open door and rapped softly on the frame. "Pop?"

A rustling inside. "That you, Mickey?"

Recognition. A correct name. This was a good day.

"Yeah. Come on out. I got you a gooey butter cake." A sudden flash of the deflated alien corpse passed across Mick's mind. Why on earth would he dream up such a thing? He had enough to haunt him already. A shrink could probably explain it, but forgetting it seemed like a better idea along with forgetting that woman. Mick pledged to get on that.

Pop came out in his plaid housecoat and slippers, wispy white hair smashed on one side.

"Were you lyin' down? I didn't mean to ruin a nap."

"Well that's exactly what you did, so show me the cake and we'll see if I forgive you."

Mick unbagged and opened the cake. "Lacy has to take some time off, so we'll have to find you a new nurse. How big a piece you want?"

"Depends. What's the occasion, Mighty?"

Mick's cake-slicing hand paused. He never got used to his dad launching right into the madness. One half of a sentence sounded like him, the back half spoken by a stranger. It always felt like a joke, one that no one was getting. "Pop, it's Mick. You call me Mickey. I'm cool with either."

"That's all wrong, Mighty Eagle. Now you listen. It's one down, so many more to go. I hear it all on the radio."

"Great, Pop. You like that cake?"

Pop took a tiny, cautionary bite, like a child. "Hmm. Not bad. What do they call that?"

"Gooey butter, your favorite. Mom used to fix it all the time, remember?" He wasn't sure what made him say that. He didn't want the confirmation that Pop didn't remember, and in this state, it was certain he wouldn't. So Mick busied himself putting groceries in cabinets while his father talked nonsense about the voices in the static on the radio. Underground spirits, bloody earth, stolen land—it was all too much for Mick, and his catfish wasn't on ice in his car. "I gotta run. Remember—no Lacy tomorrow. I'll stop by again or Kari will. Be sure to call us if you need anything before then, okay?"

"Mickey..." Pop stiffly rose from his chair to put a frail hand on Mick's shoulder. "You be careful, no matter what—"

"I'm always careful, Pop."

"Follow Mighty Eagle and listen to your heart. There's an evil livin' under this land, and when they rise there will be two paths. One of blood, and one of—"

"Hey…" Mick took his father's hand off his shoulder and handed it back to him, trying not to dwell on how bony it felt, how thin his wrist was "…don't eat too much of that cake, it'll rot your teeth." He had a flush moving from his gut into his head, and he wasn't sure from what. Stress, anger, fatigue—all of it. Unpayable bills, baby Helen's arms bruised from IVs, his father deteriorating before his eyes. A broken window, an alien corpse. The haunted black-and-white faces of Indians on the TV screen on the table. And that damn woman in the parking lot, the sad surrender of her crowbar clanging against the concrete, the blink of possibility between them. Mick didn't even know her name, and he couldn't admit how much he wanted to. She'd scammed and attacked him. She probably broke out his window. Regretting not asking her name proved to Mick how far gone he really was.

He led his nonsense-talking father back to his chair, turned the sound up on the history program, and hit the road in his GTO, foot hard on the pedal, hands solid on the wheel, speed and G's grinding his body into the seat as he lost his mind in the most voluntary of ways.

CHAPTER 4

OLD MAE'S PORCH light shone through the trees when Mick turned onto the driveway. He couldn't remember ever seeing the front of the house lit like that, certainly not the two windows above it or the ones on the side. He groaned, knowing some axe was about to fall. She'd found out about the window. She'd noticed he'd taken the key. He was a grown man, but she'd held him as a newborn and babysat him as a kid. He'd lived under her house since the day he graduated high school. She was an unforgiving landlady and an adopted grandma with high expectations and a skill for inducing a man's guilt.

Not that he couldn't handle her. He just didn't have an ounce of fight in him now.

He parked in his usual spot because she was probably pissed about the grass he drove on yesterday. Unloading the groceries from the trunk, he tuned his ear to that specific creak of the front door. The wind had died; the land around seemed eternally still in air so crisp it was intoxicating, especially after that drive. This mild December had gone righteously cold. Stars were blinking awake in a midnight blue sky still smeared with a fraction of burnt orange light in the west.

The axe never fell. It was a win he didn't expect. An escape he so desperately needed. And standing in that perfect air made it settle so true in his bones he couldn't move. He tilted his head back and felt the weight of groceries in his arms grounding him as the height of the new night's sky stretched him away. He was high on it, flying. The meditation packed into each passing second built upon itself, into something so pure it began to heal, to make everything doable, surmountable, the fight worth it, his life made okay again.

He was good. Things were good. He had catfish and French bread for dinner. He'd splurged on a bottle of craft beer. He was going to cook, eat, fix the window, clean up his place. The beer was his reward for all that, and he was going to savor it then go to bed.

Think again, said his apartment. The light was already on. His kitchen already occupied. He didn't drop his groceries, but he wanted to.

"Hello." She was more beautiful than he remembered. It wasn't a familiar kind of beauty but something one had to work a little harder to see.

And Mick found the work easy, like he was made for the specific labor of it, born with the skills to see what others would dismiss as too rugged for beauty. Too natural, too plain. He didn't want anyone to look too closely. They might get a hint of the perfection he saw with just one look, and he didn't want to share.

"Hi," he stupidly returned. That beer he bought—the glass bottle could be used as a weapon. It was in the bag in his left hand, the one in the back resting against his leg. The thought of fighting her, the physicality of it, made him hot all over. "How'd you get in here?"

"The door."

He knew he hadn't left it unlocked because he'd just felt the dead bolt slide out of the jamb. Or maybe he did leave it unlocked, and she'd come in and locked it behind her. "You picked my lock?"

She stood from the chair she'd been sitting in at his table. The height of her in his kitchen made Mick wish that glass bottle was in his hand. Following that idea for a few steps left him helpless—he couldn't hit a woman, not on offense. Defense, maybe, but even then he'd be fighting his own instincts just as hard as he'd be fighting her.

"Mind if I put these down?" He lifted the bags. If he was friendly perhaps he could avoid having to hit her—but he was friendly the first time and he'd ended up with a blade against his neck.

She swept an arm, turning to the side so he had room to pass. That close though? It was almost a dare, one Mick had no choice but to take because he was no coward. He brushed by her and set the bags on the counter, his back to her, and started unloading them into the fridge since he had no idea what else to do. He could blame himself for going so long without a date he'd gone sadly out of practice with women, but that didn't seem to matter with this one. She wasn't sweet Sammi Thompson with the nice smile. This woman didn't smile. Her lips were formed into a line of determination. If only Mick knew what she wanted.

When he turned around she was removing her brown puffy coat like she'd been invited to dinner. Underneath she wore a tan blouse, the loose neckline beaded with white and turquoise. Tight, well-worn jeans across long legs. Brown cowboy boots rubbed with age. Mick guided his eyes back to her face, those broad cheeks and high, dark eyes, naturally squinty even when she wasn't glaring. More beads dangling from her ears. The shiny hair parted in the middle and hanging down on both sides. He put it together and knew he was right enough to say it aloud. "You're Indian."

"That's a broad term, but expected from an ignorant white man."

"Guilty. I don't know my tribes."

"*Your* tribes?" Her glare cut him up, sideways and backward.

"*The* tribes. It's a figure of speech. Anyone ever tell you there's a bit of a chip on your shoulder?"

"You're making me regret not killing you."

Mick pushed past her and retrieved her coat from the chair where she'd hung it. He held it up, open so she could slide her arms in. "You're leavin'."

She didn't move.

Mick held his ground. "And not comin' back."

She licked the corner of her lip, watching Mick like she wanted to eat him. "You're terribly cute."

He felt the air leave his lungs. He had to hold it together, had to get her out the door. "I thought you said my Viking blood reeks."

One short laugh, its accompanying smile too slight to notice. "Did I say that?"

Ask her name, Mick heard in his head. No matter how desperate he was for it, he couldn't do it. It would open a door he couldn't close. He shook her coat, hoping to remind her she was being kicked out.

Her eyes didn't leave his face. She slid both hands in the back pockets of her jeans and waited for Mick to cave. The red in her eye had cleared up, but the bruised lip had gone darker purple with a yellow tinge beneath it. Now

Mick knew the wounds probably weren't the result of her innocent victimhood but the marks of a fight she started, some other guy who did act in defense when that knife went against his throat.

Mick tossed the coat at her. He wasn't going to cave. He had a big enough pile to manage, and he wasn't about to take anything else on. She let the coat hit her, unfazed as it dropped to the floor. Still watching him. Waiting.

He pointed to the door.

"Where's the other one?"

"Other what?"

She aimed her chin at his closed bedroom door where the dream alien's carcass lay in Mick's imagination. "I also need to know how you did it. But first you tell me where."

The walls fell down around him, a crumbling, quaking chaos. She knew about the alien. It was either real, or she joined the alien as part of an unending hallucination. Both options proved Mick's mind was leaving him, and there was no third option, no normal reality to tether him down. Reality was screwed-up—or Mick's brain was.

He crossed the room, threw open the bedroom door, flipped on the light. Unsure what he saw was real or fake, he turned the light off and back on. The same clean floor spread in front of him. No evidence of the gloppy trail or the deflated gory corpse he'd dragged from under the bed.

"Don't look so surprised. I'm thorough. But the other one is not here, and you're going to show me where it is before someone else finds it."

The alien wasn't real. It was the woman who was a hallucination, and she only knew about the alien because she came from the same malfunctioning brain matter that created it. Mick didn't know if this was good news or the end of his life as he knew it. It needed more thought and collaboration with Kari. He also knew ignoring the corpse this morning made it go away, so that was his plan for this woman too.

He returned to the kitchen and washed his hands. Got out the skillet. Unwrapped his catfish. She settled her hip against the counter, both hands still in her back pockets. Mick gave himself a silent command: *Ignore her*. It wasn't easy. She was so close; she seemed so real. His imagination had never conjured something so convincing, and he had no idea how—he'd never met an American Indian woman. Seen them in movies and on TV, sure, but how authentic was that? And yeah, he read a lot of Westerns, but those descriptions seemed more caricature than real. And this woman was too human to be fabricated. Too imperfectly perfect.

That's when he gave in and looked, long and hard. If this was a hallucination, he could choose to enjoy it. After all, he was the one in control.

She raised both eyebrows at his scrutiny. Still no smile—she certainly wasn't the type to fake a smile just to soften the moment. It shouldn't have been so appealing. Mick liked nice girls. He didn't go for trouble.

He also didn't feel right about eating in front anyone—real or hallucination—so his manners split the food down the middle and prepared two plates. Now there was a speck of smile only in her eyes, along with that constant glare.

"How do you pull that off?" he asked her—and himself, since he was the one responsible for all of this.

"My restraint?"

He was supposed to be ignoring her, but she was here, and he was lonely. He didn't realize how lonely until now. "And there wasn't no other one, so—"

"There was. I think you took it outside and killed it. We'll go for a walk and you can show me where." She sat at the table. "After we eat."

"I fix my window after we eat. Then I drink my beer. And then I go to bed." Mick filled two glasses with ice and water and sat across from her. Curiosity and indulgence teamed up to defeat good manners, and he allowed himself a long stare. For the first time he noticed the asymmetry of her upper ear piercings. On one ear, those two tiny stones nestled in the curve—one pure white, one a crystalline sky blue. On the other, a delicate gold hoop closer to the middle. He wondered about the imbalance, and how he could like it so much.

"I'll watch you fix the window and help you drink your beer. Then we go for a walk. And when we find the second one, you're going to tell me how you killed them."

"I didn't kill nothin'."

"You didn't just kill it, you gutted it. From what I saw, it looked like you enjoyed it." She stabbed her fish and took a bite. "I'm not sure who, or what, you are. You can tell me now or on our walk."

"I don't have to tell you—"

"You do. Because I know you like those kids, and I know where they live."

He started to say, *What?* but stopped himself. He'd understood her just fine—too fine. And a shocked, blurted *What?* would only pass the upper hand to her. Instead, he held her eye, daring her to fully own that threat. Mick Svendsen was ninety-nine percent nice guy. Few people were witness to what made up that remaining one percent, but those who were would say its number was misleading. The force of will in that part of his makeup was so condensed, so ruthless, to invoke it was to bring on something unholy. And any threat to Mick's family dialed straight into that part of him.

"It appears I touched a nerve."

"You don't know what you touched."

"Call her. Ask if there's a black Chrysler 300 sitting across the street from her house."

Mick's dinner turned to rock in his stomach. A wave of terrible calm washed over him—behind it the understanding he was about to do something stupid, something reckless, something that would make this difficult situation worse. He forced a neutral face, took a long drink of water to buy some time to think. He couldn't stick with the idea this was all his imagination, not with a threat like that. Nightmares always felt real inside them. No one in a nightmare like this would shrug and dare the monster to eat his sister's little kids. Until he was outside of it, he wouldn't be free to do that.

So he shoveled in his dinner. He got the glass frame and work light out of his trunk and ripped the plastic out of the window opening. The woman brought her drink of water to watch him drop screws and curse, drop more screws and curse some more. Mick had become the cursing type.

The window handled, Mick went for his beer. No way in hell was he sharing. He didn't even bother with a glass. So much for savoring it.

She picked up an unopened bill from his coffee table. "Michael Svendsen. Do I call you Mike?"

Mick didn't care what she called him. He'd go on the damn walk and she'd realize she was wasting her time. She came to him and took the beer from his hand. Took a long pull from the bottle. Handed it back. The stare-off that followed made war look pretty.

He'd never hated anyone like this. Never felt so invaded or at someone else's mercy. Never been so intrigued, so curious, so desperate to reach out and touch, prove it was real and not some demented nightmare. The danger and unexpectedness of it burned through him, helplessness mutating into power. She didn't have the upper hand. He did. He had information she wanted, and the only way to ensure she got it was to threaten the kids. She was stooping low because she had to.

"It's Mick," he said. *Now ask her name.*

No—he shouldn't give two shits about her name. She needed to know his, though, know exactly who he was.

He found a flashlight and put on his coat. "I'll walk you to where I went that night, but there won't be nothin' to see. That's all you get. Then you're gonna leave and stay the fuck away from my family." He didn't recognize his own voice.

She slid into her coat. "Mick."

It was nothing but an acknowledgment of hearing his name, but what it did to Mick—he couldn't even make sense of it. It was liquid pleasure enfolding him, stopping him dead. The flashlight slipped; he tightened his grip before it fell from his hand. This woman wasn't just trouble. She was criminal trouble. She was threatening-children trouble. It didn't matter what any of this did to him. He had to get rid of her.

Outside he didn't slow his pace for her to catch up. The moonless night stretched into forever above them. Her footsteps crunched the dead grass behind him, so he kept moving away from the halo of house lights, past the old barn, into the field, pushing into the hibernating underbrush at the edge of the woods. Darkness encroached around the flashlight's swaying beam. Without the light of day, Mick had no idea if he was on the exact route, but it was pointless to try to find it. There wasn't anything out there to show her anyway. They kicked through leaves under a watchful owl, their racket like a surprise raid on his quiet home.

"It's here," she said, a hand shooting out to grip Mick's arm to still him. He started at the contact; it became all he could see and feel. Standing in the dark woods beside her, he was lit up, wide awake, uncovered. She turned away, fingers slipping off his arm. They were a long-lost item, found then lost again. The yearning to have them back was too real to deny.

"Yes—very close. Shine your light over there."

He did. An animal darted away, rustling the bare limbs of a low bush. She said something else, but Mick's hearing had gone fuzzy. The flashlight dropped, hitting his knee, the beam flipping around. Mick was falling.

Then wind. Weightlessness. Fluid night curling around him. Tree tops reaching up, stars floating down. A moving shadow on the ground, darting, jumping. Getting closer, gaining on it. Wind pressing harder, impact. Thrashing. Restrained. Motionless.

MICK OPENED HIS eyes. Instead of his apartment's ceiling, he saw birds flapping across a round, risen, blue-white moon, its light spreading so far and wide it painted shadows of tree branches across his bare arm.

"No." He sat up, teeth chattering, painful shudders abusing every muscle, the hard ground cold and scratchy against his naked skin. "No, no, no—shit!"

The exclamation sent gloppy spittle against his arm. There was an unusual amount of saliva in his mouth. He swallowed, choking on the rotten tang so badly he had to turn and cough against the ground. Fleshy bits sprinkled the dead grass. A swipe of hand over his mouth brought a similar toned smear he stared at long enough to arrive at a decision: if it was his blood, there was something very off about it.

He got up and ran. Again, with no sense of direction or where to go. Ahead, the barn. This time no glint of Brazen Orange beyond it. He continued, finding the house, his apartment door leading underneath. But no GTO.

The door was unlocked this time, so he stumbled inside to the sink and washed out his mouth with cold water. No sting of broken skin. No scream of knocked teeth. He rinsed again, finishing off with a long drink. He turned around and saw the dinner dishes on the table. Two plates, two glasses, two napkins. Back outside, standing naked on the steps, he looked at where his car should be parked. Cureless anger left him unable to even curse. He was done, just done.

Inside, he cleaned off the table, took a shower, and went to bed with another new furious bleed from his arm wound, but he didn't care.

Chapter
5

THE SUN ROSE behind Waapikoona as she drove the orange Pontiac out of town. Loose cables dangled out of the hole where the radio should've been. She wondered if it had been stolen too and wished it hadn't been so she could find some music to smother unwanted thoughts.

"Mick Svendsen." She didn't know why she kept saying that. She needed to stop. It wasn't helping.

"Mick." His name was perfect but it meant nothing. For some reason it had nestled into her, too comfy to be shaken out. She liked the pleasant softness of the M on her lips, the hard ending sound on her tongue.

She'd decided not to tell The Silent One about Mick. It could've been because of his name. Could've been because of something else. She didn't want to think about it and had no time to waste on it. She had to come up with a lie about what killed her two Helpers. No one lied to The Silent One unless they had a wish of permanent death.

Waapikoona's wish hadn't been for death at all. Her wish had been for escape, but there had been nothing left to escape to. She'd dreamed of a return to the before, when her people were free in both mind and body, before their homeland had been claimed by strangers and sold to other strangers. The before was now long gone, centuries past, and she was revived in a new world with a new duty as a different kind of slave.

My terms, she reminded herself. *Only a slave if I act like one or if he thinks I care to live.* The Silent One had raised her from the earth because he needed her. She had that power over him, and she made him very aware she only cared to live long enough to help her sister. That was her only goal. She had no reason to help with his war no matter how tempting it was. And some days it was very tempting. But not this day.

Dainty snowflakes swirled against the windshield. The road crested high then fell low, her ears popping with the change in pressure. It gently curved back and forth, putting the sun beside her, then behind, then beside her again. Every once in a while the mix of evergreens and naked deciduous trees beside the road would break, allowing a glimpse across layers of rolling hazy tops of the Ozark mountains all the way to the sun-kissed horizon. She took the turn off the state highway onto a twisty county road and reset the tripmeter.

Twelve miles later and deep in a valley, she pulled off the road and got out, raising her coat's hood against the settling cold. She hiked into the woods, turning around to spy the Pontiac through the trees. It wasn't the first car she'd stolen and wouldn't be the last. This was the first time she felt so rotten about it—maybe because it was the first time the guy didn't deserve it. Mick Svendsen had been a bad pick, poetically bad. And she hadn't technically picked him. She'd been taking care of old business when he'd interfered.

She should've left him alone, and she wished she knew why she hadn't. There was so much more to him, so much she could use. Involvement in this world was bad for her. Ties would only cloud her plans.

The cave's entrance hid below a slab of limestone jutting from the earth. Waapikoona slid in on her stomach, feet first, blindly seeking out a lip on the slippery floor with her boots before ducking all the way in. She flipped on Mick's flashlight and waited for her eyes to adjust. She could see her breath in the damp air, hear water trickling deeper below ground. She only had bad news for The Silent One, and he wasn't going to be pleased.

He can't do a thing to me. He could refuse to help her sister, and that might as well be a terrible thing done to her. She hadn't been able to protect her so long ago. She would protect her now no matter what, and getting her out of the ground was the first step.

The air warmed the deeper she went. She had to go to hands and knees then to elbows as the ceiling slanted further down. As she crawled, the passageway went from narrow to squeezing. Working her shoulders through the tight rock, she forced herself to breathe, deep and easy. Her lungs were compressing but it was temporary. She shifted her hips, wiggling and kicking until the tunnel spat her into a wide black void.

Flashlight—a mini panic at its missing lump in her pocket. She checked the other side—there. Switching it on did nothing but prove how massive the chamber was. The black emptiness swallowed her puny light. She refused to feel small. That was why The Silent One chose this room, and it wouldn't work on her.

"I'm here," she called. Her voice went on and on.

Minutes later, the hiss of hundreds of legs against wet rock echoed around her. For once, he was nearby, saving her from a long wait. She kept her light steady against the ground. If she shined it in his eyes, he'd be angered, and she didn't want to anger him any more than she knew her news would. At the edge of her light, a shiny mass slid into view—his current form. A millipede so big it filled the chamber, circling, closing her in.

"Identify yourself."

"Waapikoona."

"You bring me nothing."

"My Helpers were killed. I came for new ones."

"Killed?"

"Yes—some accident. It looked like they turned on each other and both bled out." She said it straight, without pause. Worried it sounded too rehearsed, she willed herself to not allow the nerves to get into her next words.

His hiss filled the cave. He was far from silent. She could hear his body segments creaking against one another. His name came from another time, another form. "Bring them to me."

"I burned them. I couldn't risk them being seen." It wasn't exactly a lie but more of a stretch. She'd burned *one* of them. The other had gotten away—again—but with Mick around it wouldn't last long. It was already as good as burned to ash.

"Your people are unquiet. They yearn to rise, to destroy what was built on their bones. And you waste time?"

She glimpsed two dim red eyes in the pitch black beyond her circle of light. The mind invented images in such intense darkness, so she couldn't trust it was real. She wasn't even sure if millipedes had eyes—but this wasn't a typical milli-pede. A height of black more solid than the surrounding dark-ness slid beside her. She risked a shift of her light to prove it was him so close, and she was right. A ten-foot-high mass of millipede crawled by on a faint shimmer of legs, close enough to touch. She wanted to step back, but she was sure he was behind her, too.

His voice, so close to her ear it could've been inside it. "You have no new souls for me."

Her back crawled with tiny imaginary millipede legs. "I need new Helpers."

"Your sister waits."

"I know."

"Douse your torch and offer your hands."

She turned off the flashlight and stuck it in her pocket. The darkness gulped her up. She was floating in nothingness with a giant hole of unknown around her. Her heart, calm until now, decided she was very wrong in assuming this place was safe and doubled its speed, demanding she fight or run. She took a breath and extended her hands in the dark, hoping he gave her what she asked for and not something different and terrible.

A whisper of sensation against her palm once, twice. She cupped her hands against one another. "Two?" she asked. It was so much easier with two.

"Your last two. If you are careless with those, your sister remains as bones."

"Of course." She couldn't be mad. He was a practical demon. She could be a bit annoyed, though. He knew nothing about her people or what they yearned to do. He made generalizations, lumped people together who'd been separated by thousands of years. Some of them were as different from her as she was to him. And what he was doing … one would think modern Native people should've been consulted. It was their ancestors he was raising from the dead. No one like her had brought it before Tribal leadership, for fear they might say no.

The shuffle of legs against stone carried him away. She didn't move until it was so silent her ears hummed.

In the tight tunnel leading back toward the entrance, her hood caught. With her elbows lodged against the floor and the ceiling snug against her back, she couldn't reach to free it. No matter which way she twisted, it held, and she had to stop and catch her breath. She laid her cheek against the cold stone and imagined the tunnel as not rock but ice, melting away from her inch by inch. Soon she'd be back on the surface, collecting more flesh for The Silent One. Soon she'd be presenting her sister's bones to him. Soon her sister would be free from death. And then Waapikoona could shrug off some of her regret. She wouldn't be crawling through a wet cave to appeal to a demon, and she wouldn't be so alone.

Her mind now calm, she realized she should back up to release her hood—a troubling thing to do when so desperate to move forward and get out.

Aboveground, snow had turned to sleet. She could hear its tinkle against the limestone entrance as she tucked her flashlight away and squeezed out under the slant of rock. The overcast sky left the woods gray with early dusk. Time got mixed up in The Silent One's cave, and it was never consistent. Sometimes she emerged from a thirty minute trip to find herself on a completely new day.

Her hair and jeans were wet from the cave. The sleet stung like glass. She made it to the Pontiac, set the heater to its highest level, and turned around on the road, heading back the way she came. The other Helper's body needed to be found and destroyed. She couldn't risk being caught in a lie with The Silent One, couldn't risk someone else finding it.

Just outside of Wyona the Pontiac ran out of gas. Waapikoona steered it to the shoulder and watched a mix of snowflakes and ice smother the windshield. Her jeans had just started to dry. Soon they'd be soaked again. Modern times had its conveniences, but cars seemed like they brought on more trouble than they solved. All they did was make it easy to get a person too far from home.

Now on foot she could travel as the crow flies. She headed through a cow pasture, squeezing through barbed-wire fences and cutting through groves that marked one property from the other. Land carved and divided, nothing seemed truly wild anymore. Deer with snowy coats stopped to stare as she traveled past. They weren't being marched away from their homes as her people had, but their land was shrinking. And the blame wasn't placed on human spread—it was placed on them for not shrinking in number as their home was being cleared away. For that, they were being executed.

Her people's ancestors had been executed. And so many others.

She couldn't think about that. It was what The Silent One kept pushing into her head, hoping to enlist her for his big plan when all she cared about was helping her sister. She was so close to reaching her quota, and then she could return her Helpers to The Silent One and retire from this work. She'd take Pinepakatwi to some remote place and introduce her to this new world slowly. They'd settle somewhere, secure work, and find peace. The real dream was to live off the land like they did as children. She'd heard of modern people who did that, but finding a piece of land they could use was the catch. No one in this time shared. Everything was fenced off and owned. They hadn't been taught the lessons of her tribe and of many others, that humans were pieces of nature, not owners. That the plants and animals could live without humans, but humans could not live without them. Some understood this and respected Mother Earth, but too many did not.

Daylight drained from the land. Waapikoona quickened her pace and reached the woods behind Mick's house with just enough time to find the spot under the young pine where the Helper's corpse should be. Instead, all she found was a puddle of its fluid, sheltered from the snow by the pine branches. She stooped for a better look, spotting a dark purple trail leading away from the tree only to be buried under snow.

Because she hadn't stuck around to watch it be killed, she had no idea if it could have gotten away. Sinking to her knees, she burrowed into her coat. The cold had seeped through her completely, and she was finally admitting it. Her jeans and socks were wet, her fingers and cheeks numb. Winter had never been this harsh to her as a child, but she'd been more accustomed to it. Modern indoor heat had ruined her sturdiness. If she didn't get out of the weather, somewhere she could dry out, she would freeze to death.

Mick's place was—no, she couldn't. So she got up and headed for the old cemetery. Its central tomb had been easy to break into, and she'd left dry wood for burning and a gallon of drinking water. It was a couple miles away, but she was fast on foot, especially when she knew a warm fire awaited her in the peace of a sleeping tomb. Funny how she felt most at home among the dead.

CHAPTER
6

THE SIX INCHES of snow greeted Mick in the morning like cold cash dangled just out of reach. No car meant no way to get to Curly's plow and no chunk of seasonal pay Mick shouldn't count on but always did anyway. When everyone else was cursing the weather report and canceling plans, Mick was watching the sky for the first flake so he could get out in it. There were days he'd work a full shift at the auto shop, the six to midnight at the U-Fill, and drive the plow until he was nodding off at the wheel.

"Unsafe and incredibly reckless," Kari would say.

Then he'd show her his wad of extra cash, and she'd close her mouth. It didn't happen often enough to damage his health anyway.

He found his phone and dialed Curly.

"You headin' over?" Curly asked. "Real late on this one, but there's still—"

"Someone stole my car. I'd be over there if I could."

"You shittin' me?"

"Yeah, I know. Hard to believe in Wyona. I know who done it, though, so if that can explain…"

It really couldn't, but Curly didn't prompt him to finish so he left it alone.

"I'll be there for the next one, so don't go lookin' to replace me."

"No one I could trust to drive this thing but you. Also no one I could trust to give me my fair cut. Now get out there and find that car, boy, and give that crook hell."

Mick went into the bathroom and stared at himself in the hazy old mirror. Six inches of snow on the ground on a Sunday morning when he had no other job to go to, and he was stuck at home away from that plow. Today could've made him a whole heap of money to help Kari with the Santa thing this year. Christmas was a few weeks away, and he had no spare cash. A well-timed lucky break would've been nice.

He could blame the woman. He could also blame himself for picking her up.

He needed to call the police and report the GTO stolen. That was what normal people did in the world he knew, the one where terrier-sized monsters didn't get mysteriously gutted underneath beds, and strange Indian women didn't make a man walk the woods in search of more monsters he supposedly killed, only to steal his car.

Wait—the late-night walk, the surprise wake-up in the woods—

"She knocked me out," he said to his reflection. The walk was just a trick to get him out there. But why? She could've attacked him inside like she did the first time.

Mick bent, tapping his head against the mirror. Nothing made sense.

He washed, bandaged his once-again reopened wound, and got dressed, dialing Kari as he made the biggest breakfast he could fit into a skillet.

"Do the words 'Mighty Eagle' mean anything to you?" he asked when she picked up.

"Did you make another payment to Helen's hospital account?" The question was fast and low—a sucker punch. "I told you to quit that. It's just throwin' money down the drain. There's no way to pay it all off in one lifetime, and they're happy enough with the payments I'm making each month. Stop being stupid with money, Mick. This is why you work so dang hard and have nothin' to show for it."

A sucker punch followed by a pounding of low blows. Just what he was in the mood for.

"Don't go quiet on me. You know I'm right."

He didn't care if she was right. She was still his little sister, and she had three kids and no help. They were his blood, too, and *they* were what he had to show for it. "Pop called me 'Mighty Eagle' yesterday."

"That's a new one. Must be all those shows he's been watchin'—"

"Do you remember when his mind first started to go? Not when it got bad, but more like the first time he said somethin'… off."

"Ninth grade. He called me by Mom's name."

Mick closed his eyes. This was news to him. Kari must have kept it a secret. Something like this so soon after their mother's death had probably been impossible to speak of without crying. He wished she'd have told him, but he couldn't blame her. Not talking about anything had been easier back then. "So he was in what—his mid-thirties?"

"Sounds right."

Mick sat down at the table. He could smell his breakfast burning in the skillet. Kari's voice kept up in his ear, but it was far away, hushed by his fears gaining more ground. He needed to see a doctor, try to get a jump on the dementia if there was anything to be done. It would be medication, too expensive to afford. He was paying Pop's medical bills and helping Kari with Helen's, and money to cover both was frighteningly lacking. There weren't enough hours in the day to take on another job, and he'd missed out on good plowing money due to that damn woman.

"Mick, you there?"

He remembered the phone in his hand, Kari's voice loud and clear. Smoke climbed the air above his breakfast. He jumped up and turned off the stove. Dumped the scramble onto a plate, burnt side up.

"Did you hear that crazy loud crack of thunder last night?"

Thunder was the least of Mick's concerns. "Kari—"

"Seems real strange for the middle of winter."

"I think I need to talk to you."

"You're talkin' to me right now."

"Yeah I know. Over the phone though, it's…" He watched steam rise from his food. The thought of keeping this to himself for one more minute was too much to bear. "I'm gettin' the dementia, Kari."

"You are not."

"I'm seein' things. Sleepwalking. Wakin' up outside in the cold, buck naked. No idea how I got out there. You still got that nanny cam?"

"Yeah, but—"

"I need to borrow it."

"Mick, cool down. You're not losing your mind. You work too hard and you don't get enough sleep. That's all it is. If you were gettin' the dementia, you wouldn't know you were. Pop didn't."

"I left my apartment in the middle of the night two times— the first time when Dougie was here—and got no memory of it. And somehow I locked the door behind me but left my keys locked inside. You think that's just bein' tired? Bullshit."

"Well come over and get the camera, then … if that'd make you feel better."

He moved the plate of burnt food to the table and sat down in front of it. He couldn't eat, but he couldn't waste it either, even though it was nearly ruined. Ketchup might help, but he couldn't muster the will to stand and get it. Kari didn't need to know his car was stolen. She'd only offer to let him borrow hers, and she couldn't be without a car.

"I can't come today. I'll try to stop by tomorrow." He was going to find that woman and get his car back.

Mick ended the call and got the ketchup. He ate while mapping the walking distance on his phone between his place and the U-Fill to figure out when he'd have to leave to make it there in time for his evening shift. The shortest route was two hours and thirty-two minutes. He checked the weather. Temperature already below freezing and dropping into the night, a mix of sleet and snow until sunrise.

"Nice," he told his phone.

MICK SET OUT early. He'd bundled in layers, worn his wool scarf and sock hat, his hood pulled over to shield against the snow. His new work boots he'd spent too much money on were missing, so he had to wear the ones with the crack in the sole. Come to think of it, his favorite jacket was missing, too—lost in the woods most likely, since he'd had them on before he woke up naked. The energy drink he'd drained before he stepped outside was already filling his tread with power. Several inches of snow coated the shoulder of the road. It clung to the bottom of his work boots and made each step heavier than the last.

The plan was to stop by the bar in town, ask if anyone had seen an American Indian woman around. As he walked he imagined that yes, someone had and they knew where she was staying. He'd go there and get his car back, but then his dream came to a halt. What he wanted to do was send his knuckles into the car thief's face, but this car thief was a woman, and somehow the knuckles-into-face didn't fit there. He could smack her—no, he couldn't. Call the police and get her locked up overnight? Not quite satisfying enough and probably wouldn't work on a woman like her. Kill her? Yeah, he'd have to just kill her.

Pelting sleet drove him straight to the U-Fill. The interrogation at the bar had to wait. His fingers and toes were fiery cold, and the more he wiggled them the more he realized how painful frostbite would be. He wasn't there yet, but he was too close to tissue death for any kind of pit stop, even if it meant time to warm up indoors. It simply added too much to his trek. And when he finally reached the U-Fill, he only had eight minutes to spare. Stopping at the bar would've made him late. Not a good thing when it's the boss who's there waiting to hand over the reins.

Mick stomped snow off his boots and went inside.

"You on foot, man?"

"Yeah, thought it'd be a nice walk in this weather."

"I saw your GTO on my way in. Figured you'd be callin' in and I'd be workin' double. Then I thought, 'Nah, that ain't Mick.'"

"Saw the GTO where?"

"Side of Route 52. You get a tow?"

Mick took off his hat and smoothed down his hair. "Where at on 52?"

"'Bout a mile past 135. You don't know?"

"No." Well, she ditched it then. Stole it just to piss him off or to keep him stuck at home. It made no sense. Maybe she realized it wasn't the best car for the weather and decided to steal a four-by-four instead. Mick saw the look his boss was giving him and made the quick decision to keep the car theft to himself. "I mean, not exactly. I wasn't driving."

"You got a ride home after your shift?"

"Yeah, I'm good. Thanks, though."

Mick unbundled as the bells on the door jangled to the boss making his exit. Was it possible she left the key in the car so Mick could simply drive it back home? He couldn't count on that, not in this weather. It'd be hours of walking and hours back if the key was missing or if it had a flat or a blown clutch. He needed a set of wheels to get out there and check on it, see what tools he'd need to get it moving again. And at the end of his shift, a Jeep would be showing up, the perfect vehicle for a snowy night drive.

And Brenda was game. "You break it, it's yours," she said, tossing him the Jeep key.

"I'll buy you a six-pack when I get back."

"You can't afford it. Just pump a gallon in the tank and we're good."

He climbed into the Jeep and turned the heater on max. The almost-frostbite wasn't something he wanted to revisit so soon. Snow fell in fat clumps on the windshield before being brushed away by the wipers. Route 52 was frozen solid, the lanes obscured so he had to go by the tire marks left by other cars. The only vehicle on the road, he flipped on his high beams to better see and it was a good thing he did or he'd have missed the unmistakable front end of the GTO sitting in the snow on the opposite side of the road. He made a U-turn and parked behind it.

Leaving the Jeep running, he got out and tried his car's door. It opened. He got in and felt for the key—there it was. The engine wasn't having it though, almost like it wasn't getting any fuel. Then he noticed the fuel gauge: empty. She'd run it out of gas ... but heading *into* town? Mick knew exactly how much gas had been in the tank. She must've taken it on a real joyride far out of town. Clearly, she'd been coming back though. But for what?

Tomorrow would have to answer that. He went back to the U-Fill and bought a gas can and some gas from Brenda. Drove back to the GTO, poured it in, and turned the key. The engine fired up like it didn't even mind being abandoned in the snow. He drove the Jeep back and filled its tank even though it took more than a few gallons. Overpayment for favors must be another reason he worked so hard and had nothing to show for it, but so be it; it was the only way he could be. Then he set out again on foot in the cold, thankful his hat had dried during his shift, glad the snow had let up, and thrilled he hadn't lost the GTO for good.

After reaching his car it was too late to bug Kari for the nanny cam, so he went straight home. Exhaustion pushed him toward bed, but he took a detour to his tool cabinet where he found a nylon rope. He tied one end to the leg of the bed and the other end to his ankle. If he decided to sleepwalk, at least he wouldn't get frostbite.

Not enough hours later, he woke tied to his bed, his head a pulsing, heavy block. He undid the knot with sloppy fingers, showered, dressed, and shoveled in breakfast while standing at the counter. Virgil would have strong coffee brewing at the shop, so he used its image as his beacon. If he made coffee at home, he'd be tempted to sit down, and he wasn't sure he'd be able to get up again.

When he woke up a second time that morning, on the creeper staring at a hole in the exhaust system of an old Ford pickup, he went into the office for more coffee and to give Virgil crap about not having enough lifts. Virgil was speaking with a customer, so Mick turned to head back toward the waiting pickup. Not quick enough to miss the brown puffy coat with the furry hood. The silky black hair and beaded earrings. The cowboy boots.

Mick's heavy block of a head turned itself inside out. He heard Virgil say, "There's the man right there," but he didn't believe it enough to spin back around. Yes, he wanted to confront her—but not at the job he depended on. Not in this shop, his second home, a place untainted by his broken mind. He was so tired and fed up, he wasn't sure what he'd do or say and couldn't believe how sick with anger he was at a figment of his own imagination.

A hand clapped onto his shoulder. "Svendsen. Young lady here to see you."

Between the use of his surname and the hand that felt too real to ignore, he had to turn around. Now his dementia had brought Virgil inside its circus. He couldn't respond to him though; he didn't know what was fake or real and didn't want to make a fool of himself. He looked straight at his visitor. She looked right back.

She'd somehow gotten even more beautiful. The warm tone of her skin, the flash in her dark eyes—what it did to Mick was so intense it registered as a charge of pain. Hopeless, electric, incurable pain. It wasn't a good time for Mick to remember what a woman's body felt like against his, but the memory wedged itself in without consent. It had been so long, too long. It was more than loneliness; it was starvation.

Too bad he wanted her to get good and lost, maybe even drop dead. "Outside," he said, brushing past her to the front of the shop. He didn't hold the door for her on his exit.

She came out a moment later.

Instead of looking at her, he addressed the parking lot. "You don't show up here."

"I think I just did, Mick."

He looked at her then. "Never again."

"What if my car needs an oil change?"

Mick checked out the tight line of her lips, wondering how a person could be so smart-aleck yet keep such a straight face. "You bring any car here, first thing I'd do is call the cops to ask if anyone had reported it stolen."

That was when she smiled. It grew so slowly Mick wasn't sure it could be counted as anything joyful. But evil? Oh, yes. He reconsidered popping her in the mouth. Hitting a woman was vile for many reasons, but the main one was because most women didn't have the physical ability to return an equal fight. This one, though? She could hit back. She *would* hit back. And probably stab a knife in his gut as she kicked him in the balls. Popping her in the mouth would be a bad idea.

"Don't be so upset. You got it back. Not that you need it. I know what you are." She zipped her coat up against a hit of cold wind.

"Like hell I don't need it. I got three jobs and people who count on me and because of you, I missed out on work and money I need. I'm sorry you can't get your brain around that because you're some nomadic freak with no cares in the world, but you stole the wrong guy's car."

A blunt, joyless laugh. "Nomadic?"

"And a vandal and a thief."

"Where's the other body?"

Another gust of winter wind did nothing to cool the burn of anger in Mick's blood. Still with this same question, and he had no better way to dismiss it for the lunacy it was.

"I searched all over those woods behind your home. There must be some bit of it left."

"There's nothin' left of anything. And if I catch you on that property again, I'll—" Mick couldn't decide how to politely finish.

She stepped closer, invading his personal space like she expected him to back down. "Call the cops?"

"Kill you." Mick couldn't believe he'd said it. He stood and owned it, his eyes hard on hers, the rush of such unexpected words creating both a sickness and a thrill.

From inches away she searched his face. "I might like that."

The sickness ripened and swept through Mick. He'd never threatened anyone like this, and here she was egging him on. It didn't seem as simple as calling his bluff. There was something more sinister to what she'd just said. Like unapologetic honesty. "You're a piece of work."

"And you're one to talk. Do your friends in there know what you are?"

He wasn't sure what she was referring to: the thirty-seven year old man succumbing to hallucinations brought on by inherited dementia or the lowlife who casually threatens to kill a woman. "They won't believe a word you say."

She straightened her spine like this was a blow she often had to dodge. One deep breath later, her face went as cold as the wind. "Last chance, Mick. You show me tonight."

"Or what?"

"Or it's your corpse I take." She raised her hood, still eyeing him before she turned away.

Mick watched her cross the parking lot then the road. A tractor trailer passed, erasing her from the landscape. If finding an alien corpse in the woods would get rid of her, he had to do it. He'd borrow the cordless work light again and scour the yard, the barn, the field, the woods. When she came he'd take her straight to it, go back home, and lock the door. And he'd never have to deal with her again.

CHAPTER
7

MICK HADN'T WORKED out what he'd do if he didn't find the corpse. If he'd thought about it, he could've brought home some raw meat from the grocery store to drop in the woods and try to pass it off for dead alien. At least it would've been an attempt to get himself out of it. After an hour of searching ice-encrusted snow in the bitter cold dark, he found nothing but his missing new work boots, favorite heavy jacket, and the rest of his clothes he'd had on the last night he walked with that woman in the woods and woke up cold and naked. This had to be a game she was playing, one he couldn't win. She was toying with him before she killed him.

"Whatever," he said, switching off the work light and heading back to his apartment. He'd already cranked the heat up on all his electric heaters; it should be warm by now.

And it was. He never maxed the dials on those heaters, but he'd given it to himself as a salve for his recent crappy luck. He'd regret it when Old Mae handed him the electric bill, but for now he would enjoy it in a T-shirt instead of his normal thermal shirt under a fleece jacket. He set his found boots near the heat to dry out, started dinner, then got to work setting up the nanny cam. Surprised his ancient laptop could run it, he propped it in the corner of his room, aimed to take in his bed and the doorway into the main room. He set it to take continuous low-res photos; video would fill his hard drive. A figure appeared in the view on his laptop screen. Only his brain jumped. His body was too tired to put in the effort.

"You should lock your door," she said. "Bad people might get in."

He powered off the camera and shut the laptop's lid. "The lock didn't stop you the last time."

She stepped forward into the bedroom—another unwelcome invasion into his personal space. A long brown feather from some kind of massive bird hung from her thick braid. Her cowboy boot landed right by the end of the rope still tied to his bed. She picked it up as if it were evidence. "I didn't peg you for a guy who's into this kind of thing."

"That ain't—" Mick caught himself. Let her think it. Anything was less embarrassing than the real reason it was there. He left her, flipping off the light on his way out and leaving her in the dark. Childish but deserved.

In the kitchen he checked on his dinner and talked himself out of serving her too. Sharing his food with this woman wasn't polite, it was pathetic. He needed to show her the door. But an undisciplined part of him was pushing through his self-preservation, feeding him hormones and possibilities and backing his loneliness into a corner so it had no choice but to fight. Having a woman in his apartment felt too damn good, even if she was fake. Even if she was here to toy with him and kill him.

"Look..." he heard a whisper: *ask her name* "...ma'am. I don't know who you are or what you want from me. I got no idea what that thing in my bedroom was ... or how it got there or what killed it. And I never seen a second one. So if you don't mind, I'd like to have supper and get some sleep." It all sounded too nice. He was trying to throw her out, and his Midwestern manners were sabotaging it.

She was taking off her coat. Had she not heard a word he said? Laying her coat on the back of the couch, she said, "I'll wait through your meal but not through the sleeping. And don't call me ma'am."

Ask her name. "Okay, then what should I call you?"

She plucked his car key from its spot on the end table and held it, weighing it in her hand. "It's interesting you drive a Pontiac."

"No, it really ain't."

"Do you even know who he was?"

Mick had a hunch: whatever he did know was sure to be wrong in some way. So he kept his mouth shut and studied her as directly as she studied him. It annoyed him she'd avoided the question. A week ago he'd have dropped it. With any other person he'd have figured the dodge was their right, and who was he to force information out of someone who didn't want to give it? This here was a power struggle, one he might not win, but he refused to go down without war. She was the reason he was tired, pissed off, and a chunk of cash poorer, and now she was here trying to pick a fight. "What's your name?"

"Sarah."

"Sarah what?"

She hooked her thumbs into the pockets of her jeans. "Sarah Clarke."

"You don't look like a Sarah Clarke."

Her smile was artificial sweetener—it tasted good but in large quantities might give you cancer. "That's exactly what I tried to tell them."

"Them?"

"Well, one in particular."

Vagueness was only an upper hand if he cared about what she had to say. Now he had a name to call her and that was all he needed, even if it sounded wrong. He pointed toward the couch. "You can wait for me over there." If she sat down, at least her eyes would be off him.

"I'll be outside," she said, picking up her coat. "And I don't like waiting."

Twenty minutes was all he could get out of his supper, even though he preferred to make her wait hours in the cold. Not that it would make her give up and go away, but it was worth a try. He bundled up and stepped into the cold night, pulling his sock hat lower and raising his hood. Snow crunched as he found his earlier tracks, now accompanied by a smaller set that branched off behind his car. The puddle of light from his little apartment windows reached farther on the whiteness of the snow. A help, since he hadn't brought a flashlight and no moonlight escaped the overcast sky. He hadn't followed the tracks long before he noticed a flicker of orange in the distance, its light playing on the side of the old barn. Darkness engulfed him, receding once he drew near the new source of light. She was sitting cross-legged in the barn's broken doorway, feeding twigs to a small fire that had been built under the cover of the structure and out of the snow.

"You'll burn that old thing down," Mick said.

"My plan was to make a bonfire of it."

"You sure make a habit of destroying property that ain't yours."

"We'll need a hot fire when we find the other body. Unless you have a better idea?" Her words mingled with a tease, but Mick couldn't reckon why.

His luck would have this be the day Old Mae stayed up late and decided to look out her north-facing window to find him as an accomplice to strange fires in her yard at night. Probably didn't matter, though. If this woman—he couldn't even call her Sarah in his head, it just wasn't right—stuck to her word, it was about to be his corpse on that bonfire because there was no other to be found.

"Look, I searched the field and the woods. There's nothin' back here that could be found in the dark. We need daylight, and even then…" Mick didn't like the way she'd frozen in place to look at him, like she'd just had some kind of epiphany and something big was about to change.

"You really don't know." She drew the words out, unblinking, unmoving. The words themselves should've been some kind of taunt, but they were too direct, too genuine. *"Kintiwa?"*

It sounded like a question. She had to know foreign words were not going to help him.

"I don't know what you want with me."

She stood. "What I want doesn't seem so simple anymore."

"Can you quit? It's clear I don't know what the hell you're talkin' about—"

"You'll find where the other body is. And when you do, I'll come back, after the next clap of thunder." She walked to where the snow piled against the outer wall of the barn, scooped up a handful, and tossed it over the fire, dousing the flame. "I'll see you later, Mick."

It was all too strange to even be relieved. Foreboding pressed down harder than oncoming dementia and his next electric bill because this dread was unknown. A mystery he had no idea how to prepare for, much less fight. She stepped into the dense night, a walking human form fading into an upright shadow Mick had to squint to see. Then to nothing.

Imagination. Hallucination. Reality. It didn't matter. Mick's fingers and toes were starting to tingle from the cold, so he went inside and locked the door as if it would keep his mental illness outside. Now his apartment blasted with dry heat, so he set the dials on each heater back and powered on his old tube TV. He needed to make another payment to Helen's hospital account before the bill collectors started coming after Kari. He had to find a new nurse for Pop. Right now what he needed to do was stop thinking about how that woman's skin would feel against his, how her legs would tangle with his own, how her hips would slide into his hands. He'd go to the bar on his next night off—no, he was sick of trying to find women in bars. He'd go to church on Sunday and talk to someone nice. He hadn't been to church since his mother died. Surely there were single women he might hit it off with there. In fact—he checked the time—Kari would still be up. Maybe she had a friend who was looking for a date.

She picked up on the third ring. "Catch any incriminating video?"

"Haven't done it yet. Hey, any chance you got a friend who might want dinner and a movie?"

"Hmm. Dinner and a movie or a no-strings hookup?"

"Either. All."

"Amanda. She works in the dentist office. She got divorced last year and doesn't want a boyfriend. She has two little boys, one's in Janie's class. She's cute. Totally your type."

Mick wasn't sure what his type was anymore. "The Amanda you were friends with in high school?"

"Yeah, you remember her?"

"Text me her number."

As soon as it came in, he fired off a message before he thought twice about it: *Hi, this is Kari's brother, Mick. She thought you might be interested in dinner with me sometime?*

It only felt pathetic because living in the Bible Belt meant guilt grew on trees and leached into the drinking water. He cleaned up the kitchen and stripped his bed, remaking it with his nicest sheets and bedspread. Decluttering his apartment involved simply shifting things around to more logical places. After putting away the broom and dustpan, he heard a text ding.

Would love to. This weekend?

It seemed a decade away. He had a U-Fill shift tomorrow night but had the next night off. How desperate would he look? More importantly, did he care? The mountain of crap he was dealing with sure put things into perspective. He needed to lose himself in some female company more than he needed to preserve his ego.

Any chance you're free Wednesday night?

Yes, if I can get a babysitter. I'll text you back tomorrow.

One forgettable late-night talk show later, he opened his laptop in his bedroom, set the nanny cam to record, and went to bed.

THIS TIME HE knew he was outside before he woke up. The snow wasn't soft; it was shards of cold glass so sharp they'd become lodged in his skin without him feeling the entrance wounds. Every extremity felt numb, brittle, ready to crack off. He wiggled his toes—couldn't feel them. He'd lose every one of them. He should've tied himself to the bed.

His core shuddered involuntarily, each jerk a hell of pain. He got up, somehow. Brushed the snow off his legs and arms. Rubbed ice from his hair. The sun lit enough eastern sky for him to see the imprint of a human in the fetal position in the snow at his feet. Again he ran, guided by unknown native impulse, his blood so full and hot in his appendages it was like a fever burning him on the inside while the winter cold froze him from the outside. Short-term memory was a montage of dreams of pink sunrise trickling over the horizon, white snow, and dark hibernating trees far below him. Of tree limbs reaching for him to catch, swaying as he grabbed hold. Of the dead alien carcass under ice-glazed needles of a blue-green pine, its gory deflated bulk suddenly swaying in the wind below him and dropping into the open door of the old barn.

Old Mae's slate-gray roof ahead. Mick could feel his toes again, and they did not feel healthy. As he ran snow flipped behind his feet, but he didn't slow—he wished he could just pass the house and keep running, off the edge of the earth into the orange glow of morning sun.

At the old barn he had to stop and look. There it was, a lump of gray skin bruised purple, one arm flung out, the other bent underneath. A wide mouth unhinged, rows of deadly teeth stained that same shade of gory purple. He knew then it wasn't an alien but a monster. A creature from the most twisted of nightmares. If any kind of Hell existed, that was where this thing belonged. Sarah Clarke had been right—it should be burned to ash.

Not now. He needed to get out of the weather and into some clothes. With the spare key from the pot, he unlocked his door. That was when he noticed his curtain escaping the dark hole that should be housing his shiny new pane of glass. Too numb to care, Mick returned the key to its spot in the dirt and went inside straight to his laptop.

The first images showed him getting into bed. Flipping positions. Arms readjusting themselves as he slept. He skipped ahead, found an empty bed. He skipped back. One image showed him asleep. The next, a blurred object in his spot. Then an object not so blurred: the bulge of his T-shirt rising too high off the bed, a dark tear down the center. He advanced the images, turning them into a crude animation. Two giant wings outstretched. Wings tucking in. Hooked beak. Wide, round eyes on a jerky head, taking in every angle of the room. Blurred once again, in flight out the bedroom doorway. And one final image of fragments of reflective glass raining down as the window burst out and the bird dived through.

Mick pushed away from the laptop, knocking the nanny cam off its holder. He looked at the rumpled pile of T-shirt and boxers he'd gone to bed in the night before. Clearly he could tell the shirt was ripped in half. What he was doing during his sleepwalking episodes—he'd just seen it. He had evidence. But he couldn't believe it. Not now. Not ever.

Chapter 8

A CLAP OF THUNDER rang through the tomb, waking Waapikoona from a nightmare of horned water serpents and a flooded earth, and her sister too small to overcome the rise of the water. As she struggled to keep Pinepakatwi's head above the waves, a great golden eagle soared above, unaware of the serpents closing in on them below.

She fed her dying fire and went to her knees, thankful to *Kiche Manetoa* for fire and wood, for warm stone tombs and for *Ciinkwiaki.* The white men who destroyed her village and forced her and the other children into Indian boarding schools told her Thunder-Beings didn't exist; they were mere creatures of myth, and even speaking of them would send her to a terrible place they called Hell. She didn't know enough English to tell them she was already living in a hell of their own design when she watched her home burn, when they took her from her family, forced her into their clothes, and held her down while they cut her hair. And even when she learned enough English to speak it, she held her tongue. They had ways of punishing children like none she'd ever seen in her eleven years on earth. Her own people corrected children with words, not pain. In the Indian school she'd often wondered if the white people used the same violent methods on their own children or if they had special treatment for her kind. And they had called *her* people savage.

Now she wondered how it came to be that a Thunder-Being's human form was a white man who seemed to have no idea what he really was. Or could he be a creature from The Silent One's world of demons and bones? The thunder could be a coincidence—but Waapikoona didn't believe in coincidence.

As soon as the sun reached a high perch, she'd find Mick Svendsen, and this time she was sure he'd know where her Helper's missing corpse was hidden.

MELTING ICE HAD softened the land. Waapikoona's boots collected wet snow and mud as she crossed the woods toward Mick's place. The sky was lit newly blue, as if denying those days of gray had ever happened. Through the trees a powerful engine growled awake, revved, then faded into the distance. She reached the edge of short dead grass, and sure enough, the orange Pontiac was gone.

It seemed she had some time to kill. His apartment was becoming too uncomfortably familiar, so she headed for the road. Her appetite had been broken since rising from the earth, and remembering to eat had become a chore. A timid part of her wondered if she craved some kind of alternate fuel like other undead creatures of myth. Blood? Brains? She stepped onto the bare pavement of the road and stomped her boots clean, chuckling to herself. Things might be easier if she were simply a vampire.

Breakfast was a necessity, and it would taste good. She remembered the diner in the cluster of buildings that passed for the Wyona town square. They'd have pancakes and strong coffee. The hiss of oncoming tires had her moving off the road, but instead of passing by, the car slowed beside her, a "hey baby" projecting from a lowered window.

She raised her hood instead of her middle finger. It wasn't worth the effort. Guys like this were a plague on the good earth, and they thrived on both positive and negative attention. They'd been sprinkled all over the land, from her home in Oklahoma to the north, east, and south. She'd never been much farther west, but she guessed they infected every town. She couldn't remember them in her previous life—but she'd only been eleven and had worse treatment to survive. Added centuries were supposed to make people more civilized, not less. If only they'd turn into the true slippery beasts they were so the Thunder-Beings could strike them down.

The car pulled ahead and braked hard in front of her, forcing her to stop. She thought about kicking a dent in the bumper. Then she thought of something better.

"Not too friendly are ya?" The passenger had come out of the car.

"I can be friendly, when I want to be."

"You wanna get friendly now?"

She walked past him and got in the backseat of the car. The driver turned in his seat to give her a thorough look, his slimy smile so confident in its entitlement to whatever he believed she was offering she had to restrain herself from shattering his fantasy right there. She'd gain nothing from premature action. She had to do this right.

"I caught us a Latina," the passenger said as he got in and slammed the door. "Do you speak *es-pan-yohl?*"

He had no idea what he'd caught. Soon he'd experience it, but he probably still wouldn't know.

"Your place?" the driver asked.

"Nah, Angie might be home."

"Okay then, my place."

Waapikoona wished she had some duct tape. She tapped him on the shoulder. "Is your place private?"

"Private enough."

Waapikoona sat back. "Good." She might not need duct tape.

The two men exchanged a look. It was rare to find two perfect bodies at once, even rarer that neither of them had anything worth saving. Her new Helpers were in for a real treat, and her next meeting with The Silent One would go much better than the last. By the time they parked in front of a dingy farmhouse, Waapikoona was nearing on desperate to get out of the tobacco-soaked seat and back into the fresh air. Tobacco was never supposed to be used like that.

A dog barked from the rear corner of the house, its chain stretched taut. Trash littered the yard around it. A piece of plywood leaned against the house, the only visible form of shelter.

"This is so perfect," Waapikoona said, slipping on her gloves. She'd have not even a sliver of guilt here.

Inside, the driver asked her if she wanted a beer.

"Sure," she said, taking out her flint knife and burying it in his thigh. "But sit down first."

He looked down as she jerked the knife free, his mouth open and silent. Turned out she didn't need duct tape after all. She kicked his knee and he crumpled, missing the couch to land ungracefully on the floor, two hands clutching a spewing artery.

The other guy had started hollering, making enough racket for both of them. He flapped against the wall, knocking into shelves, hands busy with a search for a weapon. She waited, curious to see what he'd come up with. Screwdriver—not bad. She picked up a coffee mug and chucked it at his face. His arm flew up to deflect but not fast enough to save his nose. She got past the screwdriver, pressing in close.

"Hey, baby," she said, stabbing her knife into his stomach.

He grabbed her by the throat, some muscle memory he didn't seem conscious of. She twisted the knife. He sucked in a hollow breath and fell away. Outside, the dog started barking, raspy and incessant like all it ever did all day was bark on the end of that chain. She needed to get out of there.

In the kitchen she found a dull steak knife and her beer, cold in the fridge. It wasn't a pretty thing to re-stab them both in the same wound, but it had to be done not once but a few times each. Probably wouldn't fool good cops, but she didn't care. She didn't want to have to dump her knife if something went wrong with her new Helpers. Then she closed her eyes and summoned them. Now in her palm she released them into the room. The scent of blood would have them transforming immediately, ready to gather flesh The Silent One would use to rebuild the dead.

She'd been so wrong to release her Helpers onto Mick. It had been lazy and thoughtless. She should've questioned why she'd needed to allow The Silent One to possess her to finish the deed. It had been so long since she'd needed to mentally check out to kill anyone. Fifteen years of this work had thickened her skin and desensitized her stomach to blood. She was smart about only picking scum who didn't deserve to walk the earth. She hadn't been drawn to Mick because he was a good target but for some other reason—but what other reason was there? She had no use for a *Ciinkwia*. And all he'd ended up doing was killing her Helpers.

Her new Helpers scrambled under the couch and hid. They didn't like the light coming in the front window. She lowered the shade and drew the dusty curtain across it. In the dim room she checked pockets for wallets and found a load of cash which she shoved into her own pocket. She searched the house and found more cash in an old coffee can. A jackpot, really. It would last her a long time. She filled the inner pockets of her coat and left the house through the back door where she came face-to-face with the chained dog.

The snow inside the circle of his chain had been trampled to mud. He wagged his tail low, straining against that chain so his collar cut into his neck. Waapikoona couldn't see how a dog so mistreated could seem so friendly. Approaching might be a bad move, but she was already doing it, her hand out in an offer of peace. Hopefully it wasn't an offer of her fingers because the dog was so skinny his ribs showed and shoulder blades poked through. Breed of dog was a mystery—brown and white, ears short but floppy, a brown patch over one eye. A kid would name this dog Spot for that trait. The dog ducked low as she approached. If there was any speck of regret over those guys left in that house, it died hard then and there.

Yes, she'd been very wrong to release her Helpers on Mick. His genes were the ones that should move to the next generation. These Cro-Mags here needed to die off. What had she been thinking?

"Easy," she said, unbuckling the dog's collar. "Now go on. Find a new home."

The dog tested his legs outside of the circle of mud and came back to sit at Waapikoona's feet. She went back in the house and found sliced turkey and a take-out box of leftover chicken. She grabbed the dead driver's keys, went back outside, and dumped the meat in front of the dog. Now it was his turn for a jackpot that kept him occupied so she could walk away. She drove the car a couple miles outside of town where she ditched it at the side of the road and walked the rest of the way in to find her own food.

The diner was recovering from breakfast rush, with every table cluttered with used dishes and the wait staff looking like they all needed a nap. She seated herself at the counter and wondered what she was going to do with all that cash. She'd start with a big breakfast.

A woman in a retro waitress smock greeted her with pad and pencil. "Coffee?"

"Please. And one of these." Waapikoona pointed to a meal pictured on the paper placemat.

As the cook dropped eggs on the grill, she tried to remember the name for 'egg' in her native tongue. Like her, her language had died. Modern people were working to revive a more recent branch of it from written sources, but with no living speakers it was an unfathomable task. When The Silent One had raised her from her grave, she'd been unable to speak at all. Descendants of a tribe similar to her own introduced her to a language she knew to be related to hers as soon as she tried it with her tongue. Since then words were coming back, too slowly to rebuild a whole language in her remaining lifetime, but it was better than nothing at all. Centuries ago the white people had set out to kill her culture. They'd succeeded. But now that success was being undone.

English had returned more easily. It was everywhere, fitting back into her memory in the spaces taken up by what she'd learned from the white people in her first life. Even though she'd be lost in this life without it, she had no gratitude for the people who'd forced her to learn it. That resentment was alive and well and fed every time she visited The Silent One.

She was glad to have the word in her language for what Mick was. She could call him Thunder-Being, but it just wasn't the same as *Ciinkwia*. He was good at pretending he didn't know what he was—not just any *Ciinkwia* but the golden eagle. She'd had the word for that before but it had since slipped away. Her memories were like that sometimes—here then gone. Her spirit was dizzy from the circle of her dual lives from two disconnected times.

Her breakfast fell so deeply into her well of a stomach, she ordered a second one, with orange juice this time so she wouldn't get jittery from too much coffee. She should've been thinking about whether her new Helpers knew how to get underground and find the cave system that led to The Silent One or if she needed to go back to that house and lead them there. She also could've been thinking about what to spend her pocketful of money on. A motel room for a hot shower? A new pair of jeans? A cheap motorcycle? All three and more?

Instead she was thinking about Mick. Part of it was impatience for him to return so she could collect the missing corpse and wash away the whole thing. Being honest, it felt more like she was anxious to see him just ... because she was.

The harsh, glacial blue of his eyes. The unhurried small-town drawl. His masculine, work-broken hands. He worked as hard as her people did in her other life, not a common thing with people of this time. She shouldn't be awarding him points for that. He was still a white man, and her distrust was tattooed into her spirit, forged with fear and hate and aged hundreds of years. Nothing could change it.

"Is that a real feather?" the waitress asked, refilling Waapikoona's coffee mug.

Waapikoona had forgotten she'd stuck Mick's feather in her hair again. She pulled it free. "Yes, do you want it?"

"My little girl collects 'em. You know what kind of bird?"

"Golden eagle." She handed it across the counter. For a moment she couldn't get herself to let go. "Tell her some people believe they're great protectors."

She needed to get her Helper's corpse and leave this town before someone connected the two missing Cro-Mags and their bloody house to the strange new Indian woman in town and started lighting torches.

Outside of the diner she nearly tripped over a white and brown stump that started wagging its furry tail as soon as she stopped. "No. I told you to go find a nice home."

The dog sat in front of her, his tail still except for a chaotic flipping at the very end.

"No." Absolutely, one hundred percent no.

He put his ears back and shuffled slowly toward her as if she wouldn't notice how desperate he was for human touch. She went back into the diner and bought two hamburgers without the buns. The meat kept him on the sidewalk long enough for her to escape.

She knew he had hound blood in him when he popped his head into the doorway to her tomb an hour later. Feeding him had been her first mistake. Rubbing his ears was her second, and sharing her fire's warmth was the third.

Some mistakes she didn't want to remedy, no matter how much they complicated her day.

Other mistakes she was working hard to undo.

CHAPTER 9

MICK'S WEDNESDAY NIGHT date with Amanda was on. She'd secured a babysitter and texted to confirm. He couldn't get himself to call it off, even though he knew the potential catastrophe it would be. Either his dementia was bad enough to be turning normal photos into supernatural images before his eyes or he was shifting into a large raptor at night. Both options made him a lot worse than an unfit date. And when Virgil asked him why his tire rotation was so funny, he excused himself to go laugh out back with the dumpster. He didn't need any witnesses to his mind's spiral toward insanity.

He could show Kari the photos and ask what she saw.

No, he couldn't. If she saw what he saw—he couldn't burden her with that.

"You get those lug nuts good and tight?" Virgil hollered out of the office door when Mick was wiping off his hands to drive the car out of the bay.

Mick looked at the car. He couldn't remember. He grabbed a torque wrench and sure enough, he hadn't. The wave of shock that rushed through him lingered long enough to make him a little sick to his stomach. It was unlike him to make a mistake like that. It was also unlike Virgil to watch him work, and clearly he'd been analyzing his every move.

Virgil was waiting for him in the office. Mick got himself a cup of coffee while the customer put away his wallet and slid into his coat. As soon as the door closed and the office was empty, he turned to Virgil. "It won't happen again, sir."

"I know it won't."

Now would be the time for a person to give an explanation or an excuse, but Mick wasn't releasing the explanation, and he wasn't the excuse-giving type. So he held Virgil's eye in the hope that was all he needed to do to assure his statement was true. No more mistakes. No more dwelling on the supernatural. It didn't matter how little sleep he was getting or how unbelievable his life had become. He needed this job more than he needed to understand what was happening to him, and stupid mistakes like that weren't allowed in Virgil's shop.

"I have good mind to let you off early again, but with Andy callin' in sick and—"

"I'm not goin' home. I'm good." Mick wished his voice hadn't come out so gruff. Taking this mess out on Virgil was the last thing he wanted to do. "I got that Chevy." He grabbed the key and headed to the parking lot to drive it into the bay.

Quitting time came an hour late due to Mick staying past his shift. He got a good head start on a job for the next day and then cleaned the bathroom while Virgil wasn't looking. He wasn't brown-nosing; he was working off his guilt for screwing up. And punishment by bathroom cleaning was a fitting penance to ensure it never happened again.

"Get some sleep, Mick," Virgil called when Mick unlocked the GTO.

Mick saluted. He couldn't promise. He could only acknowledge. He knew now that even if he tied himself to his bed at night, a large raptor could shred that rope to pieces.

A QUICK CHECK on Pop left Mick without time to make dinner, so he texted Kari *Can you feed me?* on his way out to his car, fully knowing he was taking advantage even though she'd say it'd be one less favor she owed him. He headed to her place because the answer would certainly be yes. There were two extra children at her house, which made it harder to find a good moment to break out his laptop without Doug and Janie or either of the other two asking a million questions.

With only ten minutes left before he had to leave for the U-Fill, he dragged Kari by the elbow into her bedroom and shut the door.

"Tell me what you see here." He tilted the laptop's screen toward her and advanced through the images.

She squinted, taking the laptop from him and sitting on her bed. "Can't see much with it so dim. Wait—"

Mick waited, his pulse downshifting into too low a gear. A thump and a cry sounded through the wall. Kari looked up at him. "Check on them, will ya?"

He opened the door and found Doug acting as liaison between the two other kids. They belonged to a friend of Kari's who she traded babysitting with when job shifts changed unexpectedly. Doug could probably handle them better than Mick. "You got this, bud?"

A thumbs-up confirmed it. Mick went back in with Kari and shut the door. She was shaking her head at the screen, puzzled. "Some pictures are missing."

"None are missing. Look at the filenames. They're time-stamped and all in order."

"I know, but…" She looked up at him. "What's goin' on with you, Mick?"

"Just tell me what you see."

"What I see is your body disappear and a big bird take its place. That's crazy, though—is this why you think you've got what Pop has? Because the camera missed you getting out of bed, that's all." She shut the laptop and handed it back. "Never seen a bird that big. How do you think it's gettin' in?"

The problem wasn't a bird getting in, but one getting out. Mick hadn't fixed the window a second time. He wasn't going to waste the money on new glass. Plywood was cheaper. He'd board both windows up—temporarily, until he figured this all out.

At least Kari saw the bird. That was all he wanted. "Broke my window out."

"For real? You need to get it on video."

"Not enough room on my drive to record all night."

"There's a motion detection setting in the software. Click around in the options and you'll find it. Hey, come in the kids' room—do you have a minute?"

"Yeah, but just a minute."

They moved next door, where Kari pulled a big and well-used *North American Birds of Prey* coffee-table book off the bookshelf. No doubt this one was used to inspire Doug's drawings. She opened it on the bed and paged through it.

"Definitely not a bald eagle because it doesn't have that white head. Not that one either—too small."

Mick didn't want to look. Didn't want to know. It brought it much too clear, too real.

"Golden eagle," Kari said.

In Mick's head he heard a chime go off. "No."

"Yeah, Mickey, look. Has to be. Same head, same shape. Get your laptop out again. Maybe we can tell if it has these white markings on the tail."

"I gotta go."

Kari picked up the open book and handed it to him. He didn't think about taking it; it was simply in his hands. Before him spread two pages of golden eagles. Standing tall with wings tucked close. In flight, wings spanning wide. Racing toward prey, talons open, reaching, deadly. Eyes sharp, shrewd, indomitable.

"Maybe call an animal preservation group? They might be able to relocate it or at least tell you why it's tryin' to get into your apartment."

Distantly, Mick heard himself answer. "Yeah, good idea." He couldn't stop seeing those images even though the book had been closed and reshelved and Kari was gone from the room. The images were too eerily familiar, like seeing a stranger in a crowd who looks too much like you until the bodies part and reveal you'd been looking in a mirror.

Mick found Kari in the kitchen, where he grabbed his phone and keys. "I'd help you clean up but—"

"I got it. You need to go. Hey—" She paused in clearing dishes to set her eyes on his. "I hope I didn't ruin somethin' when I dropped the kids with you the other night."

The other night. It didn't ring a bell. Mick was still stuck in that book, seeing the images of those eagles.

"You know, when you had that guest. Just text me next time and tell me somethin' changed and you can't babysit. You don't have to make sacrifices—"

"No, that was…" Almost getting his throat slashed by that woman seemed minor compared to everything that'd happened since then. And he couldn't explain that night without telling so much more, and he had no time. "It wasn't somethin' that could be ruined. Trust me."

Kari tilted her ear toward the hall. "That's Helen waking up."

Mick was halfway to the GTO outside when Doug caught up to him. "Uncle Mick, see if I got it right." He handed him a page torn from a notebook. On it, a cartoonish version of the creature they'd found gutted underneath his bed when Doug spent the night, but this version's gut was still intact and it was upright, baring teeth dripping with saliva. Or blood.

"Looks good." Too good. He couldn't tell Doug there was a second carcass lying in the entrance to the old barn. Or that he was somehow responsible for retrieving it from the woods and stashing it there.

"Can I spend the night again? Maybe we can build a trap, in case there's more of 'em. We could let 'em go somewhere they won't get into trouble or scare people."

Staring into Doug's expectant face, Mick rebooted. When everything came back online, he saw the last several days with the fresh new eyes of an outsider, and he couldn't believe he'd allow a child to believe what was drawn on that paper was real. He couldn't grasp how it'd come to this or how to fix it without betraying Doug's trust. This was a shared secret, and for Mick to say it was fake would be like calling Doug a liar. He wouldn't do it.

"I'll talk it over with your mom. You know she likes you to be home with her. Can I keep this?" Mick held up the drawing of the creature. If he kept it, maybe Doug would forget about it.

Yeah, right.

NEARING THE END of his U-Fill shift, Mick dragged out the ladder to fiddle with a flickering fluorescent light above the soda machine. Not because he knew he could fix it, but just to give himself something to do so he wouldn't fall asleep standing at the counter. Kids liked to cow-tip around there, and he didn't want to be the cow. He also didn't want to be responsible for the store being robbed while he dozed.

While on the ladder, a second fluorescent panel started flickering at the opposite end of the store. "Now that's just stupid," he said, watching it blink a random beat like it was sentient and there to mock him. The fiddling wasn't fixing the first one, so he unscrewed it and climbed down.

A shadow rushed across his legs. He sidestepped, a reflex that sent him into the shelves and the fluorescent tube crashing to the floor. It popped like gunfire, glass exploding. Another reactive impulse jerked him harder against the shelves, scattering candy bars and lollipops across the tile. Reflex had stolen the wheel; it was overcompensating for a physically and mentally exhausted body and brain, and if he didn't regain control, it would drive him off a cliff.

He'd caught himself on hands and knees against the floor with no recollection of getting there. Depth perception was off, like he was looking through a fisheye lens. His fingers tingled, the numbness trickling into his hands and arms. The balance of the room tipped.

The pages of eagles unrolled in his memory. Sharply hooked beaks and talons. A flare of chestnut-colored feathers around a fierce face. Hazel eyes bright and intent. If this was how it happened at night, he'd never been awake to experience it. It couldn't be happening again, not now. Not when he was at work. He made a grab for the nearest shelf and hauled himself up on wavering legs. The blinking light brought life to the shadows all around him. Inanimate objects held hiding spots between them in each of those blinks. He looked up and found it wasn't just one light fixture blinking but the whole row. If Brenda showed up for her shift and found only a pile of his clothes, cash register abandoned, store doors unlocked, she'd call the cops. He had to stop this. He had to do something completely human, something a bird would never do. He needed to remind his brain what it felt like to be Mick Svendsen.

He crawled to one of the refrigerated beverage cases along the wall and slammed his knuckles in the door. The shock of pain was so strong, white sparkled behind his eyes. He opened the door and slammed it on his knuckles again.

Feeling returned to his arms and hands in the most nauseating way. He used the door handle to pull himself up; his legs situated themselves under him as expected. His knuckles were dented and angrily red. The pain checked in then, pure and true and as accurate as any time he'd busted his knuckles in Virgil's shop. He got a jumbo cup of ice from the soda machine and moved behind the counter to calm down. The store's spread of fluorescent light was back to bright and unblinking. Catastrophe seemed avoided, but he was still breathing hard. Another glance at his smashed knuckles gave him yet another reason to curse.

The bells jangled on the door to announce a customer. Mick straightened up, noticed the mess of candy and glass in the aisle, the potential for accident, lawsuit, his own firing. Then he noticed his customer.

She stopped just inside the door, her eyes so direct and tight on his he felt a rush of senseless delight. Behind it, a giant push broom of outrage shoved all that delight into the gutter. For her to haunt him at home, Virgil's shop, now the U-Fill—it was too much.

"You okay?" she asked.

She couldn't have known. She was toying with him again, mistaking the sick rage that must be evident on his face for something else. Delicate snowflakes were melting in her shiny black hair. He imagined what it would be like to weave his fingers through it. Or to get a grip thick enough to tug and tilt her head back so he could rest his nose and mouth against her neck and inhale. He wondered if she'd fight him or give in. He wondered what she smelled like.

"Evil," he said aloud. She smelled like an evil witch.

"You do look a bit evil right now. Is that a burn?" She looked at his hand currently plunged into a cup of ice.

She'd definitely fight him. Maybe a physical fight was what he needed—a black eye, a nice bloody lip. Something to knock him out of all of this. Or a good reason to call the police and get her thrown out of town. She unzipped her coat. He'd never admit how much it turned him on.

"You're not so cute anymore, Mick. Is this your dangerous late-night store clerk face? Does it keep the people honest?"

An old Toyota pulled up through the glass behind her, windshield wipers batting away the snowfall. Mick came out from behind the counter and got the broom and the wet floor safety cone. He picked up the candy while the man who'd entered browsed the refrigerated cases.

Mick followed the man to the register.

"Some mess. You have trouble in here?"

"Nah, just an accident." Mick handed over the change and watched his other guest walk the perimeter of the store and end up by the safety cone. "You need a bag, sir?"

Past the man's shoulder, Mick saw her pick up the broom and start sweeping broken glass. He waited until they were alone again before he crossed the store and held out his good hand for the broom.

She didn't even look at him. "I think it would be wiser to get that back on ice."

Standing there with his hand in the air he was no chump. He stepped in close, took hold of the broom handle, and yanked. She'd tightened her grip just in time for the action to yank not just the broom toward him but her too.

He could smell her, god, he could smell her. Wet stone and wood smoke and crisp snow. Female pheromones too, for how expertly that earlier turn-on ripened. Her eyes were so dark and deep, iris blending into pupil and mirroring the store back at him. If it weren't for that reflected image grounding him to the present, he might've gotten lost.

She held onto the handle much longer than any sane person would've. Long enough for Mick to realize they might be stuck like this forever because he sure as hell wasn't going to let go. His store, his broom, his life. She needed to get out of all of it.

"I take it back," she said, her breath on his mouth. "This dangerous Mick is the cutest one."

Her release of the handle was painfully slow. Once complete, she didn't step away. And the way she tilted her head made Mick fear she was about to kiss him—or let him kiss her. Some kind of dare, but he wasn't sure if the dare was to do it or not do it. He had the time to fully contemplate it, to weigh the pros and cons and give common sense time to arrive and shut the whole thing down.

"Do you want to leave," Mick said, his voice low. "Or do you want me to throw you out?"

"I want you to throw me out." Her voice lowered too, in the most god-awful sexy way.

Brenda's Jeep brakes squealed to a stop outside. Mick wasn't about to look away from those dark, daring eyes, though. He had to prove that even though he couldn't fulfill that request now, if he could, he would have.

The door jangled, and Brenda barreled through in squeaky boots. "Svendsen?"

Mick cleared his throat to get his normal voice back. "Here."

"Ah. Hey, get outta here. That crap out there is turning to ice."

SINCE MICK DIDN'T say anything and neither did she, she guessed she was there to go home with him and collect her alien corpse. He returned the broom to the closet and headed for the GTO; she headed for the road to prove his guess wrong. Snow fell silently onto ice-glazed pavement. Only crazy people walked at midnight in weather like this. Which meant it fit her, and Mick should accept it. He should be glad she'd only been there to harass him. Now he could go straight home to bed. Settling up with the corpse would undoubtedly happen some other day, and that was cool with him. His knuckles pulsed with a deep bruise, his fingers stiff with swelling. The increased blood flow down his arm brought his agitated arm wound back to his attention. He got in the car and took the turn out.

It shouldn't have been so hard to tear his eyes away from her shrinking image in the mirror as he drove away. As if the weather wasn't enough, she was covered head to toe in dark clothes. No one would ever see her on the road.

He didn't care.

The mirror was a black void. His foot eased up on the gas pedal.

Okay, he cared.

He pulled to the shoulder then made a U-turn, flipping on his high beams so he'd be able to see a dark-clothed person walking the road in the black of a snowy night. Peering down the pavement he could see all the way to the lights of the U-Fill lot but couldn't see her. She must've crossed into the woods. He'd never find her. Reaching for the gearshift he felt an odd sense of being watched and actually glanced in the backseat. Stupid, because what—now he was afraid of monsters stowing away in his backseat?

"God," he said, hitting the gas.

His tires spun. When they found grip an upright form had materialized at the side of the road, bright face pointed toward him. He hit the brakes, too hard for the condition of the slick pavement. The sideways slide wasn't the worst he'd experienced, but it was enough to give him a hefty dose of adrenaline as he waited for the car to find rest. And of course the rear tires had ended up off the road, because that was what kind of night this was going to be.

She was still in the same spot, unaffected by the new events. He rolled down his window. "Where are you goin'?" It sounded accusatory and a bit disgusted. Which was pretty damn accurate.

She didn't move. "Your place."

"You know how many miles that is?"

"I do. I just walked it."

He knew his next words would sound even more disgusted, but he did nothing to disguise them. "I'm headin' straight there."

"I figured you were."

Mick turned away from her to stare through the windshield at the emptiness beyond the snow swarming his headlights. This conversation had to be happening because he couldn't believe his brain, no matter how demented, could invent something so batshit stupid. Pitch-black midnight snowstorm. A car and a woman both heading to the same place. Yet she's going to walk?

"You want to get in or what?"

"Or what?"

Mick closed his eyes. Something pulsed red against his eyelids. Maybe he was having a stroke. Maybe he was stuck in his own mind and he'd never see the normal world again. "Just get in."

Snowflakes swirled between them as the GTO's engine hummed, a slight increase in idling RPMs making it seem the car was as impatient to move as he was. He knew he'd never get all four tires back on the road. Just knew it.

She was in. He'd missed the moment she surrendered, walked to the car, opened the door, and slid in. That was more than one moment, come to think of it, but there were worse things to deal with now because a tap of the throttle only gave him a little rev of the engine and the slightest nudge from behind that turned into tires spinning against air. Whatever lip of the road he'd been perched on he may have just lost.

He unbuckled his seat belt. "You're gonna have to drive so I can push."

She didn't budge. "I don't drive."

"You didn't have that problem when you stole this car."

"We could walk."

"I ain't walkin'."

Mick opened his door. He grabbed the flashlight from behind his seat and flipped it on. Sure enough, one tire had hold of an inch of pavement. He wasn't convinced she was a good enough driver to ease an unmaintained, overpowered car on bad tires back onto an icy road.

She'd gotten out. "You drive. I'll push. If it rolls back, I'd rather be the one back here."

That got a chuckle out of him. "Why's that?"

She planted her stance and put her gloved hands against the bumper. "'Cause I don't mind death."

Desperation for his bed left him unable to talk her out of it. He returned to the wheel, leaving his door open so he could hear her. It would be a real problem if the car rolled back. It would continue down the embankment, dragging a woman underneath it. Mick rested his hand on the gearshift and took a moment to let the situation sink in. Given enough time, his gut would tell him to step back if there was danger here.

"Ready," she called.

His gut wasn't complaining. "Say a prayer," he called.

"I don't know any."

Mick didn't either. None that he trusted to work, anyway. "Okay, push."

He found the sweet spot in the clutch and held it, catching the backward roll the moment it started. It burned through the little clutch that remained but had to be done. And yeah, that smoldering paper smell, there was nothing else like it. The car moved an inch forward. The rear end found purchase on both sides, and he was up on the road and finally able to breathe again.

She appeared beside him, sniffing the air. "I think you broke something."

"You owe me a new clutch."

"I didn't ask you to come back for me."

"Just get in." He slammed his door.

"So," she said, buckling up. "Mick Svendsen. Cute *and* sweet."

"No talking." He wished he had a radio.

"Risking this fine car on bad roads to offer a ride—"

Mick's head pulsed. "Look, I'm dead tired, and not at all in the mood—"

"—to a nomadic freak."

Was she antagonizing him ... or flirting? With any other woman the line between the two was miles wide. Right now he couldn't make sense of it, and he was too hot, sweating in his coat. He couldn't decide what was to blame: the spin off the road and stress of getting back on or her long legs, inches away, stretched out into the floorboard; her hand, freed from its glove, resting so close to his own every time he changed gears; her elbow nearly tapping his. With the road so slick, he couldn't flatten the gas pedal to the floor like he craved. He had to settle for a tame engine doing nothing to cover the unquiet between them. His awareness of her rang so loud it felt like she was stretched out on top of him.

He wondered what it'd be like for her to be on top of him. He shifted in the seat, uncomfortable, restless, so painfully alive.

"Mick."

"Yeah?"

"That car." She pointed ahead. "Is that a Chrysler 300?"

He leaned forward, willing his tired eyes to identify the taillights. "Could be." They were too far away to be sure. He let up on the gas, preparing for the turn into his driveway that would surely be covered in ice, and he couldn't let the rear end get away from him again. Ahead, the car she'd asked about took the turn. Surprise registered dreamily and dull. He was too focused on not spinning off the road to give it much thought. But then, hadn't she mentioned that make of car once? And Old Mae didn't drive and rarely had visitors, especially not in the middle of the night. Surprise kicked him in the ass then, only he didn't know what to do with it.

She went for her door handle. "Let me out here."

"I'm not stoppin' in the—"

She grabbed his sleeve. "It's not a choice."

He slowed to a stop, watching the car's red taillights trailing up his driveway through the snowy ghostlike trees. She opened her door. He caught her wrist. "Wait. Who is that?"

"Someone I'd rather not see. Let me go."

"They're headin' to my house."

"I can see that." She yanked.

He tightened his grip. "Mae's in there, alone—"

"They won't bother her. Let go!" A new anger lit her eyes, so honest and purposeful it unveiled how weak any of her anger had been up until now. But this time it didn't narrow her eyes; it widened them. And that frantic note in her voice, this desperate attempt to escape—

It was fear. And the person in that car had brought it on.

Sweat tingled cold on Mick's back. He'd lost hold of her wrist but somehow captured her other arm, the quick reach and severe hold against her resistance straining his shoulder and back. Her fear awoke something that had seized him, pushing power to muscles and adrenaline into his blood. "Are they lookin' for you or me?"

She stopped straining against him and looked at him so intently it was like she'd forgotten he was there and was now seeing him for the first time. Her lips parted, her breath held as if she were listening to something far away. But still those wide, battle-ready eyes full of so much fight-or-flight Mick barely recognized her. All he could do was stare and swallow down the urge to follow that car and demand who had the nerve to make this woman so afraid. It was a stupid idea, a reckless one, but not one cell in Mick's body seemed to give a shit right now.

"That's a really good question, Mick," she whispered.

"What is?" He'd forgotten what he'd said.

She eased her door closed and reattached her seat belt. "We both need to go."

He laughed. It was too loud, too wild. The adrenaline-fueled energy in him needed somewhere to go or he might explode. "I'm not gonna watch some asshole drive down my driveway in the middle of the night and just … *leave.*"

She laid her hand on his forearm, its weight too light to be so binding and persuasive. "Please, Mick."

Why did she have to keep saying his name?

"There's a cemetery a few miles east. It has an old stone tomb. You know it?"

Yes, he knew it. He couldn't believe he was putting the car in gear and straightening out the wheel. He couldn't believe he was trusting that the people in that car wouldn't bother Old Mae. If anything happened, it would be his fault. He couldn't live with that, not on top of everything else. Pretty soon his only out would be jumping off a cliff.

She'd withdrawn her hand, retreating to her side of the car. Because of her, strange people were stalking his house at night, preventing him from going home, going to bed, getting ready for another day of work where falling asleep wasn't an option. He didn't have any more chances.

"Tell me who they are."

By the way she quickly turned to him, Mick could tell she'd heard the same grit in his voice that he had. He knew what was owed here, and now so did she.

"Some people I pissed off."

"What kind of people?"

She turned to face the window, answering with a voice too limp to be hers. "People who want me dead and would love to find out about you."

It completely shut Mick up. All of it. The answer, the new tone to her voice. "Too fucking much," he said under his breath.

HIDING OUT IN an old cemetery in the middle of the night didn't strike Mick as odd until he'd parked the GTO on the side of the narrow access road and followed Sarah Clarke's tall frame between the first row of uneven headstones. They clustered all around like creatures wandering up to have a sniff at their visitors. Not one was straight. Tilted, broken, weathered nearly out of existence—soon the lives and deaths they marked would all be forgotten. Some of the earliest Wyona settlers were buried here. As a kid he heard stories about the ghost girl crying over her lost ghost kitten. Or the Indian on the white horse that might ride past and club you if you lingered too long. Thankfully nothing about an angry Indian woman and a gas station clerk—not yet, anyway— and he didn't want to stick around and be the inspiration for a new story. He increased his pace in the crunchy snow. The mausoleum hovered ahead, the night curling around its darkened stone walls. Large tree limbs shielded it from snow cover, and the ground beside it blended into air, leaving the whole structure unattached to the same earth Mick walked. An optical illusion for sure—yes, it was on a bit of an incline, and he could see now that she had started to climb steps that weren't obvious in the shadow.

Nearby—a creaky metallic whine. Mick stopped. He didn't spook easily but he was hopped up on adrenaline from earlier and so tired he was nearly blind. Ghosts didn't worry him. It was people he was wary of, and people were stalking his house right at that moment. There was no reason they couldn't be here too. But then the mausoleum door yawned open and out came a dog.

"I'm not really sure he won't attack you," she said. Since she hadn't turned toward Mick, he didn't know if she was talking to him or the dog.

This mausoleum was a historic place no one in Wyona had the money to care for. Trees and brambles crowded its dirty walls; dead leaves filled every angled seam of the old slate roof. Mick swung his flashlight around the side where during his high school years Tommy Caruso had spray-painted a swastika the night before he was found drowned in a nearby cave. Kids claimed he'd been lured into the water by angry Civil War ghosts. It was that story along with a ton of superstition that kept this cemetery graffiti-free. Even Tommy's little skinhead friends had been afraid to cause trouble here. The swastika remained, so faded Mick thought a person would have to know it was there to see it.

"It's interesting how your people build tombs to honor the dead in one century and then vandalize them in the next."

So it was still visible to all. Mick followed to where she stood in the doorway. No race of people were immune to their own share of criminals and scum, but he was too tired to argue that fact, and the ice collecting on his collar was starting to melt. This was also trespassing, and getting out of sight seemed like the best plan right now. Yes, anyone might see his car on the road, but in weather like this, they'd assume it was abandoned. No one would think to check inside the mausoleum unless they saw someone standing outside, and he'd rather not have to explain to the Wyona sheriff why he couldn't go home tonight. Never mind the nearest police station was exactly where he should be right now, spilling it all.

No one would believe him.

Embers of a dying fire glowed orange inside. Beside it, a stash of dry firewood, jugs of drinking water, and a rolled up sleeping bag. Raised stone coffins lined the walls, surely inhabited. One of the lids sat slightly askew, like the body inside had tried to get out. Mick couldn't believe she was really living here. It was crazy.

She tossed a few logs on and stoked the embers with a long stick. Flames came alive, throwing shadows on the walls marked with the names of the dead. A human-sized stone cross stood at the far end, reigning over the room. Watching her, watching Mick.

"We're goin' to Hell," he said.

"Only if you believe in it." She stood up, wiping her hands on her jeans. "Have a seat." She gestured at the floor by the fire, the only area swept clean of leaves and dirt.

Because his legs were about to give, he did. The dog sat beside him, thumping his tail against the floor.

"I need to go home, get some sleep. I gotta work in the morning."

The fire's warmth was perfect—a primitive comfort that seeped not only into flesh but also into soul. The stone underneath him absorbed it, radiated it back. He tucked his swollen hand into his coat. His mind erased the coffins around them, imagining white skeletons hanging in the air, bony toes pointing skyward, long arms crossed over ribs, toothy grins. Outside, a blanket of them suspended in sleep above ground, now tilting, turning upright. Facing him, a mob of bones as white as the falling snow. Crooked jaws and black empty eyes watching him, judging him, and damning him for invading their peaceful night.

Chapter

11

Waapikoona watched Mick lean against the wall and drift into sleep. An amazing thing, really, for how gracefully it overtook him and how he made no effort to fight it. That last comment was a half-assed attempt to talk himself out of it, almost like he was reaching for help he knew wasn't there. There was no help against sleep so strong it overtook even in this unfamiliar place, even on the run from people out to kill them.

Well, kill *her*. They might spare him. He had ties in this town, people who knew him and would miss him. His murder would take work to hide. But if they found out what he was, they'd surely be back with a solid plan to make him disappear.

Spot growled, standing up fast. Most of the time it was simply a raccoon or a coyote, but tonight it could be more. Waapikoona cracked the door and peeked out, keeping Spot back with her leg. Modern people were easy to see. They stomped around in the woods, believing themselves invincible, flashlights and noisy cars announcing their careless presence even when they hoped to catch someone by surprise. She saw nothing but falling snow laying a thick quiet all over the land. Even the hardy winter animals hibernated tonight.

She was about to close the door when Spot barked, body rigid, watchful eyes locked on something low to the ground. A dark shape darted from one gravestone to another; a second shape followed. Her Helpers—they'd completed their task and returned. Collecting them would be tricky with Spot around. She edged her body into the crack of the door, blocking Spot's escape.

He was barking again, but this time not in her direction. If he didn't stop, he was going to wake Mick. She had to control him and get her Helpers later, but he'd moved away, around the fire to aim those barks at something inside the tomb.

She'd forgotten what her Helpers would do to Mick.

Dark wings spread in the firelight. An eagle's cry split through the barking, a screech normally released in the spread of wide sky became a weapon enclosed in the stone walls. Spot shrunk behind a coffin as Waapikoona covered her ears. It rang in her head, rousing a need to get away before it happened again. She couldn't let the eagle out, not with her Helpers out there.

The eagle hopped onto the lid of one of the coffins, tilting his head to aim an eye directly at her. This wasn't just a bird, it was Mick. There had to be some overlap into his human form, some way for him to recognize her, for her to reason with him.

"Quiet," she said, a finger to her lips.

He stretched one wing then the other. She was dazzled by their span. One wing nearly spread the length of the entire casket he sat upon.

"You can't kill my Helpers. I need them."

He chirped, tilting his quick head all around as if search-ing for an opening in the tomb to escape. With those eyes he could spot things she couldn't see, like her Helpers hiding in the shadows of the graves, waiting to return to her palm.

"Will you promise to stay here if I go outside?"

One giant flap lifted him over Waapikoona's head to land on a coffin on the other side of the room. The fire flattened then roared high from the gush of air. Dead leaves flew toward the rafters, drifting down again and catching fire midair as he folded his wings.

She had ducked in reflex. She straightened, brushing out her hair, annoyed. Of course Mick was still a pain in the ass even in eagle form. She needed a bird ankle bracelet and a chain—but those talons would rip her apart if she got too close. Her Helpers might leave if she didn't get out there soon. They weren't the brightest or most patient of under-world beings, and she needed them to keep working to get her sister rebuilt. The Silent One could change his mind at any time.

"Stay in here for five minutes, and I promise then I'll let you out to fly." She crept back to the door, watching the bird as it watched her. As soon as she turned the knob, the bird would be out the door if he wanted to be. Spot rushed against her legs, desperate to get out of there. She couldn't blame him. He was a snack to a bird that size.

She put her hand on the knob. "Mick," she said, a final plea. She couldn't think of anything else. As she slipped outside, Spot pushed past her. The door hinge shifted as it sometimes did, causing the door to stick on the ground as she tried to close it behind her. She lifted and yanked, feeling the presence of Mick's giant form on the other side. Spot growled and took off, his hunt mode flipped on, her Helpers his prey.

"No," she said, fighting with the door. She couldn't trust Spot. He was all dog—hound dog—hot on a trail, those Helpers an enemy he was driven to protect her from. With no time to fix the door, she had to trust Mick.

She rushed into the gravestones and fell to her knees, palms open, going blind from the underground magic spilling from her tongue. The dead began to wake, excited by her sudden entry into their spirit-space. Their chatter drowned out her call to her Helpers. She raised her voice, feeling a tug downward, inward, her own bones remembering death too clearly. A tingle on one palm then the other. She closed her hands, blinking her eyes back to normal vision before she was dragged into the spirit world. The dead quieted, their disappointment childlike and much too sad. Waapikoona had long given up speaking with the dead. She had no power to help them. She could only listen, and listening was never enough.

Spot came at her as she stood, his nose to the ground, bumping into her legs so hard she stumbled sideways.

"It's okay. I got them. Here," she said, squatting to let him smell her hands. She scratched his ears until he started wagging his tail. Then she returned to the door of the tomb, unsure if she'd find a bird or a man inside.

"Mick?" A warning, just in case he was human and hadn't had time to put on his pants. She shoved the door wide and stepped back. Through it he soared, one tight flap sending his body through the opening too narrow for his wingspan. He burst into the sky, invisible in the cloud-filled dark until the top branches of a tree shed snow and creaked under the weight of his landing. The snow had stopped but the silence was as heavy as ever. A lone object twirled down, landing at her feet, a dark slash against the snow.

A wing feather this time. She picked it up and stuck it in her hair.

The tree branches shifted again. Thunder rocked the earth, just the sound without its ally of light. The eagle screeched into the air, filling the night with a cry of war. Mick was on the hunt for demons, and Waapikoona couldn't wait to see what he'd find.

Chapter 12

LICKERING FIRE DANCED in front of Mick's waking eyes. He kept still, working to figure out where he was this time. Outside, but also not. In the woods but shielded from them. A pocket of warmth surrounded by solemn chill. He raised to an elbow, the stone floor harsh on his bare skin. He nearly gagged from the taste in his mouth.

"Good morning." She sat cross-legged on top of a raised stone platform against the wall—a coffin, he remembered.

He couldn't decide if she was being literal. The room was lit only by firelight, and the porthole window near the peak in the roof showed not a speck of morning sun. He looked around for his clothes. In any other situation modesty would be a concern, but right now Mick didn't care. The night before was coming back to him, and his current setting proved it wasn't a dream. And that taste—his tongue was still swimming in it. He wiped a hand across his mouth, coming away with a smear of dark sludge. This had happened before. God, not again.

"You found one," she said, hopping down. "A small one, but it would've soon grown big."

Spotting his clothes strewn across the middle of the room, he got up. She made no attempt to avert her eyes. His hoodie was ruined, torn down the middle as if by a razor. As he pulled on jeans and tugged on socks and boots, he decided not to ask what he'd supposedly found. He couldn't trust her. Even if she saw him transform into a bird, her confirmation of it meant nothing. But when he turned around and saw her stirring the fire like her comment hadn't been dropped like the bait it was, his curiosity pushed words into his mouth.

"Found what?"

She looked up, her fire-poking stick forgotten and catching fire as she weighed his question. On her knees she waited, watching him, almost like she expected him to arrive at the answer himself. Another game, another waste of his time. He heaved a sigh, snatching up his coat and shredded hoodie. He patted down his pockets to make sure he had his phone, wallet, and keys. Enough was enough.

Before he turned away, she set down the stick and shuffled on her knees to face him head-on. The way her eyes held his breached some unwritten law of privacy and personal space. They bound him; they stripped him raw. He was too sleep-deprived to be this excited, but his hastily yanked on jeans were feeling very out of place, and his pulse was about to make him sick. And with her on her knees like that...

"*Maneto*. Horned water serpent. You killed it and brought it to me."

Lies. "Where is it?"

She licked her bottom lip. "I cooked it and ate it."

It was now beyond enough. And Mick was so stupidly aroused that the chemicals in his brain were telling him the flush on her cheeks meant she was too, and the only way to be sure was to make a move and see what came of it. Never mind he'd just woken up naked in a cold mausoleum under the evil watch of an Indian witch who claimed she ate a horned snake he'd just killed. Sex shouldn't even be on the radar. The whole thing was bonkers.

Mick saw then she had a long eagle feather in her hair. The image of it turned him flammable. He didn't need answers as badly as he needed to leave. He couldn't stand there and let her eyes keep working him over. He was afraid of what he might do. "Are you some kind of witch?"

"No."

The straight answer nearly threw him off, but he jumped back on. "Why don't you sleep?"

"I do. Sometimes."

"Why didn't you sleep last night?"

"I had to keep watch. And I walked with you."

It was a step toward confirming what he already knew to be true, and he wasn't ready to go there yet, so he simply asked "Why?"

She tilted her head, pondering a moment. "I don't know. You're very tame. It was nice."

Mick fought to keep his voice normal. "Is that mine?" He pointed at her hair.

She felt the feather stuck in her braid as if she'd forgotten it was there. Then her eyes reached into him again, and he was being wrapped, tied, hopelessly bound. Prey in her web, he'd soon be sucked dry. Prey never really wanted it, though. Not like he did.

"It was." She stood up. "It's mine now."

"Why's that?"

She was close to him now, close enough to touch, to take hold of, to draw against him. "Because I like it."

He felt an urge to take it from her, just to see what she'd do.

"You're going to be late for work, Mick."

"You've done this to me." He specifically meant his involuntary nighttime shapeshifting into a giant golden eagle. But she'd done other things to him, too.

She stood there slowly shaking her head, frustratingly close, painfully far away. Denying everything so calmly. He wanted to shake her until a rational explanation tumbled out, to put his hands on her so she'd put hers on him. He wanted to overpower her, for her to fight back so he could let her win. He longed to be overcome, to escape into being undone.

It wasn't going to happen. It couldn't happen, even though he ached for it.

The shock of cold outside turned his clothes rigid and quickened his steps. Purple spread from the lowest edge of the sky. Soon the sun would rise and tame the bite of the air but it wouldn't be soon enough to help him. The GTO was hesitant to start and unsure on the slick roads. He took it easy all the way home, hoping he wouldn't find a Chrysler in his driveway.

HE DIDN'T FIND any strange cars, but he did find the plastic taped over his new broken window had ripped free, chilling his apartment enough to kick the electric heaters to full blast. This month's bill would be a nightmare worse than waking up naked in a mausoleum.

He also found two energy drinks in the back of his fridge. They were his only hope of getting through a full day underneath cars. He had no will left of his own.

The morning stumbled by. He nearly overdosed on coffee. At noon he sat on the curb behind the auto shop and unbagged his lunch. On his phone he found a text.

Amanda: Where should we meet and what time?

"Shit," Mick said to his tuna sandwich.

Date with Amanda. Window still not fixed. Apartment a frigid mess. Sarah Clarke ready to show up anytime asking for her alien corpse. A hideous cut on his arm that had broken its scab—again—and now a set of purple-black knuckles. Probable shapeshifting into an eagle at any given time, like during dinner, or dessert, or in bed with Amanda.

Forget all of it though, if the in-bed-with-Amanda was a potential reality. An outlet for this energy that ached in him would clear a way to handle all the rest. He didn't care that he needed to handle all the rest first to get himself there. He could do it somehow. He was that desperate.

I'll pick you up, he replied. It felt more like a date and less like a hookup that way. 6:30?

Sounds good. Are we going out or in? Just need to know what to wear.

He'd love to take her out, but the thought of the check made him rethink the whole thing. Cooking for a woman was romantic, right? He could make it romantic.

My place. I'm cooking for you. ;)

Going out would provide less time for Sarah Clarke to show up at his place, but it was too late now. He'd just have to pray.

He clocked out as soon as the time rolled onto the hour and started his GTO thirty seconds later. Grocery store for fresh salad, some nice cuts of trout, fancy multicolored baby potatoes, and a quart of specialty ice cream. He went for candles and hit the checkout, almost forgetting the wine. Next was the hardware store for plywood that took forever to have custom cut. The day's sun had melted and dried the roads, so he broke every speed limit home.

It would've been nice to meet Sarah Clarke there, show her the corpse and be done with it. He wasn't that lucky. It also would've helped for her to show up while he was screwing the plywood over the windows, sweeping his apartment, or changing his sheets. After showering he checked for her outside as the sky darkened into wintery night. He washed and cut the romaine and potatoes, waiting to turn around and find her in his kitchen.

As he slid into his only nice sweater and newest jeans, he made a pact with God that Sarah Clarke was catching up on sleep and wouldn't be up for company until tomorrow. He had a bad feeling it was the Devil he should be appealing to instead, and he didn't know how to contact that guy. They didn't teach that in church.

Amanda came right out without him needing to text her. Either his car was that loud or she was as desperate as he was.

"I forgot you drove this," she said, buckling up.

Okay, so it was the car. "It's obnoxious. I plan to change out the exhaust."

"You shouldn't." She grinned, big and bright and friendly.

He had a new appreciation for women who smiled. "So, you okay with my place? We could go into town—"

"No, your place is great. The weather's been so weird, I don't want to get stuck in town."

"Good point." The temperature change had been so extreme he hadn't even worn a jacket. That's not to say a blizzard wouldn't roll in. And if it did, Mick would have no choice but to drive her home in it. If he managed to get through the evening without something unexplainable happening, he'd be thanking both God and the Devil.

He was starting to see this might be a bad idea. And no matter what words he tried out in his head, nothing fit for a vague enough explanation to counter what she might witness. He just might have to get her good and drunk. He should've bought more wine.

"So, can I help you cook? I love to cook. Never get much opportunity to, though. It's all PBJs and mac 'n cheese. Not that I'm complaining."

He laughed. She was so normal it hurt. And her wavy hair swept over her shoulder—he could really enjoy that if he could stop thinking about that feather stuck in Sarah Clarke's hair. *His* feather. And what exactly had happened that night to make Sarah Clarke say she enjoyed walking with him?

"Yeah, that'd be cool," Mick answered. "It's nothin' special, so don't get your hopes up."

"As long as it's not mac 'n cheese."

"It's not. It's shells 'n cheese."

She looked over at him as he tried to keep a straight face and failed. "Oh god, are you messing with me?"

"Maybe."

She elbowed him. "I just had a little heart attack, thinking I'd insulted you. Kari does the same thing to me. I don't know why I agreed to this." Her laugh was so genuine and contagious it filled him up with a sweet high he hadn't felt in weeks.

God, he'd been so depressed. It was hard to admit, but now it seemed it'd been pushed behind him, a ghost of a memory once latched on now released. No longer haunting him. Mick gave in to rash impulse and took her arm, sliding his hand down to find her hand and hold it. And after every shift in gears, he went back for more.

"For the record, if it is shells 'n cheese, I'm totally okay with that."

MICK SEALED AMANDA inside his apartment without any interruption from nomadic women or shark-toothed aliens. They prepped the trout and potatoes and slid them in the oven to bake. Then he found a chill-out music channel on his phone, lowered the lights, and lit the candles. Amanda was on her second glass of wine, and he'd switched to beer. She was leaning toward him over her empty salad plate, her leg against his under the table.

He couldn't concentrate. He tried with every ounce of willpower. His part of the conversation came from some low-level part of his brain, the same part that responded when he was half asleep. He knew what awaited him in maybe an hour was something he didn't just want but needed like water, food, or the sleep he was missing. And to be so out of it, so removed from a conversation with a woman he was about to take to bed—it stole his appetite. He wasn't the kind of guy who used women. And if that's what he'd become, he had to end it before it made itself a reality. The focus he could've used for that was going elsewhere, to thoughts of the mausoleum, of Sarah Clarke's direct gaze as he got dressed. He wanted to know what happened the night she walked with him. Why she described him as tame. Why she said it was nice. He wanted to switch Amanda for her, feed her food they prepared together, then crush her against the wall by the stove and taste her mouth, her tongue, her neck.

The beer made him slow, made him care less about being a shitty guy. It made him more open to mentally switching Amanda for her, made the guilt retreat, the sexual ache more insistent, less choosy, less moral. Kissing Amanda on the couch was the hit he needed, the proof all was fine. This was consensual, no strings, completely cool. He broke away to get a rubber from his bedroom to stick in his pocket. Shutting the dresser drawer stirred a folded paper on top which drifted to the floor. He picked it up. Dougie's drawing of the alien.

Mick's reality fell hard upon him, slamming doors and flipping on lights. If he went through with this, he'd never forgive himself. The woman he ached for wasn't here, and no other woman would satisfy that ache. He'd be in the same position as before, with a ton of regret he didn't know what he'd do with.

In the bathroom he splashed cold water on his face to sober up. He looked straight into his own eyes, disappointed but certain. End this with Amanda, apologize, drive her home, apologize some more. Then figure out how to find out Sarah Clarke's real name.

Amanda was in the kitchen rinsing out her wine glass. Smart, understanding, drama-free—he'd be insane to give up a woman like this, even just for one night. This arrangement could be so sweet if his life and head weren't already crammed with his own drama.

"Amanda—"

"It's okay, Mick." Her use of his name could not live up.

"My head's not in this. I got a lot on my mind and this ain't fair to you." Putting it out there should've made him feel better, but it made him feel like a dope, and a prude, and the biggest idiot ever born.

"This doesn't have to be … I'm not hung up on you being fair."

She was going to hate him, and he couldn't blame her. "Well I am. And I'm sorry about that."

"No need to be sorry. You're too nice of a guy, Mick."

"Yeah, I'm workin' on that."

At her driveway she kissed his cheek and squeezed his hand and told him dinner was perfect. "I'm open to doing this again, even if it's just dinner."

"I'll remember that."

"As long as you're okay being used for an adult dinner and conversation."

He laughed. It sounded as tired as he felt. "I'm okay being used in any way, just not the other way around."

"You need to get over that," she said, sliding out of the car.

He didn't answer because she was right. Too nice a guy all his life, and he had the sexual frustration to show for it. But if anything else changed about him, he wouldn't recognize himself, and he was already having a hard time with that.

CHAPTER
13

An early bedtime sounded so good to Mick he made a battle plan on his way home, hoping to make the steps toward the pillow more efficient. Park the car. Get inside. Lock up. Rinse dishes, stack them in sink. Cork the wine. Fridge leftovers. Take a piss. Strip down. Get in bed. He repeated the plan in his head to keep from nodding off at the wheel.

When a tingle started in his limbs, he figured it was exhaustion. More troubling was the feeling of being off-center, of driving an unlevel road when he knew this stretch was as flat as a plowed cornfield. He took a breath and held it. Ahead, a pale figure caught in his headlights, too short and upright to be a deer. He downshifted, leaning to peer ahead. It couldn't be a child walking the road alone at night. This was exhaustion, dementia, whatever. It wasn't real. He slowed to a stop six feet from the thing.

It was a child, in a pale yellow nightgown with a ruffle at the bottom just like Janie's. Her head hung wearily, her arms long and limp. She slowly turned her face toward him.

"Oh my god," Mick said, ripping off his seat belt. It was Janie. "Oh my god." He couldn't stop saying it. This was so wrong, he needed a god to help him. He needed *the* God. The one his mother had believed in, the one he prayed to as a child. Kari's house was miles away. For Janie to get this far on foot, for her to not be frozen to death or hit by a car or eaten by a bear or snatched up by a pervert—Mick was picking her up in his arms as these things were going through his head. Things that should've happened but didn't, and how didn't they?

"Janie! What're you—my god, your mom must be—" He realized then how limp her whole frame was, how it lacked both warmth and cold, how it felt like vapor in his arms. He readjusted her into a cradle hold. If she had the sleepwalking and dementia at this young an age, they were all doomed. She was set up for a life of trouble none of them could deal with right now. "Little birdie?"

She turned her little face toward him. Mick saw white eyes with the narrowest, blackest slits in the middle. He saw teeth—metal-gray and razor sharp, an upper row of all canines. He felt his hold slip. Her face morphed into a wrinkled old man's, child-sized, grinning, a laugh changing from a child's to a deep, throaty croak. The creature sunk those teeth through Mick's sleeve, directly into his healing arm wound.

Mick dropped the thing but its latch on him didn't break. The ground tilted; Mick fell into the spill of his headlights as the teeth sank deeper into muscle, bottoming out against bone. A great force inside his chest shuddered, growing still. With his good arm he grabbed the thing by the neck and squeezed, his forearm against the bulk of its body to crush it into the road. Wings snapped out against the pavement. Its teeth released their hold. Mick pushed back and away as it flapped into the sky, shrieking into the night.

Blood poured through the ripped fabric of Mick's jacket. He gritted his teeth to hold back a scream, jerking the sleeve up past his elbow. His previous wound had been made indistinguishable by this jelly-covered mess, torn flesh exposing white bone. The image was so unrelatable Mick couldn't make sense of it. Pain thrummed distantly in time with his pulse. It was a blessing to feel numb to damage so extreme, a trick of the mind, some kind of survival instinct. And it gave clarity to the absence of a piece of him—not flesh or blood but something deeper, something he'd have to lose to recognize it had ever been there to begin with.

He sat down in the road. Watched the wound gush dully to a trickle under the pressure of his grip. He waited for someone to drive by, someone with an extra hand to make an emergency call. No one came.

Clouds moved away from the moon, exposing him in white, clean light somehow stronger than his headlights. He couldn't wait for help. No one could see this. Whether in his head or real, it didn't matter. No police, no hospitals, no witnesses. Somehow he had to get himself home.

Standing up and getting behind the wheel passed in a blur. He found his driveway, the hazy path of a dream. He shut off the engine, opened his door, fell out onto the gravel. A presence nearby, one he couldn't see, seemed to grow closer. It had to be Old Mae's eyes in the window, the movement of the curtain as she tried for a better look. He silently begged her to stay in the house. Tomorrow would require some fib about low blood sugar or tripping over a shoelace. Easy. He just had to get in his door.

"Mick." She stepped from shadow into the waxen moonlight.

His name like that, the M drawn out like a long taste—she had to stop doing that. In his dreamy, post-traumatic state she was a goddess. Her voice, her solemn eyes, her halo of hood over the long fall of dark hair. He swayed on his feet, clutching his arm. Blood wept through his fingers, dripping on his boots. One step toward his apartment, he stumbled in the gravel. At once she was against him, sliding her shoulders underneath his arm to support his weight all the way to the door.

Inside. On the couch. Lights flipped on like starbursts.

"Lock the door," he bit out.

She did and shoved a kitchen chair under the knob. Then she went for his jacket. He couldn't prevent the stuttering groan that came out of him, and she ignored it, peeling his jacket off as he ground his teeth. Screaming would wake him from this nightmare, but it would also wake Old Mae and her 911-dialing fingers.

"What did—oh, *wow*," she said, rolling up his sweater sleeve.

He leaned his head back and closed his eyes. She'd materialized out of the night like an angel to help him, and he was going to let her take charge so he could check out. Footsteps took her away. Rummaging in the kitchen, the bedroom, the closet. The throbbing in his arm gained intensity as if calling to him to get on his feet and fix it.

The couch cushion shifted under added weight. He felt softness envelop his exposed flesh, heard the unmistakable squawk of duct tape ripping off the roll. Tightness surrounded his arm, one strip at a time.

"Look at this, before I finish it." She took a handful of his collar and shook him. "This is poison to your Thunder-Being."

"Thunder-Being?"

"Thunderbird."

Good, Mick thought. If that was her term for his other form, it was the best news he'd heard in a long time. Poison it dead. Poison it out of him.

"Look!"

He opened his eyes. She flipped back the edge of towel now wrapping his arm so it exposed one side of the new wound. His skin had grayed around it; black lines branched in all directions inches out from the torn flesh. It crawled before his eyes, like dye traveling through water. He'd never seen anything like it. It made no sense to him.

"What did this to you? Was it human?"

Mick had to close his eyes to breathe before he could gather his voice. "Human at first. Thought it was Janie. Turned into something else."

"Describe it." She tucked the towel into itself and ran another layer of tape around it.

"Snake eyes. Shark teeth. Wings like a … bat."

"Big or small?"

Just having the arm covered made him better able to think straight. "Small. Fifteen pounds."

"You need to see a healer."

"No hospital. They'd lock me up."

"Not a hospital. A medicine woman. She has to get this poison out of you before it finds your Thunder-Being and kills it."

"Let it die." He sat up. He needed to find some real bandages and peroxide so he could doctor himself up better once the bleeding stopped. It took a long moment for him to register the warm point of sharp pressure on his chest as her palm keeping him down.

"It's not that simple," she said.

"Move your hand."

"If it dies, it won't prevent you from changing. Your next change will be into a spirit bird, and you won't be able to change back."

She'd leaned toward him, her eyes cutting and desperate. It was almost like she cared.

Mick stared back at her. In that moment he realized she had to be the reason for all of this. She knew too much, and she was accepting it like it was a normal part of life. He couldn't continue to deny what was happening or blame it on dementia. Even if his mind was dissolving away, this woman was real. Kari had seen her that first afternoon. Kari saw the bird in the webcam photos. He needed answers, and he knew exactly where to start. "What's your real name?"

She quickly withdrew her hand and scooted several inches away. Her face, alive with concern just a second ago, cleared of expression. She regarded him, her eyes the tiniest bit narrowed, wary, headstrong. She didn't seem ready to offer "Sarah Clarke" though, so Mick was getting somewhere. Her name marked trust—he wouldn't believe anything she said until he had it. And he so very much needed to trust her right now.

"Waapikoona." It came low and plain, on an outward breath. Clearly the outcome of some internal battle where truth had triumphed.

"What?" Mick had heard just fine. He wanted her to repeat it, and his intent was clear in how grating the demand was. Pain hadn't made his voice go there, and he leaned toward her just so there would be no mistake.

She rose to his challenge, speaking it loud and clear. "Waapikoona."

"Spell it."

She did. Pain jumbled the letters in his head, but it didn't matter. Even if he retained none of this, forcing her to do it gave him such a breathless high he had to steady himself before it showed on his face. New questions lined up in his head without his conscious thought, ones he couldn't put away for another day. He might not live another day.

"What language?"

A cant of her head said, *Are we really doing this now?* His hardened gaze said, *Yes, we are.*

"*Myaamia.*"

"Your tribe's language?"

"No. The closest I've found. Your people wiped out my people's language."

"What tribe?"

"My tribe is not in your books."

Mick felt his hold on the conversation slip. "Books?"

"White men's books. The ones who write history only include what they want future generations to know."

"Who are your people?"

"Long destroyed."

A cold look Mick hadn't seen for a while settled hard onto her face. His reeking Viking blood was on her hands, but not in the way she probably wanted it to be. She was here to save him, not fulfill bloody revenge. The corpse he had yet to turn over to her couldn't be the only draw. It was too complicated to think about with the night he'd had. And he needed to get his wound cleaned and properly bandaged.

"The corpse you want is in the doorway to that old barn." Mick stood, his good arm braced against the couch until his head stopped swimming. He walked to the door, opened it. "Bye."

She stood, her lips a tight line. Good for her to know when to keep opinions to herself. Mick didn't expect her to stop as she passed before him. He also didn't expect her to make a grab for his wrapped, wounded arm or for her to squeeze it with just enough pressure to make his heart stop but not kill him. "You have maybe a day to fix this."

He said nothing. He stood there, absorbing the need to cringe, to fold in two, to shake her off, to grab her arm and twist it away as red burst behind his eyes and every curse word was broadcast in his head.

It took the dying breath of his manners not to slam the door behind her. Not to scream once he was alone. He put himself to work locating the first aid kit Kari had dropped off when he first started babysitting the kids. When he found it he set it on the kitchen table and sat down in front of it. Regular first aid wasn't going to help him. He'd been bitten by some kind of flying demon, and its venom wasn't attacking the human part of him but the other part. He laid his bad arm on the table, rotating it to check for blood flow. The only blood he saw was dried. Removing duct tape was too much a chore for his current state. He was too tired to even blink his eyes.

If he shapeshifted tonight—no, he couldn't think about it.

Pain-reliever, though, that's what he needed. He swallowed several aspirin, washed them down with water. A sick day at work—the thought made him feel even sicker, but it had to be done. As if the chronic sleep deprivation wasn't enough, now his arm wound was infected by a demon's bite. He called and left Virgil a voicemail at the shop to avoid having to wake up early and call in the morning. He didn't mention any flying demons, just that his wound had turned hospital-worthy and he needed a day to sort it out. As he ended the call, a nearby animal's growl had him turning toward the door. Another visit from a demon would end him. He grabbed a steak knife. Yes, he'd be safe sleeping behind a locked door and boarded windows even with a swarm of demons outside, but he was done being the victim. It was time for him to do the attacking. He swung open the door.

First he saw the set of cowboy boots extending from the shadow beside the wall, their owner out of sight. Then he saw the thumping tail of a friendly dog. The same dog from the mausoleum. He stepped outside and found her sitting against the house, snuggled into her coat, hood pulled down over her face. "Go to bed, Mick."

"You're not—" Mick lost all words. He'd love to see her stupidly freeze to death, but the dog? It didn't seem fair. "You're not staying out here."

She sucked her legs underneath her coat. "Call the cops."

He didn't need the police. He'd forcibly remove her himself. She'd probably break his good arm, just to be a vengeful. "It's winter."

"I'm used to it. Go back inside before I say something rude."

"The dog."

"He'll go home soon."

"To a cold mausoleum?"

"I built the fire up. Now go to bed. We have a long walk tomorrow."

He tapped her boot with his toe. The gesture was too sweet, but he had no energy to regret it. He was lying to himself anyway. Finding her frozen to death in the morning might break the remaining piece of him still intact. "I can't leave you out here."

"You can, because I need to be on watch. Your snake-eyed bat-winged playmate has friends."

If she were an ordinary woman, his masculinity might complain about this setup. The truth was he knew she was the better choice for the job, especially tonight. A strand of trust tightened in the space between them, a lifeline, its other end held by the only person who could help him. He wouldn't be able to sleep knowing she was out there in the cold. He was still human enough to care about that.

CHAPTER

14

WAAPIKOONA COULD FIGHT Mick, but she couldn't fight his sense of right and wrong. Morals ruled him with a heavy hand. She'd seen too many of his kind ruled by greed and power to ever complain about the way he was. Of course there were more people like him, but he was such a rare find, such a welcome change, so heartbreakingly … good.

And with his fierce side ready to go to war for those morals, he was too much for Waapikoona. A nice pushover was one thing. A noble fighter, selfless, disciplined, challenging this sick world in a battle for good? She simply wanted to sit next to him and absorb him. He'd been built by the upperworld. She'd made a bargain with the underworld. A union between opposing forces like these could only mean catastrophe. But if liking him was a snare growing tighter each time she tried to struggle free, she'd soon be too hopelessly caught. Her fight should be getting stronger, not weaker. Not pleasantly complacent. Not surrendered.

She'd rather stay outside. It was safer for both of them. She could keep guard to prevent another demon attack while keeping good distance from Mick to preserve her sanity—she'd never be able to revive her sister without a clear head. Even though her new modern life had weakened her to the weather, her rebuilt body demanded less warmth to stay alive. In dry clothes she could sleep outside. She wasn't ready to explain any of this to Mick. No, she could never tell him that.

"Just come inside." Too exhausted to hide the plea in his voice, he stepped back, holding the door open. The way he leaned, it looked more like the door was holding him.

Indulging him gave her such guilty pleasure. Just the thought made her heart die a little. Yes, he was indeed too much for her. She thought of all the bones in the ground. Her ancestors murdered by the hands of his. Other tribes had fought and murdered too, and she figured to Mick, all Native people were the same. To him it was only a two-sided war, his kind versus one single mass of Others. Without being personally involved, he'd see both equally to blame. His side had simply won. He couldn't begin to understand the diversity of people, of culture. Even though what mattered most was her people's land. Her home.

Stop. This was The Silent One in her head again, and yes it was true, but it wasn't going to fix anything now. She needed to get Mick to a healer, and indulging him now would make that trip much easier. But why get him to a healer? She didn't know. She had to do it, more than anything she'd ever been compelled to do—besides save her sister. Helping Mick wouldn't divert her from that. If anything, it would clear her mind to better focus on it.

She got up and went in. He watched her, too tired to even look relieved. She called Spot inside. Mick closed and locked the door, shoved the chair back underneath.

"Sheets on the bed are clean," he said, slurring the words.

She caught him before he collided with the wall. "Good, because that's where you're going."

"I get the couch."

"Not tonight. I'm locking you in the bedroom. I have no time to deal with a half-spirit thunderbird."

They'd made it to the bed where he'd dropped onto the mattress, struggling to toe off boots still tightly tied. She freed the laces and pulled the boots off. The sweater was soaked bloody. It needed to come off too, but he'd fallen to his back on the bed, eyes blinking closed, good arm batting her away. She caught it, holding the sleeve until he'd pulled his arm all the way out. The other side would be trouble to stretch over the covered wound. She unsheathed her flint knife and cut the other side of his sweater off him, revealing the toned muscle of a physical laborer set in snow-colored skin. His name should be Waapikoona, not hers.

Her adopted tribe had named her after finding her in the snow. A mysterious lost child, with no language, no family, and no name. Her name became Waapikoona when she recognized their word for *snow*, even if she didn't recognize their other words. Her people had truly been the lost ones, absorbed by time. Their language had been a strain of another, now long forgotten. The modern strain had also almost died. Its speakers were working to rebuild it, as The Silent One had worked to rebuild her and she worked to rebuild her sister.

Mick's breathing had slowed to that of overtaking sleep. She eased his belt out of the buckle and pulled it out from under him. He woke and pushed her away when she went for the button on his jeans, only to loosen them for comfort. Her reason was practical and had nothing to do with the raw excitement stirring in her that wanted those jeans gone.

White men were to be avoided. Her people taught her that in her old life, and she'd been reborn twenty-five years ago with the rule very much intact.

But rules were meant to be broken.

He watched her through half-closed lids as he unzipped and opened the fly. She stood up. A decent woman would leave. She was not a decent woman.

"Hit the light on your way out," he mumbled, wiggling himself up to the pillow where he opened his arms flat against the bed and closed his eyes, jeans open but still very much on.

Turn off the light was a very hard call. She wanted to stay there and drink him in, the almost-naked white man, the warm muscled skin, the jeans more of a temptation on than off and so forbidden it claimed her, made her promise to climb onto him next time. Should this ever happen again, she couldn't walk away a second time.

He hated her, though, thought she was evil and to blame. It seemed like a big obstacle. It only made her want him more.

She needed to go back to Oklahoma for a while and spend some time with men who weren't descended from her enemies, to get this all out of her system. She needed to find a man who'd come from the underworld like she had. There had to be some worthy substitute for Mick Svendsen, even though her heart was telling her no, there was not, there never would be. She'd traveled the circle of time, bridged the upper and lower worlds, and she'd never met anyone like him.

Waapikoona sent Spot into Mick's bedroom the next morning when it was clear he was going to sleep in. They had a long walk to the healer, and orienting her way back was hard enough in the daylight. She started coffee and unsuccessfully raided his fridge. She'd moved over to browse his cabinets when he appeared, stubbly-faced and bed-tousled and unfortunately wearing a shirt.

He seemed oddly unconcerned about the arm still wrapped in a duct tape-covered towel. "I think your dog wants somethin'."

"Yeah, for you to wake up. I could tell you about our trip today, but you won't believe me."

He brushed past her, reaching for a box of cereal. "We aren't goin' nowhere."

"We are. Unless you'd rather I release my Helpers so you change forms right now and follow me in the sky. You obey orders much better that way."

He stopped to look at her, a slight opening of his lips revealed teeth clamped tight. His eyes charged with unspent lightning he should save for the horned serpents, not waste on her. The glower held, like the unnatural stillness before a thunderstorm, the silent overhead roll of building clouds, trees straight and still when soon they'd be tossed and twisted in the wind. She stood her ground, the potency of her civil calm matching the violence of his. He was the first to break: a smile, born innocently enough but warping into a hateful grin. Full of fight but caged, resentful, at her mercy.

She wanted to grab him by the collar and kiss him hard. Mostly because she craved such a kiss, partly because she wanted to dominate him. It could be she wanted to soothe him a little, too, but she wasn't sure she wanted to claim that feeling. She poured him a cup of coffee instead. He took it from her, eyes firm on hers.

"Did you really eat a horned snake?"

"You mean the one you hunted and killed?"

"Reckon that's a yes?"

She poured herself a coffee and took a sip. "I already told you I did. What, did you lose sleep over this?"

"Sounds like somethin' a witch would do."

Not much made her want to laugh. This, though, was comedy, and if she wasn't careful the warmth pressing against her lungs might conjure a smile—or worse, a laugh. Jokes wouldn't rebuild her sister. She had nothing to smile about. "That's your mythology, not mine. So the accusation doesn't quite fit."

"It just makes it a little hard to know what to offer you for breakfast."

"Don't go to the trouble. I don't need to eat often. You know, like a snake itself." Internally, she cringed. All she wanted to do was shut him down. Instead that warmth was screwing with her mind, making her say playful things.

"You are what you eat?"

"Which means you should be grazing constantly, like the commercially raised and mechanically killed cow."

"You think you're better than me."

"You think I think I'm better than you."

He scrunched his eyes at her. Then he got himself a bowl and filled it with cereal. "Help yourself if you're due for a meal this week. Sorry I don't got any small rodents."

Now it sounded like he was ribbing her back. A hard kiss she'd take. Rough impersonal sex—maybe. Friendly banter? She'd rather die—again. She prepared her own bowl of cereal and leaned against the counter instead of joining him at the table. Distance seemed like a good thing. "It's a long way out today. You'll need to pack yourself a lunch."

No response, not even a look in her direction. Such a catastrophe to miss out on the ice-blue of his eyes, a color so terrifyingly alien to her as a child. He was accusing her of being a witch—had he looked in the mirror lately? Even after traveling through this country in her new life, she still hadn't quite grown accustomed to the shock of light eyes.

She tended to avoid looking at anyone so closely, never cared so much to see a face. She'd had a protective wall, been careful not to make an impression, to see or be seen. Now she was seeing, and she was a child again, staring into the alien blue for the first time … if only he'd look up so she could see once more.

Abruptly he stopped shoveling cereal into his mouth. He looked at his bad arm like it had just appeared there. "Oh, shit."

They'd waited too long. She should've hauled him to the healer last night. "Yeah, we need to go."

He stood up, dropping his spoon. "No, it's—" He shuddered then shook himself as if trying to fling off insects. "It just got worse. I need this off me." He found an edge of the tape and started to work it free.

"Here, let me." Waapikoona picked up her flint belt knife from the table by the couch and went to Mick's side. "Hold still."

Under the sharp blade the towel peeled away, exposing chalky gray skin and sinister black veins not only around the original wound anymore but spreading from wrist to bicep. Little of his real arm remained. Mick wasn't just poisoned by venom; soon he'd be made of it. This demon wouldn't just destroy a Thunder-Being, it would turn a Thunder-Being evil, creating a new ally to the underworld. A creature just like her. His next shift wouldn't make Mick a spirit bird, but something much worse.

"Oh, Jesus," he said. "Is this bad?"

It wasn't the moment she'd have chosen to get a full, unguarded look into his alien blue eyes, but she met them anyway and held them. An ancient buried fear of his kind crackled through her, adrenaline gone so savage she tasted blood in her mouth from centuries ago, felt the sting of the whip on her hands, heard the cries of her people as they were torn from their homes. She wasn't a child. She was strong and alive, aligned with the world of the dead, powerful and unstoppable. All she had to do was say the words and surrender her form to The Silent One, and she could do anything. Even knowing this she couldn't quiet the war-drum beat of her heart.

"I can feel it climbin' into my shoulder." His eyes, so blue, so intent on hers. His voice nearly a whisper.

And he was still looking at her like she could help. Accusation didn't fill his eyes like it should. What she saw was closer to a prayer. Her war-drum heart stuttered, picking up a new rhythm that unearthed a voice and spirit and something entirely new. Hope, compassion—*no*. It didn't mix with her memories of violence and hate. She had the urge to spit this new thing out. A new war assembled inside her, one that had no clear way to win. This is why she had that shield, why she chose to look at the people who'd settled her land without fully seeing them. Is this what would've happened had she dropped that guard years ago? Or is this the first time her shield had been punctured, her defense stripped, her decision to remain imperceptive defeated by her desire to see?

She called for Spot and went outside. She'd offered to get Mick to a healer, and she'd follow through. That was it.

Spot trotted off to sniff around the decrepit barn. In her head she mapped the route to the healer. They'd never make it in half a day, not with the venom advancing like it was. A shortcut existed but it was too risky, not just for Mick but her, too. It would expose her as a traitor, and she'd never get her sister back.

"You're not going to make it," she said to Mick when he joined her outside.

He took a moment to digest that. She refused to meet his gaze so she had no idea what he might be thinking. She shouldn't care—no, she didn't care.

"Okay," he said, turning to survey the woods. "So, what, sever the arm?"

She had to look at him then. If that was a joke, it wasn't funny. Maybe it should've been. She was so mixed up. "I guess that's an option."

A bad option. She wouldn't do it. She'd done worse, but she'd been guided by The Silent One. The images she brought back from those experiences played in her mind like hazy dreams, unconnected to reality. She couldn't claim them as her own and never felt like she should. And worse things she'd carried out herself had always been justified. Maybe her brand of justice failed the test of humanity, but she'd met Death. She mingled with demons. The test of humanity no longer applied.

"What's the other option?" He'd tightened his jaw so the muscle in his cheek stood out. He was still addressing the woods.

"A dangerous shortcut."

"How dangerous?"

It could ruin me. Voicing it would give away too much, bring her world too close to his. And that was more dangerous than the shortcut itself.

"We can drive to it." She couldn't believe she was suggesting this. But the calm that settled her heart felt right. No matter what excuses she gave herself, she couldn't revive her sister and be the person who abandoned this man. The peace she craved would be long lost. She held out her hand for his car key.

He ignored her and got in the driver's seat. *Okay, tough guy.* She got in beside him and reached into the back to make sure the flashlight was still there. It was. She flipped it on, confirming its batteries were still good.

He glanced at it in her lap then caught her eye. Decided not to say anything about the flashlight. Instead, he said, "I'm wonderin' why you're helpin' me."

"So am I."

"You must feel responsible."

"I'm not."

"For someone not responsible you seem real … in the know."

He was fishing for information she had no intention to give. She owed him nothing. In fact, it was he who owed her a Helper corpse. If he'd delivered that she'd have been on her way a long time ago.

He pulled onto the road in the direction she pointed. "Where are you from?"

That was safe. "Oklahoma."

"Why are you here?"

That was not safe. "To get you to a healer."

SHE DIRECTED HIM to park at the same spot she had left the car last time, exactly twelve miles down the narrow county road twisting through the winter trees, their skeletons branching over the road, shivering in the wind. The sun was a vague colorless orb losing its fight behind stone-gray clouds. Mick pulled on a knit hat and gloves retrieved from the pockets of his coat. He locked his car, his attention drawn to the sky. He took a big breath and held it. With his eyes cast upward, she was free to stare unguarded. Mick wasn't just worn out and wounded. On his face was the grief of a man who'd appealed to his gods and only received silence in return. A man who'd been abandoned, who'd been hopelessly cursed. He didn't see the power in what he was, only the burden. To her people, his kind didn't appeal to gods. He was a god himself.

"Mick."

He kept his eyes on the sky, clearing his throat before answering. "Yeah?"

"You can't shift while we're in there."

He released a chuckle built from disgust not humor. "I don't got much control over it, in case you ain't noticed."

"You'll have to control it. I need to trust you."

"You can't. Not about that." He gave up his study of the sky to pass beside her, hat pulled down over his ears, boots crashing through dead leaves.

She couldn't bring a fledgling thunderbird into The Silent One's den. But it looked like that was exactly what she was about to do.

CHAPTER 15

T HE FIRST SNOWFLAKES to filter through the branches overhead seemed almost a hallucination to Mick. It couldn't be snowing again. He hadn't seen so much snow in December since he was a kid. Somehow in the last ten years, snow had become a rare treat this time of year. All winter, really. Each tiny flake melted upon impact with the ground, their disappearance as dreamlike as their drowsy fall to the ground.

If he didn't find a cure for his arm and shoulder soon, his fall to the ground wouldn't be so graceful.

He slowed, allowing her to take the lead on the narrow deer trail. After she was several paces ahead, he said, "Waapikoona."

She turned, exactly as a person would when hearing their name called. So it wasn't a lie.

"What?" she asked when he came forward and stopped behind her.

"Just tryin' it out."

The sharp edge of her stare suggested she might not like him calling her by the name he'd forced her to surrender. He decided he needed to use it as often as possible. *"Wah-pi-koo-na.* Am I gettin' that right?"

"Keep up. If you collapse before we get there, I can't carry you."

Dead cold had overtaken his shoulder and was now creeping up one side of his neck. Mick wasn't sure which organ the venom would reach first and end him: his brain or his heart. He'd prefer to get help before he found out.

She was right. He wasn't going to make it. His heart pumped harder with every step, spreading the phantom nothingness of his poisoned arm into his jaw, ribs, hip. Half of his body had split away. He wished it'd at least feel numb. He didn't even have that.

"Here," she said, stopping to hand him a rock she'd taken from her pocket. "Look through this and you'll see the entrance in front of us."

In his hand he recognized it not as rock but the clearest mica crystal he'd seen, glassier and prettier than the one he'd had in a rock collection as a kid. "What entrance?"

Ahead was nothing but more trail and trees dripping melting snow in the meager warmth of the day. She stepped close, snatched the crystal, and held it in front of him, directly in line with his eye.

"Now look and follow me in."

He took the crystal from her. Although it was clear, it was more like ice than a lens and too thick to see anything through. But he narrowed his gaze as if it were indeed a lens because he had no other option but to humor her. As he stared through it, foggy scenery sharpened and an alternate view came into focus. The trail and dripping trees were still there, but new to the scene was a large bed of slanted limestone, darkness underneath suggesting the opening to a cave. He moved the crystal aside. The limestone was gone. So was Waapikoona.

With no time or desire to contemplate what he was or wasn't seeing, he peered through the crystal until he found the cold, slippery, and unyielding limestone with his free hand. Boots slid under and in. He had to twist onto his stomach and pocket the crystal as his upper half followed down, into pitch black as if a door had closed behind him.

Light flashed on, swept around to settle on his boots.

"Good," she said. "Now follow me. Crystal?" She held her hand out, and Mick dug out the crystal and handed it back.

"Won't I need this?" He didn't want to be stuck in there, unable to see the exit.

"No."

"Why not?"

She pocketed the crystal, watching him. Mick couldn't tell if she was deciding to trust him with the information or if she was just making him beg for it.

"Because once you've made it inside, you're safe if guided by an underworld spirit."

"Okay, where's the underworld spirit?"

"Already with you."

Nerves made his back crawl. He turned around, expecting some god-awful demon to be approaching, ready to act as tour guide.

"Let's go," she said.

Since she was the only one with a flashlight, he had no choice but to keep close behind, one hand raised to catch any dip in the ceiling before it caught his head. He took off his hat and tucked it into his pocket to keep it dry. Hollow black space pressed against his back, and his skin tingled with the knowledge of so much open air behind him. This 'underworld spirit' thing—it had to be superstition. Her tribe's beliefs, her religion, whatever. He couldn't understand why it felt so real to him, more real than the god he'd been brought up to believe in.

A thread of anger unrolled in his stomach. She'd led him out here completely unprepared—no flashlight of his own, no explanation for where they were headed or what they'd encounter. He'd met too many unreal creatures lately to expect the old, normal reality to be lying ahead of him. If the poison was going to kill him, he didn't want to die in this cave, lost to his family, a big gaping unknown in their world.

"I don't believe in underworld spirits," he said, his anger like a fresh wound, demanding attention.

Crouching for a low spot, she didn't stop her progress. "You should."

"Give me one damn reason why I should."

"Because you're talking to one right now."

He stopped. She didn't. Her light bobbed away, her body a shadow moving against glossy walls until they returned to nothing but vaguely lit surface. Then Mick wasn't seeing what was in front of him at all. He saw that first meeting in the parking lot, the crowbar hitting the pavement. Her knife against his throat in his apartment. The slimy alien corpse under his bed, a second one in the entrance to the old barn. His own body, replaced by a giant eagle. The mausoleum. The winged creature's teeth sinking into his arm, its laugh as it flapped away.

The last fragment of light disappeared around an invisible bend somewhere ahead, leaving Mick suspended in complete darkness. All around him the cave dripped as the black void swelled. Already crouching, it wasn't much effort to go to his knees. Palms against the cold wet stone he breathed, trying to remember which way they'd come. The exit was lost. He was in the belly of the earth, insignificant, helpless. His throat tightened, clamping off air he needed, breaths that were coming too fast, one on top of the other. A cold drop landed on his head, trickling through hair to scalp and running down to the back of his neck, triggering a shiver so violent he nearly lost his balance. Another drop, like ice-cold fingers through his hair.

Ahead, a distant call. "Mick?"

He'd been right all along. The horror movie he'd been living was her fault. She was some kind of creature from Hell, and she was probably trying to take him there now.

Her flashlight swept around the corner, blinding him. He raised his good arm to block it. The sudden movement made his head spin. With a jolt he realized he'd lost a moment because there she was, kneeling in front of him, the flashlight discarded on the cave floor between them.

Mick was pretty sure he'd forgotten how to breathe. He could see her mouth moving, but he couldn't hear anything but a building static inside his ears. A twisting pressure on his chest tightened, jerked him once. He looked down, finding her hand clutching his shirt.

"Fight it, Mick. You have to."

He didn't have to do anything except get out of there. Find the hole he'd dropped into and climb out. He couldn't fathom dying down here in this black hole. He longed to see the sky, one last time.

"Find your strength and get up. You can make it, but you have to follow me."

"Who are you?"

The clamp of her hand loosened. He raised his head, his hazy vision settling on her eyes and staying there. He felt his senses line back up, one by one returning home, all focus on her.

"It's not important who I—"

"Tell me." It was a tone of voice he never used.

She released his shirt. Her eyes didn't leave his. "There's no English word for what I am."

"Explain it."

"I'm rebuilt from bones. Given new life. A second chance."

"You died."

"Yes. A couple hundred years ago."

"You were dug up?"

"About twenty-five years ago. My spirit revived, my bones given flesh. I was a child. Native people took me in, taught me how to live in the modern world."

Mick searched her face in the dim light. The honesty he found was so bare he couldn't stop himself from reaching out to lay his good hand against her cheek. This visible, audible, tactile proof so complete it broke him apart on the inside. His body had already split into two, now his mind was. She felt human. She was something else. She was alive. She was dead. All these things couldn't be true, but they were, and he could feel those broken pieces reconnecting inside him, a new understanding of some wordless idea. He couldn't see her as an undead thing, a ghost, an underworld spirit. Her skin warmed his hand. Her voice said his name too perfectly.

Soon he might be just like her. Somehow he understood it, although he couldn't name it, couldn't believe it.

"Can you stand?"

He found that he could. She got up with him, flashlight aimed at the ceiling to light the small room.

"We can't get separated again."

He nodded. The dead cold had nearly engulfed his whole body now. His leg moved despite him being unable to feel it. His other leg burned hot in comparison. Soon it would be gone too. The cave squeezed them down to their hands and knees, compressing the light so all he could see was what escaped around her body ahead. He bumped his head, cursing, wishing it had been the dead side he'd hit instead. Ten feet farther he was on his stomach. Ten feet after that he got stuck.

"Wait," he called.

The swishing of her coat against the wet stone stopped. "Can you get through?"

"No. My shoulders—they're too wide." He brought his elbows together to gain space around him, but the stone on each side had become a vise, ratcheting down with each exhale.

She released a curse too low for him to hear.

He concentrated on not thinking about being stuck. If he didn't dwell on it, he wouldn't have to panic. He couldn't have gone too far in to get out. It only felt like the walls were impossibly tight around him because he'd stopped moving.

"Okay, back up," she said. "We have to go the other way."

His brain replaced *the other way* with *the long way,* and he decided he'd just die right there, a worm in the Earth's entrails. He closed his eyes.

"Mick, *move.*"

His body obeyed despite the will to die. Boots hooked against a lip in the stone floor, legs pulled. He could only feel one, but he knew they were both working because it didn't take long before he was far enough out of the squeeze where he could sit up. She crawled alongside him, the flashlight tucked between shoulder and chin. Backtracking passed in a blur, his thoughts replaced by the labor of moving missing limbs and breathing through absent lungs. As they pressed on she took quick glances over her shoulder at him, her constant attention keeping him from allowing his eyes to roll into his head and his knees to give. For the first time the idea to shapeshift came naturally. An eagle couldn't navigate a cave any easier than he could, but in that form he'd have no awkward strain from being of two worlds.

He followed her light through a passage into a room so large their footsteps echoed several times before fading into the nothingness. Wide open space should be comforting. Instead, it turned his remaining nerves frigid. Waapikoona stopped so abruptly she dropped the flashlight. It flicked off.

"Stay there," she said.

Again, he had to focus to not think. So deep underground with no source of light fit the worst nightmare he could imagine. Anger peeled through him again, for blindly following her without asking questions, for not having the chance to bring an extra flashlight. Wait—he had his phone. He dug it out. The screen blinked on.

She looked up at him from hands and knees, clutching the flashlight against the ground. He saw his anxiety mirrored in her eyes. Misplaced, it seemed, since she'd just found the light.

"Is it broke?" he asked.

She shushed him, standing fast, a hand on his good arm as she turned to face the hulking space in front of them. "Turn off that light."

He did, but she didn't move her hand. Grateful for the crush of her hand he'd be unable to feel anywhere else on his body, he waited as the cave dripped around them and her breathing stopped altogether.

He wanted to ask what was wrong. They needed to keep moving. A sound wormed into his ears—distant but too close. A pattern of clicking, scratchy against the stone. Complete darkness magnified it, his ears working overtime to compensate for missing sight.

"Don't move," she whispered. "Don't speak. Don't make a sound."

So asking why would be out of the question. Maybe he didn't want to know why.

She held him, fingers digging deeper into his coat as the pattern of sound grew closer until it had joined them in the room. Mick struggled against the urge to take a step back, to fumble blindly for the nearest exit and climb until that outlandish sound was a distant memory. Now surrounding them, it was clear—this was no animal he would recognize. It was what a healthy child's imagination made of the creak of tree branches against the window at midnight. It was unnamable things, otherworldly creatures out for blood.

Air shifted around them. Mick wanted to turn and face the noise, but it wasn't coming from a single direction anymore. Its scale was too big, a cacophony of clicking all around. For one sick moment, Mick believed he was the one spinning and whatever made the sound was the stationary one.

"Identify yourself."

Beside him, Waapikoona had somehow become more still, her prickly grip on his arm both a warning and a threat. *If you move I'll kill you. If you move you'll die.*

New sensation swept through his missing side quickly enough to cause him to stagger away from her hold. A terrifying thought pressed through: *I'm shifting.* He couldn't be. He'd never been aware of it about to happen. But yes, he had, in the U-Fill. Right now he had no freezer cases to slam his fingers in.

In the darkness he lacked the vision to see the truth he could feel: Human hand on one side, feathers catching the air on the other. Split down the middle and tearing apart as one embodiment tried to commandeer the other but lacked the power to complete itself. His brain, still human, formed an angry curse; his mouth, unable to scream it.

Under his boots the hard ground swayed, the tilt of an earthquake right at its epicenter. Vision smeared, blacks sharpening and morphing into shades of gray. An unholy hiss grew in intensity all around, its shockwave of power composing much more than sound. This time it wasn't terror that shook him but undaunted determination. A practical certainty of business, of duty. A calling he had no choice but to answer.

He knew the screech that answered that hiss was his own, and he fed energy into it as the rumble of thunder canceled out all human thought.

CHAPTER

16

Mick woke smelling the Halloween night of his dream in the air. The dry, nose-tickling scent of straw mazes, the burnt, rotten vegetable tang of jack-o-lanterns, the cleansing scent of damp cold earth. He raised himself up, bracing an elbow that sunk into thin blanket covering a scratchy pallet of straw.

Candlelight flickered on the dark walls around him. Some of the candles were indeed housed inside carved pumpkins, their glowing orange faces crude, as if they were there for a reason more important than decoration. Some were mounted on human skulls, wax dripping down white bone. In his dream he'd been snatched off the haunted hayride by a ghoul, clutched in its talons, wrapped in its cloak, unable to scream. With his cheek squashed against its exposed ribs, he groped for a weak spot. Such a creature couldn't have a heart, but that was exactly where his fingers plunged. Their reward: a slimy core of cold dead meat pulsing in his fist until he ripped it free.

A clatter jolted him upright. In the light of a dozen candles against the wall, he could make out a kneeling human form—long hair draping over shoulders, loose clothes, soft shoes. Her body distinctly female, with the straight back and strong shoulders suggesting she wasn't an old woman. She stood. Although too petite to be the woman he wanted to confront, this woman's face held the same high cheekbones and broad cheeks.

She approached, kneeling beside his pallet to set a small bowl on the floor beside him. Seeing her face gave him no idea of age, only a possible range too wide to be useful. She could be his sister or his mother. At once he realized how naked he was. He pulled the leathery cover up to his waist, disturbing part of the bedding that caught air and drifted to the floor. The pallet under the blanket beneath him was surely made of straw. But he was also lying in a bed of feathers.

"*Notakhv,*" she said, repositioning a candle closer to him.

Mick was surprised to find his voice so easily. "Where's Waapikoona?"

The woman pointed beyond the room's glow of collected candlelight. Mick squinted into the darkness, unable to see anything.

"*Notakhv.*"

"Ma'am? I don't—"

She pointed to her chin. Mick leaned forward to get a better look at her face. She caught his jaw, pressing a handful of warm muck against his own chin. The sting subsided before he had a chance to resist. Behind it, a flush of relief so thorough and urgently needed he had to brace himself with both arms to not collapse onto the bed.

God, what had he done to his chin? And what was she doing to it now?

"Enough," he bit out, before he passed out from the relief—or the pain it had brought to light, he wasn't sure.

She withdrew to a low stone table, to bring back a different bowl and a cup she set on the bed next to him. "*Pvpetv.*"

"Waapikoona first."

She picked up the bowl and pressed it to his lips. It tasted of dry earth, of baked clay. Steam from a heady broth drifted into his nose. He'd never found the smell of food so irresistible. He took a sip, vaguely wondering if he was drinking horned-serpent stew. The grumble of his stomach said it didn't care.

"How long have I been here?" Mick knew the woman didn't speak English but he had to talk to someone. Time away from home meant two abandoned jobs, unpaid bills, a neglected father who needed him, and a sister who didn't want to count on him but had no choice.

And his chin. God, his chin. He risked a touch, finding either the remnants of that muck she'd plastered on, ripples of shredded skin, or both. He couldn't tell where one ended and the other began. The woman noticed him prodding it and rushed over, slapping his hand away.

He glared at her. Stupid, since she was obviously helping him out. The bold set of her jaw and impassive stare-down reminded him so much of Waapikoona he felt his heart clench. The reason? Who the hell knew? Worry? Anger? Appreciation?

Appreciation his ass. It even surpassed the harmlessness of lust at this point. The yearning delved deeper, truer, making him painfully aware of how inconvenient, how wrong, how forbidden it was.

So yeah—worry, anger, and a love so screwed-up he didn't know what to do with it except flop back on the bed and cover his face with his arms. Never had he felt such ripe emotions about a woman. Even the worry and anger were new—the same feelings he'd always had but rebuilt, with more horsepower, more gears, and a much higher redline. Ready and waiting to give a ride to a woman who was some undead creature his language had no word for.

"What's your word for 'zombie?'" he asked aloud. She wasn't even that. She was too human. Too perfect. "What's your word for 'perfect?'" Damn it all. He couldn't have fallen for a woman more imperfect.

He had no recollection of why she was missing. The resurfaced worry and his new vitality prompted him to get up and find her, ensure she was safe. The haze in his head gave him reason to stay put.

Every flame flapped under the swoosh of a cool breeze. Out of sight, his caretaker spoke with more words than she'd used on him. Another breeze snuffed out several of the candles farthest from him before the room was sealed again, each candle returning to its easy dance. Mick raised himself to his elbows.

Waapikoona crossed from shadow into light. A cut slashed the plane of her cheek. Her shirt hung torn at the collar. More noticeable was the watery shine in her eyes that turned her usual fierceness into something Mick felt compelled to fix by saying, "I'm okay."

She crossed her arms. She'd braided her hair, one long rope hanging against her shoulder. The space between them felt a mile wide, as if separated by time itself. He wondered if he was really seeing her. Suddenly uncomfortable with her standing tall above him, he pushed up to sitting. "Will you ask that woman what she's feedin' me?"

"I don't speak her tongue."

Assuming they spoke the same language—the ignorant white guy yet again. He refused to apologize. Anyone would figure the healer she spoke of would be one of her own.

A breeze ruffled the candles again. Waapikoona looked over her shoulder as if waiting for the woman to leave. When the candles settled she came forward and knelt in front of him, equaling out their positions in time, and space, and everything else.

Inside Mick a gear turned, clicking into place. Like he'd been on his back, one arm stretched into the guts of a car, blindly working some part he'd been fighting for hours and *click. There.* Finally, not just any click but *the* click, the one he was waiting for, the one he knew was right, not just in its feel in his fingers but also his sixth sense, his mechanic's sense. The indescribable inner knowledge of the last puzzle piece in place, of everything set right. He didn't need to recognize his surroundings. His struggle against uncertainty fell away. She was here with him. Everything that mattered was found.

She plucked a feather from his bed and stuck it in her hair. Blood rushed south—not a good moment to embrace a growing turn-on. Or was it?

"You need to drink this," she said, picking up the cup.

He took it and drained it, wiping his mouth as he handed it back. Warm water, with a tang of citrus, a hint of sweet.

"Don't look at me like that," she said.

"Like what?"

She looked away. "Can you walk? I need to get you home."

The herbal taste of what he drank clung to his tongue. Primitive medicine, for sure. No—not primitive. Holistic. Probably supernatural. "How long we been gone?"

"Not long."

"Long enough to get me fired from one job ... or both?"

"We can't measure it in your time."

"Okay, how do we measure it, then?"

"Not in a way that would affect your daily life." She stood, offering him a hand. When he didn't budge, she added, "We crossed the circle of time. I can't tell you where we are. Or when."

"But you knew to come here."

"Yes." She reached for the leather bed cover, a threat to tear it off so he'd have to get up.

He caught her hand. "I'd like my clothes back."

She retrieved them from a pile at the foot of his pallet and dumped everything on the floor in front of him except the jeans. "Show me your arm."

"Give me the jeans."

Power flexed between them. In this place, outside of time, the game of it didn't frustrate him. It gave him hot pleasure strong enough to bring him to his knees in front of her if he hadn't already been on the ground. He'd let her overpower him if she'd let him do the same. He wanted it both ways. He wanted to experience the tug of it, the back and forth. He wanted her to say no; he wanted to take the jeans from her anyway.

He got up and snatched them from her hands. Bracing for an expected head rush from standing so fast, he missed her grab for his arm and the twist that jacked his body sideways. He dropped the jeans in favor of a grip at the back of her neck, fingers sliding up to clench into hair. They locked eyes. In hers was a dare: *pull harder*. He returned a dare of this own: *twist farther*.

"Your arm looks better," she whispered.

There was no way she could've gotten a good enough look at that angle in this weak light. He remembered then what had happened to him. Rested muscles and health so good he tingled had pushed the memory of that demon's bite far away. Opening his hand to release her hair prompted her to untwist his arm so they could both view it.

"Back to normal," he said.

"You're welcome."

He crouched for his jeans and held them against his junk. She wasn't going to get a thank-you from him. As he stood she extended her fingers, letting them trail down his chest to his stomach where they lingered before she pulled away.

Not a spoken thank-you anyway. He could thank her in other ways. "How long until the healer comes back?"

"Get dressed, Mick."

She collected two more feathers from his bed before retreating into the shadow. Mick tucked himself into underwear and jeans, aware she was watching. It wasn't the first time. He hoped it wouldn't be the last, even though it should be. Another ruined shirt, zipped inside his coat, which was miraculously okay. "My phone?" he asked. Please let the phone be intact. It would cost too much to replace.

Seeing her step into the light with two more of his feathers fanned out in her hair drove him wild. She handed him his phone. It was all he could do not to take her hand instead, yank her against him. "I need to thank the healer."

"She needs no thanks."

"I disagree."

"Of course you do."

The words were the calm facade of an exchange taking place on some other level, a chaotic mixture of eye contact and pheromones, friction and desire. If a soul existed, and if it could speak, Mick's had just learned a new vocabulary from hers. Understanding rained through him. *This is what real love feels like.*

But didn't she—what did she say she was again? An underworld spirit. Mick couldn't surrender and believe in it, which meant she was crazy. And Mick had responsibilities, bills to pay, and barely any time to sleep before she had arrived with her entourage of biting demons and other forms of trouble. It didn't matter how compatible their bodies and souls were. They clashed in life.

Real love didn't happen so fast anyway. Attraction was a better word. He just had no idea attraction could be so absolute. So painful if not fed. So exhausting.

So exhilarating.

Mick hadn't felt this happy to be alive in years.

"Coming?" she called.

He ducked into a dark tunnel she'd disappeared into at the far end of the candlelit room. Earthen floor turned to stone, dry at first, but the damp air fell across him like a shroud about a hundred feet in. He wasn't sure where they'd been, whether it was a dry part of the cave system or an earthen home built against its mouth. He didn't know if it was day or night. Once again he was helpless, completely dependent on her to get him back above ground to the real world. He remembered how frustrated he'd been with this arrangement on the way in. This time, he embraced it. To release responsibility to someone else and simply follow, unburdened and unthinking, offered reprieve to a part of him he didn't know was so tired.

They splashed through a stream against the current, the ceiling high enough for him to straighten up. He didn't recall water on the way in. It felt like he'd woken from a monthslong coma. If they returned to the surface to find spring instead of winter, he'd have a lot of explaining to do to a lot of people. Ahead, she stopped and turned around, aiming her flashlight at his knees. "You okay with taking a different path out?"

How would he know it was a different path? He didn't remember the one they'd taken to get there. "Lead the way, Waapikoona."

"Okay, Mick." What she did to those four letters should be illegal. "Just stay close. I don't know what lives down this branch."

What could live this deep in a cave?

Reaching a fork, she took the smaller opening. Mick had to fill his lungs several times before he felt stable enough to go to hands and knees and crawl in. His boots were soaked, and his pants were cold and wet from the knees down. Crawling through mud wasn't going to change a thing. He thanked the ceiling for staying high enough he didn't need to drop to an army crawl, but the farther they got in, the more he felt separated from open space, from room to breathe, from fresh air. He tried not to imagine the walls closing in. He had to keep reminding himself he still had the same amount of room to move. Waapikoona stopped to tuck the flashlight into her pocket and aim it forward. With the cease of their rustling clothes silence fell hard. Mick's ears filled the void with a pulsing hum that didn't go away even after they started moving again.

"You hear that?" he asked.

She stopped to listen. Water dripped from inches above, cold and slimy, working its way under Mick's collar. New sweat tingled across his neck and back. Panic sweat, prickling on top of the exertion sweat.

"You can't shift here."

"I told you I can't control it." He didn't notice the anger in his voice until hers matched his.

"You have to."

"Okay, any idea how?" If he could just stand up, stretch his body, breathe. He was so far from the open space behind him, who knew how far to the exit ahead? If the tunnel stretched backward for a thousand feet, it might stretch ten miles in front of them. The farther they went in, the farther he'd be from being able to stand up. He wasn't in a tunnel but a box. A coffin.

But the only reason he was desperate to stand up was because he couldn't. He was fine.

That hum—was it getting louder? "You don't hear that?"

"Keep going. How fast can you crawl?"

She moved, and he moved toward her. His leg caught, stretched to its length. He tugged, turning to look behind him, but everything past his waist was swallowed by black pitch. "Hey, shine that light down here. My foot's caught."

The beam swept along the wall and blinded him. He blinked away the black spots in his vision and turned to see what had snagged him. Too much shadow danced around his feet to see anything, so he shifted his body to the side and tugged his leg hard.

One of the shadows moved independent of the light. Something coiled around his ankle, clamping the leather of his boot against his skin. Adrenaline surged through him; he yanked his leg with all his strength.

Three feet of wet stone slid under his palms as whatever had hold of him yanked back.

"Shit, somethin's got me—somethin' is—go, go, go!"

Instead of pushing forward like he needed, she scrambled backward over him—boots, knees, stomach, chest. Braid trailing against his cheek then his neck then gone. Once she crossed over his feet, he flipped onto his back to try to twist free so he could turn around and help her. It was too tight a space to turn around, and he couldn't stand up. He extended his arms above him, pressing against the slimy ceiling as if it would do any good. God how he wanted to stand up.

The flashlight had dropped by his head. He snatched it, aiming it past his feet as the clamp on his ankle released. A shriek peeled his eardrums. He couldn't cover them in time.

A noise from some alien world at circular-saw volume. It cut off abruptly and a dull thump hit the tunnel wall near where she'd disappeared. She cursed; he swung the flashlight, trying to find her. The beam fell upon her arm stabbing down, that flint knife in her grip.

A gurgling hiss filled the tunnel. Mick's vision sharpened. The floor under his back tilted. He tapped his head hard enough against the stone to hurt—once, twice. Gravity righted itself. A third time brought his vision back to normal. Brain damage he'd take. If he shifted now, he'd never get out of this place.

With a final stab the hiss cut off, and Waapikoona shoved a heavy object past her then folded her legs and kicked it farther away. She collapsed, her head rolling against his boot.

"You all right?" he asked.

"Fine. Just need to catch my breath."

"What the hell was that?"

"No idea. It's dead now." She gripped the toe of his boot and pulled herself up. "Are you bleeding? It had a wicked set of claws."

"Don't think so. Nothin' gets through these boots." He felt winded himself. And he wasn't the one who'd just killed a clawed cave-dwelling varmint. Picking up the pace made sense so they didn't have to repeat it, but lying on his back made the space feel taller, and he needed to experience it just for a minute. That creature's hiss still rang in his ears. At any moment the gravity and vision could turn again. Staying in an easy place to bash his skull against rock and bring himself further from eagle mode sounded like his best plan.

She wiped her knife on the bottom of his jeans and put it away. Then she was crawling over him, and he froze, his admiration of the space above him on hold as it filled with her body. Palms walking between his legs then over, her breasts brushing his pelvis, his stomach. Her knees between his own then one sliding over to straddle his leg. She stopped, her lips nearly against his, the silky tip of her braid hanging against his bare neck.

"Close call," she said.

The only thing missing was her weight settling down. That was all it would take to undo him.

"Thanks," he whispered.

A smear of something dark streaked her chin and cheek. He reached to touch it, gathering it on his finger to hold up to the light. It shone like wet paint, glossy black and sticky enough not to drip.

"Demon blood," she said, shifting her thigh so it pressed against him *just right*.

He didn't dare move his hands because he knew once given motion they'd head straight to her ass, and he wasn't going to be the one to give in to this. He was no toy, not in her game. If he wanted to kiss her, he'd do it when he was damn well ready to. Her legs were open against his own thigh, and it was all he could do not to lift the slightest and make contact against her like she'd just done to him. No matter how slowly he did it, there would be fire, like flint striking steel, their friction a spark, their bodies flammable.

He frustrated women by being too nice. And since this was the woman he wanted to frustrate most of all, he lay like a corpse and prayed she'd move before he stopped being nice and lost himself for good. One thing was certain: The man in him was so turned on the eagle had retreated a million miles away.

CHAPTER
17

The tunnel was too narrow for Waapikoona to crawl beside Mick instead of straight over his face. She'd paused to consider the best way to do it; now she was stuck in place, one leg over his, the other resting against him in the perfect unintentional tease, glued by the heat packed between them. It was hard to say if his reaction was simple physical male reflex or true attraction, if his body and brain were in agreement, or if his body had gone rogue.

With every second she spent lingering over him, the static charge of the air fizzled further away. If she was right, and her goose bump-driven feeling of a storm building so deep underground did truly signal the arrival of his Thunder-Being, this sexual temptation appeared to be its antidote. In the future she might have to get creative, run a few tests to be sure. It might spoil this battle they seemed to be engaged in, the battle of who would break first. Who was the strong one and who was the slave. As she watched his eyes for any hint of which role he played, she felt him rouse even more against her. She realized then she had it wrong. Whoever broke first wasn't the weak one but the one in command, the one to start it all.

The role of power could be hers. She had him there. All she had to do was press her lips against his. The thought gave her a new round of goose bumps, not a mark of anticipation but danger. Fear. And a hatred she could harness and use to conquer him.

Below her, Mick's chest rose and fell, his breath gaining speed and stirring the loose hair on her neck. When had he become more to her than just another faceless white man? She closed her eyes and she was back in the healer's den, stepping into the room to see Mick in human form, awake, alive. In the relief that had frustratingly made her eyes fill, she could see a different path. Instead of using the hatred to conquer him, she could conquer the hatred itself. Tear it up, throw it away. Take the high road of peace and forgiveness. She could raise her sister, move closer to her people, finally be free.

There was no peace in her heart.

She climbed over Mick, careful not to boot him in the face. When he didn't move to follow her, she called, "Let's go."

"In a minute."

"We don't have a minute."

"You should've thought about that before you gave me a hell of a hard-on."

She took a moment to stifle a laugh. "You can't crawl with a hard-on? Please. And you—"

"I can. Just don't want to."

"—can't blame that on me."

"Then who? Oh, I got it—the ankle-grabbin' cave demon gave me a hard-on, and I need a minute to simmer down."

She did laugh then, bright and full. She couldn't help it and for once didn't regret it. "That's twisted, Mick."

"So are you, Waapikoona."

The darkness hid her smile too powerful to strike down. Friendly banter was here to haunt her again, and she couldn't deny how it sang inside her. In the past she only allowed this type of thing before she killed the guy and released her Helpers to consume his corpse. Bones digested, flesh delivered to The Silent One to raise one of her own. And she'd never told a white man her real name, never heard it spoken by enemy tongue. He seemed to know that, but his torment seemed more playful than vindictive.

She sat up and crossed her legs, facing his prone frame. He hadn't budged from how she'd left him, flat on his back, arms relaxed against the cave floor beside him. His hair, darkened with wetness and dirt, glued against his forehead. The skinned chin made him more rugged, more like the fighter she knew he was.

"Thought you said I'd be safe if guided by an—"

"Safe from getting lost, not attacked."

He flipped over and crawled toward her. She wanted to lie back, let him crawl over her like she'd done to him.

"Are you over it?" Aware it gave her power to make him wait, she didn't turn around and move ahead until he answered.

What she got was a thoughtful, calculating "No" that sounded more permanent than the question she'd asked. Then he sat back on his heels with a gaze that met the intensity of her own.

With one look he'd turned her from the leader calling the shots to a guide employed to navigate him out. The dominance he'd just flipped on wasn't the Mick she knew. She might be worried he'd been possessed by the clawed cave demon if it didn't fit so perfectly on this Mick, the one who hunted horned serpents and lay coolly while she so thoroughly seduced him. Seeing this side of him did nothing but give her a tempting challenge she didn't need.

"I got a lot of questions for you," he said.

His take-charge tone of voice did things to her. Anger was expected. The melt of nerves was not. "Keep them."

"When we get out of here, you're mine until I've asked every one."

When they got out of there, she'd be gone. Back to Oklahoma to regroup—no, straight to Illinois to retrieve her sister's bones and demand The Silent One complete his side of the bargain. She'd worked long enough. The damage she'd caused by bringing a Thunder-Being into his cave couldn't be undone. She had to use it as an advantage. A threat.

She returned to hands and knees and moved forward. Mick's phone was dead, and she had the flashlight. His choice was to follow her or die. Her knees were raw and bruised from all the crawling. Sharp electric ache shot through her shoulders. She focused on all that instead of the gash on her ribs she'd collected fighting the demon. That one was too painful to give any thought to, and she wasn't sure what she'd do if its claws were venomous like Mick's biting demon's teeth had been. But maybe it didn't matter. She'd been built by their leader. Surely she'd be immune.

She didn't spot the first trickle of light hours later until Mick uttered a thanks to his god so nearly broken she turned around to make sure he hadn't collapsed. Which he had— on his knees, one hand against the cave wall that had risen to walking height not long ago. Sunlight slashed across his fingers. She followed it to a hairline crevice straight above, lit with light so pure she had to look away. Her flashlight had gone so dim, her eyes were adjusted to almost darkness.

She tugged his sleeve. They'd long given up on words. The energy used to speak couldn't be wasted. Mick got to his feet, and she led them forward, new slashes of light spraying across the floor and walls until their combined effort rendered her almost dead flashlight useless. The floor tilted up, forcing their exhausted legs into a steep climb. A few steps later she stumbled, catching herself with palms, a current of pain shooting up both arms. Mick took her by the elbow and hauled her up, pointing ahead at a horizontal line of mottled light.

He pushed ahead. By the time she reached him, he'd ripped away enough broken tree limbs to get an arm through to the surface. She used the bottom of the flashlight to chip away mud. The intensity of the light blasting in made her eyes water so much it spilled down her cheeks. Snow fell in, coating her arms and face. Mick made a stirrup with his hands beside her foot; she stepped in as he lifted, and she pulled herself out into the day.

She wasn't sure how Mick would get out. She needed a minute alone with the sun, her sky brother, to let him warm her face and neck through the cold winter air. To embrace the upperworld, to praise it. She'd been so wet and cold for so long the snow-covered ground made no difference against her skin. All she could feel were those rays of sun baking all the dark cold away.

Mick's boot sailed through the cave's mouth, followed by his other one, then his coat, tied in a bundle, and a wad of jeans. Too exhausted to even call his name, much less ask what he was doing, she shuffled on her knees to the opening. If she slid halfway in, her arms might reach him. She could lock her feet on a nearby tree root and pull him out.

A dark mass burst from the cave mouth, sending her scrambling back as feathers fluttered down. Her coat flapped against the wind from his great wings as he lifted into the sky. She zipped her coat and gathered his clothes as he circled. With his boot laces tied together and hung around her neck, she waited, hoping his bird's-eye view would locate the car. She had an idea which direction to head, but it wasn't certain enough to be the direct path, and she had no energy to waste on wandering. So she stayed put even as he disappeared from sight, hoping he'd understand why she was waiting.

The trees bent around her, shedding snow as the wind blew through her. She put Mick's coat on over hers. The cold was penetrating now, and she was soaked to her skin. She had to start moving before the water in her clothes froze and she herself turned to ice. They'd taken the north branch of the cave, so she should walk west to find the car. How far north they'd gone was the unknown. She set off, hoping she had the right angle.

Five minutes later she heard a whistle—human, definitely Mick. She whistled back. When she came upon him he held a hand up. She tossed him his jeans and started on the knot to free his boots.

"Car's straight that way," he said, zipping his fly.

"How'd you do that?" She held his eye so he'd know what she was asking.

"I still had that demon blood under my fingernail."

"You...?"

He walked toward her and took a boot from her hands. "It tastes disgusting. Hey, that cut on your cheek looks bad."

She took off his coat and handed it to him. Her head spun. She wasn't breathing deeply enough. She was sapped—every muscle, her head, her bones. She had a prickly, raw demon scratch across her ribs. And she couldn't tear her eyes from his, couldn't mask her surprise, her awe, her reverence. She couldn't brush away the warmth he returned. Half white man, half thunderbird, he was poison to both her halves.

They were enemies not in one way but two. She'd be disowned by the underworld and by Native people. She and Mick had become unimaginably tangled, unified by more than platonic circumstance. She had to get away from him.

She started walking in the direction he'd indicated. Each gust of wind pressed the wet clothes against her frigid skin as if she needed a reminder. The fire in the tomb would be dead. It would take some time to get it hot enough to dry her clothes. She had cash for a motel room, but that would be a drive out of Mick's way and she was finished asking him for favors. Accepting help from him was how this all started, and she needed to end it now.

As they walked the sun slid toward the horizon, woodland shadow stealing its rays. Mick passed her, increasing the pace. The cold bogged her down. She was too tired to care about how fast her legs were moving. Having him in front of her gave her something to focus on, something to follow.

At the car she weighed a reckless thought: decline the ride altogether and walk to the tomb herself. He got in without a word. The Pontiac roared alive as she stood outside her unopened door. He revved the engine, the sound invading the silent woods like an underworld beast. She didn't know whether he was reveling in his return to civilization or impatient for her to get inside. Choosing to walk would rid her of Mick Svendsen right here, right now.

He lowered her window. She leaned in. "Bye, Mick."
"Get in."
She raised her hood, wishing she'd ditched him in the woods when he was in eagle form, before she'd entertained the quick ride in a car to a fire warming a dry shelter of stone inhabited by the quiet of the dead. She hadn't made it but a few steps away before his door opened and his footsteps closed in on her. He took her by the elbow. She yanked

it back, straining her arm already so fatigued it pinched a nerve in her neck and pounded in her head.

"Don't be stupid."

"Put your hands on me again and you're the stupid one."

"It's below freezing. You're soaked. I don't care where you're headed, you won't make it on foot. Get in the car."

The remaining light reflected off the snowy ground, high-lighting his chin scrape like a shocking blight on his cave-slimed face. The healer's salve had completely worn off. Without a scab, the wound was a glistening red flecked with mud. He needed to get home, clean it, and bandage it. She wanted to do it for him. She shouldn't. Couldn't. She had to get away.

"You owe me answers, and until I get them, you're mine."

"I'm not yours in any way." It was so loaded she wished she could take it back.

"I'll take that demon corpse straight to the sheriff's office."

Oh—would he? And expose what he was? But no—he'd gained control of it now. If he'd figured out how to shift, he would know how to not shift. That Helper was tied to her. It wouldn't take long for news to find its way to The Silent One, and then she'd never have her sister back. She'd given up on reclaiming that corpse. Come spring it would decompose to nothing, but not if it was preserved in a freezer at the police station.

"Okay, then ask. And be quick." She turned her back to the wind.

"I'm not askin' shit until I'm in dry clothes and a heated house with a big meal in front of me. Get in the goddamn car."

The need to shove him warred with the need to kiss him. Hate and passion consumed her. She roamed the alien blue landscape of his eyes, looking for clues to escape this snare she'd been caught in. Wondering how matted wet hair, a dirt-streaked face, and that gory chin could stoke a fire in her so hot, so obscene. She had to have him, just once. Meaningless sex, that was it.

But there was too much meaning already. If she got any closer to him she'd be poisoned by it all. She'd be knocked off her path, irreversibly changed. And if she was the one to start it, she'd be his slave. She could work for The Silent One and not be his slave—it was cold business, a straightforward exchange of services. It could never be like that with Mick because it wouldn't be work. If she gave in, she'd be his slave forever.

He had her with the demon corpse, that was for sure. Still burning to kiss him, she shoved him back instead. The impact shocked every one of her spent bones, but it was worth it. She got in the car. He got in beside her, jammed the car in gear, and hit the gas so hard they spun in place for a good few seconds before they lurched forward.

Once he'd torn through the gears, he said, "Shove me like that again and—"

"Don't threaten me."

She wasn't sure how either of them found more fuel for combat. They seemed to be powering each other, some kind of grotesque symbiotic cycle with no beginning or end. Somehow she had to end it, before she yanked the parking brake, dragged him out of the car, and peeled off all his clothes. The sweet Mick was tempting enough. She couldn't handle sitting next to the angry, combative one. Dirty, domineering, calling her 'his.' She wanted the angry Mick with a hunger she couldn't deny any longer. Conquering this one promised such a high. But now there was something else, something pure, ready to even everything out, balance it all in the most perfect way. An appeasement she hadn't felt since her old life, her life before the white man had destroyed her world.

Mick could never give her that. He was one of them.

Now they were turning into his driveway, parking beside the house. Her thoughts had distracted her from telling him to drop her at the tomb, and now she had another hike ahead of her when she could barely lift herself from the Pontiac's seat. The sky was still lit, but the sun was long gone. The land had gone gray. Soon the sky would be moonless and black.

"Who the hell's that?" Mick was looking past her, through her window.

She turned. Across the field a man crouched in the doorway of the broken old barn, his face aimed her way. Recognition flared between them in the dying light. She was out of the car crossing the field before she could think. Her plan: *Get rid of him.* She hadn't yet figured out how. Then she saw what lay at his feet, and she remembered what Mick told her the night he got bitten by the winged demon: *The corpse you want is in the doorway to that old barn.*

"Is this yours, Sarah?"

He'd cut his hair short. The last time she'd seen him it'd been as long as hers. It was so against his character she wondered who he'd joined, what people he was trying to fit in with. He toed her Helper's lifeless body.

She refused to look down. "You seem to have forgotten what I told you."

"I didn't forget." His gaze shifted behind her as Mick's footsteps arrived. "I also didn't forget The Silent One's rules."

Mick joined her side. "Care to tell me what you're doing on my property?"

It was the exact wrong thing to say to Jeremiah. She didn't know his real name, and he didn't know hers—unless Mick spilled it, which would be bad. They needed to get rid of Jeremiah, not give him any information. Not incite him.

"Land as property is a concept of your people I don't follow."

Mick chuckled. "That workin' out okay for you?"

Jeremiah raised his chin to study Mick. Battle-dirtied and scarred and pushed to the edge of his anger by Waapikoona herself, Mick didn't look anything like the tame, nice guy he normally was. She knew Jeremiah was getting a false first impression, but she was okay with that. She'd gotten a false first impression of Mick herself. And she could handle surprises a lot easier than Jeremiah.

"Are you two related?" Mick asked.

Jeremiah said, "Yes," as Waapikoona said, "No."

It was the second time Mick assumed two Native people were related, but she'd have to save her annoyance with him for later. The relationship Jeremiah confirmed wasn't at all what Mick was asking.

"Here's what's gonna happen," Mick said. "I'm goin' in my house, and when I look outside in three minutes you're not gonna be here no more."

"Works for me. Three minutes are all I need with her."

"She's comin' with me." Mick looked at Waapikoona. The look said, *You're mine.* He snatched the Helper's corpse by the arm and dragged it toward the house.

Jeremiah's narrowed eyes proved he read the look Mick gave her exactly as she had. She could deny it, claim she was leading him on, pretend she planned to kill him—but the stunned disgust on Jeremiah's face was too priceless to shatter. Let him take this news back to whomever he was working with now. Maybe they'd finally understand she wasn't on their side. Maybe they'd leave her alone. She didn't work with The Silent One for the same reasons they did. And using Mick to sever ties with Jeremiah turned Mick's favor of a ride to a warm house into a tool she'd be stupid not to use.

CHAPTER 18

Waapikoona surprised Mick by coming through his apartment door. She was making this too easy for him. There had to be something else at play. His use of the demon corpse as blackmail couldn't be that effective.

"Where's the body?" she asked.

Or maybe it was. "Hidden. You get the shower first." He could still sense the presence of that corpse like a lingering residue in the air, still had to concentrate on remaining human.

She slid off her coat, watching him. The cut on her face leaked black ooze, the skin around it tinged with gray. Kind of like what his arm used to look like but on a smaller scale. Declining a shower was on the tip of her tongue, he could tell. Compliance was so unnatural on her, he had to watch closely or he'd miss it. Maybe he shouldn't savor it so much. It seemed wrong to get pleasure out of using blackmail to wield such a powerful upper hand over someone so fierce.

Her boots came off next, and she didn't stop there. Jeans unbuttoned, unzipped, sliding down long legs. One sock then the other. She still watched him, daring him to stay or leave—he wasn't sure which. Then her fingers gripped the bottom of her shirt, and he felt something inside him cave.

No. Not like this. His terms, not hers. "Don't use up all the hot water." He went in the bedroom to find her something to wear. He didn't come out until he heard the shower turn on. She'd left the bathroom door open. He closed it, picked up her discarded clothes, and tossed them in the laundry basket with his own.

Above him, a child's voice filtered through the ceiling. Old Mae's slow tread squeaked the old wood. The child's voice became frantic then crying. The only children Old Mae would have in her house were Kari's. Mick threw on sweatpants and a hoodie, grabbed the laundry basket, and ran outside and up the front porch steps. A glance at the old barn showed no sign of Waapikoona's friend.

"It's Mick," he called as he opened the door.

The crying cut off and Janie came into the hall, face streaked and eyes wet. He put down the basket and crouched to her level. "What's the matter, little birdie?"

She didn't move so he went to her, taking her shoulders to look at her. The last time he saw her, she'd changed into a biting demon. Even though he knew that hadn't been her, seeing her now relaxed a strain in him even though she was crying.

"What's that?" she asked, pointing to his chin.

"Just a little scrape. It don't hurt."

"It's all dirty."

"Where's your mom at?"

Doug came down the stairs. "Uncle Mick, where were you? Mom's worried. You didn't answer your phone."

"It's dead. What's goin' on?"

Old Mae had come into the hall behind Janie. Her usual hunched shoulders seemed more weary. "Helen had a relapse. Kari took her to the hospital in the city. You need a bandage for that scrape … and a bath.”

“Yes, ma’am, I’m on it. Just need to throw some laundry in. Janie, help me out?”

She nodded, reaching for his hand. He hadn’t yet figured out how long he’d been gone from his life, and the guilt was creeping in. Kari would only leave the kids with ancient, reclusive Old Mae if she had no other option. He picked up the basket.

“Mickey.”

Old Mae’s all-knowing tone stopped him cold.

“Your guest walks unholy ground.”

Whispered in her croaky voice, it pushed him further to the edge. No response fit. Agreeing would admit too much—to her and to himself. Disagreeing would make him look dense. What he wanted to know was how she knew and why she cared. Old Mae wasn’t the church-going type and had enough cats to make small-minded people think she walked unholy ground herself.

“It’s under control,” he said finally.

“I live a quiet life.”

A tabby swarmed him, rubbing his legs so aggressively he had to shift his weight to stay balanced. “You know I respect that.”

The clock on the wall chimed the hour. The kids needed to eat and get ready for bed soon, and he couldn’t leave them in this big old creaky house. Janie would beg to sleep with Doug, and Doug’s imagination would keep them all up, including Old Mae. His apartment was in the same building, but was enclosed by the ground on three sides. The wind didn’t whistle through it at night. The moonlight didn’t trickle through tall windows, filling spacious rooms with roving shadows.

"Let me get this load in and take a shower, and I'll come back up for the kids." He gave Janie one handle of the laundry basket, and he took the other. They walked it crookedly to the closet that had been converted to hold a washer and dryer, and he set Janie on top of the dryer and dabbed her teary cheeks with his sleeve. "You wanna push the button?"

Back downstairs, his unholy guest stood in his kitchen, wrapped in a towel, wet hair hanging flat and loose down her back. He handed her the clothes he'd found for her and got in the shower, mentally bulldozing the picture of those long naked legs and bare shoulders. Hot water soaking his muscles felt so good he almost fell asleep standing up. He got out and wiped the steam from the mirror, examined his chin, decided the scrape was too big for any bandage he had on hand. Then he heard Doug's voice, not coming from upstairs but from his own place. He threw on clothes and opened the door.

His couch held his niece, nephew, and a cave-demon-killing underworld spirit who walked unholy ground and probably shouldn't be anywhere near children.

"Hey, Uncle Mick, where's that drawing I gave you of the alien?" Doug had his sketchbook open on the coffee table like he'd been giving Waapikoona a full show.

Waapikoona only looked serious to the uninformed. Mick could see the smile in her eyes, the tease in her firmly held lips. He could also see Janie on her lap, and that she was braiding the little girl's hair. Too normal, too surreal—he couldn't get it right in his head.

"In a minute, Dougie. Let's get you kids somethin' to eat."

"Sarah said you have no food."

"She did?" The look he flung at Waapikoona said, *Sarah, huh?*

"Sarah also said you went spelunking. Will you take me sometime?"

"You'll have to clear that with your mom. It's kind of dangerous."

To get himself out of the conversation, Mick busied himself with a search for food. He needed to get the kids fed and asleep so he could deal with Waapikoona. He had to keep her from telling the kids anything else.

"Sarah said her favorite animal's a golden eagle. I'm gonna draw that next, but I ain't sure what to cross it with."

"A horned serpent," Waapikoona said.

"Horned?" Doug said. "Sweet."

"Hey, Sarah," Mick said, heavy enunciation on her name. "Help me out over here? I got some canned green beans. And we can heat these leftovers from my last date." He stressed the last word, too, just for the hell of it. If she was going to goad him, he would do the same, even though he wasn't sure what mentioning his date would do.

All smile left her eyes. His comment had hit the mark. He scrambled for another one with more firepower, but Doug and Janie were both talking, and he could barely keep the can opener straight in trembling fingers. He was on the verge of shock. Hunger, exhaustion, dehydration, or all three. The last thing he'd had to eat or drink was that medicine woman's broth, and who knew what strange crap was in that. He filled a glass with cold water and chugged it.

When he lowered the glass, he saw Waapikoona had taken over the can opener. She added a second can of green beans to the pan. Standing there in Mick's flannel and sweats, rolled at the waist so they'd stay up, she looked more at home in his kitchen than he was. She'd turned him into a creature unfit for his own life then pushed in and hijacked it all. This wasn't help. It was dominance.

"How old is this?" She stood in the open fridge door, sniffing the extra piece of fish he'd bought on his date night for the next day's dinner. "It smells fine."

Mick checked his phone he'd plugged in to charge on the counter. If it was right, his date with Amanda had been the previous night. There was no way. "How long we in that cave?"

"Impossible to know. I thought I told you that cave sits outside the circle of time."

Mick gauged Doug's face to make sure he hadn't caught that. He'd take it and run with it, and there'd be no end to it. He was bent over his sketchpad at the table, going to town. Janie sat next to him, chin propped on both fists, staring through the drawing like she'd missed her nap and was about to drop.

Waapikoona handed him the fish in its wrapper and bent to open a cabinet. Mick stepped back into the side of the fridge. She hadn't just turned compliant. She'd become willing. In his flannel and sweats. His kitchen, his domain. He was wrong—this wasn't her barging in to overtake his life. It was him, sucking her into his. She was wearing his clothes, for god's sake. He'd gotten her out of the armor of her puffy coat and cowboy boots.

"What?" she said. It sounded so accusing, both kids turned to look at them.

His clothes swallowed her narrow frame, making her look smaller. Let her try to get a knife to his throat right now. Things would be different.

Mick didn't feel like such a nice guy anymore.

"Nothin'," he said, taking the pan out of her hand and pushing by her. "Go sit down. Away from the kids."

She stood there and watched him long enough for him to sense her defiance, to understand this would go differently if there weren't two innocent witnesses a few feet away. And he stared back, promising her just how differently it would go. She retreated to the living area, but instead of sitting down, she leaned against the far wall under his boarded windows and crossed her arms, her unbroken gaze like an unending gust of cold air.

When he put the food on the table, he called her back. She came like an obedient guest and sat across from him, the cold gaze now a staring contest he didn't remember entering.

"Laundry. Be right back." Because he wasn't doing this in front of the kids.

The frozen night didn't seem so cold after the frigid air he'd just endured. Old Mae's porch steps were now shiny with ice. He got up them with the handrail and many carefully planted steps. As hungry as he was, salting steps felt more pressing and less unappealing than Waapikoona's attitude, so he grabbed the bag of salt from the corner of the porch and threw down a few handfuls.

Inside, the house was dark. Yellow cat eyes glowed at him from the hall. He could hear the dryer spinning. Old Mae must've moved the clothes for him, and sure enough, the dryer clicked off as soon as he flipped on the light. He shooed a cat out of his laundry basket and scooped everything out in one big clump so he didn't have to handle Waapikoona's bra and underwear. He locked the front door behind him and let himself out into the winter night.

On the porch he waited. His excuse was to let the salt do its work so he didn't break his neck on the way down the steps. Reality? He needed the freeze to suffuse him like a cold shower and shock the nuclear turn-on back into hiding. Hating that woman made him so hot he couldn't function. It stripped away all the pain of a long-empty stomach, the bone-deep fatigue. It turned his and her mental combat into foreplay so delicious he couldn't imagine filling his body with food. It was her he craved. To be filled by her. To fill her. To conquer, to be conquered. He wanted both so badly, he throbbed with it.

Forget the salt. All he had to do was walk down the steps, and the heat radiating from him would melt a path six feet wide.

He filled his lungs with air, felt the cold trickle into his stomach, willing it lower. Down the stairs and around the house gave him enough steps to walk it off. Her dog waited at his apartment door. He opened the door and let him in.

"Doggie!" Janie squealed.

"Settle down. You're about to go to bed, little birdie." The irony of his nickname for her smacked him in the face.

"I'm done. Can I pet the dog before I brush my teeth?"

"Take him over by the couch."

Mick put down the laundry and started clearing plates. Kids only ate this fast when starved. He knew it wasn't his fault, but he felt guilty anyway. Doug bolted for the dog, too, leaving Waapikoona at the table, slowly eating, eyes back on Mick like they'd followed him all the way to the dryer and back. Her cut looked better after her shower but still held a ghostly smudge.

"Thanks for dinner," she said. "Yours is cold."

"I don't mind." He took his plate and stood at the counter to eat, watching her right back.

She got up and joined the kids. Mick took them to brush their teeth and tuck into his bed. He gave Doug a look of death when he started talking about aliens, which shut him up fast. Janie would never fall asleep if she knew what happened in that room, and Doug was old enough and protective enough to understand that.

Mick closed the bedroom door and found the kitchen cleaned up, Waapikoona leaning against the counter, drinking out of the open bottle of wine from his date with Amanda.

"Is she nice?" she asked.

"Yes," Mick said, adding emphasis that said, *Unlike you.*

"Is she your girlfriend?"

Mick didn't want to answer. It was none of her business, but an easy answer meant she held nothing over him. "No." He snagged the wine bottle from her hand and took a quick pull. "Who was that guy out there—an ex?"

She took the bottle back and drank long enough to avoid the question. He wasn't letting her off. He'd told her she was his until he had everything he wanted from her—everything but one thing. Right now, anyway. Taking her to bed could be on the table if he let himself go there, and so far he hadn't. Didn't mean he wouldn't. As long as he held that demon corpse, he could get anything he wanted from her. He knew that, and so did she.

"Do you have some ointment?" she asked.

"You didn't answer the question." He took hold of her chin to aim her cut cheek toward the light. It was more a power move than anything. She let him do it. No protest. No change in expression. So obedient it turned him rock hard without warning. "And that ain't bad enough to need anything now. You heal like a vampire."

"I'll answer if you give me some."

"Give you … what?" If she crossed the line he'd just laid between them, if she asked him for it, he'd give it to her so good.

"Ointment," she said, so deadpan it almost wasn't.

He went to the bathroom. Looked at himself in the mirror. Hair still messy from the shower, half-dried so it could be sweat, not water. Crazed, sleep-deprived eyes. Chin scraped so deep it was nearly bleeding again after the shower dried it out. *Stop it. Be the nice guy you are. Don't do this.*

He could shapeshift at will into a giant golden eagle. He didn't know who he was.

She hadn't moved from where he'd left her. He handed her the ointment. She twisted the cap, squeezed a blob onto her finger, and instead of raising it to her own face, she raised it to his.

The contact was such a battle of cold and hot—the slippery chill of the ointment, the primal heat of her finger—it set him loose. He stepped back, for her protection, not his. She moved forward. "He's Blackfoot. He and I work for the same being, but for different reasons."

"He got a name?"

"Jeremiah."

"He said you're related."

She came at him again. He'd already backed into the counter and couldn't retreat any farther. To avoid her, he'd have to step aside, flee. He wouldn't do that. She dabbed the raw wound on his chin, her eyes intent, the heat of her body pressing against his. "He said that to fuck with me."

"Why?"

"He wants me to do his work. They all do. He thinks that's what relates us."

"Who do you work for?"

She stopped dabbing to look him in the eyes. "The creature we met in the cave. The one that made you shift."

"You brought me in there—"

"No," she said, shaking her head like she meant it. She handed him the ointment. "He wasn't supposed to be there. It was the only quick path to the healer."

"And how'd you get me to her?"

His question dropped away, his mind now invaded by the image of her lifting her flannel—*his* flannel—to expose the creamy brown of her side. First he saw the fiery red slash across her ribs—thick, weeping, the mark of the most savage claw. But what really captured him was the swell of her breast, its underside, the silkiest, softest part of a woman.

He took her hand, smearing the ointment from her finger onto his, then he slid it across that slash, inches away from that soft breast he could so easily touch instead. The proximity of it made him hurt.

"You fought The Silent One," she said. "I don't know how, it was so dark. You surprised him, ran him off. I heard your body hit the ground, so I found you with the flashlight and carried you to the healer."

The answer was crazy enough to pull his attention away from her skin. "Carry me? How?"

"Eagle form. You didn't shift back until the healer had done her work."

He tried to imagine that. A golden eagle weighed what—ten pounds? Fifteen? His eagle form stood nearly twice as tall. "Twenty pounds?"

She shrugged. It was doable, therefore believable.

Believable his ass. Tell it to last month's Mick—he'd laugh and tell you to jump in a lake. He bought thinking time by applying ointment to the other end of her wound. Then he dabbed some across her cheek scratch, even though her shower seemed to have cured it.

"That one's from you. Your talons are just as wicked."

"Thanks."

"Makes me wonder about the rest of you."

He steeled himself. She couldn't flirt, not now. He'd never last. To turn it around, he raised his fingers, nails facing her. "Trimmed short. For once not caked in grease. Nothin' to be afraid of."

Her eyes said, *That's not what I was referring to.*

Exactly what had she told him she was? Dead—undead. Rebuilt from bones. A spirit given new life. "When did you die?"

She withdrew, picking up the wine bottle. "Late 1800s. I don't know the exact date."

"How old?"

"Eleven. Your people—" She hadn't raised the bottle to her lips, hadn't moved. But the bottle was now trembling in her hand, and her lips had gone tight, her eyes glazed.

Mick's turn-on uncoiled so fast it flipped his stomach, washed him through with morbid dread. He whispered, "My people … what?"

"Destroyed my village and took us. So I lied to my little sister, told her—" Her breath hitched. The bottle slid.

Mick caught it before it hit the floor.

"—lies. So she'd follow me. I took her hand and we—I ran us off a cliff." She wasn't looking at him anymore. Instead, she focused past his shoulder at a distance that didn't exist in his small apartment.

From nowhere, that still image from Pop's television program surfaced in Mick's memory: an old black-and-white photograph of young Indians with haunted faces, wearing the clothes of his own people instead of their own. The strangeness of it collided with what he was about to say, and he lost the words. If what she'd said was true, she was only separated from that volatile time of pioneers and Indians by a couple decades. Two hundred years after a war against her people, she rises from the grave, the injustice still fresh, the hatred armed. It was no wonder she'd tried to kill him.

CHAPTER 19

WAAPIKOONA ACCEPTED THE wine bottle from Mick's offered hand. Strange—it had been in her possession, and she didn't remember giving it up. She couldn't drink, not until she caught her racing heart. A minute ago she'd been back there on the edge of that cliff, Pinepakatwi looking up at her. *Before we hit the ground, we'll turn to birds and fly into the sky. Give me your hand, we'll do it together. The white people will never find us.* It was just a memory. There was no reason to choke on air hitting her face, or despair at her hand slipping from Pinepakatwi's, or panic at the ground rising so fast underneath her.

Even the last part had been a lie. The white people had found them and buried them in their Christian graveyard, under stones marked with their English names. Jeremiah's cousin had unearthed her bones for The Silent One to revive. A few years ago Waapikoona and Jeremiah had gone back for her sister's bones and reburied them in Illinois, near the grounds of an ancient Native civilization now preserved as a national landmark. It was surely a crime to dig into those mounds—they now belonged to the white people. But Jeremiah lived to break their laws.

She'd said too much. It was a first for her, and she didn't know what to do now that Mick was looking at her with such numb awareness. Killing him was off the list. She needed to get back on her path, dig up her sister's bones, demand The Silent One revive them. Surely by now the price was paid. Her threat in bringing a tamed thunderbird would help convince him.

Too tired to answer Mick's questions and dodge them at the same time, she walked past him and fished her clothes out of his laundry basket. If she couldn't keep her guard intact, she couldn't do this today. She needed rest, distance, time alone to plan the best way to deal with Mick.

The best way was to not deal with him at all, ever again.

"Hey—" he started.

Ignoring him, she locked herself in the bathroom. Admitting how tired she was would do no good for her long walk back to the tomb, so she avoided the mirror and her reflection that would prove just how worn she was.

"You ain't leaving," he said through the door.

She sat on the toilet lid. Even getting dressed seemed like an impossible undertaking.

"Where do you think you're gonna go? Back to that cemetery? On foot?"

How had she let it get this far? She should've never climbed back into his car. Somewhere along the line her brain had started associating Mick with her path, like he was her guide, blazing the trail in front of her. She touched the scratch on her cheek. She'd flushed the itchy sting of poison with cold water from her shower. In eagle form he was poisonous to her, as he'd be to any underworld creature. In human form he might as well be poisonous, too, for all the trouble he caused with lending her his damn cozy clothes and warm apartment. The hot meal and cute kids. The soft couch just waiting to be curled up on. He'd even invited Spot in.

"You can't leave until I'm finished with you."

Right, because he was still holding her Helper's corpse over her. She couldn't summon the mental power to remember why it mattered. Let him keep it. It was no use to her anymore anyway.

Her eyelids were closing on their own. She could give in, just this once. It wasn't surrender if it was blackmail.

When she opened the door, Mick had raised his fist like he was about to pound. She ducked under his arm and went to the couch, folding her clothes in a tidy pile. "You don't have enough beds if I stay."

"If you're cool with the couch, it's yours. I'll lie down with the kids." An answer so direct he must've already planned for it. He opened a closet by the door and retrieved a sheet and blanket and set it all on the end of the couch. "We talk in the morning."

She'd spent too many nights with him already.

"Do I need to block the door to keep you in?" he asked.

"It wouldn't work. My Helpers could tear through it."

"Helpers." He looked aside, thoughtful. He was putting it all together. "They're dead."

"I have more. They'd make you shift, too. In front of those kids."

"I can control it."

"Can you?"

He took a step toward her. Provoking him to shift when he didn't want to was an advantage she could use. Was the threat of it higher than his threat to expose her Helper's corpse to the police? It could be stalemate. It could be war. It all depended on who chose to strike and if the other chose to strike back.

His voice rang low, restrained. "You okay with the couch pillows, or do you want one from the bed?"

She wanted one from his bed so she could inhale against where his head had been. She wanted to crawl over him, sink her nails in like he'd done to her cheek. She wanted it rough, against the wall, the hard floor, the prickly pine needles outside. Discomfort mixed with savage pleasure.

"I don't need anything," she said, her eyes not leaving his.

"Good." He flipped off the kitchen light and closed himself in the bedroom.

He expected her to obey, to camp on his couch until he was ready to interrogate her in the morning. To trust him, as if his kind could be trusted.

She waited until the shifting noises in the bedroom turned to quiet. Then she slipped into her clothes and sneaked out the door, thankful Spot was tagging along. She wouldn't succumb to fatigue on the icy ground if he was there. He needed a fire in that tomb, and she was going to drag herself there to make it for him.

Her boots crunched against the frozen dead grass. There had never been a stiller night. Any moment Mick could burst through the door behind her. Human or eagle, either form would catch up to her, and she wasn't sure she'd fight back. Entering the woods gave her cover, but it didn't seem like enough, with the full moon drenching the snow with white reflective light and the crunch of every footstep resounding far across the land.

Spot noticed their tail before she did. When he stopped and whirled around, she figured he'd caught the movement of some earthly nocturnal creature out looking for food. A possum or raccoon for sure—she simply had no energy to deal with a roused bear. Moving through the animal's territory would eliminate a confrontation, but she couldn't tell that to a hound dog pointing into the dark woods behind them, ears and hackles raised, every muscle tense. This was what he'd been born to do.

He'd have to catch up. Her body couldn't take a delay. She kept going, getting so far ahead she was afraid that in her near-coma state she had followed the wrong trail and lost both Spot and her tomb. She paused to whistle; an owl hooted back. Probably a friend of Mick's, taunting her. She ought to build a bow and some arrows, provoke Mick to shift then shoot him out of the sky. A bloody thunderbird corpse as a gift for The Silent One, an encouragement to fulfill his side of their bargain.

Ahead, the gray strip of cemetery road lay like a ghostly ribbon through the trees. Dry branches rustled to her right; a thunder pounded the earth. No animal in its right mind would attack so boldly, but she slid behind a tree anyway, knowing she'd never fool a bear but the delay would be enough to release her Helpers and scare it off. Not a good use for them, but she had no other option. The ruckus gained on her in cold air so steady she already felt closed in her tomb, listening as some creature tried to breach its walls.

Spot leapt onto the trail, wiggling with pride for finding her or chasing off their tail. She spared a moment to rub his ears then headed for the cemetery road. Too tired to mask herself from the dead, they awoke at her presence like children who'd been told to be quiet for too long. They leaked from the shadows, building themselves like an upward rolling fog. The more desperate spirits clustered at the edge of the graveyard, their wispy white forms pushing against one another to get at her first. Others hung back, watching, regretful, mourning their own deaths in place of the living who should've been. Only one generation honored these dead—maybe two, for the lucky ones—then they were forgotten. Her people had honored their dead forever.

"I won't speak to any of you if you act like that," she said to the pushy ones, careful to stay on the road. "I'm too tired to help you now anyway."

A few at the front turned their murky faces away, dissolving toward the ground, elation and hope turned to sullen gloom. Spot had gone rigid again beside her, eyes and ears trained on the door of the tomb, where another group of spirits created a stagnant fog near the door. Spot wasn't built by the underworld and couldn't see those spirits. He'd fixated on the tomb steps in front of them, on the human form standing in greeting.

Jeremiah had been their tail. She'd led him close enough to figure out where she'd been holing up, and he overtook them to reach it first.

We're on the same side. There's no reason to suspect him of anything. Except there was. So tired her head throbbed, she had no idea how to play this. The spirits parted, drifting away as she approached. "I'm in no mood for guests."

"You can't exactly make them leave."

Spot growled; she lay a hand on his head to calm him. Maybe she should let him run Jeremiah off. A conversation with him would be a battleground. He'd twist more of her words, pretend to miss her meaning, dance around her questions. She'd speak clearly; he'd somehow make it unclear. They both knew the guest she wasn't in the mood for was him. Clarifying it would only goad him into the confrontation he'd come for, having missed out on it at Mick's house.

The spirits had faded into the winter air. To see Jeremiah give them the same cold shoulder she did made her promise to help them tomorrow. She could spare some of her time, especially if it kept her from being like Jeremiah.

She blinked to focus her eyes. She was seeing double. "Unblock the door."

"Or...?"

"Or this dog and I will unblock it with flint and teeth."

He glanced between her and Spot. "Whose flint and whose teeth?"

The energy required to draw her knife couldn't be mustered. She concentrated on the soft side of his neck where the artery lay. Maybe all she did need was her teeth. Leave Spot out of it. Jeremiah was one of The Silent One's raised army—the millipede demon would kill her if she went that rogue. Then he'd raise her sister and send her off with Jeremiah to be fully indoctrinated into their plan. Her sister's second chance at life would be wasted just as her first had, and both would be Waapikoona's fault.

Jeremiah still blocked the door. Anger and guilt powered her grab of his collar like she'd fantasized doing to Mick, but instead of kissing him, she sent a knee into his gut. The last ounce of strength she had, and it took a moment to understand it hadn't made contact, he'd gotten hold of her coat; they'd switched positions, and her breath was being knocked out of her as he slammed her against the tomb's closed door. The second slam snapped her head backward so it made its own pronounced, star-filled contact against unforgiving wood. The third one—delayed, due to Spot's bright white fangs appearing under a curling lip, his growl chilling an already cold night.

"Okay," Jeremiah said, releasing her.

It wasn't fast enough. Spot lunged, those white teeth clamping on his arm and shaking so violently Waapikoona prepared for a spray of blood from an armless shoulder. It didn't pay off. Spot had already let go and backed up into a slight crouch, ready to spring. Like the most noble bodyguard, he seemed to be giving Jeremiah a chance to leave.

Stumbling down the steps, Jeremiah cradled his crushed arm. "You won't get many more chances. You've used them all up. Soon you won't be a volunteer anymore."

"I don't need chances."

"You think he just raises family members out of the goodness of his demon heart? That's not a favor, it's easy recruitment. You don't put in time and then get to walk. He raised you, he owns you. Until the end."

"He doesn't own me."

"Keep telling yourself that. I feel sorry for you, Sarah. That's why I'm here."

"You're here because you're his errand boy. Not to help me."

He sighed heavily, closing his eyes. "I'm here because our people finally have a hope. And if you don't see that, you may as well lie down and let the white man have you. Just like he had you in your first life." He opened his eyes. In them played a thought he didn't need to voice: *Like he has you now.*

She didn't want to think of Mick, but that's exactly what Jeremiah pushed her to. It should only be met with her silence, but she was too tired to stop herself. "There is no 'our people,' Jeremiah. And to let The Silent One trick you into thinking we're all the same ... you're as ignorant as the white man. So you lie down with them. Give up on war. You've already lost."

If Spot hadn't parked himself between them, Jeremiah would surely be ripping *her* throat out right now. The anger wouldn't last long with him. He'd hand it across the circle of time to his imagined future self who was living in the world of what would come. Millions of Native people raised from their graves by The Silent One, a living army built and fed by the underworld. People who once shared this wide land, people who were once allies and enemies, neighbors and competitors, newly united against a common goal: overthrow the ones who stole this land. Destroy them; take it back. Then open the trapdoor and let the underworld leak out.

It would never work. Native people who inhabited this land during her first life were too dissimilar to meld. The land was too vast, language and lifestyle too varied. Going back a thousand years like The Silent One planned? It was laughable. Those people knew nothing of European colonialization. Of borders and stolen hunting grounds, of illness and starvation, of being marched away from their land. Of being torn from their families, stripped of their culture, their language, their spirits killed. With no common enemy to fight, they'd demand to be returned to their graves.

And all this was too much to have in her mind when all she wanted to do was sleep.

Jeremiah said, "If you don't kill that guy soon, I will."

She watched him turn and leave, wondering why it was any of his business. He had seen Mick pick up her Helper's corpse, as unsurprised and familiar with it as if he weren't an enemy white man but one of them. A simple daily act, like he was taking out his kitchen trash. Jeremiah didn't know what Mick really was, and she'd love to be around when he found out.

That didn't mean she was a traitor. It meant she was free.

CHAPTER 20

OF COURSE SHE was gone. After seeing the empty couch and untouched blanket and sheet, Mick didn't need to check the bathroom or the yard. The emptiness of her leaving had infected his sleeping form and laced his dreams with gloom; he'd woken to find that gloom still alive and well.

"Stress," he said to the empty couch. That's all it was. Anger. Annoyance. He'd have to wait for his answers, have to seek her out. More trouble added to his pile. It wasn't loneliness. Heartbreak? No way. Maybe over his situation. Certainly not over her.

He was searching the fridge for something to feed the kids when Doug appeared and reminded him Old Mae was going to have breakfast for them. So he walked the kids up to her kitchen and found her already at work on pancakes. His appetite had been consumed by the gloom, but he'd be dead at work if he didn't eat. So he helped her serve the kids then sat down with them and shoveled it in. Back in his apartment he showered, dressed himself and two kids, and did his best to comb Janie's hair while Doug searched the bed for her missing barrettes.

His shift at Virgil's shop started before school did. If he left them with Old Mae, they'd have no ride in, and he didn't have the numbers of any of the women who traded babysitting with Kari.

Except for one.

God, there had to be some other option besides calling Amanda.

"Please don't let this be my life," he said, scrolling through the contacts on his phone. But there was no one else. If Waapikoona had stayed, he could pack them all in the GTO, get himself to work, and leave the kids and the GTO with her—

"What? That's crazy." So was talking to himself, but that ship had sailed long ago and joined a whole fleet of crazy. He could text Kari and ask her, but he didn't want to bother her at the hospital, where nurses checking on Helen interrupted crappy, anxiety-laden sleep on the cramped corner bed all night long. He could handle one morning with kids, or a week, or however long she needed him to keep them.

He could also be an adult and call Amanda. It was a favor for Kari, not him. He didn't need to feel guilty that it was a different woman's help he craved for some ungodly reason. He dialed. It went to voicemail.

"Dang it," he said after hanging up without leaving a message. She'd have a missed call from him, and it was all for nothing because by the time she called him back it would be too late. He should've at least left a message so if she got it too late to help, she'd know she didn't need to call back. He felt like such an asshole. What bothered him more was how little he cared.

"You kids are comin' to the shop with me," he said, ushering them to the GTO. The barrette search had wasted too much time; he was going to be late, and the thought of speeding to work on frozen roads with two kids in the car didn't appeal to him at all. In the rearview mirror, Janie hugged herself and shivered. He'd forgotten her hat and gloves. He left the car running and sprinted back in for them. Her backpack, too, handed to him by Old Mae off the front porch. If this was Kari's life, he didn't know what the hell he had to complain about.

"Dougie, you got everything?" He backed straight onto an unshoveled patch of solid ice but couldn't curse out loud with the kids in the car.

"Yeah—oh wait. Forgot my homework."

That, along with the tires spinning impotently against the sheet of ice, brought a curse out of him that was very unfit for children's ears. Both kids gazed at him, eyes so big and white it sucked him into their fear of men who spoke like that to kids. Maybe not Janie's fear—she'd been too young to remember—but certainly Doug's.

He was failing at this, failing Kari. He had to get a grip.

"Sorry, kids, that was bad to say. I—" No lame excuses. Kids saw through that. "Dougie, run on in and get the homework, and I'll get the car unstuck."

Doug didn't budge. Mick turned in the seat to look at him, and Doug jumped into action, fumbling the door handle he tried to get out so fast. He sped up Old Mae's porch steps now free of ice due to Mick salting them last night. At least he'd done something right.

He eased the throttle, but every go was spinning him farther away from the clear spot he was aiming for. He tried it in second gear. He wondered what kind of an idiot would buy a car like this as his only car and let winter roll right in without at least replacing the bald tires. With what money, though? He could barely afford to put gas in the damn thing. He was stuck, in more ways than one.

Doug returned and stood by the car, waiting for the cue to climb back in. Mick got out and walked around to Doug's side.

"Dougie." He opened the passenger door for him, put a hand on his shoulder. "I'm real sorry for sayin' that. I wasn't mad at you."

"You sounded real mad."

"I know. I was. Just not at you. Are we good?"

Doug glanced into the back seat at Janie. He wasn't good unless she was good. The protective big brother to the end. "Yeah, we're good."

"Okay, do me a favor. Get in and pull that emergency brake if the car starts rolling too fast. Can you do that?"

Doug got in. Mick released the brake and replaced his hand with Doug's. "I'll holler if I need you to pull it. Ready?"

"Ready."

Mick walked behind the car and braced his feet. His boots had better grip than his stupid tires. Once he got it rolling he moved into his open driver's door and took the wheel while he continued to push, steering the car into the tire ruts that would lead him to a hopefully salted road.

"You need a truck," Janie said, once all the doors were shut and they were moving down the road.

"Go to college and get rich and buy me one."

"Nah," Doug said. "He just needs a better winter setup on this one."

Winter setup? The kid had learned well. "Okay, buy me a winter setup and a truck. And a garage to park them in."

"Mommy wants me to buy her a maid," Janie said.

"That too." And pay off Helen's medical bills, move Pop into a nice nursing home, chip away at his and Kari's credit card balances … but if Janie and Doug inherited the family debt, they'd never get ahead. They'd be stuck just like he and Kari were stuck, accumulating their own debt on top of it all. He didn't hope for them to be rich. He simply wanted them to be secure and not have to work three jobs and still be driving around on old tires.

He couldn't believe kids born poor stayed poor. Somebody had to catch a break. Hours—days?—weeks?—spent in a timeless cave, as both human and eagle, must have rewired his brain because he couldn't just accept this was his life anymore. He couldn't wake up and go to work, pay his bills, go back to work and pay more bills without wondering what it was all for. Up until now he hadn't needed anything but his routine, his packed days sometimes ending in a blissful hour or two in front of the TV. Many people in his position needed religion. He didn't even need that anymore. There had been nothing to question, nothing to puzzle him, nothing to make him curse at the sky.

Now he was parking at the shop, trying to figure out where he could stash two kids while he changed oil and tires and brake pads.

Which seemed like a silly problem to have when mixed with the things he knew. He could shapeshift into a thunderbird. He'd been bitten by a flying demon, healed by a witch in a cave. He was in love with an underworld spirit. How could he just go back to small talk with Virgil between brake jobs and wheel alignments? His life had fractured into two halves. If he didn't get one sorted out and buried, they'd rub together and detonate.

With the kids settled in the waiting area, he went in back to clock in. Virgil sat at the desk, scowling at the handwritten schedule. The part-timers were always asking to alter their hours and giving him a headache. He looked up at Mick over his reading glasses. "Now what've you done?"

His chin. He'd forgotten all about it. The arm wound he'd called in sick for was healed in one day without a trace, and now he had a new wound with no prepared explanation. He should've wrapped his arm at home, pretended it was still healing. But as long as no one asked about it, he'd be fine.

He just needed to remember not to roll up his sleeves. "It looks worse than it is."

"How's the arm?"

"Better." Mick flexed his elbow to demonstrate.

"Have you thought about taking some time off?"

"Can't go without the pay."

"I got it worked out to give you another paid week of vacation. You been here long enough to earn it."

"Virgil, I can't…" Can't what, take a handout? That wasn't what this was. Even though the too-nice part of him thrashed against taking something that didn't feel like his, he absorbed the struggle.

"There's one condition. You have to take it now. Starting Monday."

"You don't got enough guys to cover me."

Virgil set his pen on the schedule, flipped an adjacent ledger closed, and stood. "You let me worry about that."

"Is now a bad time to tell you my niece and nephew are sitting in the waiting room, and I'll need to skip out to take them to school in a bit?"

Virgil waved a hand to dismiss that, close enough now to scrutinize the amount of flesh chipped off Mick's chin. "That didn't happen here, not that I know how it could've. Did you run into some trouble, son?"

Trouble? Mick shouldn't laugh, but he did. "Yeah, maybe. It's real embarrassing. I'll spare you." That was the truth.

He got a full-body analysis then, and he was grateful for the long sleeves on his coveralls. He could think of no excuse for the missing wound on his arm.

"Those kids gonna behave?"

"You betcha."

"Fellow came looking for you on your day off. Said his name was Leo, that he needed to talk to you…"

Mick's ears turned off even though Virgil was still talking as he moved past, heading to the front like this was a casual thing and Mick would follow. There was nothing casual about Leo Boyle being in town, coming to find Mick—because if he went straight to Kari, she'd call the police. Or maybe he did go straight there to find her car missing and house empty. His brother, Kari's ex, was still in prison. His brother who'd wanted Kari punished for divorcing him. Leo now wanted Kari punished for sending his brother to prison.

Mick already had Waapikoona and her crap showing up at the shop. This was a new level of worse. If he could drag the asshole into that cave and leave him there, he would. Right in that massive black cavern with that creature from Hell that had made him shift. He'd never be able to concentrate on work until the kids were safe at school. The parking lot and road were only visible at the shop bay doors, and he couldn't work on cars from there. And once Kari and Helen returned home, he'd never be able to sleep.

He needed to find that guy. Give him a good reason to never show up in Wyona again.

Virgil switched the waiting room TV to kids' public television and flipped over the OPEN sign on the window. Janie positioned her backpack as a footrest, and Doug gave Mick a sleepy smile. A meth addict brother of a convict wouldn't be up this early. And if he showed up again and saw two kids in the waiting room, he probably wouldn't even recognize them as his brother's. Even if he did, he couldn't carry them both off without a commotion that would reach Mick in the bay. So Mick slid his biggest socket wrench into his coverall pocket and got to work on a job that didn't need a socket wrench.

When his phone rang later, his hands were too full to see who it was but he knew it was Amanda. Of course she'd call back all helpful. She'd probably want to stop by and drive the kids to school with her own, an offer that would be too convenient to pass up. She'd insist because it'd be on her way, and he'd agree. Then he'd be in deeper with a woman he should be pursuing instead of the underworld spirit who ditched him last night. The one who'd left her earrings on his bathroom sink and her imprint on his every thought.

He needed to flush it all away. Forget the answers he needed. His attention should be on his family, on finding a new nurse for Pop, on helping Kari with the kids while she tended to Helen. And now dealing with Leo. He'd use his week of vacation to get all that settled, and then he'd reestablish his routine. Waapikoona would leave, and he'd be back to his non-shifting human self. He wouldn't need a socket wrench to make her go away. All he had to do was return the corpse.

AFTER WORK HE grabbed some groceries for himself and Pop. Amanda had called back and convinced Mick to let her pick up the kids from school and keep them at her place until he got off work. He'd forgotten he had to check on Pop, but he could do it quickly enough, and she said Kari's kids entertained her kids so she could get dinner started. It was a win for both of them.

He traded a few texts with Kari. Helen was stable but needed a few days. She insisted she owed him. He swore she didn't, because Janie was going to buy him a truck and Doug was going to take care of him when he was old and sick with dementia.

It had never been dementia all along. He kind of wished it was. The things he knew now disturbed him too much to trust the world he knew. It turned outlandish deeds into possibilities, like murdering a guy with a socket wrench and dumping him in a haunted cave. The murder part hadn't been included in his earlier plan, but now it was. And that disturbed him worse than anything.

A thunderbird could kill someone and leave no human trace. There was also that. It was a line of thinking he didn't want to follow.

Pop's driveway got the full light of the day's sun, so the ice had melted to the asphalt. Mick parked and rebagged the groceries in the trunk, separating his from Pop's in the shadow of approaching night. He'd bought the better coffee, one step up from bargain brand. Not because he expected Waapikoona for breakfast again. It would be his reward for getting rid of her and for not looking back. It wasn't all for him anyway. He'd give half of it to Pop.

He called out a greeting as he opened the door. Shutting it behind him, he could still feel the cold embrace of winter, still see his breath. "Pop?"

The nearest floor vent blew hot air. He checked the thermostat, finding it set as usual. The TV blared in the kitchen, but its audience was an empty room. Then Mick noticed the back door hanging wide open. He dropped the grocery bags on the floor and rushed outside. Boot-sized footsteps led away from the door in the slush. He flipped on the floodlights, pulled the door closed, and followed the boot prints to the edge of a long stretch of very unilluminated woods. His internal warning siren shrilled to a higher register.

Pop could be miles away, dressed for the weather or not. He'd need a police search party, search and rescue dogs. Mick cupped his hands around his mouth and shouted Pop's name loud enough to rouse an animal in the brush and set it fleeing.

Shift.

"No." He wasn't sure it was himself he was answering.

His other self had razor eyes and night vision. Whether that was true for regular eagles he wasn't sure, but the kind he morphed into could find his dad in the thickest forest on the darkest night. He would not do that, couldn't even entertain it. He was done with that. He wanted his normal life back, which meant getting a damn flashlight, a hat and gloves, finding Pop himself. His car held all of those, so he trudged around the house in the rigid north-facing snow. Everything would refreeze tonight. The sky had that dead-of-winter blackness that went up forever. The landscape and shadow wrapped around him like that cave.

Someone stood beside his car. Blue robe, snow boots. Pop.

Mick's relief melted through him, even though Pop was assessing the car like he'd never seen it before.

"Nice set of wheels."

"God, Pop, how long you been out here?"

"Been checkin' on them. They're comin' alive, all around. A few out there..." he gestured toward the woods behind the house "...but they hide from me."

Groundless anger advanced on Mick. This behavior from his father, this nonsense, it wasn't new. It shouldn't bother him, but it was eating through him like that toxic demon bite. At least Pop hadn't strayed too far. He should be grateful for that. "Let's get on inside before we freeze to death."

"I been in and out all day. Ain't no warmer in there."

"That's 'cause you left the door open."

"No, they left the door open. They check on me, too. But I hide from *them*."

Forget the nurse. Mick needed to hire a babysitter. In fact, yeah, that'd be cheaper. Some high school kid to come by every day after school and check on things. Make sure the doors were closed and the stove was off, and the old man was happily watching TV. The hard part would be finding a high school kid in Wyona who had a car or a parent who could lend one. It'd be a lot easier if Pop lived closer to town.

"You need to stay inside. There's nothin' out here you need to see." He opened the door and guided Pop in. "Take off those boots or they'll mess up the floor."

Mick considered hiding them. Maybe if Pop had no snow boots to go outside in, he'd give up on the idea and stay inside. But he could also decide to go without them, which would be worse. Mick found the TV remote and lowered the volume. His nerves were taut enough without the noise. Leo wouldn't dare come by and bother Pop—would he?

"Hey, you have any visitors lately? Besides me."

"Just you and the ones comin' alive."

The thought of humoring the dementia—Mick couldn't do it. He didn't want to see his relationship with his father flipped like that. He was a grown man, yes, but he was still the kid. Pop was the father. He was okay seeing them as equals. He couldn't handle humoring Pop as if he were the child. But there was a nag, pushing through Mick's frustration. What if this wasn't the dementia talking but the new reality he'd faced, the one he was determined to swear off? The twist in the world that he thought was dementia in himself? What if Pop knew the things he knew? Technically, Waapikoona had come back alive. There could be more like her, and they could be living in Pop's woods just as he believed.

"Okay, Pop, who are they?"

"That's what I'm tryin' to find out. They're not like us though, and they want us gone." Pop started unloading groceries onto the counter, sorting cold stuff and pantry stuff like his mind was all there.

"If I told you it's handled, would you stop worryin' and stay in the house?"

Pop paused to look him in the eye, as clear-minded as ever. "Depends who's handlin' it."

It was a dare. A bluff called. Two people who knew the same secret, locked in a standoff of who would admit it first. Mick wanted to deny it all. He wanted out. He wanted to stick fingers in his ears and blinders on his head and move forward, forgetting all he knew until life spun back around to normal. One small problem now: he had started this conversation, and he wasn't going to back down. "Mighty Eagle."

He couldn't believe he'd said it. Pop's crazy words, validated. His shapeshifting self, introduced to someone who wasn't undead. He wasn't admitting it was him, so at least he had that.

Pop put a hand on his shoulder. "I knew you wouldn't let me down."

Chapter
21

Mick didn't expect to spend a Friday night planning how to find Leo Boyle, or what to do about him when he did, but with Kari out of town, the urgency to do something had animated his bones. If he could get it good and done, she wouldn't even have to know.

Back at home he switched his coveralls for clean jeans and a flannel, scrubbed the grease off his hands, and gulped down a hastily made sandwich and a can of bargain cherry soda. The light coming from the house lit the GTO like a puddle of sunset on the frosted driveway. Cold embraced him; testosterone and resolve burned against it. The startup roar of the V8 broke the night. It fixed him, though, like ointment on a skinned chin, like an ally in war. Just as he released the brake, his phone rang. He checked it: Amanda.

"Hey, can you keep them one more hour—"

"Leo Boyle's here, looking for Kari. I think he's on something…"

Adrenaline surged so hard Mick nearly choked. "Leo—there? Get the kids, get out—"

"He's waiting in the other room. The kids are here with me."

"He's in the house?"

"Yeah, did the custody agreement change? He says the kids need to visit their dad, and if Kari won't take them—"

Mick switched the phone to speaker and hit the gas too hard, catching his mistake just before the back end flipped out from behind him. "Tell him to go outside. I'm on my way right now."

"He won't, I already told him. He's on the couch. I don't know what he's on, but he's talking like crazy, and he's just about scratched a hole in his cheek. Does he do meth?"

Yes he was on meth, had been for years. "Can you get the kids and leave?"

"I don't think that'd go over too well. I'm being nice, trying to keep him calm. Should I call 911?"

The old Mick would say yes, would have already hung up and called it himself. But this Mick didn't want police there when he showed up. The GTO fishtailed onto the main road as Mick tried to lighten his foot.

"Oh, hold on, I think he's coming." Amanda's voice drifted away. She told the kids to stay put and keep the door closed before the call cut off, leaving Mick in a panic made worse by icy roads and speed limits. He hit the state road, its surface clear enough to bring his speed up. It didn't matter. Seconds were years; minutes were centuries. He caught up to a semi, held his breath, and passed blind. The v8 roared its victory over the double yellow lines just in time, the oncoming van's horn blaring. He knew all the legal passing zones on this road by heart. Following the law would not serve him now. But spinning off the road or getting pulled over wouldn't either. He gritted his teeth and eased up.

A lifted black Dodge pickup rounded the bend ahead, riding the middle line close enough to make Mick swerve halfway onto the shoulder to avoid a head-on. Scraggly goatee, baseball cap in winter—it was him. In the rearview mirror the pickup was already gone around another curve, speeding on better tires with a more reckless driver than the GTO's. Even though Mick knew a U-turn would be a waste of time, he felt ripped in half by his options: follow him or get to Amanda and the kids. If Mick didn't have an idea of where Leo was heading, he'd have followed, but he did and checking on the kids was more important. He also needed to know how much trouble the dirt bag had given Amanda before he decided how he'd deal with him.

He parked behind Amanda's ancient Jeep Cherokee as she came onto the porch. She held a white pack against her mouth, the other hand tight in a fist against her chest. For one dark moment, he stopped to roll the image around, to compare it to the worst-case scenario still alive in his head. It wasn't so bad. Bad, but not worst-case bad. He could deal with this.

"Don't freak out," she said.

His heart reacted to that by pumping double. He was going to kill him. Now at the top of the porch steps, he waited for her to lower the white pack and confirm it was in fact an ice pack held against a fat lip and that he was in fact going to kill him.

"Oh god…" her big eyes focused on his screwed-up chin "…did you catch him on the way out?"

"No, but I saw him on the road. I know where he's goin'. Tell me what happened."

She extended the hand not holding the ice pack, flexing the fingers as if stiff. "I clocked him real good. No one ever says how bad it hurts to punch someone."

"Lemme see the lip."

She lowered the ice pack. He looked away, swore, looked at her again, swore again. It wasn't just fat. Blood oozed from the corner of her mouth like her teeth had cut the inside of her cheek.

"He touch the kids?"

"Tried to. Doug kicked him square in the knee, and Janie screamed until the bastard left."

"They hurt like you?" He needed a warning before he saw them, so he could process it out here in the winter chill instead of in front of them.

"No, just me. He got real mad 'cause I wouldn't tell him which kids were mine and which were Kari's. Deadbeat piece of trash doesn't even know what his nephew and niece look like."

"There somewhere you can go tonight, in case he comes back before I get to him?"

"Yeah, my mom's. But you can't do anything, Mick. You don't need that kind of trouble—"

"Trouble's all mine. Sorry it became yours tonight. I'll..." He didn't know what he was going to do, but it would surely be premeditated. "...deal with him."

Mick stayed until Amanda had packed overnight bags and buckled her kids into her Jeep. Then he buckled Doug and Janie into his car and led the way to the state road. The night was a blanket of black, the headlights of oncoming cars blinding. Behind him, Amanda slowed for a turn onto a side road, her lights swiveling, then disappearing. Leo knew Amanda was a friend of Kari's, but there was no way he'd know where Amanda's mom lived. They'd be safe.

"You wanna hear how I screamed?" Janie asked.

In the seat beside him, Doug plugged both ears. Mick didn't have a chance to answer before she let loose a shriek more animal than human, its pitch tearing eardrums, its volume popping blood vessels. Predatory, punishing, and delightful.

"Okay!" Mick hollered over her, lowering both front windows to allow wind to drag it away. The onslaught of winter air turned her scream into shouts of *Too cold! Too cold!* from both kids. He rolled the windows back up. His ears rang. "That's great, little birdie, but maybe save it for the bad guys."

Old Mae didn't question him when he dropped the kids with her.

"They've been fed."

"When's bedtime?" She directed the question to Doug instead of Mick.

"Midnight?" Doug tried, the word too drawn and slow to sound like anything but a shameless stretch.

"The witching hour," she said. "That'll give us plenty of time to eat heaps of cookies. With sprinkles."

Janie and Doug looked at each other like they'd just struck gold.

In his apartment, Mick grabbed his own socket wrench out of his toolbox. A pair of winter gloves he didn't mind tossing. A roll of duct tape. A flashlight with fresh batteries. He plugged his nearly dead phone into the wall and paced in his kitchen. Was he planning murder? A mafia-style shake-down? Blackmail? The guy had enough drug crimes to go away for a long time, and Mick could fabricate some evidence anyone would believe. All of Wyona would believe hardworking, good-natured Mick Svendsen over Boyle scum. Drug crime was much easier to prove than the assault on Amanda. And it probably carried a heftier sentence.

The real problem was the future assaults he knew would someday become reality, their degree of harm very much unknown. Against Amanda, her kids. Against Kari, Doug, Janie, and Helen. Even if Leo went to prison, parole could happen. His sentence would end someday, and he wouldn't be reformed. He'd be worse—more toxic, more hateful, with new tricks.

So murder, then. It'd get rid of him once and for all. It should be out of the question. The old Mick wished he could find some moral reason it was; the new Mick said it didn't matter. The old Mick worked against him, drafting a conversation he'd have with the sheriff's office first thing Monday morning. Trying to prove it could be done, that this was someone else's job and not his. He didn't have to take matters into his own hands, even if he wanted to.

The new Mick could shift into a golden eagle. It wouldn't even *be* his hands committing a human crime in the jurisdiction of nature, of gods and thunderbirds and demons. He'd be unfindable, untouchable, unkillable.

He wasn't planning murder. He was planning dinner.

"Execution," the old Mick said.

Whatever it was, Mick wanted his normal life back. He didn't want this option in the future, didn't want it to become so easy to fall back on solving every problem in his life as a damn bird. One last go, that was it. He would return the demon corpse to Waapikoona, tell her to leave Wyona or she'd be his last hunt instead of Leo Boyle.

He scooped her earrings off the sink and pocketed them. He dragged the trash bag full of semi-rotted demon out from under Old Mae's side porch. Too frozen to offer any flesh or blood, it sat on his kitchen table and thawed while he waited with an open zipper sandwich bag. It was taking too long. He was losing the nerve. So he got a box knife, hacked off a piece near its neck, and put it in the microwave. Thirty seconds made it ooze black goop. After sealing the warm pliant flesh inside the bag, he had to plant his palms on the table and breathe through an oncoming shift. It was like stifling a sneeze; if he caught its first hint, he could stop it.

The box knife rinsed, it went into his pocket. The socket wrench and other tools he'd gathered into the GTO's passenger floorboard. The trash bag of demon shut into his trunk. Mick behind the wheel with an easy foot on the pedal. There was no room for haste or carelessness or spinning an overpowered car off an icy road. This would be done right.

HE DROVE AS far into the cemetery as the roads would allow. The air outside the GTO smelled of burning leaves and rich V8 exhaust. He tugged the trash bag out of his trunk and let it hit the ground with a deliberate thud. The last thing he wanted to do was surprise Waapikoona and her dog. He needed to save all his energy for Leo Boyle. This was the easy part, and he didn't want that to change.

The gravestones stared like pale faces as he zigzagged between them in the dark, his flashlight glancing off one then another. A shaving of the moon had risen, glowing so silvery bright it lit the rest of the orb in a supernatural blue. Any other night Mick might stop to take a mental picture, to breathe in air so cold and crisp it burned on the way down. He couldn't pause among these graves, not on a night like tonight. Not when they regarded him so blankly. So expectantly. He couldn't remember the last time he'd visited his mother's grave. He owed her flowers for many holidays. Years' worth. He wasn't superstitious, but the graves around him seemed to know this. They'd conjured his guilt, and they were watching.

Halfway to the mausoleum he had to turn around and remove the plastic zipper bag of thawed demon flesh from his coat pocket and return it to the GTO. His eagle mind had zoned in too closely and was itching to possess him before he was ready. Having the frozen corpse so close was temptation enough, and if he shifted now, he wasn't sure if he'd be able to later. Tonight he was driven by new rules, a new power. By a black-and-white right and wrong where he was the judge and the sky was the courtroom. It filled him up, primed, his fuse awaiting flame.

With the trash bag slung over his shoulder, he stopped at the mausoleum door and gave it a polite knock. The weight of his knuckles set it creaking inward, revealing the hot orange glow of a healthy fire.

"Come in," she said from some dark place he couldn't see. She must've heard his car pull up.

He entered, dragging the door closed. He dropped the bag to the ground. "Here's your corpse. I'm done."

"Badass self-control, Mick."

He needed to banish her from this town just for saying his name like that. She hopped down from her perch on one of the coffins, brushing off her jeans. Instead of the puffy coat she wore a body-hugging zip-up fleece. And no cowboy boots—her feet were bare. The stone around him pulsed with heat. Mick had a sudden need to shed his coat. But no, this would be quick then he'd leave.

"I'm givin' you one day to get out of this town."

"Or?"

"Or I shift and rip you apart."

She licked her bottom lip like this had just gotten interesting. Other than that she remained perfectly still, the only motion the dance of fire in her eyes.

An unpleasant thought sparked in Mick's head: *I'm going to kiss her.*

No he wasn't. No way.

"You have that look in your eye. Are you planning to hunt evil tonight?"

Interesting words. He wondered how she knew. "Sure am. So if you'll pardon me—"

"What kind? From your world or from mine?"

Because it felt like she was calling him a liar, he had to answer, to prove her wrong. "Mine."

"Who?"

"A guy I know who hits women and tries to steal kids."

"This guy have a name?"

"He does." And she wasn't getting it, because that would link him to whatever he was about to do. He'd already said too much.

She backed into the stone wall, resting her shoulders against it, her arms tucked behind the small of her back. Firelight licked her body, a flicker of light and shadow, of real and unreal. She was dead—undead. A risen spirit. Bones buried in another century then revived in this one. And he wasn't just going to kiss her, he was going to make her his— if he didn't stop himself.

"What are you going to do, Mick?"

He fell out of the conversation. He could only think of her and what he was going to do, right now, to her. With her. Primed with this new energy and new set of rules he could only entertain tonight. Tomorrow there'd be no more. His normal life would be back—no more shifting, no more fitting justice. No more Waapikoona.

He slipped a hand into his pocket and drew out her earrings. She didn't come forward to take them; she was a fixture against the wall, making him come to her. He weighed that a moment, trying to determine where the power rested. With her, demanding he walk across the room and deposit them in her hand. Or with him, if he advanced on her, pressed them into her palm, and walked away.

One final option hit him then: keep the earrings. Let her watch him leave this place with a token of hers since she made no move to take them herself. It occurred to him that he wanted to keep them, to put them back on his bathroom sink as a reminder of what he'd exiled, what he'd chosen to live without.

He turned, stepped over the trash bag, and left through the door, letting it close solidly behind him. Not bothering with the flashlight this time, he rounded the first group of gravestones and stopped. The unnatural silence of the night fell hard around him. He tilted his head, listening for the shuffle of naked branches in the wind, a hiss of tires passing on the nearby road. All he could hear was his breath coming faster—too fast. Bitter in his lungs, chilling his chest and stomach. What he needed to do tonight would be spoiled if he didn't release a coiled-up need. The unrest in his system would sabotage it all.

The mausoleum door stuck when he tried to re-enter. He shoved until it gave, and he burst into the room. Cold air whipped into the heated space; he kicked the door closed with his boot. She watched him in the firelight, half annoyed, half amused. Eyes as dark as an undead creature's should be.

Mick didn't observe the steps it took to get him to her, he was simply there, her shoulders in his grip, his mouth on hers. She gave him teeth; he gave teeth back. His hands now on her face, holding her. Her fingers on his ribs, digging in. He ground his pelvis against her, the zippers of their jeans a painful obstacle. She absorbed the pressure, squirming against it for more. The kiss warped from violent to sweet so fast Mick shuddered, finding her punishing fingers turned soft, his grip delicate, sliding to the back of her neck into her silky hair.

In a flash they separated. Breathing hard, they glared at one another. The blame of who'd stopped first mutual because neither could be sure who it was. Mick couldn't decide which he'd liked better: the beginning of all that or the end. Vicious or gentle. It seemed he liked the combination most of all, that he'd like neither without the other.

"What is this?" she demanded.

"I don't know."

"Do it again."

"Nope. I'm done." He gave her shoulders a meaningful shove, forcing her back against the wall she'd stepped away from.

"Coward."

Name-calling wouldn't get her what she wanted, and what she wanted was what Mick wanted so badly it stung him in every erogenous zone. But if denying himself meant denying her, he was all for it. Even though he was so hard he could barely walk. Even though she smelled like fire and female spice and promised a ride between Heaven and Hell so delicious he'd lose his mind to something worse than dementia, be infected by something scarier than a demon bite. He was going to walk away, to leave her hot and desperate and breathless and looking at him like she was the one about to perform murder. He held the power, and he was about to prove it by walking out the door.

CHAPTER
22

Waapikoona watched the door close, unsurprised that calling Mick a coward had the opposite effect on him. No matter what she did she couldn't seem to draw the ugly behavior out. He couldn't be that wholesome. And she couldn't blame him for wanting her gone. Someone had to stop this. But she was searching the shadows for where she'd left her boots because she had to go after him. Whatever part of her now calling the shots couldn't be stopped. Threats, pleas or bargains wouldn't work. She was her own pawn, and she couldn't find her damn boots.

She'd never known a kiss like that—it was so much more than a kiss, but she didn't know what else to call it. An ambush? A capture—but instead of her escaping, he had? A tease so wild her teeth chattered? It was the first battle of a war, and it was her duty to retaliate and end it. She couldn't live until she had the rest of him, until he was laid out and drained, until she conquered him. She'd never been so close to begging a man to stay so she could fill herself up with him.

The whole thing was illogical. She found her boots and yanked them on along with her coat, not caring about how she'd let hormones and heart blaze the path toward the most unsuitable man.

Whatever mission Mick thought he was on would turn out differently once he found that guy. Mick would never pull it off. Anger and bloodlust were one thing in a person like Mick's mind, but in reality, he'd screw it up as soon as his conscience showed up. And the guy he was hunting sounded like a perfect target for her. So here was her logic: she'd been slacking on her work for The Silent One, and Mick had found her some perfect prey. She wasn't just following him. She was cashing in.

The graveyard's spirits surrounded her as she went outside.

"Which way did that car go?"

They gestured. She rolled a stolen motorcycle from behind the tomb and started it up. Dying in a crash on an icy road wouldn't be any worse than falling from a cliff.

The wind lashed with a desperate cold even before she hit the main road. Once there and up to speed, she could barely breathe. Mick didn't have much of a lead. Hopefully once she caught him she could ease up on the throttle. Every extra mile per hour pushed the dagger of wind deeper into flesh. Her face numb, her nose ice, she pushed forward, unrelieved at the set of taillights she was gaining on because it was too soon to have already caught up to him. No one else had a car that orange, though. And no one but Mick would be calmly driving the speed limit on a mission of vengeance.

She hung back, allowing some distance to build between them so he wouldn't think he was being tailed. After two turns, it started to look obvious. The third took him into the entrance to Lucky's Tavern, an Appalachian-style bar in an old log cabin that had probably been built in her time. She passed it, rounding a bend to put her out of sight, then she rode off the pavement into the woods and cut the engine.

Robbed of all body heat from the ride, she plunged into the woods on foot, wiggling her frozen fingers and pumping power into her legs. Ahead, the parking lot's light sparkled between the frost-coated tree trunks. She had to get there before Mick made a scene people might remember. She'd been to the tavern for dinner a few times. The people were nice enough, the food home-cooked. But she could see it might attract a shady character now and then, the kind Mick might be after. She emerged from the woods, crossed a used car lot, then passed a laundromat. At the edge of the tavern's lot, she slowed to an unhurried walk. Mick had backed his Pontiac into a spot at the side of the building, aiming toward the exit to the road.

She parked herself behind the car, against the tavern's log wall, close enough to the rear corner so she could slip behind it and out of sight should Mick emerge from the front. The chimney poured smoke above her, filling the air with a scent of fire and food that made her long to go inside. Voices rose behind her shoulder—the rear entrance. The low one Mick's. A gruffer, more aggressive one talking over him.

"—not going nowhere. So you tell that bi—"

A slap so biting it sounded wet. She shouldn't be so thrilled by it. This guy needed to be swiftly gutted so she could release her Helpers, not be smacked around. But maybe she could relax her need for efficiency a little, just this once. It was a special occasion to see Mick Svendsen dole out a little punishment to a guy who deserved it.

"I know you didn't just slap me, you piece of shit."

"You're goin' for a drive with me."

A glob of spittle hit the pavement. "Fuck off."

Waapikoona slipped behind a large cab pickup. Convince the guy to go for a drive—that was Mick's plan? Why, so he could give him a lecture in the car and then drop him off at home? Guys who beat up women and kidnapped children couldn't be politely asked to stop. They couldn't be reformed. They were tiny gears in the terrible machine that had rolled into her land and destroyed her language and culture before exterminating her people. Machine oil had leaked and coated the landscape with inequality and hate, not only against Native people but also against their own. It gobbled land with jaws of genocide and had only recently stopped actively working to exterminate the remaining Native people who had survived. But these little gears still turned, and if not broken to pieces, they might latch on to others and gain momentum. Racism and sexual assault were still a very real thing. Sneaky politics still a threat to what remained of Indian land. Native culture alive and well in small pockets that were still struggling to be heard, recognized, allowed the human rights they'd been promised. She remembered what these little gears could do with larger power, and she had to stop them.

Drawing her flint knife, she walked around the corner of the building and stabbed the guy under the ribs. He wheezed and lost his legs; she yanked the knife free and let him fall. On the ground he held his side, his body trying to cough and breathe but not quite getting either action right. Even though he was a piece of trash, she couldn't be inhumane about it, so she snaked an arm under his chin, lifted his head, and cut his throat.

She looked up at Mick standing utterly still above her. "What?"

He choked, putting a fist against his mouth. Throwing up might be good for him, might keep him in human form after what she was about to do.

"Don't shift. You need to stay human just a few more minutes." She uncurled her hand against the ground and released her Helpers. "And back up, they need space."

Mick was already backing up, straight into the side of the building. Already so close to the scent of running blood, the Helpers grew to working size quickly and started at the feet. She usually didn't like to watch, but she couldn't risk leaving Mick, who was glued, watching the scene with dead eyes like his mind had checked out. Maybe she should have warned him with more detail.

Watching her Helpers devour a corpse always felt like a dream. The unceasing snap of their jaws gobbled shoes, clothes, flesh, and bone so fast it seemed viewed in fast motion. As they ate they grew, their stubby bodies extending in length until they became so fat and bloated their legs sucked into their bodies, nearly disappearing completely. Teeth still sharp, they ate into the ground like giant earthworms and burrowed out of sight. Soon they'd return to home base, to The Silent One, to deliver the flesh. She'd have to be on the lookout for them later when they came back to her.

"What about his car?" Mick asked hoarsely, still gaping at the twin circles in the ground that had refilled with dirt behind each Helper.

She wrapped her bloody knife in a handkerchief and slid it into her inner coat pocket. "What about it?"

"It's—" He frowned, looking at the spot where the body had been like he'd just lost his thought.

"Let's go in and have a drink. People saw you leave with him and they need to see you back inside, before you've had enough time to kill and dump a body."

"I'm not—"

"You have to. And settle down. You have to act normal."

"I am actin' normal."

"Your hands are shaking."

He shoved them into his pockets but didn't budge when she started toward the door. "You just—they—"

"Come on, Mick." She hooked her arm in his and took a step, but it was like trying to move a tree. "You have to walk. This foot first." She nudged his ankle with hers. Once she got him going, he didn't stop until he'd plopped onto a barstool inside, looking at her like she was a stranger who'd just bumped into him. He needed to act normal or people would catch wind of something not right. "Mick."

"Don't—" He leaned his elbows on the bar like he'd just drained of all energy. "Please stop sayin' my name."

She flagged down the bartender and ordered two beers. Mick was about to collapse from shock, and now he was making pointless requests about his name. She had to dull his brain. When the bottles arrived she handed him one. "Cheers?"

"You kiddin'?"

"You're making too much of it. Bottoms up and you'll feel better. I'll drive you home."

He stared at her—and through her, somehow at the same time. His eyes reflected the tiny Christmas lights woven around the liquor bottles behind the bar. And suddenly— violently—she remembered that kiss in the tomb. A vicious tingle crawled through her from the memory of it or the anticipation of more. She realized then he'd somehow turned on his stool so she was straddling the space around his knee. Without contact it was an innocent position at a tightly packed bar. Without contact it was a toe-curling tease.

She lifted her leg over his knee, crossing it on top of her other one. Teasing him now would probably send him into cardiac arrest. "Do you want to order some food?"

"Food—after *that?*"

"It might settle your stomach."

He finished his beer in one long gulp. She handed him hers.

"Booth," he said, sliding off his stool. By the way he fell into the booth on the opposite wall and put his forehead on the table, she understood he wasn't so much looking for a quiet place to talk as he was trying to hide out.

"Please warn me if you're going to pass out."

"I'm goin' to pass out," he said to the floor.

"You want something harder than beer?"

He raised his head, threaded his fingers into his hair. "I want to go back a few minutes and stop you."

She leaned forward. "Your problem's fixed."

"That ain't how civilized people solve things."

A good, long look at his face told her he didn't know the baggage attached to that word. He was too far removed from it. And she was still too close to her past, to being called a godless savage, an animal. To being forcibly recultured by her home's invaders. "Civilized people—the ones who build countries on genocide and slavery? Tell me how they solve things."

"Just say 'you.' That's what you mean."

"Tell me how you solve things."

He straightened up like he'd just been called on, and he knew the answer but didn't want to give it. He drained half her beer, set it on the table too hard. "You need to get out of the past. This country's changed."

She held his eye in the most uncivil way she could. "Are you sure? I've seen the news."

"You think your kind didn't war? Didn't have slaves?" He stood. His voice was too loud. "Wouldn't have killed us all if you could?" He shoved her beer bottle back at her. "Go back to the hell you came from."

Ambient tavern noise crashed in, like Mick had been the dam holding it back and something had blown straight through. So many eyes and ears around them. This was the scene she'd come to help him avoid. She could speak back and bring this cusp of confrontation into the light, or she could play it cool, save what she wanted to say to him for later. Or she could bury it forever. She took a casual glance around, finding other diners had already turned back to their own conversations. If Mick raised his voice again, they'd notice something wasn't right. And now that he'd walked away, if she came back at him, she'd be the one causing a scene.

She watched him pay the tab at the bar. A gentleman, maybe. More likely he knew it would irk her since the beers were technically her treat. Then he went out the door. It was the second time he'd walked away from her tonight. She'd followed him once. She wouldn't do that to herself again.

After allowing a few minutes for Mick to get lost, she stepped into the night and raised her hood. Already too far into the parking lot to turn back undetected, she noticed Mick's car still parked in its spot, engine humming, exhaust pipes breathing steam into the cold air. The dashboard lights illuminated his pale face, head tipped back against the headrest, eyes closed. He couldn't be waiting for her, and a thought that pathetic needed to be doused fast before it infected her. She lengthened her stride, found her stashed motorcycle, and started it up.

The ride home to her tomb was a new kind of cold, one that not only sapped her body heat but also her strength. The might of her shivering wiggled the steering; she had to lock her arms to keep the motorcycle on the road. By the time she found the graveyard entrance, every muscle had seized and her cheeks were so chapped she mistook tears from the cold air for blood. She ditched the bike behind the tomb and headed to the entrance, telling herself the scent of her fire was only missing because her nose was too cold to smell it. Her fire hadn't gone out. She wouldn't have to shiver in the dark while she worked to rebuild it in a freezing stone tomb. She wouldn't find Spot frozen to death.

She didn't make it inside. Her graveyard had become overrun with cars and bodies. Human. Not undead. Very much alive and very unhappy with her. She backed away from one, collided with another. Struggling was useless. There were too many. *You've been sneaky, haven't you?* they said. *Well, we have you now, and you won't get away this time.*

Duct tape smacked over her chapped lips. Wrists bound behind her back. As she was shoved into the trunk of a Chrysler 300, she glimpsed Spot's white face in the woods, big eyes taking it all in.

Chapter 23

Mick's mind had surely warped. He'd watched a guy get his throat cut and die—barely—before being consumed by demon worm creatures that grew from palm-sized to human-sized before his eyes. He'd had a beer with the murderer instead of turning her in, because what would he tell the cops? Where would he say the body was? And what was his role in all of it?

All that fit, though, with everything else. The world had warped, not his mind. The real problem was bigger than demons and dead bodies. Because after all that, he was still thinking about the give of her lips against his. The nip from her teeth, the rush of perverse pleasure. His fingers sliding into her hair. He'd watched her casually kill a man, and he couldn't do anything but dwell on that damn kiss.

It was too late to go into Old Mae's and check on the kids. Too late to do anything but climb into his own bed. But he couldn't muster the strength to get out of the GTO once he parked at home, and now that he'd killed the engine the cold was seeping in fast.

A smudge of gray-white passed through the dark in front of the car's nose. He didn't have to look twice. It didn't matter what it was. He'd reached the end of his tolerance for supernatural events tonight, and his socket wrench was about to keep him from going over the edge.

When he got out of the car his gut said *stop*, so instead of swinging the wrench he lowered it. Waapikoona's dog barged into his legs, whining and flopping all over him, frantic. Which was strange—Mick had watched her cross the parking lot and disappear into the woods only to reappear a minute later on the road, the only person insane enough to ride a motorcycle on such a wintry night. She would've made it back to the cemetery by now, unless she decided to camp out somewhere warmer tonight. He couldn't see her leaving Spot out alone in the cold. She might be from Hell, but she wasn't that heartless when it came to the dog.

But what did he know? He had just met the woman. And tonight proved she had some bad habits he hadn't been previously introduced to.

He didn't care. Not one damn bit. The dog could sleep inside with him, and tomorrow if it didn't leave—well, then he'd have a new dog. He wasn't going back to that cemetery. The kids would keep him busy during his week off until Kari came back. If the weather thawed, he'd have them help him do some work on the GTO. He'd take them to the big junk yard in the city to hunt down some decent used tires and a stereo head unit out of a compatible Pontiac. Maybe he'd get lucky and find a GTO with a good tail light to replace his cracked one. Then he'd ask Amanda if she wanted to bring her kids for dinner. They could cook together and feed the whole pack like a family. The thought of it was so nice it put a dent in his chest, and he was too damn old to cry, but he was at the end. Something had to change.

"Inside," he told the dog, ushering with his leg. It only made the dog more frantic. "Quit that. You wanna freeze out here?"

Spot clamped down on Mick's pant leg and pulled. Mick didn't tug back. He wanted to spend his money on tires, not new jeans. Hollering might wake Old Mae and the kids. The socket wrench—no, he couldn't do that, couldn't even swing it as a threat. So he let the dog drag him a few yards before he was able to wiggle free. Spot took off in a hard sprint, making it into the deeper grass near the woods before he skidded to a stop and turned to face Mick.

The request to follow couldn't be any clearer. Well, too bad. Mick was done with all of it. Tonight and forever. He headed to his apartment's door. Spot beat him to it. This time it wasn't aggression he played but puppy eyes. The more Mick stared the more he saw. This dog didn't just want a warm bed or an ear scratch. He was begging for help—alone, afraid, desperate. Something about it reminded Mick…

That car. Is that a Chrysler 300?

Some people I pissed off.

People who want me dead and would love to find out about you.

The toughest woman Mick had ever met, reduced to fleeing in fear. That car had driven down his driveway looking for someone, and Spot might be trying to draw him away to safety. Mick looked up at the dark windows of Old Mae's house where his niece and nephew slept. He had to fight; he had to catch these people before they came back. He had to convince them to leave, like he'd planned to do to Leo Boyle. And the quickest and easiest way wasn't in a GTO limited by indirect surface roads and bad tires. The most efficient way was a bird's-eye view.

Mick unlocked his apartment's door and pushed it open. He pulled the zipper bag of demon guts from his pocket, stripped off all his clothes, and tossed them inside. One whiff of the guts sent his head spinning; he barely managed to get the zipper bag sealed before the ground tilted and he stumbled into the frozen grass, finding forward motion on bare feet that fell into a jog, a run, a pump of arms, of wings. Legs tucked, ground falling away, a streak of white dog his beacon, the night no longer so dark.

THE CEMETERY NOW a parking lot, cars shining like melting ice. The swarm of human bodies, the noise of shouts. Not friendly but combative. His circling caught by a pair of eyes, he dove into the woods, found a branch with a view. Bodies slipped into cars, slamming doors, starting engines. Like a funeral procession they moved out, a shiny, segmented serpent through the trees.

He followed.

Prey flitted through the forest beside the road below him. His energy waned. He craved. But he pushed on. Two darting bodies stood out to his eye—not just prey creatures but enemies. The world's litter he needed to clean up. But he followed the shiny snake, the true enemy to both his worlds.

And when the cars slowed, those two darting demon bodies stopped with them and hid just out of their view. But not his. Rays of sun trickled over the horizon in colors he couldn't name. Cars unloaded. Demons watched and waited at the periphery. An opening trunk threw a reflection of sunlight into the sky and a woman rolled into view. Her knife sunk into a stomach. Her hand ripped a holstered pistol free. Bodies swarmed to her like ants, and Mick released a screech into the sky and dove, ripping jugulars like fish plucked from a lake. On his sixth he missed, his talons no longer sharp, his wings unfit for flying. He rolled like a ball into the brush beside the gravel lot and found fingers that could dig into earth and knees that could crawl away.

Vision dulled and darkened; sound swelled with new understanding of gunshots and language he could understand. He crawled around a thick tree trunk and pressed his back against it, hard bark chafing his bare skin as he tried to make out who was shouting and what they were saying. Twigs pricked his feet but they were quickly growing numb in the biting cold. Each slight shift of air felt like a deeper freeze that sliced and chapped his skin. The clothes thing he'd failed to plan for. Transportation back, too, since he wasn't sure how he'd shift again without the demon guts or if he even had power to do it. He could barely stay upright on human legs.

A lone gunshot split the air, reducing the voices and sounds of conflict to wind whispering through the trees. Mick had to know who the last one standing was. His only way home was one of those cars, and if Waapikoona was dead, he'd have to surprise the guy, get a set of keys, and get out. *Waapikoona dead*, echoed in his thoughts, but he was awash in adrenaline and couldn't let that concept in just yet.

He spotted a thick downed branch, rotted on one end. Rising to his feet blackened his peripheral vision; he took a gulp of air and breathed himself away from a blackout. Stomping the rotted end of the branch gave him a perfect sized club but the sound of it ruined his chance of surprise. He steadied his legs and pushed from the underbrush onto the gravel lot. Headlights from idling cars angled harsh white light in several directions. Club in hand, he was weary but alive and not going down without the most savage of fights.

Blood splashed cars like graffiti and painted the gravel. Bodies lay twisted and limp. Waapikoona rose from behind a Chrysler's hood, wiping her knife against her jeans. There was something not right about how she held herself. Contorted, almost. Shoulders stiff, chin at an odd tilt, eyes reflecting in a way like she'd been crying, or drunk, or high. She sheathed her knife and covered her face with both hands. As she drew her hands away from one another, she took a long breath in and opened her eyes. All oddity vanished, like she'd woken from sleepwalking and reclaimed her waking self. She blinked a few times, her gaze now on Mick.

"Hi," she said.

Mick wasn't sure his human voice would work. "Hi."

Blood leaked from torn skin across her cheekbone. Above it, her eye swelled, a dark smudge in the white. "Stay there. I'll get you some clothes." She surveyed the battlefield until her eyes landed on a guy about Mick's size. Mick didn't want to wear clothes soaked in another man's blood, but what choice did he have? So when she tossed him a pair of jeans and combat boots he put them on. She moved to a different body for a shirt that wasn't so gored up. Then she went after a jacket, and Mick stopped her—somehow he'd stepped in close enough to take her arm, pull her up from her body-pillaging crouch. Up close he saw another trickle of blood from a torn earlobe. Her nose had bled too but since dried. Her lip was cut in the corner, and her neck was chafed red and starting to turn purple where fingers had obviously gripped hard.

She gazed at him, surprised. Through her coat sleeve he could feel her pulse in her arm, kicking against his hand, gaining speed. His shifted gears in response, and it didn't seem to matter he was tired, starved, and probably in a state of shock. He could smell her on the air between them. She was alive. She was beautiful. He wanted her so deeply, more than warm clothes or a ride home, more than food or sleep. She wasn't pulling away from his grip on her arm. Her eyes anchored so calmly on his, like she could feel the impossible tug between them, like she was as hooked as him. And she had no fight left to get away. She released a slow, resigned breath, and Mick breathed it in.

He closed his eyes. He was red-hot, wicked with desire. If he didn't release her arm, he'd be taking her against the closest car in a sea of corpses. She'd risen from the underworld, and he'd go there right now to be with her.

"You have blood all over your mouth," she whispered. With the way she'd tucked her top lip in, she looked far from disgusted. She looked hungry.

"I think I might've torn some of these guys' throats out."

"I saw that."

He relaxed his hold on her arm. Slid it up to shoulder, to neck, to jaw. She took a step against him as if he'd commanded it, her eyes still on his. Docile, submissive, waiting for something they both wanted but she'd granted him the power to give. He wanted to fuck her. He wanted to cry. He wanted to wrap an arm around her, hold her against him, never let her go.

Her steady patience slid into a dare. It always seemed to go that way, and for the first time Mick recognized this act of giving in wasn't what it seemed. She wasn't submitting; she was waiting for him to do what she'd ordered. What she expected. His next move would be a response to her silent command. Stepping against his body wasn't a surrender, it was a tightening of the chain she'd clamped around his neck.

Sucker, he thought. He didn't care. He liked it too much. And now that he'd figured it all out, he liked it even more.

But hadn't there been something wrong with her just a minute ago? If she'd been on something, she'd sobered up fast. And just how does one woman clean up a whole group of men so efficiently? Mick needed to know something, but he wasn't sure what. "What's wrong with you?"

As soon as he asked he heard how stupid it sounded. She was undead, a creature from the underworld. Everything was wrong with her.

"I need to drag the bodies into the shadow so my Helpers can clean up."

"What about the cars?" he asked. It was an echo of their earlier conversation at the tavern, and he felt the dried blood crack along his mouth as he smiled. He'd turned evil, and right now, he didn't want to stop it.

"What about them?" She couldn't deliver the line as blankly as she had at the tavern, and he knew his killer's smile had something to do with that, along with his withholding of the kiss she seemed so breathless for but one he wasn't going to give. Not here, not now. Because once he did he'd want more, and he'd regret it once he found his morals again.

He wanted her in his bed. With his good mind, his right mind. Not the one that'd just come out of the skull of a bloodthirsty raptor.

"Try not to leave any prints," she said, stretching her sleeves over her hands like mittens.

How often did she do this? Mick yanked a sock hat off a nearby body to use as a mitt and helped her drag the corpses into the darkest shadow. She raided pockets for cash. Her demons bounded over and latched onto the bodies, sawing through them like living, walking tree chippers before Mick had a chance to clear out. More blood splatter was the last thing he needed. He avoided all glimpses of faces and had to remind himself that these guys had no problems locking a woman in a trunk of a car. And who knew what they'd planned to do to her next? Being murdered themselves was a likely part of that scene. They'd chosen this life. And technically Mick hadn't murdered anyone. All the credit went to his other form.

"Pick a car," she said when her demons had drilled into the ground and away.

Mick surveyed the cluster of vehicles. "Charger."

She opened its door and slid into the passenger seat. Mick got in the driver's and found her separating a thick wad of pillaged cash into two piles on her lap. Watching her search pockets and cars had made it all too concrete, and he didn't want to dwell on it. She'd found so much money it didn't even look real.

"Half this is yours."

"I don't—"

"Shut up and drive, or you're getting all of it."

"Yes, *ma'am.*"

He felt the blaze of her glare and started the car, loving it all too much.

Once they made it back to Wyona, Mick became very aware of dawn lighting the road, empty except for their very stolen car. He'd been up all night, but he was too alive to feel sleepy, and now his nerves had come online, turning every parked vehicle into a police cruiser.

"Your place," she said. "I'm keeping the car." It was the first thing she'd said the whole drive.

He headed to his place, hoping Old Mae and the kids would still be in bed so they wouldn't spot the unfamiliar

Charger coming down the driveway. Not that it mattered. It could be hers. They didn't have to know it wasn't.

After pulling in behind the GTO, he took the cash she handed him. He could give it to a church, a charity. He didn't have to spend it himself. "You're welcome to come inside and get some sleep—"

"I can't."

"Don't be stupid. That mausoleum will be a freezer."

"I'm not going there."

"Then where?"

She held his eye a long moment then got out of the car and came around to his side. He unbuckled and got out; she slid into his spot behind the wheel. "There's something I need to do."

He remained in the open door so she couldn't shut it. "Right now?"

"Yes."

"Somethin' more important than a shower and some sleep?"

"It's ... urgent."

To go the entire drive and not say a word about this something—well, maybe it wasn't Mick's business. But he'd just done the unthinkable for her. Her business had become his. And anything urgent was probably dangerous and might lead another gang of guys down his driveway. God almighty— was this night for real?

"It doesn't concern you, Mick."

Funny she'd say that. It sounded almost like she was trying to convince him it didn't, when she knew herself it sure as hell did.

"How 'bout you tell me what it is, and I decide if it concerns me." His jaw had frozen in the cold. All he had on were the stolen bloody clothes and ill-fitting boots, and even though the sun was above the horizon, it would take a good several hours before the rays would chase the night away. And what he'd just witnessed, what he'd just *done*, was starting to feel less like a distant dream and more like a nightmare. If he'd stayed in eagle form, maybe he could dismiss it as some episode that didn't much concern him. But he'd been there. As a human. He'd dragged dead bodies. He was wearing their clothes.

"Mick—"

"And I'm real cold, so come inside." He snatched the car key before she could reply and headed inside his apartment door, where he immediately stripped. It didn't matter if she came in before he'd found new clothes. She'd seen him naked so many times already. He dumped the stolen clothes in a trash bag and stashed it under the kitchen sink. He'd have to find somewhere to burn them later.

In the bright bathroom light, he took a look at his face in the mirror. It wasn't him but a ghoul. Gray circles under his eyes, skinned chin, dried blood around his mouth his hasty shirtsleeve cleanup in the car had missed. He washed up and came out, found Waapikoona inside, staring at him. He went to his bedroom for clothes.

She came in behind him. "I'm going to dig up my sister's bones." She held out her hand. "Now give me the car key."

He didn't have it and couldn't remember where he'd left it. Exhaustion was creeping over him, slowing his brain function. She had mentioned a sister before. They'd died together. He didn't remember much else, if there was anything. "Why?"

"No reason."

"That's a crap lie. You must need sleep worse than me."

"I don't need sleep. I need to get on the road." She didn't withdraw her hand.

"To where?"

She sat down on his bed, closed her eyes. The swelling had gone down, leaving a purple-red bruise under one eye spreading toward her temple. "Illinois. Can we not do this right now?"

"Fine by me. You want the bed or the couch?"

She opened her eyes to give him a look that might have made him pause a week ago. Her droopy-lidded exhaustion wasn't ghoulish like his, it was sinister. He couldn't let her get behind the wheel. It didn't matter where she came from or how many times she'd come back to life. She was still in a human body that had just taken a harsh bashing and hadn't had any sleep.

"If they find out what we just did, they'll go straight there, beat me to it."

"No one's gonna find them cars in the middle of nowhere. Not for a while, anyway."

"But if they did—"

"Who?"

She held his gaze long enough to prove a steely unwillingness to answer, and he was too tired to push.

"Stay. We'll sleep a few hours, and then I'll go with you." What was he saying? He couldn't go anywhere with her.

"You can't."

He could. It was Saturday, which meant a U-Fill shift, but he could finally redeem the favor Brenda owed him for covering her shifts for weeks when her mother was in hospice. She'd only have to work one double, maybe two, depending how far into Illinois they had to go. He was off Virgil's shop for a whole week. And Old Mae could keep the kids. They wouldn't need a ride anywhere until school on Monday, and if he wasn't back, Amanda could act as carpool. He needed to call her and check on her.

A cold jolt pinged through him. Leo Boyle—dead. Just like that. How had this become his life?

Waapikoona swayed, her eyes rolling a little, fatigue nearly taking her down. She righted herself, bracing her arms against the mattress, so stubborn it was almost cute.

"You get the bed," Mick said. He went into the kitchen and rifled through his first aid box for a butterfly bandage. When he went back in the bedroom, she had succumbed, flat on her back on the bed, boots and coat still on. She didn't fight the bandage he carefully applied to her split cheek. He slid her boots off, which prompted her to struggle out of her coat. It was tempting to threaten her in some way should she attempt to sneak out like last time, but he didn't want to plant the idea in her half-asleep mind. So he said nothing and fell onto the couch, hoping her exhaustion would keep her glued to the bed until he woke.

CHAPTER
24

Thundering footsteps above his head brought Mick out of sleep gradually enough for him to revisit the night before, determine it was too messed-up to confront, and cover his head with a pillow for a second attempt at sleep.

It failed. As soon as he noticed how quiet his apartment was, aside from the children about to break through his ceiling, he scrambled off the couch and into his bedroom. In the windowless dark, she slept, one arm flung over her forehead, her ankles twisted in the sheets. He reached for the doorknob to seal her in so she could rest, but the shift in light slanting into the room caught in a reflection on her cheeks.

Curiosity walked him into the room. Manners kept him from spying too closely. But he didn't need to be overhead to understand what he saw were tears, one line from each eye running down her temples.

He had to fix it. He didn't know why. He didn't even know how. But it didn't just feel like he'd stumbled across something broken; it felt like he'd broken something. Like he was broken himself. If he backed out of the room, he'd have to pretend he hadn't seen it.

"Rise and shine," he said.

She slowly opened her eyes at the ceiling, like she knew at once he was there but was making an effort not to acknowledge him.

"Breakfast?" he asked.

She brushed her hands across her cheeks, removing the evidence.

"Bad dreams?" It came out easily with no hint of how much he was dying to know what they were about. Murdering people? Her past? Her dead sister?

Her answering glare told him it was none of his business. Well, she was wrong. She was the one who kept showing up in his life. He was the one trying to get away. And right now, he wasn't sure why. Seeing her in his bed felt right. Every unexpected encounter with her like it was somewhere he'd chosen to be.

She kicked her feet free from the tangled sheets and sat up, gathering her hair. "I have to go."

"I said I'll come—"

"No. I'm used to being alone."

So was he. Surrounded by people for most of the day but so very alone. Mick couldn't say he was used to it. He'd grown sick of it. And this—whatever it was—felt like the cure for that, as twisted as it all was. Being around her only made it more pronounced, more promising. Which is why he'd pledged to stay away. She'd risen from the dead. She carried two man-eating demons around in her hand and cut a guy's throat with no remorse. More importantly, she had a major, and somewhat validated, hatred of his Viking blood. Nothing between them would ever work out.

But what if he gave himself one more go, one last lap? Go with her to Illinois then swear her off. Forever.

"I'm goin' with you."

"Why would you do that, Mick?" She picked at a spot of dried blood on the knee of her jeans.

It didn't seem like a question that needed to be answered. "If you want a shower, I can wash those for you upstairs."

"Don't like to be reminded of what you did last night?" No smile, not even in her eyes.

He had no idea if she was flirting, but at this point he didn't care. "I didn't do nothin'. But if your conscience is feelin' guilty, I could help take your mind off all that."

She raised her eyebrows the slightest. "By doing what?"

"Cook you a nice breakfast and wash your clothes." He grinned.

She stood, pulling her shirt up and over her head before Mick could even step back. Her jeans, unbuttoned, unzipped, she wiggled them down her thighs to the ground. The view of half-revealed breasts, of muscled navel and soft hips— Mick took a breath then, common sense telling him this is where she'd stop. Down to her pale yellow bra and silky silver bottoms was good enough to prove her point of who could tease best. It was plenty for Mick, who had pushed his limits of temptation and knew the next time he'd lose, he'd be the one to so willingly give in.

But she didn't stop. The bra was off; the bottoms were sliding down those long legs and meeting the jeans on the floor, and Mick had to step back, had to get his malfunction-ing lungs working again before he choked. Naked women weren't a new thing. He'd seen his share. He liked them all equally—until now. He'd never liked them as much as this.

Bending for her socks, she clutched his arm to steady herself as she removed them one at a time. Mick knew it had to be normal speed, but what he was seeing was slow motion and in eagle vision, tiny details brought into light, analyzed, processed, saved for use later in some future hunt. It was so much data he was glad the bedroom light was off and all he had was the light streaming in from the other room. Any more and his head might explode.

"There you go." She dumped her gathered heap of clothes into his arms and left him there, stupid and nearly drooling. And counting to ten before turning around so he wouldn't catch a glimpse of her nude backside heading through the door because that'd be too much.

It wasn't his head that was about to explode.

MICK ENTERED THE thawing day with a feeling he'd forgotten to do something. He couldn't remember the last time he'd had a real day off, one that could be spent wasting time with a strange woman on an even stranger road trip. Most days off were spent on chores and non-work work. Greeting a true vacation day made everything feel upside down. Especially this day, with its midwinter springtime sun that had turned the ground to slop and coaxed the birds into the trees. When she caught him looking at them, she asked, "Hungry again already?"

"Funny." He locked his apartment door behind them. He wasn't sure if golden eagles ate smaller birds. It was always the little scurrying animals he was spotting on his flights. That—and the demons.

Her black eye looked worse today as black eyes often do. A half circle around her eye had filled with purple, the socket dark against her skin. The scab on her eyelid and abrasion on her cheek set the whole thing off. There was no not noticing it, and he knew what he'd be labeled as by every person who saw them. At least he still had the scabbed-over chin. Maybe they'd just look like a matching pair of troublemakers instead of a domestic assault. Mick hoped they wouldn't need to go out in public together.

He'd talked to Brenda about taking his U-Fill shifts. She'd even offered to check in on Pop, an unexpected offer too helpful not to take. He still had to talk to Old Mae about babysitting and say goodbye to the kids, and he wasn't sure he wanted to bring a murderer up into the house with him. He offered her the Charger key. "Warm up the car and I'll be back in a couple minutes."

On second thought, no. She'd drive off without him. He'd already extended his arm though, and she'd placed her hand underneath his, waiting for the key to drop.

When it didn't, she looked at him. "Oh, dangerous store clerk face. I promise I won't steal anything." She smiled, an arrow into his heart.

Instead of dropping the key, he lowered his whole hand against hers, the key sandwiched between them like a bargain made. If she tried to make a break for it, he'd catch her. "My GTO is faster."

"So are your wings."

He let go. She left her hand in the air, key perched on top, waiting for his next move. Her breath steamed the morning sunlight between them. On her face was the look of a woman who expected a kiss, who wanted a kiss. It couldn't be nearly as much as he wanted to give one. But he stood there and let it build as retaliation for what she'd done to him earlier.

She made a good point. He didn't need her trust. In eagle form he could find her anywhere. If she was right, it was his duty to seek out and destroy creatures of the underworld, to keep the upperworld clean. And it didn't matter whether she was right or not—he felt it, as sharply as he felt the need to kiss her. If she took the car and ran, hunting her and killing her would simply be his job done well.

"Just a little road trip," he told the kids. They'd found a chest of old toys in one of the spare bedrooms and were dividing them between the two of them. "You two be good for Old Mae."

"Can Spot stay with us?"

The dog had somehow invited himself in last night, and all the cats of the house were sulking. "If that's okay with Old Mae."

"It was okay with her before."

"Well, there ya go." He bent so Janie could give him a strangling neck hug. It was a trap. She wouldn't let go. "You're killin' me, little birdie." He faked a cough.

She pulled back. Mick saw in her sleepy brown eyes how much she wanted her mother, and he felt a tug against her, demanding he stay until Kari came back. It was all in his head. He was no substitute just as Old Mae wasn't, and it didn't matter which one of them stayed with the kids; the end result was they'd still be missing their mother. Guilt grew the more he ignored it, and he couldn't let that happen. "You want me to stay?"

Janie shrugged.

"Is that a yes or a no?"

She shrugged again.

"You just want your mom."

She nodded. Mick drew her in again, let her strangle-hug him to near death. "She'll be back real soon. Couple days. 'Kay?"

Doug came to the rescue. "Janie, Mom don't let us eat cookies for dinner. And I think Old Mae said she's gonna make brownies this time."

Janie released Mick to check Doug's face to see if it was a lie.

"She said we can stay up late as we want again. And you can sleep with Spot."

Behind Janie's head, Mick gave Doug an appreciative thumbs-up. Then he got himself out of there before he caved. Staying would only ease his own guilt. It wouldn't help Janie.

Waapikoona had taken the driver's seat in the Charger—a surprise he could work with. Driving away from those kids demanded a power he might not have. He slid into the passenger side and buckled up.

"What's that face?"

He could pretend to not know what she meant, but why? He could guess his expression matched his need to punch a wall, and there was no fix for it. "Children's diseases," he said. "Fuck 'em."

"All of them, or a specific one?"

"All. You gonna drive or what?"

"Not until you get in your car and follow me. We need to dump this car on a road somewhere, and I'd rather not have to walk the rest of the way."

"Since when is that the plan?"

"Since I made it just now."

"I ain't drivin' my car across the state on bald tires to do whatever illegal crap you got planned."

"Then you're not coming. Get out." She put the car in reverse and looked at him, waiting for him to leave.

Now he was sure his face matched his need to tell her to get lost for good. Take her stolen blood-spattered car and get the hell out of his town before he shifted, ripped out her throat, and gutted both her pocket demons. Before he carried out instinct and duty and set the world a little more right.

If only it were that simple. Without her, a new, vivid part of his world would go gray. Whatever had been supplying the invigorating breaths of oxygen would deflate. He had to admit that. Someday he might find a suitable click of connection with a woman, but it would never be like this, the perfect match of OEM parts. He'd have to force the fit, maybe rig it a little. It would never match up clean, never feel exactly right. She wasn't just a selection from a shelf of compatible pieces. She was the only part machined just for him. He didn't just feel it. He knew it.

But getting out of the car, even if just to get inside his and follow, would be her win. Her commands, his obedience. Right now he was in no mood for that. "You drive away without me, I'll hunt you down."

"And do what, Mick?"

He responded with a slow shake of his head, a lazy shrug. Nonchalant and mocking, the best threat of all. If his bird self was doing the hunting, it was kind of up to him, not the man she expected to answer. The smile he felt on his face must've come from that bird, because it wasn't his, didn't feel like his. Terrified him just a little. And got his heart beating hard enough to make him question how long he was going to last before he proved their physical fit was just as perfect as their mental one.

The thought leaked from his head into the space between them, ripening the air with oxygen-dissolving chemicals. She shifted the car back into park, a slow deliberate motion that made it look like her mind was somewhere else. Her lips parted for more breath like Mick wasn't the only one about to suffocate. A vibrating, parasitic creature had invaded his stomach. Each time he noticed it, the thing was flitting around with worsening frenzy. Today it was out of control.

He was in love. So stupidly in love. He had to get out of it.

"Maybe…" she shifted her body to face him "…we should go back inside and handle this. Get it out of our system."

If her way of handling it was the same as his, she wouldn't be purged from his system, she'd be implanted. He knew that with the same certainty that told him he was in love to begin with. It would only lead him to want more, want it all. Even if she was the perfect fit for him, she didn't fit his life. And the creature she'd woken in him didn't fit either. As exhausting and pathetic as his normal life was, he wanted it back.

But not just yet. One more weekend. Two more days with her.

He opened his door. "I need to fuel up. Meet you at the U-Fill."

The vibration in his stomach spread to his legs when he got out, making them clumsy and heavy and unwilling to bend as he got in the GTO. What they really wanted to do was walk him inside, dragging her by the hand behind him. Inside, he'd kiss her just like he had before. She'd grapple for control, and he wouldn't let her have it. Not until he was ready. And then, near the end, he'd give in. He'd turn on his back and let her dominate him.

He stabbed the GTO key into the ignition and turned. The engine was supposed to pull him back to reality but it wasn't enough to dissolve images of Waapikoona handing him her bundle of clothes, of her fire-lit eyes watching him dress in that mausoleum, of her lips wet from his after that kiss, of his feather in her hair.

Chapter
25

Several hours on the road did nothing to mute Waapikoona's desire to be sharing space with Mick. It didn't matter where. His cozy apartment, the icy woods, a damp cave full of clawed demons. The appeal was all him. Years ago she'd have hated herself for it, but now she'd lived long enough among his kind to see it as something simpler than a punishment or inconvenient streak of rebellion. It was simply bad luck. And she knew bad luck was just bad circumstance allowed to get out of control. All she needed to do was exert control. Turn the bad luck good.

She checked the Charger's rearview mirror and there he was behind her as he had been the whole time. Some misguided part of her had assigned comfort to that orange Pontiac trailing her for hours, and she couldn't digest it. So there it sat, a lump in her stomach. Unexplainable, unsettling, a comfort that made her uncomfortable. Her ancestors' judgment weighed on her, but should it? Why care so much what they thought when she didn't care what her living people thought? These times she lived in were different. She hadn't admitted that to Mick, but since it had come up she had accepted it herself. In her time, being followed so deliberately by Mick would be a completely different thing than it was now.

A hundred miles outside of St. Louis, she steered to the shoulder and shut off the engine. Mick pulled in behind her. She left the key in the Charger and joined him, ignoring the gush of feverish excitement brought by meeting his eyes as she slid into his worn leather seat. Sometimes she couldn't help herself. She'd lived so long avoiding any type of connection with his kind, and here she was overdoing it.

Okay, maybe this was some kind of punishment.

"Buckle up," he said. His amused tone and half smile acknowledged something else: she'd been caught staring. He knew what she wanted, and he was going to withhold it just like he withheld that second kiss in the tomb. Well, fine. The longer he waited, the bigger her victory when he finally gave in.

Back on the road, the city grew around them. Lone gas stations were replaced with shiny hubs of shopping and food. Large glass office buildings stretched enclosed walkways across the interstate. The highway gained lanes and cars.

"I can't get over how close these people drive," Mick said, glancing in his mirror at the van that slid in behind him. "I think that guy just skimmed paint off my bumper."

Waapikoona could never get over how many people could pack into one area. She braced herself against a sudden stab of homesickness for her first life in her uncrowded village. For dirt paths traveled by foot, for the peace of a close-knit community sharing land. Open, borderless, respected, free.

"Dang it," he said. "That was our turn."

"There's no turn until we cross the river."

"I didn't want to drive through downtown."

"Small-town boy afraid of the big city?"

"Just not up for gettin' carjacked. You wanna drive, since you know so much?"

She felt the squeeze of white civilization tighten around her throat. She cracked her window for air. Through the glass, red-brick row houses crowded the highway, packed nearly on top of one another. She'd accused him of being afraid but she was the one about to crack. She didn't like modern cities and they didn't like her, but there was no way this one was going to put its foot on her throat without her standing up to face it. "Get off at this next exit."

"What for?"

"Food."

"You don't just pick a random highway exit in St. Louis…" He checked her face, finding exactly what he seemed to expect. "Unless you're an Indian witch who carries killer demons, I guess."

"Or a merciless Thunder-Being with a taste for human throats."

He downshifted and took the exit, skipping several gears so the engine roared. The car was mouthing off so he didn't have to. At the red light she assessed their surroundings and found herself face-to-face with the OPEN sign on a tire shop. "Pull in here."

"That ain't food."

"I'm buying you new tires. Pull in."

"No way I'm lettin'—"

"Light's green. Do it."

The driver behind them tapped the horn. Mick found first gear and aimed his tight-eyed annoyance at her. Should she tell him it only got her fantasizing how she could irritate him further? And once she achieved it, how she'd so quickly undo it? Anger into pleasure, combat into passion.

Fierce, pissed-off Mick turned sedate, lustful, wanting. She craved that exchange of power, how languid he became, how zoned in and attentive. And when he so easily followed command and parked in front of the tire shop, she struggled not to show how badly she wanted to grab him by the collar and kiss him.

"You got any idea how much a set of tires for this car's gonna set you back?"

She leaned to dig under the seat for the money she'd hidden. Hopefully the purchase would eat through a couple stacks. It wasn't good driving around with so much cash in one spot. Police didn't like that. Thieves did. She didn't want either to find it before she could spend it. She unfolded bills, stacking them on Mick's leg. "Will that cover it?"

He gripped the wheel and looked away from her, out the window at the cars passing on the street. "I can't believe this," he mumbled.

It was the closest thing to a yes she was going to get. She got out of the car. He followed, shoving the cash into his jeans pocket. "I don't just trust anyone with my car."

"What's the worst that could happen?"

"Damaged rims. Bent frame. Any kind of—"

"Be daring, Mick. It feels good."

He exhaled frustration, like he was about to explain something to an impatient child. "Daring might cost money I don't have."

She poked him in the pocket. "There's more where that came from, if you're okay owing me."

He stopped, his hand on the shop door ready to pull. "Owe you what?"

Wind flipped his hair, fanning it in a way that made him look boyish and cute while he delivered the blackest of looks. On the road they'd caught up to gray clouds that blocked all sense of that warmth shining down from Wyona skies. Now she saw they'd found wind, too, and a temperature that was at least ten degrees chillier. The tops of his ears already tinged red by the cold, next would be his nose. Then cheeks and lips and she'd have no choice but to kiss him to warm him up. Words weren't needed to explain what was owed, what was overdue. He knew as well as she did by the tight way he held her eye as she held his. That black look had been summoned for protection, to mask the pressing, inescapable desire that disturbed the air between them. She didn't want to name something if there was any chance it would influence what plans he already had in his head. She wanted to find out what he'd give her.

"Owe me lunch." It didn't sound nearly as innocent as it had in her head.

At the counter inside, Mick talked tires with the mechanic for so long Waapikoona went back outside to look around. If it was English, it was vocabulary she'd never learned. One thing was absolutely clear: Mick was being both picky and frugal, which didn't at all fit with being daring. The man just couldn't break free from that mold, and she couldn't stand there and listen. It annoyed her. It intrigued her. Witnessing the power of his character, his soul, his inner Thunder-Being driving him toward righteousness—it was too much. Respect and admiration she reserved for those who deserved it, not his kind. Not the invaders, the settlers, the murderers. Not their children, grandchildren, great-grandchildren. She couldn't give Mick a free pass just for being part Thunder-Being. He was part *them* too.

She raised her hood and walked to the edge of the parking lot, surveying the street for someplace to eat. When she heard the shop door open and close behind her, she stayed in place, forcing away the tingly need to turn around and steal a glimpse as he crossed the lot. She needed to stop looking at him. Stop enjoying what she saw. End this warmth of liking before it turned into something worse.

He stopped beside her, their coats brushing together like a long stolen kiss. "Burgers or tacos?"

"That's our only choice?"

"It's all I can see from here. Wanna walk?"

She took off without answering. She didn't know why she hadn't just taken the stolen Charger all the way herself, left Mick back at his home and never looked back. Here he was, catching up, now walking beside her. And fine, she'd use him for a ride to the site. Once she got her sister's bones, she'd send him off for good. But why wait until then? She could steal her own car and drive away right now.

Ahead, he turned around. Said her name. She hadn't realized she'd stopped, and with her name so fresh on his lips, she couldn't get herself to move just yet. He'd put on the knit hat he kept in his coat pocket. Navy blue tugged so close to his eyes made them light up like blue flames. His kind called her looks exotic. He was made of glacial blue ocean and sharp white ice. *He* was exotic.

He was gorgeous.

And she hadn't thought it the day she'd met him in that parking lot. Something had turned her, had knocked her off-center. She took a breath—behind it, in the space that should have been an exhale was the sensation of falling. He closed their separation with a few quick strides, grabbed her by the coat, said her name again.

She looked at him, begging. *Kiss me.* So she didn't have to kiss him. The crime should be on his hands, not hers. And where was that exhale? His eyes, a frozen blue, an arctic ocean. He was speaking but she couldn't hear. She'd gone halfway into the realm where she existed when she let The

Silent One possess her. Alive but inoperative; present but uninvolved. Mick dropped back and away, bending down, reaching for the nearest object—a light pole—for support as he appeared to be losing the stability of his body as it prepared to change. She could kiss him to bring him away from the edge of a shift, but she couldn't kiss him, not again, not ever. One more time and she'd never return to herself. She knew this now.

She kicked him in the shin. He went down to one knee, shaking his head as he blew out breath that rose in the cold, both hands on the ground now. She found her exhale and sucked in, air freezing all the way through to her toes.

"What the—" He looked up at her. Those eyes. Those wind-stung cheeks.

"Sorry. I think I need to eat."

"I thought you said you don't eat."

She offered him a hand, which he took. His grip sent a warm wave through her, and she instantly regretted it. No more physical touch. No more looking into his eyes. No more Mick.

BUYING NEW TIRES hadn't turned Mick daring, but having them sure did. "Testing them out" had also turned him into a show-off and a spectacle on the road that attracted many admirers. He'd also gained a new smile, and Waapikoona had to twist in her seat to avoid a glimpse of it. She needed to ditch the man and his tires, but the thought was like a funeral she dreaded attending.

"I'll pay you back," he said once he settled down.

"I don't want it. None of it was mine anyway."

His silence was so loaded she wished she'd kept quiet. His phone navigation interrupted with driving directions, and he moved over a couple lanes to be ready for the upcoming exit. It was great timing for a changed subject, but Waapikoona couldn't come up with a thing to say, and if she didn't soon, he was going to ask—

"Who were all those guys you killed?"

"You mean *we* killed?"

"Not we." He pulled his knit hat off, tossed it into the back seat. "You and a golden eagle."

"Denial. Nice. I like that."

"Who were they?"

She plucked his phone from the cup holder and checked the screen. Fifteen minutes until they reached the site. Fifteen minutes in which she could be telling him the truth or feeding him lies to get herself out of this.

"And how in hell did you do it? All those guys, and I heard gunshots. I don't care what you are. That's ... nuts."

"Unless a thunderbird shows up."

"Yeah, okay. But you didn't need the help."

"Then why did you come?"

"Just a wild guess you were in trouble. I—"

He caught it the same moment she did: The Gateway Arch, rising bright from the concrete of the highway, so close it was hard to believe this was the first glimpse. In the glint of stark winter sun, it appeared in white, not the silver steel she knew it to be, one side in shadow that set the brighter side off like a mirror. Skyscrapers clustered before it, separated by space and sky like a gathered audience.

"Wow, that's neat," Mick said. "Never seen that in person."

She had. She'd stood at its base and placed her hand upon its cold body, wondering how such a strange monument could exist so close to her home just a few generations after she'd left the earth the first time. To downplay what it stood for was to cope, which had made her helpless and angry. Jeremiah had tagged it with some derogatory phrase, escaping seconds before security wandered close. Such a cowardly thing, to sneak a mark onto some monument. So passive aggressive. She never understood why he bothered with such trivial things when they had the power to do so much more. All they needed was a little patience.

The cityscape now in full view, Mick had his hands full taking in the sight while keeping the Pontiac in the lane. He slowed for a ramp that elevated them off the ground, curving into a short merging lane where he had to hit the gas to squeeze into traffic. All at once the Mississippi stretched underneath them, a rushing brown living thing, impossibly wide. In the distance on the north, a cable bridge spanned shore to shore, sun lighting it so bright it glowed. A train crawled beside them on the other side, its bridge rusty and utilitarian, colored by blocky graffiti.

"Whoa, you seein' this? That's a big river."

He'd dropped his speed to stare, taking quick glances back at the road so he didn't drive them over the concrete barrier and straight into the muddy deep. Waapikoona wished they were on foot. Modern cars could get a person someplace fast, but the life and experience that were missed in that race just didn't seem worth it sometimes. She leaned forward, looking ahead for somewhere they could pull off to the side and relish the view with their feet on the ground, but the lanes were being squeezed down by construction cones, and Mick had already started moving out of the disappearing lane. There wasn't even a shoulder for an emergency stop. At the end of the construction they were well past the water, the river not even visible in the side mirror.

The moment was over. Not that she should care—she'd seen this river many times. She grew up near it. But Mick obviously hadn't. She wasn't sure he'd ever stepped foot outside of his little town. To experience a sight like this with him made it brand-new ... but no, she shouldn't. It wasn't a missed moment. It was better this way.

A sign welcomed them to Illinois. Her eyes stung but she couldn't wipe them, couldn't let him see her like this. Her people's land before they'd been forced to give it up. Her origins stolen and buried. The mounds so hazy in her memory plowed down, plowed over. Farms erected on the sacred burial sites. Houses built on her people's bones.

Maybe it wasn't exactly here. She couldn't remember and had no proof, but it was close enough to matter. She wasn't sure if she remembered real mounds or had just heard stories of them. Even if her people had lived a hundred miles farther into Illinois, a people very similar to hers had lived here at some point in time. This was her ancestors' land, and her heart wept.

"Sorry," he said. "Lost my thought there. What were—"

"Forget it." Truth or lies, she no longer felt like giving him anything.

"Them guys you killed. I need to know."

"No, you don't." She closed her eyes and reached for the hate she should have for him. She needed to hate him right now, and she couldn't find how.

"They friends of that guy who showed up at my house lookin' for the demon corpse?"

Interesting he'd make that connection so easily. Not that it was true. But it wasn't false either. She tried to remember what she'd told him about Jeremiah. She didn't want to contradict herself. "Yes ... and no."

"I figured maybe we'd be past vague answers."

He didn't like vague? She'd have to make it clear, then. "I'm not telling you about my problems."

"Why not?"

Because confiding in him would only do harm. She didn't need a friend. Right now she needed a driver. Later on she wouldn't mind a one-night stand. Then she'd recover her sister's bones, and she'd be gone. "I need to be able to hate you."

Without looking at her, he narrowed his eyes at the road. Contemplation, confusion, anger—it could be any or all three. She didn't care; she couldn't care.

Under his breath, he repeated it. "Hate me."

When he said it like that, it made her rethink the whole thing. She didn't like this new gray area he'd created, this heady uncertainty that made her question what she wanted in her life, made her think it wasn't so simple anymore.

He offered nothing more but an iron silence, hands readjusted on the steering wheel like he was settling in for a long silent drive.

In that moment as he closed himself off, she regretted everything. Every reckless, selfish decision, every fast call made in the vacuum of her own disconnected life. Going home with him that first day. Pursuing him after that. It was as pointless and trivial as Jeremiah marking the leg of the Arch with a tag in a language no one would know. She never really needed her Helper's body back from Mick. Now she saw it for the excuse it was. And she could go further: Dragging her sister off the cliff. Joining up with The Silent One. Killing in his name to fund a war for revenge.

Regret was something she'd died with, something she'd spent centuries with in the spirit world, something she'd been reborn with. Her relationship with it was so tired she hated herself for continuing it. Soon she'd have her sister's bones and they'd be revived. She'd rid herself of The Silent One.

Her regret would dry out in the new life she'd give her sister. She had to kill this regret with Mick. She didn't want it to tag along, didn't want to live with it any more.

"Stop it," she said.

He made no indication he heard her.

"Whatever you're doing. It's immature and pointless."

He looked over at her. Looked back at the road.

"I'll tell you, but I have to be able to trust you. I'll tell you everything."

CHAPTER
26

MICK WASN'T SURE he wanted to know everything. It'd be nice to be prepared if there were more hostile guys out there—and if they knew who he was and what he'd done to their friends. He'd love to know how to permanently turn off the shifting. And he wouldn't mind being educated on the more intimate parts of Waapikoona's body, even if it meant swearing her off after this day and not looking back.

Not if it meant getting caught up in any games. Or giving her any kind of platform to preach history at him again. Holding him accountable for the brutal stuff done centuries ago, whether he was descended from the guilty parties or not, it was absurd. He might be a hick, but he was no racist. He was no fan of slavery, genocide, invasion—any of it. And she'd have a hard time finding any American who was.

Or maybe she'd have an easy time. It didn't matter. It wasn't him, and she needed to back off.

He was relieved to hear his phone warning him of his next turn so he didn't have to respond to Waapikoona. Once they got out of the car he could face her the right way. He wasn't going to allow her to give him information freely, not if there was a chance he'd be sucked further in or get into any facts someone might want to kill him for knowing. He was going to ask questions, and she was going to answer.

She said, "Those guys—"

"Not now."

She angled toward him in her seat, giving him a deep look when she'd been avoiding his eye since they'd crossed the Mississippi. Good, let her get pissed. She'd already pissed him off. Now it was his turn.

MICK EXPECTED THE historic site of a massive Indian civilization to be more noticeable from the road, especially with how flat this state was. Without a road curving around swells and valleys like he was used to, he could see for miles. "Did I just pass it up?"

She said nothing. Which meant he did. But when he found a residential area to turn around in, she found her voice. "We have hours to kill."

Earlier, she'd produced a new set of earrings from her pocket and threaded them into her earlobes. They were beaded like the others, but these had a new feature: short, golden brown feathers that dangled from the beadwork like they'd been added later. He took a long look, determined they were his feathers, and suffered a silent, clenching heart attack as he answered her. "So we oughta check out the visitor center, then."

"Mick—"

He loved the irritation in her voice. He had no idea why. The fifteen minutes of cold silence between them had darkened her agitation but leveled his. And every corner gripped by his new tires raised the lumens on his mood. By the time he turned into Cahokia Mounds State Historic Site, his mood had been reborn. He'd question Waapikoona like the good cop. He wouldn't need to play bad cop. But not yet. This was a road trip, a mini vacation he'd never had. He planned to experience the hell out of it, disgruntled woman and all.

To his right earthen mounds covered in brown hibernating grass huddled in a small cluster. Set against the rolling hills of his southern Missouri home, they'd be a natural part of the landscape. Out here, rising independently out of flat Illinois farmland, they stood as human invention on display. Nothing about their looks proved their age. As far as he could tell from a glance, they could've been built last year by a crew with a couple Caterpillars and some dump trucks making a few passes.

He found a parking space at the empty end of the lot where they could have a view of the land if they did need to kill time. Then he got out, went around the car, and opened her door. It was the large mound on the opposite side of the road that had made him miss the turn-in. He thought he'd seen a set of stairs, and he wanted to climb to the top. Coaxing information out of Waapikoona would have to wait.

"I'm not going in there," she said.

"Well I ain't goin' alone. You want me to beg?"

She caught her smile, but not before it lit her eyes. "That's tempting."

"Please, ma'am. Do this lonely man the honor of your unholy company." He offered a hand. "Waapikoona, undead goddess—"

"Shut up." She took his hand, let him haul her out. Without the resistance he expected, the force he'd used was all wrong, and she ended up so close she'd raised a hand to stop herself from colliding with his chest.

His silliness fizzled away fast. It'd been an attempt to irritate her, to flaunt his sunny mood. Not play with her. Not get her pressed against him, resisting only to the point of breathtaking temptation. In the open front zipper of his coat, her hand slid sideways, across ribs, around him, opening herself up to him. Her other hand, still glued in his, he couldn't let go of even if she shook him off.

"Told you we should've gone inside to take care of this."

He had to swallow to find his voice. "Take care of what?"

That sliding snake of a hand moved up his chest, latched onto his collar. He got his own hand back, but all it did was free hers to put a second latch on his collar. But she didn't lean in. She was expecting him to.

The buildup in his groin had reached a point of fury. He felt himself splintering in two, one side powering up to fight it, another ready to part earth to be with her. But no, he wouldn't be played. His terms, not hers. He took a step back, control clamped hard onto every resisting body part. She let go.

His phone was ringing—for how long, he wasn't sure. He dug it out of his pocket, fumbling it on its way to his ear. Too late he realized who it was. "Amanda?"

"Mick, where are you at? The sheriff just left my place, asking about Leo—"

"Shit—I mean, what? What'd he want?" He tried to breathe. He needed to be cool and wasn't doing a great job at it.

"Leo's missing. And now the sheriff's looking for you. I couldn't lie, Mick, not that I needed to. I didn't see you ... do anything. It was scary, though. The way he was talking—"

"I'm—"

Waapikoona jabbed him in the arm, hard. Her face said, *Stop talking, dumbass.*

"I'm on a little trip. Should be back tomorrow. Tell him, I don't know. I'll stop by the sheriff's office and talk to them."

"I told him he attacked me, and what he's fixin' to do. He said they'd send a patrol to my house. You don't think Leo'll come back, do you?"

"He's not comin' back."

Waapikoona widened her eyes at him. He got the warning loud and clear but wasn't going to let Amanda be scared when there was no reason for her to be.

"Wyona sheriff's office has got it covered. You don't need to worry."

"Okay, but did you find him last night?"

Mick closed his eyes, trying to remember what happened in the presence of witnesses and what didn't. "Yeah, found him at Lucky's. Told him to get lost for good. Then I went back in and had a beer. I don't know where he went to, but trust me, he's not gonna bother you no more."

"The kids with your dad? You need me to look in on them?"

"I left them with Old Mae. They'll be fine till I'm back. Amanda—" For some reason he looked up, met Waapikoona's eyes. "You're too good to me."

"Aw, I'll get it back outta you someday. It's really for Kari. You know that."

Mick hung up after she did, staring at the phone. New worries added to the pile. The plan for what he'd say to the police thrashed in his stomach like a pecked worm. If it fed on anxiety instead of food, he was growing a monster.

"You'll tell them nothing."

He put away his phone. "I'll tell 'em what I tell 'em."

"I'm glad we agree."

"I think there's only one thing we agree on, and that ain't it."

She crossed her arms and shifted her weight—a sarcastic position to hear him out, when she seemed to know exactly what he was about to say. "Okay, then what is it, Mick?"

"That I needed some new tires." He smiled, big and overdone.

Wind pushed against him, biting his ears. He zipped up his coat, retrieved his sock hat from the GTO and tugged it on. Waapikoona had turned away to watch a whirlwind of dry leaves travel across the parking lot. As it collided with the wall of the visitor center, it broke apart, and Mick spontaneously took her unsuspecting hand in his like it was something he did every day.

After two dragged steps she was walking with him, her legs matching his gait with precision, her hand a willing captive. Inside, Mick took off his hat and got a brochure from the counter after stuffing cash for two adults into the donation box. A glance at the brochure told him the large mound was open to visitors and yes, those were stairs climbing ten stories to the top. Waapikoona had wandered over to the nearest exhibit, where a mother had parked her stroller to rummage through its underneath storage. Her little girl waited beside her, openly staring at Waapikoona. Old enough to know it was rude, but too overcome by curiosity to remember her manners.

In that moment Mick saw what everyone else saw. Brown-toned skin. Black silk hair, natural and loose against her arms. The fake fur along the hood of her stylish puffy coat, the feathers dangling from her ears. He saw the rare sight of a real, in-the-flesh Native American. Not in traditional costume, not on the movie screen. Not overt about her

Nativeness but not hiding it either. Alive and present just like they were.

He'd been guilty just as everyone else was. America relegated its native people to the past. It didn't matter how many were still around. No one expected them to live in cities or suburbs, and knowing they lived on reservations made them seem put away and somehow irrelevant, made them historical and extinct. They only persisted as the magical people on TV and in movies. The seers, the prophets, the healers. They were different, abnormal, otherworldly, unreal. They weren't neighbors; they weren't tourists. They didn't walk among everyday Americans.

In this context they were one combined group. Mick wasn't the only one who didn't see a difference between tribes, who couldn't recognize one or the other. He sure could tell the difference between a Scottish person and an English person, from accent alone. French, Spanish, Italian, all distinguishable. Maybe it was a new thing, but people knew Chinese and Japanese too. Indian tribes had to be as distinct, but no one bothered to learn or see differences.

Two young men several paces past Waapikoona caught sight of her, one elbowing the other with a hey-check-that-out nudge. Not that they'd say or do anything. Maybe it was her black eye capturing their interest. Such a thing was a shock to see on a woman. But no, the angle was wrong for them to even see it. Mick appreciated the proof they'd added to his thoughts, but it didn't make it any easier to face. The whole thing stunk of a million wrongs.

So did the feeling of moving onto Waapikoona's side. He didn't want to admit there were sides. He didn't want there to be. His stomach churned; he got that distinct cold rush of urgency and prickly tongue that meant he might throw up. He headed toward the men's restroom, hoping Waapikoona noticed where he was going. Not that she needed him out there. She could handle herself. Even though it felt like he was leaving her surrounded by territorial wolves.

He remembered the term as he wiped his face down with a wet paper towel. *White knight.* Well, whatever. There was no way to win this. He needed to stop reading crap on the internet. All it did was fill his head with stupid terms designed to out injustice when all they really did was divide people further. He got a Snickers bar out of a vending machine and joined Waapikoona.

"What's wrong?" she asked. It sounded like she already knew, just hungered for the satisfaction of him confirming it. She couldn't possibly know.

"Guess I don't travel well. Want some?" He broke the Snickers in half.

"You can't get culture shock in a town just like yours."

The chewy chocolate and peanuts helped him ignore that comment, especially since it was mostly true. The difference was Wyona's remoteness, its pleasant isolation from the buzz of thick traffic and noisy civilization, the swell of uneven land surrounding it. Noise traveled too long and far across this flat land, and it unnerved him. "You wanna do the exhibits or head straight to the big mound?"

"The wind up there is going to freeze us dead."

"Okay, so, exhibits?" He unfolded the brochure and scanned the page, surprised at the dates. It wasn't just an Indian civilization, it was ancient. A thousand years old was well before any Europeans settled here. So these weren't people his kind had destroyed. This prehistoric city must've been abandoned before that. "You know anything about this place?" he asked her.

She said nothing, but the weight of her gaze meant she had much to say. "I'll wait for you outside."

He caught her arm before she could take a step away. For once, she didn't jerk out of his grasp. She simply turned to face him, her eyes carrying an unstable mix of weariness and disgust. The urge to kiss her sped through him, an upward burn that had nowhere to go once it reached his head because he wouldn't do it here. Sweet kisses belonged in public spaces, not the obscene, beastly one waiting inside him. And he still had questions to ask her before this day ended. She needed to stay nearby.

"Zip up, then. We're doin' the mound." He released her arm, stuck the remainder of the Snickers between his teeth, and gently raised her hood with both hands, drawing her one step closer as he did it. He didn't consider himself a cool guy, but the move was so smooth it surprised him. If only he didn't have the damn Snickers in his mouth, he might've pulled off a sweet kiss then, just to tease her. Just to tease himself.

She leaned closer and took the Snickers out of his mouth with hers. The surge from his stomach to groin felt more like climax than foreplay, and he released her fast before he lost all control.

"That was my half," she said.

To give his hands something to do, he took his hat out of his pocket and pulled it on. She looked quickly away, as if she'd caught herself watching something she shouldn't. She hadn't zipped up yet, but he led them outside into air he didn't remember being so frigid and gusty. She was right— they were going to freeze to death. Good thing she'd had the forethought to set him on fire.

THE CLIMB TO the top became an unspoken competition over who could make it there without breaking stride. Mick could tell by her rapid breath she could do with a rest, and he knew his own panting gave him away. They stopped halfway up, in unison as if the pause had been planned, the synchronized rhythm of their breathing steaming the air in puffs of white. Her eyes sparkled, wet from the cold wind. They calmed their heart rates and filled their lungs, watching each other. Land stretched behind her as wide as her unguarded smile. Mick wanted to preserve the moment, to capture it and hold on. He took out his phone, put an arm around her, pulled her close.

"Say cheese."

To his surprise she yielded to his arm and the selfie, and he captured her perfectly. Breathless, cheeks nipped by the wind, the challenge in her eyes tempered by the easy curve of her lips. In his own face he saw freedom, and a weightlessness he hadn't felt in years. He was soaring, and he wasn't even in the sky.

"Ready?" he asked, pocketing his phone.

They took off, the second half a more difficult climb on already shaky legs and muscles ready to seize in the cold. Mick was aching to stop but couldn't, not with her fighting to the top beside him. It didn't need to be spoken: together or not at all. And since they'd begun side by side, there was no choice but to finish the same way. They reached the top, both bending with hands on knees to gasp for air and calm their hearts. He couldn't decide if it had been a race or a team effort. Somehow it felt like both. He wanted to laugh but didn't have the breath for it. She straightened, turning away from him to take in the view.

He noticed a complete lack of barrier first—nothing to stop a rolling fall to the bottom should a person get too near the edge. But there wasn't much of an edge either. The side of the mound sloped too gently; weather and time had tamed its earthen side. This may have once been a dangerous place, with evidence of walls built against enemy invasion and the likelihood of human sacrifice, but a thousand years later, all Mick felt was peace. They were alone, standing ten stories high over flat Illinois farmland with gray winter clouds dipping almost low enough to touch. The road at the base of the mound was quiet, any noise generated by a nearby industrial area carried away on the wind. Even the hike to the mound was deserted, unless a person counted the smaller mounds framed by naked trees, their brown twiggy branches swaying in the wind. It seemed the two of them were the only ones committed enough to brave the winter hike, and that was fine for Mick. He had Waapikoona all to himself and didn't have to fight the need to shield her against curious eyes.

A turn toward the west gave him a startling view: a miniature Gateway Arch and its entourage of buildings glinting white in the sunlight, so far away it sat right on the horizon. The gray clouds above him must've cleared in St. Louis just in time to show it all off.

Waapikoona wasn't seeing it. She faced north, rigid and unmoving, wind flapping her hair against her arms as silent tears coated her cheeks. The peace Mick had found retreated as far away as that steel arch. He stepped to her side, arm against arm. Considered taking her hand, decided against it. He should say something. He tried a few options in his head but everything sounded dimwitted, and he had no idea what could be bothering her without some kind of hint. It could be several things: dead sisters, home sickness, history. It could be none of that. They weren't happy tears, that he knew. And what he ended up saying wasn't meant to tease her like he had before—it was plain recognition of her, of something he didn't grasp, and might not ever understand. "Waapikoona."

She turned to him, so sharply it had to be propelled by anger. But as he studied her face, her eyes so red it seemed she hadn't been crying for minutes but hours. Years. Centuries. In her drawn-together brows, there was no anger, just a straightforward, questioning demand. *Who are you? Why do you care?*

He took her face in his hands. He cared, so much, he couldn't even speak it. He didn't even know what he cared about—but he did. The wind encircled them; he drew her closer, a cocoon of warmth on a day determined to rip heat out of their coats, push cold under their skin. The kiss wasn't a thought. It was a happening. A strike of the unexpected. An overflow of a mighty dam, overcome, overpowered. Nature reclaiming its path, its pattern, its determined carve into the earth.

It wasn't the kiss that had been threatening for days. This was new, sweetened to a level beyond any past experience and any expected future one, pressing them together from knees to lips, body to soul. Bright, wide sky crashing upon fertile, deep earth. Upperworld and underworld linking, eclipsing. Sunlight and life, moonlight and death, nothing in between but the two of them. She tasted like secrets and perfection, like candy for the most deprived sweet tooth. She was the deepest breath of crisp morning air. A call echoed across the sky of his mind: one of his kind, calling to another. Breaking away, she gathered a breath, gazing at him. Her arms still so tight around his neck she loosened her hold. A dare, to see if he'd let her go.

He'd never let her go.

"Again?" he asked.

She nodded.

This time he tasted the salt of her tears, the depth of her anguish. He felt a burden unloaded, a new one stacked in its place. And freedom, like he'd seen on his face a moment before, swelling through him. He unzipped her coat and sunk his hands into her warmth, wrapping his arms around her so tightly she gasped, releasing his mouth.

He buried his nose against her neck, inhaling her all the way into his lungs, his stomach.

"Mick—"

"Shh."

The feathers on her earrings landed on his cheek, a tickle riding the breeze. *His* feathers. He pulled back, a force of will greater than starting a shift—or stopping one.

"You wearin' my feathers ... I can't stand it."

Her teary eyes narrowed. "In a good way? Or a bad way?"

"A real, *real* good way. So good I can't—"

She touched his bottom lip, her fingertips cold, silky soft. Not an action to shut him up. She admired his mouth, her eyes no longer sad but awed. "Can't what?"

He didn't know what. "Stand it." He smiled.

Her hand flattened against his mouth, and she looked away quickly like she had before. "Stop smiling like that."

He found his mind had changed, without any thought from him at all. "I need to know everything about you."

Chapter

27

Mick pulled his hood over his blue knit hat and zipped his coat to his chin. Now with those eyes and his smile dulled in shadow, she could more easily talk to him. Recovery from that kiss was hard enough without standing in front of its godly source.

"Sit?" he asked.

She sat. It was as good a place as any, and she didn't want to return to the visitor center, a tourist attraction paying homage to the ancestors of a people conquered and driven to near extinction. She couldn't understand any of it. It made more sense to just plow over these mounds like they'd done to the rest of them. Build some houses, gas stations, warehouses, and roads, make no apologies for the bulldozing of sacred land. And it seemed most of the people in that visitor center would be more comfortable with her inside the exhibits instead of viewing them. Except for the park ranger, who'd asked what tribe she belonged to in a friendly, welcoming way, not the morbidly curious one she was used to, complete with a raised phone ready to snap a photo. She had to remember her world had changed, that some people, although rare, were good. Her world now included Mick.

He sat facing her, his knees against hers, hands in pockets, strong shoulders hunched against the cold. His cheeks were rosy, and his lips, instead of being drained of color, were pink from the contact with hers. And even though his hood had dulled his eyes, when he looked right into her like he was now, she saw their blue like they were lit by the sun. Blue was rare in nature. Nothing on Earth dared to rival the beauty of the bluest sky. Mick's eyes had accepted that dare, and could she admit they'd won? They were the blue sky on this gray day. He was master of the sky. He reigned in that endless blue.

"I used to live…" she turned, gazing north "…not too far from here. My tribe told stories of these mounds, but there were more of them, on both sides of the river."

"Do your people come from the people who built them?"

"I don't know. Maybe."

"I know you don't shy at murder, but human sacrifice? You into that too?"

"My people didn't kill. We were nonviolent. If our ancestors were Cahokian, we'd abandoned that violence. We only fought for defense. In my time, the war was more centered around your kind. And it was a type of war we couldn't fight."

"You mean, guns and horses?"

"Politics and cultural cleansing. Lies. Disease."

Mick looked away, into the distance she'd admired a moment ago. "I'm startin' to think I might need to read up on this. I wasn't all that good in school."

"White schools aren't going to teach you the truth. I was taken from my family and sent to a white school at age ten. My sister too. Its purpose was to wash the savage Indian-ness out of us." She closed her eyes against the memory of that paddle hanging in the headmaster's office, the lye soap sitting on the window sill. Of her sister being dragged into that room every time she forgot the rule: English only, Native language forbidden. "My people didn't beat their own children. We knew nothing of that. But at that school…" She looked at Mick, watched him go still. "Tell me who the savages were. It wasn't us."

And still wasn't. Native people were trying to live, trying to get ahead, just like every other American. A few generations worth of time had mercifully dulled some of their anger. But even though the struggle and violence was a ripe, recent feeling to her, that didn't mean modern Native people didn't feel it. That kind of trauma was everlasting. It carried into new generations to press struggle onto children who've never felt it firsthand. It sowed poverty into culture, strengthened by politics and racism perpetuated by the invaders. The rulers and conquerors didn't want to make it right. They didn't want to see their captured rise up, succeed. They didn't want their own children to face the consequences of their actions. They wanted their violence erased. The people they invaded to be silent long enough to die out.

"We will never die out," she said aloud, knowing Mick didn't hear her thoughts and couldn't connect it. Somehow she knew he'd understand.

"You know…" He looked down at the scraggly brown winter grass between them. "I think most folks in this country today would live in peace with your people, if they'd got the chance. We believe in the story of Thanksgiving. Of Indian heroes."

"The Thanksgiving myth is a lie."

He looked at her like she'd just spoiled his day. "Well, fine. But what I'm sayin' is … Blame the rulers of countries who sent explorers to America. Not the common people who came here for a better life. Most folks today would agree this land was stolen, but what can be done about it now?"

"Things are being done. Do you really want to know everything, Mick?"

He took his hands from his pockets, placed them on his knees. It was the body language of action, not listening. "I want to know exactly who you are, what you're doin'. Who's after you. And if there's more people out there who'll come after me."

"I'm a Native person of unknown tribe, born once in another century, died at age eleven. Twenty-five years ago my body was revived, and I lived with a tribe in Oklahoma. Fifteen years ago I left Oklahoma with Jeremiah, who introduced me to the creature you met in the cave."

"The one I accidentally shifted for?"

She tilted her head at him, impressed. Referring to that shift as accidental meant he could feel a difference between doing it on purpose and not. "He's called The Silent One."

"What is he?"

"In his current form? A giant millipede. When I first met him he was a horned serpent. He didn't like what that form gave away."

"No, I mean, what *is* he. Where'd he come from?"

"The underworld. He's taking advantage of the bad history between my kind and yours. He wants turmoil and war. He wants this country turned upside down."

"Why?"

"To split it in half, open a rift to let the underworld leak out."

Mick looked up. A hawk soared down from the clouds, long wings working to hold steady against the turbulent sky. It was so close Waapikoona could see the longer wing feathers flapping individually, the predatory eye angled right at her.

"Is he one of yours?"

Mick stood. "Should I know that?"

A stray raindrop plopped onto her waterproof sleeve. A few more pelted the ground around them. In her first life, *she* would've known that. The elders had been training her to be a guide, a Thunder-Being handler. If only the elders knew she'd found one now as a child of the underworld, wholly incapable of handling him.

A second hawk joined the first, diving from shadowed darker grays that hung in low swells, ready to spill. She didn't know how long the rain clouds had been up there, if enough time had passed for them to move in or if they were some force at work against her.

"I think they're here for me," she said.

Mick spun slowly, surveying the sky as if looking for more birds—possible allies for him, enemies to her, and she was standing on a ten-story platform rising into their domain. She saw his place in the middle and wasn't sure how she could possibly ask. *Come with me. Let's run away.*

Before she found the nerve to speak, he snatched her hand, and they took off down the stairs, a conjoined mass of opposite forces moving in the same direction. The clouds spilled as they crossed the road. They ran, cold rain turning to sleet as they approached the visitor center. She tugged Mick away from the front door and aimed for the Pontiac.

Sleet showered the asphalt as they crossed the empty lot, the noise so pervasive she could hear nothing over the wide hiss of a million falling particles. Closing herself inside the car narrowed the sound into an onslaught of ice against glass and metal.

Mick started the car and raised the dial on the heater. "You as soaked as me?"

Maybe not as soaked, but definitely not dry. Her hood had fallen in the run so her hair was wet, along with the stretch of jeans between her boots and the hem of her coat. Her feet would probably be wet as soon as the icy pellets that had migrated into her boots melted. She removed each boot and shook it into the floorboard.

He took his hat off and laid it on the dashboard. "What now?"

"We wait for this to stop so we can dig up my sister."

"What if it don't stop?"

"Then we get wetter." It occurred to her then—she didn't need Mick. She'd have to send him home soon. Traveling anywhere with a sack of human bones wasn't safe, and Mick didn't need to be a part of that. She'd been waiting for the cover of night, but why? No one would be out in this. It was the perfect time to rob a grave. She turned to him, taking a breath to speak.

He beat her to it. "Sorry I don't got a radio to pass the time. Want to drive somewhere, get some supper?"

"No," she said fast. She couldn't entertain that, not even for a second. Sharing a meal with Mick in a cozy small-town bar while ice dropped from the sky outside was the perfect dream right now, but she had to keep her mind on import-ant things. She couldn't do this anymore. "And being real, I need to do the rest myself. So ... thanks. And have a safe drive home."

She pushed out of the car into the hard sleet, slammed the door. Her hood blocked most of the weather, but the wind found a way in and cut as badly as the ice. She stepped into the crunchy grass in the direction of the mound where she'd buried her sister's bones. Behind her, the Pontiac horn blared through the falling sleet, its raw sound crawling up her back like one of her Helpers might devour a corpse. The temptation to turn around and face that sound nearly broke her. Anger, distress, alarm—even without looking she could clearly see it, see Mick's eyes driving into her, ordering her back into that car before he got out to retrieve her. She increased her pace to a near sprint as she heard his door slam, footsteps pounding through the assault of sleet behind her. She could outrun him—she had the lead. She couldn't outrun him if he shifted. And the weather was too bad to hide from him and wait until he left. She needed to dig up the bones and leave, and he'd be on her as soon as she stopped at the temporary grave.

He was closer than she thought when she turned around. She only had time to raise her arms before he tackled her. Skidding in the icy grass, he managed to keep them both upright; she threw an elbow, he cursed and dodged. She didn't want to hit him, but if she needed to, she would.

"Cool it!" he hollered, his face close to hers.

"Leave, Mick. Go home."

"I said…" he let her go, stumbling a step back, trying to catch his breath "…I'd help you."

"You have."

"I can't leave you here in an ice storm."

"You can. Because I can't have you with me after I do this."

Ice was quickly collecting in his wind-blown hair. "We ain't done talking."

"So what? None of this matters. You'll go back to your life, I'll go back to mine."

"That what you want?"

No, it wasn't what she wanted. But what she wanted for herself had never been on the table. The only task was to raise her sister, give her a good life. Nothing else mattered; nothing else could get in the way. She could feel sleet sneaking into her boots, melting against her feet. It was warm underground. She had to get there, and time and the cold were working against her human body. "Forget about this, Mick."

He grabbed her by the shoulders of her coat like he was going to shake her or throw her to the ground. "You've changed me."

"I'm sorry."

"I can't forget about you."

"Then don't. But let me go."

He released her. In the break of his latch was a desperation mirrored in his eyes. Instead of looking away, she stepped into him. She had to make him understand; she had to douse the regret before it grew. "We're on opposite sides of an unfought fight that will soon be war."

"It was fought. Your people lost."

"My people are buried all over this country, waiting to rise. Many tribes united against a common enemy. The Silent One will possess them just like he can possess me. They'll be joined. Single-minded and unstoppable. Your cities built on top of their bones will fall. And once The Silent One has built his army, the land will be reclaimed."

"For him or for you?"

She watched him watch her, their breath white in the air. That was the question, the one that had tested her loyalty to everything. She knew there were two parts to this effort. One, power returned to her reborn people. Two, their restored land stolen yet again by The Silent One, as the underworld spilled across it, burying everything in its wake. He was capitalizing on the unrest, on the history of her people. She'd been a part of that, but soon she'd be out.

"Doesn't matter. I'm getting out."

"You don't want this fight?"

"Maybe I do. But on my terms, not his."

"So you reclaim your land. Destroy everyone. Then what?"

"Then nothing. Let it go back to the spirits. Let the white man be cleared away like he tried to clear away us."

"So … revenge. That's it?"

It would be simpler to admit that. It would make sense to him. "That's it."

Mick brushed a hand against his hair, clearing ice, flipping water off his fingers. She could see he was thoroughly soaked now and needed to seek shelter and heat more than she did. She was powered by The Silent One, could surrender her form to him at any time. Cold weather was inconvenient and uncomfortable, not deadly, and The Silent One's cave was waiting for her, if she could only lose Mick. It seemed her plan to push him away had backfired. Jaw clenched against the cold, taking ice into already wet hair, he stared into her. Either he didn't buy it, or he was too angry to back down.

"You're a slave," he bit out.

"I'm no one's slave."

"A victim of your own past."

Now it was her turn to step toward him. "I stopped being a victim when I took my sister's hand and convinced her to jump off that cliff. I told her we'd soar like eagles, and she believed me." New tears flowed hot into her already gritty eyes, but he'd never see them against the sleet melting on her face. "Don't pretend to know anything about me."

"You murder for him. You're his—"

"I work for him so he'll raise my sister. I shouldn't have let you help me. It has nothing to do with you."

"It has everything to do with me! Another person raised from the dead by you is another enemy for my other half to kill. Unless it gets you first, with a little help from *them*." He flung his arm toward the top of the mound where the hawks had been patrolling.

"Is that a threat?"

"No, it's the truth. It's a job I never asked for but got now because of you. And the only reason I'm not going eagle and killing you right now is—" A stillness washed across him, smoothing the furrow in his brow, melting the fury in his eyes. "You know what? Forget it. Freeze to death if you want. I'm done."

She watched him turn and walk away. It was the right thing, the thing she needed, but it stung worse than every hit of wind and every sliver of ice. Nothing had ever felt so wrong.

It was her fault for involving herself. For falling for a man too kind to hate. A Thunder-Being, a white man—so many wrongs had mutated into a right, and she had to cast it away.

Yes—forget it. Forget him. Get to the mound. Dig up Pinepakatwi's bones.

Cutting through the woods saved her some time, but it didn't matter. The scene she walked up on made no sense to her: fresh earth piled beside a shallow hole, the shovel she'd stashed laying out in the open as if tossed hastily aside. She lost her bearings, had to consult her memory. The sack of bones had been buried here, three stones placed to mark its location, the shovel hidden under a fallen tree. She hadn't been back since. But someone had, recently enough for that pile of dirt not to settle. And whoever it was had stolen her sister.

On her knees, she clawed the loose earth that once held a sack of bones, searching for evidence it had been raided by an animal and had simply been scattered. That shovel sat there in the periphery like a curse. She'd fallen out of reality; what she saw couldn't be truth. She was the only one who knew they were here—she and Jeremiah.

She sat up. Jeremiah knew, and he'd beaten her here. She would've made it, but she'd been stalled by Mick, insisting she spend the night, demanding they tour the visitor center, climb the mound. Jeremiah must've gone to see him, given him some lie, told him to delay her. And Mick didn't just fulfill that favor; he'd satisfied a duty of his own. He didn't want her to find the bones. It would mean one more person raised against him, one more child of the underworld he must kill. He'd betrayed her, and he'd kissed her on top of that mound like he was on her side.

The sprint back to the parking lot passed in a blur. All she found was a cloud of ripe exhaust and two wiggly tire tracks in the accumulated sleet that straightened out and aimed for the road.

She knelt, releasing her Helpers.

"Find me the shortest path to The Silent One."

They scurried off, and she followed.

CHAPTER
28

MICK WAS GOING home. It was where he should've stayed. This trip had been a stupid choice, an irresponsible teenage fling, and he was a grown man. His life had forked and he knew which road was the right one and which was wrong. Now he was backtracking on the wrong one, praying the turnoff to the right one hadn't fallen out of time.

He reviewed the past few days, trying to find the moment he'd gone wrong. He'd returned the demon corpse—that was supposed to be the end of it. He'd kissed her in the mausoleum. A mistake, maybe, but it didn't feel like one. It had been part of that night of impulse, instinct, and anything-goes. The night he was going to kill Leo Boyle, as himself, or as an eagle, it didn't matter to him as long as it was done. As soon as Leo was dead it should've ended there, but it didn't. He had sensed trouble from the dog. He'd shifted. He'd gone after Waapikoona.

That was his misstep. His mistake.

If he'd ignored the dog and stayed home, he'd have never killed bad men as a golden eagle. The blood on his mouth would've never dried, never been admired by her, never made him feel justified and right and alive. He'd have never shifted back into human form and helped her dispose of bodies in a dead man's gory clothes. He wouldn't have convinced her to spend the night, wouldn't have welcomed the impulse to accompany her to Illinois.

That prickly, urgent feeling that had sent him into the sky to save a woman he'd already sworn off—that was what did him in. It hadn't been a conscious thought, not one he could remember. It had been an instinct he had no idea how to fight. He hadn't even known he *should* fight.

Well, now he was aware. If she came back—she'd better not come back—he'd be wise. He'd made his choice, and it was his old life he wanted. Not the new one. This war she spoke of was supernatural. Superstition. It wouldn't hold up to reality, to getting coffee brewed and bills paid and kids off to school. He was too busy to join a war between life and death. He was a man. He wasn't a god. Didn't want to be one.

He hadn't made it but a few miles before he detected two eagles trailing him in the sky. Without actually seeing them he wasn't sure how he knew they were there, but he felt them soaring above like one might sense a direct gaze from across a room. At a stop for gas and a soda, they circled overhead, as shadowed as the night that had folded around him, as present as his own dark thoughts.

He left the GTO at the pump and trudged across a field layered in ice behind the gas station, expecting them to adjust their circle and follow. They did. He crossed a commuter parking lot, vacant except for a few rusty trailers. As he climbed down a snowy decline and headed toward the woods, they dipped low, anxious for contact. He didn't want to chat. He wanted a rifle with a night scope to shoot them out of the sky.

"Go!" he hollered, stopping at a pile of rocky debris. He volleyed rocks at them into the dark, rapid-fire. "Get off me! I'm outta this!"

One of them dived, the violent flap of feathers diverting just above Mick's head, but he didn't flinch. The next time he'd be ready to punch the bird out of the air. He waited, but they climbed higher, screeching their complaints. He sent a few more rocks, knowing he'd never hit targets that flew with such power and grace. It was the message he wanted them to get, and he wasn't returning to the GTO until they gave up. He didn't care if demons flooded the woods right now. He would not shift. Never again.

He wanted to tell them to go back there to those mounds, do their job, kill that undead thing before she unburies more undead things. The words halted on their way to his mouth, making him sick, ashamed. A coward? No, just a human being.

Come to think of it, the rifle with night scope made him sick, too, which made him angrier for a reason he couldn't nail down.

All at once the sky was empty, like it always had been. Mick dropped his handful of unfired rocks and retraced his steps. If it weren't for the glare from the gas station's lot, he'd be blind and lost. He shivered in the cold as he reached his car, unsure how he'd found his way out there in the dark the first time.

THE WYONA WELCOME sign gave Mick a pang of relief so sharp it hurt. He noticed the clock, figured it was too close to the kids' bedtime to check on them. His return would only wind them up. Straight to his apartment, straight to bed.

He'd make up for ditching them tomorrow. That dinner he'd imagined with Amanda and all the kids sounded real nice. If he kept it in his mind, maybe he'd go to bed and dream about it, and tomorrow he'd live it.

He kept the throttle easy all the way down the driveway, hoping to sneak in undetected. He parked, giving half a thought to all the serial-killer paraphernalia still in his car. Putting all that away tonight would give him a fresh start tomorrow, might make it easier to put all that happened behind him. But his rock-firing arm ached, and his eyes were dry and road-weary. And he'd be damned if all that wasn't already behind him. He'd left it at the Mississippi. It didn't matter what was in his car in the morning. The bridge was burned. There was no road back.

"Michael." It drifted across the field and fell into his ear as he got out of the GTO, the wind given voice, the night stopping his feet, taking hold.

He turned, knowing no one was there. It wasn't a human voice, and no living soul called him that. There had been one person who'd used that name, but his mother was long dead. He took in a breath, let it out slowly. It was in his mind, the one that had belonged to him before he took the fork in the road. The mind on its way to succumbing to dementia.

"It's okay," he said. Talking to himself again. It would have to be okay. Dementia was normal. It fit reality.

"Michael...?"

"What?" It came out harsh and irritable, like it was too early and he was too sleepy. His mother was nagging him to get up, get dressed, let's get a move on, and he was too young to know not to be crabby to his mother in the morning. He didn't know she'd so soon be dead.

Beside the old shed, an upright shape wavered into view. Mick braced himself against the play of shadow and light, the ruffle of space, knowing his witness to it would bring him to the brink of a shift. He held his ground, going lightheaded with the effort. And he missed the man who'd approached from behind, waiting to be acknowledged. Mick turned to face him, wishing he'd grabbed the socket wrench from his car.

"Welcome back," Jeremiah said, his face revealed as a cloud gave way to moonlight sliding across the land.

Mick worked to catch his breath. The shift still pressed against him. He backed up, bracing himself against the GTO. And again, his name, in his mother's faraway voice, sprung into his ear.

"Sorry. She won't stay where I put her." Jeremiah crossed the yard in pursuit of the wavering grayness, which changed direction as if it didn't like being chased.

Mick used the distraction to bow and breathe, bending at the waist, his head low, imagining warm human blood flowing back into every extremity. Thinking of human things like food and cars and sex, Christmas presents and Fourth of July fireworks, his heavy boots planted on solid earth. He ran a hand over his scabbed chin, remembering the pain. He swiveled his rock-throwing arm, glorifying its deep-muscle ache. Then he got the socket wrench out of his car and waited for Jeremiah to join him.

He did, towing the reluctant gray form behind him. It seemed to be pulled in bursts, a battle of resistance against Jeremiah's tight arm. Up close it stabilized into shape despite being made up of a constantly shifting mist, both human-like and not. Mick averted his eyes. A close-up might be a bad idea.

"Now stay down," Jeremiah said to the mist. "Or the tether never comes off."

Mick took a quick glance. The shape now resembled a person crouched low on the ground.

"The only Svendsen in the cemetery with a recent date. I decided there was a good chance you'd know her."

"Thought I told you to stay off my property."

"I thought I told you I don't believe in that concept."

Mick weighed the socket wrench in his hand. "Think this might make you a believer?"

Jeremiah laughed. "Okay, dumb hick needs it spelled out. This here..." he gestured toward the hunched misty shape "...is your mother, lifted from her grave. I took the liberty of..."

Mick closed his eyes and tried to imagine a bed he was in or a roadside where he was camping out for a catnap to revive him for the remainder of the drive home. This wasn't what he'd come home to. He was dreaming.

The voice traveled into his ear. "I'm lost, Michael. Where do I rest? I shouldn't be here."

It could be a trick, like the Janie he'd picked up from the road who'd morphed into the flying demon. Whatever conjured the image could've picked his brain, found a memory of his mother, her voice, her specific use of that name, and used it against him.

Jeremiah snapped his fingers in front of Mick's face. "Pay attention. Your mother, she'll remain unquiet unless—"

"I'm done with Sarah," Mick said. "Put my mother back."

"Oh, but I'm not done with Sarah. So here's the deal. You come with me, and I'll return your mother to her grave unharmed. Refuse, and this big old house gets its very own ghost."

Tempted to look at Old Mae's house where Doug and Janie spent so many nights, Mick leveled his gaze on Jeremiah so hard his eye twitched. His mother wouldn't be capable of haunting her own grandchildren, but what did Mick know of the underworld? Jeremiah could curse her to do it. He could feed her a lie, make her think they were the ones who'd locked her there. She didn't know them in her life, and even if she recognized Kari in them she might be easily poisoned against that warmth.

"I also have a set of hungry demons who'd love to devour children, if that sweetens the deal for you."

Shift. Kill his demons, kill him.

One last time, for a good reason. It would only prove how Mick needed that part of himself he'd sworn off, and he refused to allow it. And if he killed Jeremiah, and this ghost really was his mother's spirit, how would he return her to her grave?

"Or I could just take them. I know how your kind like to handle children. I was very educated on that. I'll be sure—"

"Michael?"

Jeremiah kicked the ground at the base of the ghost. "Shut *up!*"

Mick took a good look then, and the ghost lifted what might be a face at him. Inside its form he could make out hollow features that hinted of his mother, but her hair was too thin, her bones sharp. Her weathered mouth shifted with a confused sorrow he'd never seen in her. He knew where she should be, as unfair as it was, and he had to get her back there.

"I'll come with you. But first you put her back."

Once his mother was safe in her grave, Mick and his socket wrench would convince Jeremiah he'd renounced this world of ghosts and demons and no one could drag him back.

"QUITE a lONG walk for a … guy like you."

Mick could guess what Jeremiah wanted to say. That the insult to his culture, his way of life would in any way rock him. The natural response was a ground out *fuck you*, but Mick refused to give him that. He wouldn't be baited into racial division. He wouldn't go there, not ever. He clung to everything he'd said to Waapikoona—no, Sarah. He wouldn't use her real name anymore, not even to himself.

He turned to glimpse his mother's misty form following behind, mustering a fragment of positivity to flash her a smile. The dark gray line where her mouth would've been fluttered—her own returned smile, he imagined, because he couldn't handle it being anything else. He longed to tell her everything about his life, about Kari, Doug, Janie, and Helen, but there was too much hardship mixed with the good stuff, and he wasn't sure he could separate it out. And with this undead asshole walking with them? Forget it. When all this was over, he'd visit her grave, prepared, with flowers and an hour to fill her in, once a month for the rest of his life.

"Not much of a talker, are you?"

Mick bit back another *fuck you*. That kind of an emotional reaction would only give this shithead pleasure. He couldn't determine the source of his violent shivering. The temperature was near freezing, but his core blazed with a fire so angry he'd started to sweat under his coat. Blood pulsed hot in every fingertip, every toe. Walking the winter woods at night should be a risk for hypothermia. Instead, he feared he'd pass out from heat exhaustion.

Opening his coat allowed the chill to settle against him. He took a breath into his lungs, held it, let it leak slowly out. Still he shivered. Still he burned. Inside, the eagle thundered against him, ready and alive.

He didn't need it. Not for this. Not for anything. Too bad he'd been forced to leave the socket wrench back at home.

Having that cold metal weight in his hand would remind him how human beings shut down blackmailing grave robbers. Its purpose would add promise to each step, making them lighter instead of heavier. Branches snagged his clothes, each one a barrier to overpower, sapping his strength bit by bit. He couldn't afford to let it all tire him out, but his legs were dragging, and his willpower was nearing surrender.

He barely recognized the entrance to the cemetery once they arrived. It had been too long since he'd been there. Someone had landscaped the driveway by the front gates, and the pine trees that had been planted a few years after his mother died were nearly growing into the overhead power lines. Jeremiah had shortened the tether so Mick's mother had to drift right behind him. He veered to the side, gesturing for Mick to lead the way.

With the two of them behind him, the eagle thrashed. Too tired to fight it, Mick's impulse was to shed his coat and shirt—it was happening whether he allowed it or not. He could fight it with them in sight and under surveillance. But being forced to walk while two representatives of the underworld trailed him—it was too much.

He thought of Waapikoona. Of the weight of her body when she climbed over him in the cave. In the mausoleum, her teeth on his mouth, his tongue. And the feeling she was made for him, that saying goodbye meant he'd lost something he'd never find again. His human heart beat a wound into him. His anger cauterized it. The eagle hunkered down, subdued but watchful.

"Here," he said, finding he'd reached his mother's grave.

"Not so fast." Jeremiah took a coil of rope from his inner coat pocket. "I don't untether her until I tether you."

"I'm not goin' nowhere."

"That's fine. But the word of your kind means nothing to me. Hold out both hands."

Mick stared him down. Outwardly it may have looked like opposition, but really he was frantically searching for options. For sharp objects nearby he could somehow palm before those ropes went around his wrists, for a strategy that could get his mother back in her grave and Jeremiah simultaneously knocked unconscious.

There was nothing. Mick lifted his hands together in front of him. The rope burned his skin as it tightened—so tight his bones felt fused.

Mick had a thought that didn't belong to him. It was simply born of revenge, something another person might say just to hit where it would hurt. He tried to squash it from becoming words but failed. "Guess there's a reason they called you savage."

Mick tasted hot blood, knew he'd been hit but wasn't sure how. That's how it always happened—a punch only made contact when you didn't see it coming. Now his jaw flared; he found his head hanging at a slant, the strain in his neck so severe stars pulsated in the outskirts of his vision.

"Michael?"

"I'm okay." It came out slurred—too much blood and saliva for him to deal with, so he spit what he could and swallowed more than he should've. He couldn't make sense of what would be bleeding so much. Every thought felt a thousand times too slow—so slow that by the time each one completed, he forgot how it started.

The rope jerked his arms forward, popping several vertebrae in his neck. His brain felt too big for his skull. Jeremiah was pointing his mother's ghost toward her grave, and she was lying on top. Soon she'd be gone.

"I'll visit soon, Mom," Mick said. "Soon as I can."

Her wispy form settled onto the ground as if in sleep. Slowly, it melted away. He wasn't sure if what he'd just seen had only occurred in his mind. Everything felt languid and dreamy. Around him, the night had darkened despite the moon still hanging high. Finally he felt the real cold. The blood on his upper lip and chin was drying, freezing, now cracking if he moved his mouth. For a long moment he lost sense of where he was, what he was doing.

"Time to walk."

The rope jerked again, yanking Mick from his knees to his feet when he didn't remember sinking down—or maybe he was always down? The last time he'd been punched he'd punched back, but he was younger then. Less exhausted. Less tied up and less blackmailed. His mother was safe again, but Jeremiah still had those children-eating demons.

They'd made it to a sedan, and Mick took a shove that landed him in a musty backseat. A bad seal somewhere, gone long unchecked, many rains and snow melts allowed to seep in. Parts of his brain were coming back online, one at a time. Diagnosing cars was good—it meant instinct and critical thinking were working together. He wasn't ready to fight back, but soon he would be.

CHAPTER 29

As Waapikoona waited in the cavern for The Silent One, she worked on finding the right words. She couldn't reveal she knew Jeremiah or that he knew where the bones were.

My sister's bones have been stolen.

It sounded too guarded, like she was hiding something. She could accuse a thunderbird—her employer's enemy should also be her own. Even though she'd brought one into his den.

A thunderbird helped someone steal my sister's bones, and we need to stop it.

We need to kill it.

The duty that brought her to say those words toiled against the memory of Mick holding her on that mound. His arms, binding and sure around her even though looking out over the flat land where her people once lived freely filled her with such chaos. Perhaps it was a mistake, but it felt so true: Allied with him, this imbalanced world felt a little more right.

He was no ally. She knew that now.

Deep in one of the tunnels branching from the echoing room, something skittered against the wall. A falling rock finally loosened by eons of quiet erosion. A crawling cave demon hungry for flesh. The sound reverberated so far away on the opposite side of her it seemed more like a new one, answering the first instead of the echo it was. Her Helpers scampered back to mill around her feet, anxious for a job to do. She bent, gathering them up in her palm. If the noise had been a threat, she'd rather kill it herself than risk one of her Helpers being injured. She wouldn't get any more, and now she didn't just need to reach her flesh quota to ask The Silent One to raise her sister—she needed to locate her sister's bones first.

The cave's stagnant air shifted. She flipped off her light. The great demon was coming and all she could think of was Mick and Jeremiah, working as a team to betray her. She wished she'd been able to confront Mick at her sister's temporary gravesite. Her own suspicions were all the proof she had, and after all she and Mick had been through, it didn't seem like enough. The accusation didn't sit well with her. It was too big. It was too … not Mick.

As The Silent One's many legs scratched against the rocky cave floor, she suppressed her instinct to run. This was her employer. He needed her and she needed him, until what they both wanted was fulfilled.

"Identify yourself."

"Waapikoona." For the first time, she regretted giving him her real name. Mick was a betrayer, but so was she. Bringing a thunderbird into The Silent One's cave would have its own consequences, and she had to be sure to play it right.

A staccato clicking trailed around her. "A brave return."

"I think we understand one another better now."

"You test me."

"I hold you to your bargain."

"Yet you bring me nothing."

"My Helpers were here not long ago. Alone, but they brought a haul. It seems a waste of my time to come every—"

"And now you waste my time."

"I have news."

The motion of his body that had quieted rose up around her again, hard body segments clicking against one another, its sound somewhere between insect and monster. "Speak it."

"I need—"

—a more powerful Helper, one strong enough to slay a thunderbird.

Could she really sic The Silent One on Mick before confirming his guilt? There could be some other explanation for the missing bones and his attempts to delay her. She was underfueled, underrested, and thinking in narrow terms. These were the hasty, reckless decisions that could so easily end in regret. And if Mick was innocent...

She closed her eyes and imagined moving through life, knowing there was no longer someone like Mick in the world. She visualized her life five years from now, her sister reborn, growing up on land so changed that would never be the same. It didn't matter whether it was still the modern country run by the same people it was now or if it was a colony of the underworld, ruled by The Silent One. Mick's absence in either would cast the darkest shadow. She'd never find a way out from under it.

"I need help finding my sister's bones. They've been stolen."

"They have been brought by one of your own. They rise upon reassembly in the cloak of night."

Soon her sister would come alive somewhere, alone. Waapikoona hadn't planned it that way, and Jeremiah knew that. And he certainly wasn't one of her own. Explaining this to The Silent One would get her nowhere, and she had bigger issues than planning how she'd deal with Jeremiah.

With a start she pieced it all together. Of course Mick agreed to delay her so Jeremiah could get the bones. They both had a prize in mind. For Jeremiah, it was power over her. For Mick, it was his godly duty. Once revived, her sister would be Mick's prey. He'd said it himself: another enemy for him to kill.

Getting to Pinepakatwi first was all that mattered. "Where will she rise?"

He laughed, hissy like a snake, wild like a demon. "Do you think I know anything of the upperworld?"

She tried to remember how the awakening happened. The only one she'd been present for was her own. Her memories began years after that. Jeremiah told her some things, but she couldn't mention him here. The Silent One forbade his workers from contact—a rule she and Jeremiah broke many times long ago. He preferred his slaves independent, disorganized, unable to mutiny.

A cold, segmented wall of giant millipede slid against her back in the direction from which The Silent One had come. If she didn't get the location of Pinepakatwi's bones now, she'd never find them in time. The Silent One knew. He shared the eyes of many beings. He could see through every Helper, every horned serpent, every flying demon. He had access to human eyes every time someone like her opened herself to possession. He could be anywhere at once; he could know anything he wanted. She bent and released her Helpers. "Tell them to take me there."

HOURS THROUGH DRIPPING tunnels trickling with water from the icefall above, she climbed. Her Helpers never tired. Her flashlight grew dim. When they finally led her to the surface she fell to the ground, sharp ice stinging her cheek, exhaustion making her ambivalent about the urgency of this trek. Her sister would know to stay put. She'd be cold, but she'd be undead. She'd know to hide from soaring thunderbirds and she'd survive.

No. Waapikoona got up, brushing her jeans free of ice. The haze of early morning light filtered through dark glossy branches. Her legs wobbled; she latched onto a nearby tree trunk. Her Helpers were so far ahead she could no longer hear them. She couldn't be certain if she was still in Illinois or back in Wyona. Time and space worked differently in The Silent One's cave than in the upperworld. There was nothing flat about this land. She stood in an old growth forest on a ripple of earth, looking out across more tree-covered ripples in the distance as far as she could see. These were Mick's rolling Missouri mountains, and it wouldn't surprise her if she'd surfaced right in his wooded backyard. Without her Helpers guiding her, she had no idea which way to turn, and calling them back might break The Silent One's command over them.

If there was ever a moment to give her form to The Silent One, it was now. She closed her eyes and called to him, and when she opened those same lids they were no longer hers but his. She was hanging behind, watching her legs pump, her boots sail over banked snow and fallen trees, faster than a doe, more graceful than a golden eagle. Reality and dream merged. The cold of winter was an idea, not a truth. The Silent One didn't know much of the upperworld but this was how he learned, and his mind was insatiable.

THE HOUSE WHERE she arrived plucked at a memory, but her active mind hung too far away to make sense of it. She pushed, edging closer until The Silent One relented. As she slipped back into her body, a strong current of panic filtered through her heart. How could she ever be sure The Silent One was completely gone? The haunt of it faded as feeling returned. The dull cold in her toes spreading up skin chilled by wet jeans. The ache of overused muscles, the empty cave of her stomach.

She bent to gather her Helpers, setting off the motion lights on the porch. This house sat in shadow, the slow sunrise blocked by the forest behind. The place wasn't familiar, but some higher sense told her it was special for some reason, and not only because it was the place where her sister would rise from the dead. Jeremiah chose this house, and she couldn't trust anything of his, especially not now. She needed to find out if someone lived here, and if they were home. The windows were dark, and there were no cars parked nearby. She walked around the corner and found a detached garage, untouched snow spreading before it.

A semitruck rolled by on the road, carving a notch in the winter silence. She hiked toward it and took a look down the pavement in both directions. At the farthest curve she could make out a sign: HWY 29. It had to be the same 29 that ran through Wyona. So here she was, back where she didn't want to be.

Light blinked on inside the house, illuminating the window beside the front door. Someone home. The temptation of warmth, food, and clean water from the tap walked her back to the house and onto the porch. She'd meet them, get a judge of character. If they were scum she'd kill them. If they weren't, she'd have to come up with a good story fast. Modern people were territorial and strict about their fences and property lines. They treated any wandering creature, human or animal, with unhealthy suspicion.

The door opened before she could knock. An old white man in a plaid robe assessed her head to toe. His hair stood up on one side like he'd walked straight from his bed to his front door. "You one of the good ones or bad ones?"

"Good ones," she answered, her eyes unwavering from his.

"Bad ones tell lies, though. That makes this part tricky."

"Bad ones would have already started trouble." A smile would soften this exchange, but she couldn't force herself to do it.

"True." He leaned out, squinting at her earrings. "Them eagle feathers you got there?"

"Golden eagle."

He stepped aside, holding the door open for her. She savored the dry heat as she stopped in the tiny foyer, hoping this house was the right one. She had no time to waste.

"Well, come in, if you're comin' in. It's warmer in the kitchen."

She propped an arm against the closed door to yank off her muddy boots, using the messy effort to piece together a story to tell this man. Her jeans were caked and her coat dripped. "Sorry, I'm making a mess—"

"Nah." He waved a hand. "You're soaked to the bone, girl."

She looked deeply into his eyes which were so startling in their familiarity she forgot to lie altogether. "I got lost in a cave."

"We got plenty of those. And who's been roughin' you up?"

She'd forgotten about the shiner. In others' eyes she was always the victim, an untruth she could often work with.

"Here, you head on down the hall. Bathroom's there on the right. I'll put some coffee on."

When he chinned her toward the hall, she realized she'd been staring. There was something about this man, some stray bit of knowledge she couldn't find in her head. As she locked herself in his bathroom she caught her reflection in the mirror and took a quick breath, holding it. Was he some prey she'd spared? Did she kill his family but find something redeeming about him? Or maybe it hadn't been her but The Silent One in her body, taking souls as he saw fit but missing this man for whatever reason. Surely he'd remember her—unless—

In the mirror she saw herself flinch at a knock on the door.

"Clean clothes for you out here. Come get some coffee when you're done."

She was so stung by not remembering that it took several minutes of staring at herself before she realized why she was really here. Her sister was either shivering under a tree somewhere right now or would rise tonight. She had no time to change clothes, no time for coffee. No human bones could be laid out inside this house without that old man dialing 911, so she had a major search of the muddy woods in front of her.

Outside the bathroom door she found a tidy pile of a man's flannel shirt and jeans, much too big for her, but they were at least dry. Ill-fitting clothes would only hinder her search, and they'd be just as wet as her own clothes as soon as she got back out in the elements.

The scent of coffee filled the hall with such intensity she nearly swooned. The old man was sitting at the kitchen table, the coffee maker trickling away. A boxy television played a history program in black and white, the sound muted.

She set the clothes on a kitchen chair. "Thanks, but—"

"Aw, I didn't mean for you to wear 'em out. Just temporary, so yours could dry. They're not gonna fit. Them's my son's. Old ones he left behind."

Missing son, clothes left behind. So she had killed his family. She tried not to stiffen, not let her guilt show on her face. They'd probably deserved it. "I can't stay. I'm looking for my little sister. She's … also lost. I'll need to check the woods behind your house."

"Too wet and cold out there for that, but I won't stop you. At least let me put some coffee on, so I can send you off with a warm belly and a hit of caffeine." He stiffly rose from the chair and took the coffee can from a cabinet, frowning once he spotted the coffee maker finishing its brew. He watched as it clicked off, returned the can to its spot and closed the cabinet, rubbing at his temple, his eyes a little lost.

"Okay, I'll take a cup." Sympathy made her say it, to shift the attention away from his embarrassing lapse. She had no clue when the sympathy had sprouted or how it had grown to this kind of maturity without her realizing. She had no time for how it complicated things she must do.

She never felt so veered off her path. Killing this man would steer her right back onto it, and the sympathy would die with him.

She watched his bony hand retrieve two mugs, his arm tremble under the weight of the full coffee pot. His kind had spared no sympathy for her people, yet here she was, struggling. She felt for her flint knife, found it on her belt where it should be. Grab his hair, yank his head back, cut his throat.

He wasn't the scum she usually went after, but it was okay to slip up once in a while. She'd messed up choosing Mick. He'd turned out to be a worse thing than a good person who didn't deserve to die. Even though she only had the room to care for one person—her sister—somehow Mick had found his own spot right there beside her. He'd slipped into her every thought, a constant presence, summoning all kinds of inconvenient questions and judgments. She knew right now he couldn't be in the sky, but she sensed him there, gliding above her like a guiding spirit—

"Wait," she said. "Your son—what's his name?"

The man handed her a mug, spilling it over the brim in his shaky hand. "Mickey. You might call him Mighty Eagle, though sometimes he don't respond to that. He's a stubborn one."

"Svendsen," she said.

"You know him?"

She let that question fall because her thoughts were spiraling, and she had to catch up to them before she could figure this all out. Mick's father. This was his house. She'd been brought here by her Helpers, commanded by The Silent One. Was he playing with her? Did he know about Mick? Or was this simply the truth, and Jeremiah had indeed brought her sister's bones to Mick's father's house? The Silent One only knew of this place for that reason. "Did you have another visitor here, an Indian guy who looks a little bit—"

"Have lots of visitors, all the time. Not to the house though. Just out there." He aimed his mug at the back door.

It wasn't The Silent One playing with her, it was Jeremiah. She handed her untouched coffee back to Mick's father and picked up the stack of Mick's clothes. Pinepakatwi would need them when she rose. "I have to find my sister."

Chapter 30

MICK WOKE WITH his chin on his chest and a strain in the back of his neck so tight he was afraid to raise his head for fear the muscle would seize. He licked his upper lip, found it wet with blood and connected the scent in the air to his fresh blood and not the damp stone it smelled like. Then his vision came online and confirmed the damp stone—mausoleum stone to be exact. Cold as December ground through his jeans even though his legs were asleep. Arms bound behind his back—not good. He wiggled his wrists, testing the binding only to find it tighter than expected. A little give would offer something to work with. There was no give.

Each breath felt jagged on its way in, hot and raw on its way out. His nose was surely busted. A few good swivels of the neck loosened the strained muscle but sprinkled the stone with blood from his face. Unable to wipe his nose with hands, he pressed it against his shoulder and looked around, finding Waapikoona's abandoned pallet bed and clump of ash and charred wood that had been her fire.

Sarah—her name was Sarah from now on. He had a new reality to follow: He knew nothing about her, and she knew nothing about that other side of him. And neither did he.

He scooted away from the wall for a better view but only made it a few feet before his tied wrists yanked backward, all slack stretched to its max due to the binding being also attached to something behind him. Kicking the rope did no good. In the scant light he could see he was tied to one of the raised coffins set against the wall.

Footsteps shuffled outside. Mick pushed backward into his original spot, leaning flush with the wall and resting his head back so his face was in darkest shadow. Now that his eyes had adjusted and he faced the width of the room, he could see hazy human shapes disrupting the blackness. They shifted around, finding coffins, slipping back inside. He hadn't been alone.

The door swung open on the opposite end, letting in a slant of dust motes in grayish light. Colder air sneaked in and clung to him. He shivered, wishing he could control it. He feared it wasn't just the cold making him shiver, that it was some primal response to being tied up and awaiting death. Being actively afraid could be stifled. He could put his mind somewhere else, talk himself out of it. A lower-level fear instinct wasn't something that could be managed. It would manage him. And it might set off the reaction he'd vowed to suppress now and forever, in order to preserve his humanity. Willing participation in murder and corpse disposal had no place in an honest man's life or anywhere near his family and everything he cared about.

Everything but one thing. One *person*. No one could care so sharply for a stranger, though, so he was being irrational. He'd forget about her and all would be fine, as soon as he got himself out of this.

Small logs were being tossed through the door, disrupting the dust motes. Mick couldn't picture who it could be, and his head swam with the effort of remembering. Couldn't be Waapikoona—Sarah—he'd left her back … somewhere. Birds … eagles … he'd left them too, but he couldn't recall why it mattered. Those dry logs clanking together as they hit the pile meant one thing: fire. And he'd welcome that now more than anything. He couldn't be sure if he'd lost the feeling in his hands due them being bound behind his back or due to the cold, but his toes were also numb and his nose was so cold it felt like ice through his coat as he tried to warm it against his shoulder.

"Good, you're awake."

Mick couldn't focus on the moving person in front of him. He had to close his eyes to reset his brain, stabilize his senses. And when he opened them again, a column of dread collapsed hard in his stomach and it all came back. Jeremiah ambushing him outside his apartment, his mother's spirit used as bait to get him here. Mick's noble but foolish effort to fight Jeremiah while his hands were tied, Jeremiah's elbow to Mick's nose, knee to his gut, arm tightening around his throat, and Mick with no arms to fight against it. Then, nothing. Until waking up here.

"I'm building this for me, not you, so don't think I've softened. I need some answers."

Nothing mattered to Mick but the idea of that fire and the warmth it would bring to his feet. He was numb to the knees now, convinced he'd already lost both legs. His need of heat was too urgent and Jeremiah's act of building it too casual for it to be of any comfort, so Mick rested his head back and closed his eyes. All brain function could then go to a plan of escape—once his muscles and bones thawed.

Waking a second time gave him a view so bright it stung his eyes. Light flooded the room from the cracked window under the peak in the roof. Daylight made a liar of the darkness that claimed ghosts left the confinement of their coffins and roamed free. In this starkly lit room all that nonsense proved impossible. Even more impossible was the ferocity of a headache, pressing against the inside of his skull as well as gripping the outside, a flexing stab with every heartbeat and every breath so severe he turned his head to vomit but nothing came.

Jeremiah sat cross-legged beside the fire, eating from a cup of ramen. "I'd offer you a cup … ah, no I wouldn't." He gave a half smile that seemed aware of the bad joke but willing to own it anyway.

Missing the time it'd taken for water to boil over a campfire meant Mick had passed out. He felt dizzy enough to go down again right then. The muscle in his neck threatened to seize like before. Afraid to move, afraid to sit still, he breathed against the anger rising in him that would surely twist that muscle until it spasmed. He couldn't have that happen, not tied like this and unable to stretch and ease it back into place. And now he was smelling chicken broth and noodles and a growl rumbled through his stomach that brought the pounding head back to its drive into nausea.

"Tell me what she sees in you."

Mick licked lips so dry they'd cracked in several places. "Who?" He had to try twice. The first time the word came out hoarse. He'd die for a drink of water. Or maybe he'd die without it.

"Sarah."

Shifting his weight to sit straighter amplified the throb in his head and gave him sparkly vision. The fire had warmed him enough to bring attention to a soppy cold mess on his chest. He looked down, found his nose had bled a hell of a lot. So much, he wondered if he had some aggressively weeping gash on his chest or neck he'd been too cold to feel.

"Doesn't ring a bell? You have a habit of bedding strange Indian women?"

He didn't, but let Jeremiah think it because he couldn't muster the care. Anger was rising again, making his heart pump too fast for what his bleeding and disoriented body could handle.

"Yeah, there you go. *That* Sarah. Tell me why she won't kill you."

"Tell me why she should, you piece of shit."

Mick felt the sting of boiling water long before he saw the cup of ramen fly at him, but somehow he'd turned in time for it to smack him in the collar instead of in the face. The skin on his neck and shoulder flared with the scald, the burn trickling down as the liquid migrated, leaving trails he knew should feel hot but felt cold instead. Add burns to the list of wounds inflicted by this path of life he'd taken. All it did was add more proof to how wrong it all was. Soon it'd all be behind him. He'd heal, move on, never look back.

"Because she loves killing white trash like you. So if she's keeping you around, I need to know why."

As if Mick knew why. Forget the physical attraction. His new other half existed to destroy things like her, and that first day she'd recognized it and attempted to kill him. Why she hadn't tried again was as much a puzzle to him as it seemed to be to Jeremiah. "Guess me and you have somethin' in common."

"What's that?"

"Neither one of us understands that witch."

Jeremiah stood, brushing himself off as if stalling an action he wanted to savor. From his boot he drew a shiny fixed blade, and Mick closed his eyes knowing this was it. His life, his death, the thin seconds between them. He gave his wrists one last twist against the rope just to be sure it was still there, that he had no last minute self-defense. Other than shifting, which a human being couldn't do, not in the world Mick had returned to. Jeremiah turned the steel point toward the ground. Mick's heart thudded hot blood into his head, his ears, his neck, his chest, as if anticipating where that knife would land. He'd die stubborn, like a human. He wouldn't live as a supernatural creature ripping free from his binds. He was too broken to do it even if he wanted to.

The blade came down, so much lower than expected that he frowned up at his captor, wondering why the shin, why that bony ridge of bone. Why not a fat artery, a vital heart. As the blade sliced thin skin and gouged tender bone he fell out of the feeling. He remembered countless shin traumas—playground accidents as a child, icy stair slips as an adult. In their moments nothing could be more painful. But every single time he'd been wrong. This could be more painful. All those other bumps were just meant to temporarily offend, not upend you like this. Not defeat you so completely. A cold blade sinking, tearing, chipping bone won. It was worse, so much worse.

A long distance call screeched deep in the now insignificant ache of his migraine. The call of his other self, rising, coming to his aid. He struggled for the grip of this new pain, the shin damage, the bloody, slippery rush down his leg, soaking his jeans. Shifting now wouldn't just break Mick's oath to himself, it would give Jeremiah an answer. Not the answer to his question but a different one, one that carried its own set of questions. Mick's body convulsed against the ropes but inside he was serene. He would not give himself up.

The door opened and closed. Mick was alone with the crackle of fire, the blinding beam of sunlight through the broken window, and his own screaming agony.

THE NIGHTMARE WAS on repeat. Blurry eyes blinking open to a room warmed by firelight, the same evil fucker eating another cup of ramen. Mick's chest and neck seized, violent coughs taking him over. With his throat as dry as it was there was no way the coughing would ever stop. At least this part was new.

His arms were completely dead now. If there was a maximum time limbs could be bound and wrenched backward and keep their living tissue, he'd reached it long ago. He twisted, flexing his wrists, and found he still had feeling in the tips of his fingers. Not that it mattered. If his arms were indeed dead, he'd have no use for his hands.

"Ready to talk now?"

Mick said nothing. But he stared that fucker down so hard his head spun.

"You guarding that answer just makes me think it's so much more interesting than I thought."

The urge to cough gripped him again, but he stifled it, knowing it would only shred his dry throat further. He risked a glance at his shin, spotted the shiny puddle below it, and wished he hadn't looked. Closing his eyes allowed him to gather himself. He breathed, putting himself at the U-Fill with a secondhand paperback and a cup of coffee. He didn't know what time it was or what day it was, but chances were that was where he should've been and where he would be in a week's time when all this was over.

A tug on his foot snatched him back to his present where he found Jeremiah loosening the laces on his boot at the end of his unharmed leg. Mick yanked, prepping to kick, but Jeremiah held tight and pulled back, removing the boot while Mick tried to kick with his other leg but found it too sluggish and heavy to make contact. A shockwave of violent pain in his shin traveled every nerve until it slugged him in the brain. That other leg was his wounded one. He needed to remember that.

Jeremiah had extracted a stick from the fire, glowing orange on one end. He lowered that end toward Mick's bootless foot. "Do you remember the question?"

"You're gonna have to ask her."

"Well she's not here. All I have is you."

Mick watched him, unblinking, his mind drifting away because it knew what was coming even before Mick could name it. And down that smoldering stick came, simply a hot spot on the other side of Mick's sock until it was through it and burning layers off the coarse flesh on the pad of his foot. He'd never experienced such burnt, ripened air that made him want to both vomit and scramble away from that hellish stench and run. And now the scorching pain had hit deeper, more sensitive skin, and between the smell and the pain, Mick choked, his stomach rolling upward as he coughed nothing out.

"I said you're gonna—have to—ask—*her*," he bit out, surprised at how violently potent the words sounded when inside he was crumbling. He realized he was struggling against the ropes holding his wrists when fire erupted against live nerves where the skin had torn from the friction.

Jeremiah sat back, withdrawing the smoldering wood from Mick's smoldering foot. He looked away from Mick as if some new thought demanded all his concentration and his torture victim was too much a distraction. He tossed the stick toward the fire and leaned back on his heels, fully taken over by an idea he'd just found, a plan he must put in place. A new and much worse torture to inflict.

Every part of Mick worried about this except for his conscious, thinking brain where only one idea flourished: *Shift.*

He couldn't. Didn't need to. Jeremiah was a sadist but he had no reason to kill Mick. If he wanted him for the underground demon, he'd have done it by now. Soon he'd let him go. All of it was so optimistic and so wrong, but he couldn't admit that shifting was his only option here.

Dry leaves scattered across the stone floor, and the mausoleum door closed, leaving him alone again. Exhaustion lay heavy upon him, along with a pressing need to think himself out of a shift that could not happen. He gathered every bit of effort for that task as time ticked and the fire waned. He didn't notice the heavy chill seeping into him or the spill of blood growing beneath his ruined leg. Chained by the cold, seduced by the solace of the quiet tomb, he rested his head on his shoulder and surrendered to the underworld.

Chapter

31

Waapikoona hadn't abandoned her search yet, but defeat stalked her, made itself feel inevitable. The cold nipped like a cornered animal. If it had been this frigid on her walk from the cave to here, being possessed by The Silent One had shielded her from that. A recent snow clung to the land, spreading bright white over gray stone jutting from the dark loam. The hill behind the house slanted toward a ridge, everywhere she looked covered in that same grayish stone that mimicked human bone in the most troublesome way. She'd thought she'd found her sister a dozen times already, only for the faraway little skull to become a lifeless stone once she drew close.

Above her, heavy blue storm clouds hung dark against the struggling rays of a noon sun. If those clouds spilled in this temperature, she'd have more snow or worse … sleet. She'd thrown herself into the middle of a sleet storm to get away from Mick. It seemed unfair now that her choice was sleet storm or Mick's family home and kind, hospitable father. She'd already made a similar decision, and she didn't want to have to do it again.

She pushed through a wall of ice-crusted pine needles. There in a circle of evergreens sat a slumping canvas drawstring bag, looking very out of place as the only thing not coated with old snow. The imprint of a human body had melted into the shiny white beside it. She wanted to call out to her sister, see if she was hunkering somewhere nearby. But something about that shape in the snow made her hold her sister's name inside as she closed in on the bag.

Of course it was empty of bones. They'd been reassembled last night just as The Silent One would have instructed. They'd been rebuilt with flesh to leave that imprint in the snow. And calling the name she'd given her sister wouldn't do much good. Even if Waapikoona remembered the real one, her sister likely wouldn't recognize that either. She dropped the bag back to the ground and studied the snow, finding footprints leading away, too large to be the feet carrying her sister's eight-year-old body. She took a step back and saw the human imprint in a new light. This wasn't the body of a child. It was adult, wide at the shoulders and long in the arms like a man.

This was a decoy.

Her sister's bones were somewhere, and it wasn't here. Someone new had been raised, and she had no other options but to follow his steps and hope he could help in some way. He'd just fallen through the circle of time and would be disoriented, lost, lacking memory, and probably mute, but if Jeremiah raised him, Jeremiah must have known him. He might know something about Jeremiah that could help her. This newly raised man would be ripe from the grave, but he was all she had.

She followed the prints through the grove of pines and into deeper forest, where they turned sharply and headed uphill. If he was mute, she hoped it'd only last minutes and not months like it had for her. She hoped he spoke English.

Ahead, a plume of white steam from a heated home emerged through the bare treetops. Another visit to Mick's father's house wasn't something she could tolerate right now, but it was the only house on this stretch of road, and she knew those prints were heading straight there.

An animal brushed through the snow to her right—a large one, judging from the noise. She stooped, trying to see under pine limbs if it was one she'd be better off avoiding even though she knew it would be rare to encounter an animal that could hurt her. The white man hadn't just worked to kill off Native people. He'd targeted apex predators too. She'd welcome the sight of a wolf or bear and then move quickly out of its territory, but that was not what she saw.

It was a muscled human shoulder, a splash of sandy hair. Not a Native man. She tried to remember ever hearing of a white man raised by The Silent One. It seemed wrong. Warriors didn't question their leaders, and maybe that was her problem. Maybe that's why she'd hit so many obstacles, why time seemed stuck and she couldn't find her way ahead.

"Hello," she called. She didn't want to spook this man who'd just been yanked from the peace of death. "I have some clothes for you. Be still and I'll toss them."

She balled them up and threw them through the branches separating them. Warm clothes would earn anyone's trust, something she needed if she was going to interrogate him about Jeremiah. Something she especially needed if this man was from her time like she expected. As soon as he saw her he would despise her.

A shuffle against the frozen ground meant he'd picked up the clothes. A flap of fabric in the breeze meant he was shaking them out, probably putting them on. She risked a glance, hoping to assess him before he had a chance to assess her. He'd moved behind a trunk, giving her only a stretched arm sliding into Mick's flannel. The thick fingers of the hand that came out of the sleeve sent her back a step. The pinky was short. Severed just under the nail.

She'd known a man with a pinky like that.

The coincidence doubled her heart's beat. Tripled it. Made her gulp air high in her chest, too fast, erratic, prey-like. She'd drawn her flint knife, its handle warming in her hot hand. This was a mix-up, a traumatic memory surging free, warping her present. She'd learned to block these hallucinations, and now was not the time for them to return. The Silent One wouldn't raise the man her mind had tricked her into seeing. To the army of Native people he was building, this man was its enemy. He'd haunted her childhood and still menaced her in dreams. In the Indian school he was the one they'd all feared, the one who caught them breaking rules so he could dole out punishments. And when they'd learned not to break them, he'd set them up so they'd break new ones. He was a devil in the daylight and a predator in the night. Inescapable, ever-present, and watching. Always watching.

And he wouldn't have died young like this man who stood before her. He was the kind of criminal who'd live a long life spent serving terror to children. So she swallowed her wild heart and breathed it back into its spot, and she stepped around the trees to face this other man.

Bent slightly, he was trying to make sense of the clothes he'd put on. With his head bowed and at a tilt, she could tell his hair was starting to gray at the temples and in the beard covering his cheeks. Just like that man with the short-ened pinky who'd terrorized her as a child. The man who'd driven her to take her sister off that cliff.

This man looked up at her. In her eyes he was the same. For one stuttering moment she thought she had his name— she hadn't remembered her sister's or her own, but she remembered her torturer's—but it fled. Distantly she realized she'd have to make one up for him like she had for herself and her sister, but not in her tongue. Never would she grant him that.

In her hand, her knife swiveled, sharp flint point now aiming downward. The effort subconscious, its goal was for her to leap on him and plunge it into his neck with the force of her body weight driving it through his spine.

He was pointing at her lazily, his eyes sparking with recollection. Too soon for him to recall anything from his previous life if she compared this to her own reviving. She could see this one might be different than her own. She'd died young, traumatically, a tragedy of her own making. Of course a grotesque thing like him would leave the world peacefully. Isn't that how it always seemed to work with the white man? Committing all those crimes against Mother Earth and never seeing one consequence for it.

As much as she avoided modern people, now in front of this man she could see how much worse he was than any person in this time. He hadn't been enlightened out of his narrow world and selfish views. He hadn't been made to find common ground with people different from himself. He wasn't like Mick.

This was no hallucination. The pinky was real. *He* was real, as real as she was.

Even as she recognized him there was no way he'd recognize her, a grown woman he'd last seen as an eleven-year-old child. He'd called her savage and uncivilized; he'd claimed the terrible things he did were for her own good. Now, in this time, in her second life, he was right. She was undead and perfectly uncivilized. And the terrible things he'd done may not have been for her own good, but they were for something: her glorious revenge.

He was newly raised. Weak, disoriented, vulnerable. Snatched away from his time, his people, from everything he understood. Just like she and her sister had been. Just like all the children he'd abused. The roles had reversed and it couldn't be more perfect.

Her strike went unblocked. He staggered backward, arms thrown over his face as if that's where she'd aim a second time. She wanted his heart. Cut out, held in front of his eyes as it beat its last beat. Then she'd gut him and turn him inside out. She wouldn't call her Helpers to eat him; she'd let him rot, let the sun thaw him so the waste of him would remain, frozen by night, thawed by day, carrion slowly scavenged by the birds. But as soon as the tip of her blade sunk into skin, a red-hot current lit her nerves as if she were the one being stabbed, not him. Instead of driving it deep, she sliced downward, gasping as she pulled away.

The recognition came like a punishing bolt from the mightiest Thunder-Being. She couldn't kill this man. He'd been rebuilt by The Silent One just like her. They shared a creator; they were part of the same truth. Her bones had come from the cradle of Mother Earth, but her flesh and life had come from the father of the underworld. They were like siblings, reborn of the same parents. Even if she succeeded in killing him without crumpling under the act of doing it, The Silent One would find out. The least he'd do would be refuse to raise her sister. The worst? She couldn't imagine.

"Tell me your name." Her voice calm and even. It betrayed nothing.

He pressed a hand over his chest where she'd cut him. The questioning recollection had vanished from his eyes. In its place an aloof, calculating hatred she remembered well.

"Your name," she repeated, stepping forward. She had to name him, place him, call him out. She wouldn't give him a name in her language, and nothing in English was foul enough to fit.

"I suspect you know it, s—"

She saw his mouth start to form the slur his kind had used against her, and she was at him again, a clump of his hair tight in her fist, the handle of her flint slamming into his ear. He grabbed her around the waist and threw himself against her. Their height matched but not their mass, and she spun, throwing his heavier weight behind her, but he spun back, the force of it too unexpected for her to counter. The ground came at her, and she tucked her head to take the blow on her shoulder instead of her skull.

She was a killer, not a fighter. This would not do.

In their fall he'd lost his grasp, so she wiggled away, but he scrambled forward and tackled her again. As he restrained her arm, she groped the ground with her other, searching for her flint. A flare in her ear—her earring ripped out. The flint found her hand and she reached, but her grip was wrong and it slipped away. She took a weak blow to the mouth— he didn't have enough range for a worse one—that sent her teeth into her lip and blood swelling against her tongue. She gave up on the knife to move closer against him so he couldn't create room for a worse blow, jamming her forearm against his windpipe. He choked, recovering just enough air to cough spittle into her face. She repeated the blow, simul- taneously shifting her hips so she was out from under him and hopping to her feet while he sputtered and fought for breath. There—her flint. She snatched it up.

With a fist of his hair, she yanked his head back. As it hung in the air she imagined what came next: his face in violent contact with the gray rock peeking through the blanket of snow. She had a fraction of a second to decide if it would kill him, but her decision was interrupted by a shout of her English name.

She looked up. Jeremiah stood several paces away.

"You might want to think this through," he said, nodding toward the flint she'd positioned under her enemy's jaw.

Waapikoona steadied her rough breath. "You might want to run. You're next."

"The Silent One might forgive you for him. He won't for me."

"It'll be worth it."

"And you'll never find out where I stashed your sister's bones."

The man she held shifted his weight, preparing to fight out of her hold. She tightened her grip in his hair and her flint against his throat. "You lie."

"I have someone else, too."

He tossed a man's work boot to her. It looked very much like the one Mick had been wearing when she'd left him in the sleet storm. The boot he'd worn as he held her up and kissed her on top of that mound and made the world feel right, for the first time in this life.

But this was her proof. Jeremiah and Mick were working together. She had been betrayed.

"You can have him."

Jeremiah sighed. "Sarah."

But she wasn't looking at him. A splatter of rusty brown on that beige work boot had caught her attention. She and Mick had hiked the frozen Illinois ground, but she hadn't remembered any mud that color. It was blood. She was quite familiar. She looked down at her own boots which were now cleaned but recently had been splattered just like that and were about to get splattered again.

"You killed Mick."

"Not yet. He won't answer my questions. I thought you could help me out with him, and I'll pay you back with a nice little sack of bones."

Suddenly she felt the strain in her arm from holding her enemy by the hair. She released him, kicking him hard in the ribs to get him down and away from her. He grunted and rolled, staying there on the ground, clearly assuming he was outnumbered by the ones he deemed most savage.

"Good." Jeremiah produced a roll of duct tape from his inner coat pocket and tossed it to her. "Bind his hands. I'll help you convince The Silent One to let you kill him later."

It all made sense then: Jeremiah had asked The Silent One to raise the monster, just so she could kill him. A twisted little gift, just the thing Jeremiah might do to win her back. The odd part was this man who'd had so much fight in him a moment ago was now lying still, allowing her to secure his wrists with tape. But she couldn't dwell on it. Jeremiah's games didn't matter. Her concerns now were getting to Mick. It was pointless to decipher Jeremiah's games until she could see with her own eyes whose side Mick was really on. Then she could determine if he needed saving.

As she ripped a final piece of tape off the roll, she heard the swish of Jeremiah's gait and an intake of his breath and then—nothing.

A GALAXY OF orange stars pulsed against her eyes. Under her cheek, a vibration running through a cushion both plush and scratchy. Her head bounced against it in time with a rattling, bumpy ride—a car. It came together so fast she wondered why each detail had been so slow.

An attempt to brace her arms against the seat and sit up was denied by her wrists bound by the very same tape she'd used on someone else. Twisting her head allowed her hair to fall out of her face so she could see the ceiling of an unfamiliar car, its driver's arm lying along the middle arm rest. Strong jaw against an upturned collar, black hair ruffled by wind or a struggle. Or both.

The swollen sore spot on the side of her head was his doing. A sucker punch from a coward. She thought back, remembering she hadn't refused to go with him. She'd wanted to, to check on Mick. So knocking her out to get her in the car seemed a bit overdone, even for Jeremiah. The bumps in the road brought out every other injury she'd gained from her tussle with—she hadn't gotten his name out of him. Now that her eyes had fully opened, her vision looked like it had cracked, like she was looking through shards of broken glass. Her mouth and nose leaked watery blood. And her eyes, now that they had figured out where she was, kept trying to close.

When the car stopped and engine shut off, she wasn't sure she'd be able find her legs to get them moving.

"Get out." Jeremiah opened the car door.

Normally she wouldn't so easily follow a command of his, but she didn't like being tied up and horizontal with him standing over her. So she wiggled herself to the edge of the seat, and Jeremiah grabbed her by the coat and launched her upright. Now out of the car, she was able to see he'd brought her back to her cemetery. Wind pushed against her, bringing the scent of smoke from a nearby fire.

"What'd you do with him?"

"Hammond?"

Yes—Hammond was the name. Gilbert Hammond. *Headmaster* Hammond.

"He went in a car with a friend of mine. He'll be safe until you and I can kill him. Together, like old times."

"Killing a raised body is a great way to make an enemy of The Silent One."

He reached, freeing her hair from its tangle inside her coat, straightening her collar. "Which is why I had him raised. We'll defy The Silent One together. There's a mutiny building, Sarah, and now's the time for you to join up."

Mutiny … against The Silent One? She laughed, straining sore ribs. New blood trickled from her nose and something in her mouth began to bleed again too. She was a mess, and she was laughing, and Jeremiah was smiling at her like this was a happy response to exciting news. No, this was a joke.

"So many of us have been raised," he said. "And are raising so many more—"

"It'll never be enough. The Silent One lies to keep you working. Native people will never become the army he envisions. Most of us just want to be left alone." She had to get the tape off her wrists. Having her arms glued together and wrenched behind her back was very close to making her crazy, and the more she struggled the crazier she felt.

"Don't you want to be on the winning side? For your sister?"

She flexed her arms, and they seemed to have somehow gotten tighter together. "Don't talk about my sister."

"Your sister—"

Enough. The tape, the immobile arms—it was a torturous claustrophobia in the openness of the outdoors. She took a step forward and head-butted Jeremiah in the nose. The crack against her skull jarred so deeply into every bone she tried to recover with a step backward but stumbled against the car instead, off-balance and unable to determine up from down. She was more a mess than she thought. And now that she was eating dirt she realized what a bad move it was. She couldn't get up. Jeremiah had her by the coat, and she couldn't defend herself. He slammed her into the car enough times for her vision to shutter away. She sagged, and one more hit brought the sore spot from the sucker punch in her head right against the glass and then she lost all structure in her body. Jeremiah let go; she fell to the ground.

Laughter—was that her? It sounded like her. She'd lost her mind.

Now she was being dragged, and all she could see were the wavering spirits sliding from around tombstones and slipping from the frosted trees. Curious, worried, helpless. She kicked, trying to gain purchase so she could buck loose from Jeremiah's cruel grip, but the ground slid against her boots too quickly. Then her shins were crashing against the stone steps and at the top she was thrown through the door.

He hauled her toward the fire. For a terrifying moment she thought he'd pull her straight on top of it, but then he stopped, resting her in a sitting position against the wall. She smelled blood, thick in the fire-warmed air. Strange she'd suddenly smell it now when she'd been bleeding for a long time.

"You two catch up," Jeremiah said. "I need to get more wood."

The door closed, but she wasn't alone. Across the room, slumped against the wall, was Mick. And the warm air flushed to instant cold around her because that unnatural droop to his frame meant he was long dead. Bled out, due the dark puddle he was sitting in. Frozen to death, from the way his shoulders curled together in his wet coat. His hair was matted around an ear darkened with dried blood. The bottom of one foot was bare and blackened and the other leg was soaked, having fed that puddle. She couldn't call his name to see if he'd wake. She knew he wouldn't. Her voice was stuck, stopped by a sob that wouldn't release, and she couldn't breathe, couldn't remember how to, couldn't do anything but sit there while her eyes stung and her teeth ground, and she had to get up, kill Jeremiah, make him pay.

A pang hit her from nowhere: she missed Indian Country. Hushed, star-filled nights and days being surrounded by people who accepted her unconditionally. Poverty reigned but so did peace and community, and she'd been so ungrateful. So defiant. Mistakes had been left there, apologies never spoken. Her burden couldn't accept more load. She would not leave mistakes here in this tomb.

"Mick," she said, just to make sure. Scarcely a whisper, all she could bear.

He opened his eyes. Such a tiny miraculous movement, unaccompanied by any other hint of life. She could've easily convinced herself it never happened, that his eyes had been open that way in death. But he held her gaze like a living person would, his eyes silver in the light of the tomb. He was part himself and part something else, like the blue in each iris had drained away to allow the gold-flecked amber eyes of his Thunder-Being to enter, but had gotten stuck before the color was complete. Everything about his eagle was golden—the feathers of his head, his sharp eyes, his presence. He was a piece of the sun, chipped off, liquid in the sky. If all that had been doused, she'd never forgive herself for leading him here.

She'd found peace and shelter in this tomb among the dead, but it would never recover from the taint of Jeremiah being inside. From the memory of Mick slumped there with his wasted eyes.

A Thunder-Being could end this battle now, with the added glory of surprise. If Mick couldn't get himself there, she'd have to help him.

She'd release her Helpers—no, Jeremiah would kill them. The Silent One would give her no more and refuse to raise her sister.

She'd summon the surrounding dead. But could Jeremiah use them against her? It wasn't worth it, and her head felt fuzzy with the effort of coming up with options.

No good options meant no surprise thunderbird to save them. If it was all up to her, she'd have to accept that. Mick wasn't dead but he soon would be. Jeremiah had done this to him, and she was going to be ready for him when he came back.

New strength pressed through her. She scooted to the edge of a coffin and rolled her shoulder against it, using it to stand. The room spun; she squatted, gathering herself on planted feet to keep herself from toppling. Up once again she moved to her stash of belongings in the corner and rooted through the pile with her feet. There—a smaller version of her flint knife. She knelt, picked it up with her teeth—too late. A shaft of light swung across her from the opening door.

Jeremiah crossed the room and grabbed her. Raw heat peeled through the corner of her lip where the flint ripped free. She aimed another head butt, received Jeremiah's hard forearm instead. Unable to catch herself with pinned arms, she fell against Mick's wounded leg, the impact of stone floor against shoulder so intense her brain decided not to feel it at all.

Somehow she'd draw Mick's Thunder-Being out. Even if she had to open her own body and spill her own underworld blood. The shock on Jeremiah's face as Mick tore out his throat would be worth it.

CHAPTER
32

Wind moaned through the mausoleum, sleepy and mournful like the graveyard outside. Subdued wind touched at Mick's cheeks, stirred his hair. A shaft of direct light framed two figures. One Jeremiah, the other—Waapikoona? So it hadn't been a dream? He leaned to get a better view—too far; his head swam, his vision blurred. Flashes of bloody hands and gore-soaked pant legs and charred feet weeping strange excretions onto the stone floor. Images he'd never unsee, even in death. He'd be haunted forever.

The two people collided, the action too fast for Mick to follow, so he closed his eyes, trying to steady his senses so he could figure out if he was dreaming or dead. His fingers—still there, but burning with such fever he knew they were on their way to frostbite. Legs—worthless they were so numb. He opened his eyes to find them still attached. Movement—above him—his wrecked leg exploded with renewed pain. The bend of his body against the blow automatic, his upper half slid halfway onto the floor.

His view became Waapikoona's tangled hair, sticky against her bloody cheek. A torn, crusted ear lobe missing his feather along with the earring that once held it. The spider web of red around her eye and inside it, purpling before his eyes. Her proud straight lips, swollen and glazed with glistening red. And the vision before all this that hadn't made sense until just then: Jeremiah shoving her down, the crack of her shoulder against the stone floor, her wrists bound like Mick's, useless.

She rolled onto her side. A laugh meant to stay inside shook her shoulders, curling her lips into the most unfriendly smile. Evil, carved by the underworld. She lay there and let the laugh build until Mick couldn't bear it, not one more second of it. He wanted to say her name. Didn't want to say it in front Jeremiah. He leaned to reach out, bring her back into his world. Too far away and helpless against the ropes, he retreated, his clothes scraping against the stone wall.

Startled by his movement, she turned her face toward him. The evil smile washed from her face. And Mick was glad Jeremiah had busied himself rebuilding the fire because the new look she gave him wasn't one he wanted Jeremiah to see. It carried too much heart. Too much care. The bright, startled relief shadowed by worry for someone in danger, the dark despair of not being able to help. These feelings were a liability Jeremiah could use against them. She must've understood this at the same time Mick did because she blinked, all evidence of the emotion falling away. In its place lay anger. Not at the situation, but at him. And a look that said, *You know how to save yourself, why aren't you doing it?*

He shook his head. He was just a slow, spent brain in a broken body. He couldn't shift, even if he hadn't made a vow to himself never to shift again. He tried to remember the words he'd used to explain it to her.

I'm done, he mouthed. In so many ways he was done.

Her eyes widened, angrier than before. She seemed to understand those words clearly now, as if she hadn't grasped their full meaning when he'd said them in Illinois right before he'd walked away.

A canvas bag dropped beside them. Jeremiah's boots stood behind. Mick refused to look up at him.

"Your sister's bones," he said. "I'm going to untie you, Sarah, and you're going to kill him."

Waapikoona spit on his boots.

Jeremiah squatted to root around in the bag and withdrew a small bone. In his other hand, a hammer glinted against the dark. "Or I'll start crushing bones."

He stuck the bone in his pocket and yanked Waapikoona's arms out from under her. She made no effort to fight him as he slit the tape at her wrists and hauled her upright by the coat. He pressed the blade into her hand and spun her to face Mick.

"However you want to do it. He's half dead already." Then he took the little bone out of his pocket and inspected it in the weak light. "I think this is a finger, but I can't be sure."

"You're just like them." Waapikoona stared into Mick, but her eyes were far away. Unseeing or seeing too much no one could see but her. "Like Hammond himself. Doing this evil for my own good. Right?" She turned her attention to Jeremiah then, and Mick realized she wasn't talking to him but to Jeremiah. Mick shivered at the bare hatred that simmered there, more wicked than her laughter, more troubling than every murder committed by her hand.

Jeremiah set the little bone on the edge of a coffin and raised the hammer. "Don't wait until there aren't enough pieces to rebuild her."

Waapikoona laid a hand on the coffin, her eyes on that hammer. Sweat trickled down Mick's back. He knew she'd choose family over him. He hoped she would—he was nearly dead already. He wouldn't survive the wound in his leg and didn't want to. But it didn't stop a fresh supply of adrenaline from dumping into his veins at the knowledge that he'd avoid death no longer. Without voice he begged her to see him, to accept his willingness to die. He'd rather die by her hand than Jeremiah's.

But what he saw when she turned her eyes on him wasn't resignation at what she had to do. It was a vicious defiance. Her hand would not be forced. Mick knew she would watch her sister's bones be crushed to powder one by one, and Mick would live only minutes, maybe hours longer, knowing what he caused. Her heart would break a second time over her sister, and it would be his fault. It would be permanent and it would be for nothing.

"Do it," he said to her. It was the ground out, gritty voice of a ghoul, not his own.

A shake of her head, so slight.

"Yes—" Mick choked. Hot blood bubbled into his throat. "You will."

She set her jaw, breathing hard. "I won't choose..." she shot Jeremiah the darkest of looks "...between the only two I love."

The hammer came down, pelting Mick with particle and dust. Adrenaline surged; he tugged at his restraints with the last trace of life he had left. Waapikoona watched Jeremiah select a second bone from the bag, her breathing now steady and sure. Mick felt the skin on his wrists peeling away from bone, but there was no slippage of the rope, no give to the stone wall. If she was crafting a plan it wouldn't be quick enough—the hammer halted in the air above the second piece of her sister—Jeremiah tilted his face toward her in a final warning—

With the second strike against stone, Waapikoona closed her eyes, shiny tears slipping out of her good one and her wrecked one. She stood with wet cheeks, shoulders stiff, breath impossibly slow. Mick couldn't find his voice to holler at her, bring her toward reason. He swallowed and choked as Jeremiah grabbed her by the back of the neck and swung her toward Mick, shoving her to her knees in front of him. He forced her hand into a grip of Mick's hair, wrenching his head backward. Jeremiah's other hand squeezed her fist around the handle of the knife. He guided that blade against Mick's neck then released his own hand, whispering something in her ear too faint for Mick to hear.

Jeremiah got up. Her hand remained a claw in his hair, the blade a promise against his thudding pulse. Mick waited for her eyes to open. He needed to pass along a message: He heard her, and he loved her back. He didn't know why or how, but he knew it was truer than anything he'd ever felt. And as he walked the border between life and death, the complications of their love lurked far away. Outside of this moment he wanted her in his life, in his bed, in his always. And dying now—he couldn't live without her, but he could die without her, as long as he died for her.

And he forgave her for killing him.

Beside him, Jeremiah unbagged a small human skull. He was no longer playing. Mick knew this third test was it, that no demon of any world could rebuild a human being without its intact skull.

"Final chance to rid yourself of *this*." Jeremiah waved a hand toward Mick even though Waapikoona wouldn't see with her eyes still closed. "You've been seduced. You can't see what he's done to you. Someday you'll thank me for this."

She opened her eyes then, and Mick's message halted because of that supernatural cataract over her eyes, the same one he saw on that first night in his apartment when she'd tried to kill him. The one she'd worn while killing all those men from those cars alongside his eagle form. He'd agreed to surrender his life to her, to sacrifice himself so her sister could live. He didn't count on this stranger to do the final deed.

Waapikoona. No sound came out. His voice had vanished, but he tried again, hoping her name would travel the air in some form and find her. It was a whisper of a whisper. "Waapikoona."

She shuddered, flinging the strangeness off. Her eyes opened, teary, but her own.

Jeremiah set the skull on the edge of the coffin beside them.

"I won't do this," she whispered. The blade's pressure eased on Mick's neck. "Where are you, *Ciinkwia*?"

"What did you say?" came from above.

She ignored the question as if their captor hadn't spoken. She scooted closer to Mick, her hand now gentle in his hair, lowering his head so his eyes perfectly aligned with hers. "Help us, Mick."

A tingle spread through him, wild and unstoppable. Dead limbs filled with newfound life, arms slimming, lengthening. Lightness took over the corpselike weight of his old body as his new body wrestled free, trembling in the air, flapping into position.

All he saw was a plump artery in a human neck, and he aimed straight for it. Talons sank into flesh. Wings flapped once, twice, as the talons separated artery from muscle and bone. The body fell, its attempt to escape hindered by a second attack of talons crushing spine, snapping the bone to powder in the air.

The body thrashed and flipped to face the ceiling. Prey eyes stared up at him, unaccepting of death. It was a crippled prey, but still a living prey. He could toy with it or he could end it. He latched onto the body near the heart, not close enough for a kill. One set of talons hung useless, so he pushed extra force into his good one and made use of his beak, carving eye sockets clean. Movement some space away—he tilted his head, found her flattened against the wall, the fire dancing beside her. She was not his prey. She was his guide. He called to her; she called back, her language foreign, but understood: *End it.*

He dug out the heart and tossed it onto the ground. Flapping away, he found a perch nearby and landed, tucking his bad leg against his body. She approached. He held still, curious. She'd never come this close before. When she reached he settled himself, watching her, watching the doorway, the window, the fire, the stone slabs covering the dead. Her arm breached the distance between them, and he held still as she stroked his neck.

He tilted his head to watch her walk away.

She couldn't go, not before he spoke to her in a language they both understood. So he shed his feathers and gripped the edge of the coffin with human fingers, but it wasn't enough to keep him from sliding to the floor.

He rolled, his forgotten wounds now screaming alive. She came to his side, wiped blood from his mouth, and lay the tips of her fingers against it. "Shh."

So many words raced to but died on his tongue. She was busy wrapping his leg, not even aware of his need to speak.

"This wound—it's bad, Mick. You need a doctor."

There was something important he needed to tell her, but his thoughts were stuck between eagle and human, and everything was fading.

She was rolling him, tugging clothes on, jamming feet into boots. "I'll summon my Helpers to clean this up, but when they return to The Silent One he'll know who we killed, and I have to go—"

"Can't—"

"Shh, Mick."

"Don't summon—"

She stopped to look at him. He couldn't think of how to explain, but she needed to know that was a bad idea. There had to be a way to avoid implicating herself. She turned, looking at the shredded human corpse lying several feet away. "Okay, but I have to leave."

"No, Waapikoona."

"There's someone I need to find. And you need to get to a hospital."

He risked a glance at his leg. For the first time it felt dry, her improvised bandage doing its job. His eagle blood had revived every nerve, and new warmth pumped through his veins. He sat up—she tried to hold him down, but he found strength to fight her, and she let him up.

"You and me—"

She put her fingers against his lips a second time. "I should have left a long time ago. You don't need the trouble I bring. And if I don't get The Silent One to revive my sister now…"

Mick finished her thought: something like this might happen again, but it wouldn't end in her favor. She recognized the understanding in his eyes and stood. He watched her tuck the little skull into the bag and linger at the side of the coffin, where the two bones had been destroyed. Mick knew those bones were inconsequential, that a human body would function just fine without them. It couldn't be any other way, and he wouldn't accept it if it was. Waapikoona gathered a few other things from her pile in the corner and stopped at his feet, a hand offered to help him up.

"You leave," he said, "and all we've got is lost."

"I lost a lot of things I loved. I know how to move on."

"But you don't have to." He searched for the words that would make her stay. He'd help her. He'd fight The Silent One, force him to rebuild her sister. He'd take on anything for her. But she already knew all that, and saying it would only delay what he should be saying instead. If only he could figure out what that was.

"I'm bad for you, Mick. Go home to your family."

He let her haul him up and tested his weight on his leg. It buckled—he righted himself on a coffin. In the time it took for him to straighten, she was gone, the mausoleum door swinging in the breeze.

This form impaired him, with its maimed leg and slowing blood. He'd lost too much of it and he was faint, hungry, exhausted. He looked around for something to use as a cane, at least that might ease the pressure on his burnt foot so he could hobble after her. There was nothing but stone and blood, firewood and shredded human flesh. And spirits, sliding from under the lids of their coffins, calling for someone to hear them, to rid their resting place of this unwanted crime, to restore the quiet.

Inside, his eagle heard them. He took a step, his next one had wings to guide him off the ruined leg and into the air. One flap took him through the door, and then he was up, shooting through branches sparkling with fresh snow. He crested the treetops, tiny snowflakes swirling all around to lay a hush on the land. Below him, she walked with purpose, one he knew he couldn't sway until she was ready to be swayed.

As he circled above her in his gray winter sky, he made a new vow to himself: wherever she went, he'd find her. And once he did he'd have the right words to say. She'd be his, every day, every night. Bad for him, yet so, so good. He'd unearth his life, rebuild it, find a way for her to fit.

Until then he would remain both human and eagle, waiting, watching, and unquiet.

FOR DETAILS ABOUT THE NEXT BOOK, PLEASE VISIT
KAYCAMDEN.COM